BEWARE OF RODENTS
WITH GOOD INTENTIONS

"Some fun," Tazli said. "Me and a blue chipmunk, having a Festival party in the northeast tower."

"Not here," Rikiki said impatiently. "Fun place."

"But they won't let me leave the palace," Tazli said.

"Don't care," Rikiki declared. "Nice Tazli want fun; Rikiki fix." He scurried over to the window and up the wall to the window ledge. "Hold tail," he commanded.

Tazli stood up and reached for the chipmunk's tail. "Careful!" Rikiki warned, and walked out of the window, pulling Tazli behind him.

Afterward she had a clear memory of crawling down the outside wall of the tower like a three-legged fly, headfirst with one hand clutching Rikiki's tail. Partway down it occurred to her that this was not a very dignified position for the Levar to be in. She lifted her head, intending to point this out to Rikiki, and saw the flagstones on the courtyard far below. Her hand tightened on Rikiki's tail, and she decided not to mention the matter just then . . .

—From "The Levar's Night Out"
by Patricia C. Wrede

Ace Books Edited by Will Shetterly and Emma Bull

Ace Books by Will Shetterly

Ace Books by Emma Bull

Liavek:

FESTIVAL WEEK

edited by *Will Shetterly*
and Emma Bull

ACE BOOKS, NEW YORK

LIAVEK: FESTIVAL WEEK

An Ace Book / published by arrangement with
the editors

PRINTING HISTORY
Ace edition / May 1990
•

ISBN: 0-441-48192-2

Ace Books are published by The Berkley Publishing Group,
200 Madison Avenue, New York, New York 10016
The name ''ACE'' and the ''A'' logo
are trademarks belonging to Charter Communications, Inc.

PRINTED IN THE UNITED STATES OF AMERICA

10 9 8 7 6 5 4 3 2 1

**To you—all of you—who have
spent your holidays with us in Liavek**

Contents

————◆————

LIAVEK: FESTIVAL WEEK

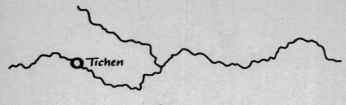

EMPIRE OF TICHEN

Tichen

THE GREAT WASTE

SILVERSPINE

Trader's Town

Liavek

Ombaya City

Hrothvek

Saltigos

Crab Island

THE
SEA OF
LUCK

N

Gold
Harbor

Ka Thow

Ka Zhir

·wlx·84

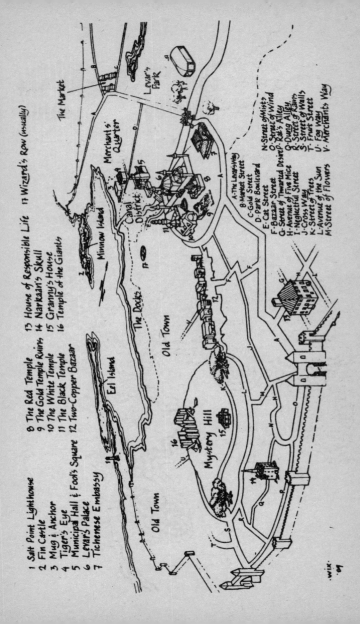

1 Salt Point Lighthouse
2 Fin Castle
3 Mug & Anchor
4 Tiger's Eye
5 Municipal Hall & Fool's Square
6 Levar's Palace
7 Tichenese Embassy

8 The Red Temple
9 The Gold Temple Ruins
10 The White Temple
11 The Black Temple
12 Two-Copper Bazaar

13 House of Responsible Life
14 Narkaan's Skull
15 Granny's House
16 Temple of the Giants

17 Wizard's Row (usually)

A - The Levar's Way
B - Market Street
C - Gold Street
D - Park Boulevard
E - Cat Street
F - Bazaar Street
G - Street of Thwarted Desire
H - Avenue of Five Mice
I - Neglectful Street
J - Cross Way
K - Street of Trees
L - Avenue of the Sun
M - Street of Flowers

N - Street of Mists
O - Street of Wind
P - Rat's Alley
Q - Dung Alley
R - Street of Ravens
S - Street of Walls
T - Fruit Street
U - Fog Way
V - Merchant's Way

Levar's Park

The Market

Merchant's Quarter

Canal District

Minnow Island

The Docks

Old Town

Eel Island

Old Town

Mystery Hill

— wjw '91

THE FLEEING YEAR

Consequences

by Walter Jon Williams

WHITE SAILS CUT precise arcs against a background of vivid color: green sea, blue sky, black volcanic sand. Spindrift shone like diamonds as it spattered over the weather rail. *Birdwing* heeled in the strong gust; timber and cordage groaned as they took the strain. Captain Derec SuPashto adjusted his stance to the increased tilt of the deck: his mind was on other things.

Birdwing and its convoy was about to be attacked by the Liavekan navy.

"My compliments to the ship's wizard, Facer," he said. "Ask him if he can veer this wind two or four points."

"Sir."

A veering wind would be useful, Derec thought, if Levett could conjure one up. But whatever happened, let it stay strong.

"Starboard a point, Sandor."

"Starboard a point, aye aye."

"Break out our colors, SuKrone."

"Sir."

Derec's first reaction on seeing the three Liavekan warships was not one of anxiety, but rather relief. *Birdwing* would finally have a chance to prove itself to Ka Zhir, and that chance was desperately needed.

As the streaming black-and-gold Zhir ensign broke out overhead, Derec studied the enemy with narrowed eyes: three bright ships on a shallow sea the color of green baize. The lead galleass was a big one, thirty oars or more per side, white foam curling from its massive ramming prow. It was painted purple with scarlet trim; a rear admiral's blue pennant fluttered from its maintop and gold leaf winked from the carved arabesques that decorated the stern. The second galleass, three cables astern, was smaller and lighter, its rigging more delicate: it would be at a disadvantage in this strong wind, this choppy sea. It hadn't been painted; its sides were the bright color of varnished wood. Astern of the second enemy was a small xebec—its military value was negligible unless it could get under an enemy's stern in a dead calm, in which case it could pound away with its bow chaser until its opponent was nothing but driftwood. Likely it served as a tender, or was used for chasing down unarmed merchantmen. Derec's impulse was to discount it.

A brave sight, these three, on the green ocean. They seemed entirely in their element.

Derec knew that appearances were deceiving.

He wondered what the Liavekan admiral was thinking as he stood on his fine gingerbread poop. The Liavekan squadron had been lurking along the coast between Ka Zhir and Gold Harbor for the obvious purpose of attacking a convoy: and now a convoy had appeared, twelve caravels and two huge carracks, all crammed to the gunnels with trade goods. The Liavekan squadron, waiting behind a barren, palm-covered islet, had duly sprung their ambush and were now driving toward their prey. But what in hell, they must wonder, was the escort?

A ship of *Birdwing*'s type had never been seen in these waters. The stout masts and heavy standing rigging marked her as northern-built, a Farlander ship able to stand up to winter gales in the high latitudes, but even in the north she would cut an odd figure. She was too narrow, flat-sided, and low for a carrack. The forward-tilting mainmast and bonaventure mizzen would have marked her as a galleon, but if she was a galleon, where were the high fore- and sterncastles? And where were the billowing, baglike square sails the Liavekans had come to associate with those heavy, sluggish northern ships? *Birdwing*'s square sails were cut flat, curved gently like a bird's wing, hence her name.

To the Liavekan admiral, Derec wondered, how did this all add up? A galleon with its upper decks razed, perhaps, in an effort to make it lighter, and furthermore cursed with an eccentric sailmaker. Some kind of bastard ship at any rate, neither

fish nor fowl, with a broadside to beware of, but a military
value easily enough discounted. Everyone knew that northern
ships couldn't sail to weather—unlike the oar-driven galleys
and galleasses of the Levar's navy, galleons were doomed to
sail only downwind. And the Liavekan's tactics were clearly
aimed at getting the escort to leeward of its convoy, where it
couldn't possibly sail upwind again to protect it.

You're in for a surprise, milord admiral, Derec thought.
Because *Birdwing* is going to make those wormy hulks of yours
obsolete, and all in the next turn of the glass.

"Wizard's compliments, sir." Lt. Facer had returned, sunlight winking from his polished brass earrings; he held his
armored cap at the salute. "He might venture a spell to veer
the wind, but it would take twenty minutes or more."

Within twenty minutes they'd be in gunshot. Weather spells
were delicate things, consuming enormous amounts of power
to shift the huge kinetic energies that made up a wind front,
and often worked late or not at all.

"Compliments to the wizard, Facer. Tell him we'll make
do with the wind we've got."

"Sir." Facer dropped his hat back on his peeling, sunburned
head. For a sailor he had a remarkably delicate complexion,
and these southern latitudes made things worse: his skin was
forever turning red and flaking off. He was openly envious of
Derec's adaptation to the climate: the sun had just browned the
captain's skin and bleached his graying hair almost white.

Facer turned and took two steps toward the poop compan-
ionway, then stopped. "Sir," he said. "I think our convoy
has just seen the enemy."

"Right. Cut along, Facer."

"Sir."

The Zhir convoy, arrayed in a ragged line just downwind of
Birdwing, was now showing belated signs of alarm. Five minutes had passed before any of them noticed an entire enemy
squadron sweeping up from two miles away. Derec had no
illusions about the quality of the merchant captains: the convoy
would scatter like chaff before a hailstorm. None of them were
capable of outrunning a squadron of warships: their only chance
was to scatter in all directions and hope only a few would fall
victim to the enemy. Still, Derec should probably try to do

something, at least to show the Zhir he'd tried to protect their
cities' shipping.

"Signal to the convoy, Randem," he said. "Close up, then
tack simultaneously."

The boy's look was disbelieving. "As you like, sir."

Derec gave him a wry grin. "For form's sake, Randem."

"Aye aye, sir. For form's sake."

Signal flags rose on the halyards, but none of the convoy
bothered an acknowledgment: the merchanters had no confidence in the ship's fighting abilities and were looking out for
themselves. Derec shrugged. This was nothing more than he
expected. At least they were clearing out and leaving an empty
sea between *Birdwing* and the enemy.

Birdwing gave a shuddering roll as it staggered down the
face of a wave; Derec swayed to compensate and almost lost
his balance. His heavy breastplate and helmet were adding
unaccustomed weight to his upper body. The helmet straps
were pressing uncomfortably on his brass earrings, and the
helmet was warming in the sun, turning into an oven.

Carefully Derec calculated his course and the enemy's. The
wind was holding a point north of west: the convoy had been
moving roughly north along the general trend of land. The
enemy squadron was racing under oars and sail as close to the
wind as their characteristics permitted: they were trying to gain
as much westing as possible so as not to be pinned between
Birdwing and the coast. Their course was more or less northwest: *Birdwing* was moving nor'-nor'east on a converging tack.
Unless something prevented it, the ships would brush at the
intersection of their paths; and then the enemy would be to
windward of the *Birdwing*, which was just where they wanted
to be.

At which point, Derec thought confidently, they were going
to suffer a terrible surprise.

Birdwing's crew were already at quarters; they'd been doing
a gun drill when the enemy appeared. There was nothing to
do but wait.

"Wizard's compliments, sir." Facer was back, his leather-
and-iron cap doffed at the salute. "The enemy is attempting a
spell."

"Thank you, Facer." Suddenly the brisk warm breeze blew
chill on Derec's neck. He turned to face the enemy, touched

his amulet of Thurn Bel, and summoned his power.

Awareness flooded his mind. He could feel the protective shields that Levett, *Birdwing*'s wizard, had wound around the ship; from eastward he could feel a strong attempt to penetrate those shields. Derec called his power to him, but held it in reserve in case the onslaught was a feint. The attack faded grudgingly before Levett's persistent defense, then disappeared. Whatever it was, the probe had failed. Levett's protective spells remained intact, on guard.

That was the strategy Derec and Levett had formed weeks ago. The wizard's magic would remain defensive, and *Birdwing*'s bronze cannon would bring the war to the enemy.

Derec let his hand fall from his amulet. He saw his officers standing around him expectantly; he gave them a smile. "Done," he said. "We're safe for the moment." He saw them breathe easier.

He looked at the enemy. Brightness winked from the enemy's decks: marines in their polished armor. He could hear the thud of kettledrums and crash of cymbals as the enemy quartermasters beat time for the rowers. A mile to leeward, in deeper, bluer water now, the galleasses were laboring in the steep sea, the smaller one having a particularly hard time of it.

Derec's awareness tingled: the enemy wizard was making another attempt. Derec monitored the assault and Levett's efforts to parry it. Once again the enemy was repulsed.

There was a flash from the flagship's fo'c'sle, then a gush of blue smoke that the wind tore into streamers across her bows. The thud came a half second later, followed by a shrieking iron ball that passed a half cable to larboard. The range was long for gunshot from the pitching deck of a ship beating to windward. Jeers rose from *Birdwing*'s crew.

Another thud, this time from the smaller galleass, followed by another miss, this one coming close to clipping *Birdwing*'s stern. The enemy were giving their gun crews something to do, Derec thought, rather than stand and think about what might come, their own possible mutilation and death.

There was a bump and a mild bang from *Birdwing*'s maindeck, followed by a hoarse bellow. Derec stepped forward to peer over the poop rail; he saw one of the marines had stumbled and dropped his firelock, and the thing had gone off. Marcoyn, the giant marine lieutenant, jerked the man to his feet and smashed him in the face. The marine staggered down the gangway, arms windmilling: Marcoyn followed, driving another punch into the marine's face. Derec clenched his teeth. Hatred roiled in his belly.

"Marcoyn!" he bellowed. The lieutenant looked up at him, his pale eyes savage under the brim of his boarding helmet. His victim clutched the hammock nettings and moaned.

"No interference with the sojers!" Marcoyn roared. "We agreed that, *Captain!*" He almost spat the word.

Derec bit back his anger. "I was going to suggest, Marcoyn, that you blacken the man's eyes later. We may need him in this fight."

"I'll do more than blacken his eyes, by Thurn Bel!"

"Do as you think best, Marcoyn." Derec spoke as tactfully as possible; but still he held Marcoyn's eyes until the marine turned away, muttering under his breath, his fists clenched at the ends of his knotted arms.

Marcoyn's strange pale eyes never seemed to focus on anything, just glared out at the world with uncentered resentment. He was a brute, a drunk, illiterate, and very likely mad, but he represented an element of *Birdwing*'s crew that Derec couldn't do without. Marcoyn was the living penalty, Derec thought, for the crimes he had committed for the ship he loved.

Derec remembered Marcoyn's massive arms twisting the garrote around young Sempter's neck, the way the boy's eyes had started out of his head, feet kicking helplessly against the mizzen pinrail, shoes flying across the deck. Derec standing below, helpless to prevent it, his shoes tacky with Lt. Varga's blood . . .

His mouth dry, Derec glanced at the mizzen shrouds, then banished the memory from his mind. The enemy had fired their bow chasers once more.

The smaller galleass fired first this time, followed a half second later by the flagship. Interesting, Derec thought. The smaller ship had the better crew.

A strong gust heeled the galleon and drove it through the sea. The waves' reflection danced brightly on the enemy's lateen sails. The enemy squadron was half a mile away. If the ships continued on their present courses, *Birdwing* would soon be alongside the enemy flagship in a yardarm-to-yardarm fight, a situation ideal for the northern galleon.

Another pair of bangs, followed by a buzzing and a smack: the smaller galleass's ball had pitched right through *Birdwing*'s main topsail. Derec saw blond and redheaded countrymen looking up in surprise, heard nervous laughter. This was the first time most of them had been under fire. Derec realized he should probably say something now, offer an inspiring comment to drive any thoughts of fear out of his sailors' heads. He could think of nothing.

"Run out the starboard chaser!" he finally called. "We'll answer that!"

There were some scattered cheers, but Derec could see puzzled expressions. The enemy were within range of the broadside guns: why not open fire with the whole battery? Derec kept his counsel. He was saving the first broadside for close range.

The bronze starboard demiculverin rumbled as it thrust its muzzle from the port. Derec could see the gun captain bent low over the chaser's barrel, timing the ship's motion, linstock in his hand. There was a gush of fire from the priming, then a roar; the gun flung itself back like a monstrous bronze beast. Derec turned to leeward and saw the nine-pound ball skip on the waves like a dancer twenty yards ahead of the enemy's prow. A groan of disappointment went up from *Birdwing*'s crew.

"Chaser crew, fire at will!" Derec called.

The chasers banged at each other for another three or four rounds apiece. The Liavekans showed no sign of changing course: were they really going to let Derec lay alongside and fight exactly the kind of battle he wanted? Ignoring the artillery duel, Derec studied the enemy, the changing relationship between the ships. Tried to get into his enemy's head, wondered what the enemy admiral was thinking.

The sound of kettledrums and cymbals was very loud now, carrying clearly upwind. The enemy sweeps moved in beautiful synchrony, the blue water boiling at their touch. The distance between *Birdwing* and the lead enemy narrowed, and Derec was considering running out his starboard battery when flame blossomed from the enemy's sides and the air was full of shrieking. Derec's heart turned over at the sound of a slamming noise from below—a shot lodged home—followed by another smack as a ball tore through the fore topsail. The enemy had fired its full broadside, maybe ten guns in all.

His nerves wailing in surprise, Derec bit his lip and frowned at the enemy. Something had changed, but he couldn't say what. Something in the pattern of drumbeats and cymbals. Another level of his awareness sensed the enemy's magician attempting a spell. With a start he realized what the enemy intended.

"Hard a-starboard!" he roared, and ran to the break in the poop. Just below him, sheltered by the poop overhang, Sandor the timoneer controlled the ship's whipstaff. "Hard a-starboard!" Derec shrieked again, and he felt the change in the ship's motion that meant the timoneer had flung his weight against the whipstaff and the galleon was beginning to respond to its big rudder. Derec suddenly felt the nature of the enemy spell—it was an attempt to paralyze them for a few seconds, but Levett had parried it, again without the need for Derec's assistance. Derec glanced at the surprised faces of his crew.

"Both broadsides, load and run out! Starboard guns, load with doubleshot! Larboard guns, load with roundshot!" He glanced at the enemy to confirm what he suspected, and found it true—the bright silhouettes were narrowing as one set of sweeps backed water while the other continued driving forward. Lateen sails billowed and snapped as the yards were dropped to the deck. The enemy were changing course, driving straight into the wind under the power of their sweeps alone.

Birdwing lurched as the waves caught it at a new angle. "Braces, there!" Derec shouted. "Rudder amidships!" The galleon filled with shouting and stamping as the crews bent to their work. Heart in his mouth, Derec gazed at the enemy.

The relationship between the ships had changed drastically. The enemy vessels had simultaneously turned straight into the wind while preserving their relationship to one another, from a line ahead into a line of bearing. They had attempted to cut behind the Farlander galleon, head upwind and into the convoy without the necessity of a fight. *Birdwing* had just turned downwind and within the next two minutes would pass along the flagship's starboard side. The ships would exchange broadsides on the run, and then race past one another.

If *Birdwing* were a caravel or high-charged galleon, that would have been the end of the fight: Derec could never have turned into the wind to pursue the enemy. The Liavekan admiral would have got between him and his convoy, a master stroke.

But *Birdwing* was something the Liavekan hadn't seen, and savage exultation filled Derec as he realized he had the enemy in his hand.

There was a massive rumbling as the guns were run out, all fifty-four of them, heavy demicannon on the lower deck and lighter, longer culverins on the maindeck. Derec stood on the break in the poop and shouted through cupped hands.

"Larboard gun captains and second captains remain with your guns! All extra crew to the starboard guns!" Bare feet drummed the planks—the crew had practiced this many times. *Birdwing* didn't carry enough crew to efficiently fight both sides, and Derec wanted his starboard guns served well.

Enemy kettledrums thundered over the water. The purple-and-scarlet galleass was frighteningly close.

"Starboard broadside, make ready!" Derec shouted. "Fire on my order! Sail trimmers, stand by the braces! Timoneer—starboard a bit!" He'd pass alongside the enemy and drive *Birdwing* right through their starboard bank of sweeps if he could.

But abruptly the kettledrums made a flourish, then fell silent. The enemy sweeps rose like white teeth from the water, and then drew inward. The Liavekans were prepared for Derec's maneuver.

"'Midships!" he called. And suddenly there was eerie silence—no kettledrums, no shouted orders, no guns running out, only the whisper of the wind and the deafening beat of Derec's pulse in his ears.

The galleass came alongside, and the guns spoke. The enemy fo'c'sle guns bellowed first, so close their fires licked *Birdwing*'s timbers, and the air filled with splinters and moaning shot. Then Derec shrieked "Fire!" and the galleon lurched as all its guns went off more or less together, from the demicannon on the lower decks to the little sakers and minions used by the marines. Abruptly there was a chorus of screams from the galleass as shot and splinters tore through the close-packed oarsmen—the weird and awful cries sounded clearly even to Derec's deafened ears. The enemy quarterdeck guns went off last, massive iron cannon firing fifty-pound stone shot that burst on impact and laid low a score of Marcoyn's marines.

But all that was anticlimax: as soon as *Birdwing*'s guns fired, Derec was shouting new orders. "Hard a-starboard! Starboard guns, reload! Larboard guns, fire as you bear!''

Kettledrums and cymbals punctuated Derec's cries: the enemy admiral's galleass was losing momentum, beginning to swing in the wind. They had to get under way, and quickly. Derec saw sweeps beginning to run out, and saw also that his salvo had blown gaping holes in the galleass's sides. The rowdeck must be a shambles. Triumph filled his heart.

Suddenly he was aware of the pressure of an enemy spell. Levett seemed to be handling it; but suddenly there was another strike, moving fast as lightning, a white-hot flare in Derec's mind. Derec's own power lashed out without his conscious effort, turning the spell away. A hollow feeling overtook him as he realized the spell's nature: the enemy wizard had tried to set off the powder cartridges on the gundeck. The powder magazine itself was well guarded by spells renewed yearly, but the powder was vulnerable as the ship's boys carried it to the guns, as the gun crews ladled the cartridges into the breeches and rammed shot atop them. This closely engaged, explosions on the gundeck would be disastrous.

The purple galleass fell off the wind a bit before its sweeps finally struck the water. *Birdwing* turned like a dolphin under the enemy stern, the starboard guns running out again, barking as they drove iron lengthwise through the enemy, wreaking hideous destruction on the narrow enemy vessel. Derec pounded the taffrail, roaring encouragement to the guncrews. *Birdwing* was now close-hauled between the two enemy galleasses, and the larboard guns—manned inefficiently by two men apiece—fired as the smaller vessel came into line: the range was much longer, but Derec saw the foremast come down. The fully crewed starboard guns ran out again, driving another broadside into the admiral's port quarter. The kettledrums fell silent. Sweeps flailed the water in panic.

"Stations for tacking! Helm's a-lee!'' Derec's heart beat fire: a bloodthirsty demon howled in his soul. He wanted the enemy smashed.

Birdwing pivoted on its heel like a dancer, running along the purple ship's larboard side. Two full broadsides lashed out; the enemy timbers moaned to the impact of shot. The main- and mizzenmasts fell: the enemy rudder hung useless from its gudgeons. Nothing but small arms replied: the Liavekans hadn't reloaded their larboard guns after the first broadside, either because they hadn't the crew or hadn't thought it was necessary. Now they paid for their neglect.

The enemy flagship was left astern, a near-wreck pouring blood from its scuppers. *Birdwing* tacked again, heading for the smaller enemy; the lighter galleass had bravely turned toward the fight in an effort to succor its admiral. Useless: *Birdwing* forged ahead and yawed to fire one broadside, then the other. The guns smashed enough enemy sweeps to stagger the galleass in the water; the next broadside brought the mainmast down along with the enemy colors.

Derec saw the third enemy vessel's colors coming down—the xebec had surrendered, even though it had stood away from the battle and might have got away.

Then there was silence, filled only with the gusting wind and the eerie sounds of the dying. Wreckage littered the sea: broken sweeps, jagged splinters, torn bodies of the dead. The enemy were drifting toward land: Derec would have to order them to drop an anchor, 'til he could jury-rig masts and get them under way.

Suddenly the silence was broken by cheers, *Birdwing*'s crew sending roar upon defiant roar into the sky.

Derec looked down at the capering men, laughing and dancing in the waist of the ship, dancing in the blood of their crewmates who lay where the enemy's shot had flung them.

Then he remembered the mutiny, the way the men had danced in the blood of their countrymen, and the taste of victory turned to bitterness in his mouth.

"Ah," said Prince Jeng. "My mutineer."

"Your serene and glorious Highness," Derec said, and fell to his knees, bowing low and raising his hands to his forehead.

Jeng was a balding man in his late thirties, tall for a Zhir, bearded and portly; he was heir to the throne, and head of the Regency Council while his father the king was ill and recuperating at the Obsidian Palace inland. It was Jeng who had intensified the undeclared naval war against Liavek, and who as a means of forwarding his policy had welcomed *Birdwing* to Ka Zhir. This was Derec's first lone audience with the Prince—he had met Jeng twice before, but only as one petitioner among many.

Jeng seemed a bit surprised at Derec's submission.

"Rise, Captain SuPashto. This is an informal audience, after all. Would you like a sherbet on the terrace?"

"Thank you, Your Highness." Derec rose and suppressed a feeling of discomfort. Back in the Twin Kingdoms, on the continent the Zhir called Farland, he'd never had any dealings with high nobility, and despite Prince Jeng's hospitality he was not at home here. Derec was also uncomfortable in Prince Jeng's language: his tongue was rough, and he desperately wished for an interpreter.

Jeng's cool summer silks whispered on marble as Derec followed him to the terrace. The sherbets were already laid on a wrought-iron serving table: obviously the Prince had not expected Derec to refuse an offer of refreshment. Below the terrace, cliffs fell away to reveal the Inner Harbor of Ka Zhir.

A strong sea breeze blew through the palace, but below the harbor was windless. A hundred ships of burden stood on their perfect reflections in the still blue water. Among them, small guard boats scuttled like water spiders under oars. Thirty war galleys were drawn up on the shelving pebble beach of Great Kraken Island, safe beneath the guns and curtain walls of Fort Shzafakh, which was perched atop the old volcanic dome. Beyond, between the Inner and Outer Harbor, thousands of slaves were toiling to build the New Mole, at the end of which a new defensive fortification would rise, one from which a massive chain could be raised to block the channel and keep the Inner Harbor safe. The new fort was coming to be known as Jeng's Castle, just as the intensified conflict with Liavek was gaining the name of Jeng's War. Neither term was official; but language was, in its inevitable fashion, reflecting the realities of power.

Jeng scooped up his sherbet in one broad paw and walked to a brass telescope set on the terrace. Touching it gingerly— the metal had grown hot in the sun—he adjusted the instrument and peered through it.

"Your conquests, Captain," he said. He stepped back from the telescope and, with a graceful gesture, offered Derec a look. Derec nodded his thanks and put his eye to the instrument.

The bright varnished galleass leaped into view, anchored in the Outer Harbor next to the xebec. The Zhir ensign floated over both, black-and-gold raised over the Liavekan blue. The admiral's purple galleass was just behind, drawn up on the shelving beach where it had been run aground to keep from sinking. *Birdwing*'s distinctive silhouette, a total contrast to every other vessel in the harbor, shimmered in a patch of bright, reflective water.

"I understand the xebec surrendered without a fight," Jeng commented. Derec straightened and faced the Prince. The sea breeze tugged at the Prince's cloth-of-gold silks.

"Yes, Your Highness. The xebec captain witnessed the loss of the two larger vessels and concluded that mighty wizardry was at the work. He surrendered rather than be blasted to the bottom."

"But wizardry was not at work, was it?"

Derec shook his head. "Nay, sir. We had a wizard, and so did they; but the magics canceled each other out."

Jeng raised his delicate silver spoon to his mouth. "We have interrogated Tevvik, their wizard," he said, sipping sherbet as if it were wine, "and he confirms this. In return for his testimony, we have released him on parole."

Derec shrugged: the wizard's fate meant nothing to him.

"A pity that Admiral Bandur was killed in the fight. He might have brought you a large ransom."

"With Your Highness's blessing," Derec said slowly, staggering through the foreign phrases, "we will capture more admirals."

Prince Jeng smiled catlike and licked his spoon. "So you shall, Thung willing."

"If Your Highness will modify our privateer's license to permit us to cruise alone against the enemy . . ." Derec began, but Jeng frowned and held up a hand.

"There are those on the Council who say your victory was a fluke," Jeng said. "They say the winds were kind to you. What should I answer, Captain?"

Derec hesitated, an array of technical terms running through his head. How much did Jeng know of the sea? Ka Zhir depended on ships and trade for its livelihood, and Jeng was an intelligent man who took an interest in the affairs of the kingdom; but how much practical seamanship did the Prince know?

"Your Highness has seen galleons from the Two Kingdoms before, and from Tichen?"

Jeng nodded. "They come with the annual trading convoys, yes. My mariners do not think well of them."

"They are slow, yes. And cannot sail into the wind."

Jeng finished his sherbet and scoured the dish with his spoon. The sound grated on Derec's nerves. "So my advisors tell me. You say your ship is different."

"It is, Your Highness. We call it a *race-built* galleon," stumbling, having to fall into his own language, "to distinguish it from the old style, which we call *high-charged*."

Jeng reached for a bell on the table and rang it. "Race-built?" he said. "Because it is faster?"

Derec was surprised at Jeng's conclusion: the Prince understood Derec's language better than he'd suspected.

"With respect, Your Highness, the root of the word is *razor*," Derec said. "Because the upper decks, the high stern- and forecastles, are *razored* off. The race-built galleon is lower in profile, and also lighter, without the weight of the castles."

A servant appeared. The Prince ordered more sherbet, then looked at Derec and frowned. "The castles, my advisors tell me, are the galleon's great advantage in combat. The castles can hold many soldiers, and the soldiers can fire down into enemy ships."

"The castles also make a high profile, and a high profile can catch the wind. The wind catches the ship and tries to push it to leeward. This is called *leeway* . . ."

Prince Jeng's eyes flashed. "Any Zhir child knows this, Captain. Please do not inform me of matters I learned at my mother's knee."

Derec's heart skipped a beat. He lowered his eyes and looked at Jeng's feet. "Your pardon, Your Highness. I was merely trying to make the point that with a lower profile, the race-built galleon makes much less leeway and is therefore able to point higher into the wind."

"Yes." Curtly. "Very well. I understand."

"Also, Your Highness, we have a new form of square sail called the birdwing. It's flatter, rather like your own lateen sail. Although it holds less air, it's somehow able to drive a ship nearer the wind."

Prince Jeng's sternness dropped away, replaced by frank curiosity. "Is that so? How can that be?"

Derec shrugged helplessly. "I do not know, Your Highness. It appears to be a property of the wind that we do not yet understand."

"It works, but you don't know why?" Jeng considered this. "I shall have to inquire of my philosophers. We know why the lateen works so well, of course—it's the triangular shape, which reflects the universality of the Triple Unities of Heart, Wit, and Spirit."

"Perhaps Captain-General Collerne understands these matters," Derec said, "I don't know. The birdwing sail had been in use on some of our smaller craft for two or three generations, but it was Captain-General Collerne who thought to use it on a warship. It was also his idea to raze the upper decks, after he noticed that some old ships that had their castles removed became better sailers." A fire kindled in Derec as he thought of his old captain and teacher. "He wanted to create a fleet taking its orders from *sailors*, not generals appointed to command at sea. A fleet that fights with broadside guns instead of rapiers and firelocks, that uses the wind and water to its own advantage . . ." His thick northern tongue stumbled on the Zhir words.

"Yes, yes," Jeng said. "That's all very well, but it's practical issues I'm concerned with." A servant arrived with another bowl of sherbet. He gave his catlike smile as he tasted the treat. Derec understood how the man had grown so stout.

"I am trying to speak practically, Your Highness," Derec said. "Your galleys and galleasses are built lightly, so they can be driven through the water by muscle power. Because they must have so many rowers, they must water and victual frequently, and they must stop and let the rowers off every few days, so that they won't sicken and die. If the enemy attacks while your ships are beached, your fleet is in grave jeopardy. Your ships can carry only a limited number of guns, because they are built lightly.

"Because it is powered by the wind, *Birdwing* is built stoutly and can resist punishment that would sink one of your galleys. Our holds are deeper and our crews are smaller, so that we can carry more provision and stay at sea much longer. *Birdwing* carries twenty-seven guns on each broadside, twice as many as your largest ship—and that's not counting sakers and minions. The Liavekans simply won't be able to stand up to a race-built ship, and a fleet of race-built craft will sweep them from the Sea of Luck. I'll stake my life on that, Your Highness."

Prince Jeng looked at him darkly. "You may have to, Cap-

tain SuPashto.'' Derec felt a cold touch on his neck. Prince
Jeng took a deliberate sip of sherbet. ''You are from a northern
land, where political realities are somewhat different. Your
King Torn is bound by custom and by the House of Nobles.
There *is* no law of custom in Ka Zhir, Captain. The King is
the law here, and in the absence of the King, the Regent.''

''I understand, Your Highness.''

Jeng's eyes were cold. ''I think not, Captain. I think you
do not comprehend the ... *necessities* ... of life in Ka Zhir.''
He turned, facing the Inner Harbor, and pointed with his silver
spoon, an oddly delicate gesture in such a big man. ''You see
the New Mole, Captain? I ordered that. One order, and thousands of slaves were set to work. Many of them will die. I
didn't have to apply to the Regency Council, I didn't have to
speak to a treasurer, I didn't have to get the permission of a
House of Nobles. I merely gave an order one fine morning—
and behold, the slaves die, and the mole is built.''

''Yes, Your Highness.''

''Perhaps our political character,'' Jeng said, turning philosophical, ''is derived from our volcanoes. They are unpredictable, inclined to sudden violence, and prone to massacre.
So are the Zhir. So is my family.

''I am a tyrant, Captain,'' he said. He turned back to Derec,
and his smile sent a chill through the northern man. ''My very
whim is law. I am an educated man and am considered an
enlightened tyrant by my philosophers''—his smile was cyn-
ical— ''but I would scarcely expect them to say anything else,
as I would then be compelled to have them crucified. That is
the problem with being a tyrant, you see—I can't *stop* being
tyrannical, even if inclined otherwise, because that would encourage other would-be tyrants to take my place, and they
would be worse. I am not as great a tyrant as my father—he
had his unsuccessful commanders beheaded, and I only have
them whipped, or make slaves of them. But I promise *you*,
Captain SuPashto,'' and here he pointed his spoon at Derec;
and the gesture could not have been more threatening if the
Prince had held a sword. ''I promise you that if you fail me I
will have you killed.''

Prince Jeng fell silent, and slowly ate two bites of sherbet.
Derec said nothing. From the moment he had entered into

conspiracy with Marcoyn and the two of them had raised the crew, he had expected nothing but death.

Jeng looked at him curiously. "You do not fear death, northern man? I can make the death unpleasant if I wish."

"My life is in your hands," Derec said. "I have always known this."

"Then you understand the essential character of our relationship." Prince Jeng smiled. He finished his sherbet and put the bowl down, then put his arm around Derec's shoulders and began to walk with him back into the palace. "I have in mind to give you a squadron, Captain," he said. "It will be under the nominal orders of a Zhir, but it will be yours to command, and my admiral will understand this. Bring me back lots of the Levar's ships, and I will favor you. You will be able to replace those old brass earrings with rings of gold, and diamonds and emeralds will gleam like reflective water on your fingers. Fail me, and . . . well, why be morbid on such a lovely day?"

Derec's mind whirled. "Thank you, Your Highness," he stammered.

"I will send some slaves aboard to replace your casualties."

Derec hesitated. "I thank you, Your Highness. Could I not have freemen? They——"

Jeng's tones were icy. "Slaves can pull ropes as well as anyone."

Derec sighed inwardly. Jeng would send his slaves aboard and collect their share of the pay and prize money. The slaves would not work hard and would prove cowardly, because they hadn't anything to fight for. It was a persistent evil here, one Derec had hoped to avoid—but now he must concede.

"I thank you, Your Highness. Strong men, if you please."

"No women? Not one?"

"Women are not as strong. On a galleon, the sailors must move heavy cannon, and fight the yards when the sails are filled with wind. . . ."

"Really? But surely there are less physical tasks. Scrubbing the planks, or cooking, or serving the officers."

"Then there are discipline problems, Your Excellency. If you will look at the complaints in your navy, I'm sure you'll find more than half having to do with officers playing favorites among their prettier crewmates."

"But how do your sailors keep warm at night?"

Derec smiled. "Abstinence makes them . . . fiercer fighters, Your Highness."

Prince Jeng looked shocked. "I would never deprive my men and women of their pleasures, Captain. They're prone enough to disobedience as it is. But if you *insist* on your barbaric customs . . ." He shrugged. "The least I can do is rescue *you* from this cold regime—one of my commanders must learn to enjoy life, yes? Until your ship is ready, you will stay in the palace and accept my hospitality. I will send a woman to your room tonight." He hesitated. "You *do* like women, yes?"

"Ah. Yes, Your Highness."

"You *did* make me wonder, Captain. Perhaps you would prefer more than one?"

Derec was surprised. "One is generally sufficient."

Jeng laughed. "I'm unused to such modesty. Very well. One it is."

"Thank you, Your Highness. For everything."

The Prince had steered Derec back to the audience chamber, and he dropped his arm and stepped back. "The major-domo will show you to an apartment."

"Thank you, Your Highness." Derec knelt again, raising his hands to his forehead.

"One more thing, SuPashto."

"Your Highness?"

Prince Jeng was smiling his catlike smile. "No more mutinies, Captain."

A day later, coming aboard *Birdwing*, Derec was surprised to meet the Liavekan wizard, Tevvik, at the entry port. The pleasant-looking young man smiled and bowed, his expression cheerful. Derec nodded curtly and stepped below to his own wizard's hot, airless cabin. He rapped on the flimsy partition.

"Enter." Derec stepped in to find Levett sitting in his bunk, reading a Zhir grammar by the light of a tallow candle. Derec stood over him.

"I've come for my lesson, wizard," he said.

Levett was a short, thin man. Though he was young, his hair and beard were white. Diamond chips glittered in his hoop earrings. His green eyes studied Derec.

"As you like, Captain. I was just chatting with a colleague.

Tevvik's an interesting man. Shall we go to your cabin?''

Derec turned and moved down the passageway to his cabin. The stern windows were open, providing relief from the heat. Flitting reflections danced on the deckhead above.

"I have been comparing notes with Tevvik," Levett offered. "The Liavekan."

"He's Tichenese, actually. That's why he's so dark. It was a matter of chance that he was in the Liavekan navy—it might as easily have been Ka Zhir, or the Two Kingdoms. He's seeking adventure and foreign lands; he doesn't care whom he serves. He's on parole; now he'll set up on his own, here in town. Of course," Levett said rather deliberately, "he has no family. No one depending on him. He can afford to wander."

Derec sat at his table and held the wizard's eyes for a long moment. The wizard looked away.

"I have promised you your liberty, wizard. As soon as I know your weather spells."

"I have never doubted your word, Captain."

"Just my ability to keep it."

Levett said nothing.

"This situation was not of my making, Levett," Derec said. "I'm sorry you are without your wife and family; I know you love them dearly. As soon as I can spare you, you will be free to take the first ship north. With money in your pocket."

Levett licked his lips. "They will call me a mutineer."

"The mutiny was mine, wizard."

"I understand. You were left no choice. I had no choice myself—when the fighting broke out, I wrapped myself in illusion and hid."

"You had no part in the mutiny, true enough."

"Those in authority at home . . . may not understand."

"There would have been a mutiny in any case. My choice was to try to control it, lest everyone die."

The finest ship in the Two Kingdoms' fleet, Derec thought bitterly, and the man who had conceived it, fought for its building, sweated through its construction—Captain-General Collerne—had been denied command. Instead *Birdwing* received a courtier from the capital, Captain Lord Fors, and his venomous lieutenant, Grinn . . . and within two months, with their policy of vicious punishments mixed with capricious favoritism, they had destroyed the morale of the crew and driven

them to the brink of violence. Derec—who as a commoner
had risen to the highest rank available to the lowborn, that of
sailing master—had tried to stand between the captain and his
crew, had tried to mitigate the punishments and hold the crew
in check, but had only been mocked for his pains and threatened
by Grinn with a beating. A sailing master, the senior warrant
officer on the ship, flogged . . . the threat was unheard of, even
in a service accustomed to violence.

After that, Derec knew that mutiny was only a matter of
time. Derec approached Marcoyn first—the man was constantly in trouble, but he was a fighter. Derec then chose his
moment, and as an officer had the keys to the arms chests:
Fors and Grinn both died screaming, begging for their lives as
maddened crewmen hacked at them with swords and pikes. Lt.
Varga, a good officer who had been appalled by his captain's
conduct, had nonetheless tried to rescue Fors, and was stabbed
and flung bodily into the sea for his pains.

Derec had tried to hold the killings to three, but the mutineers
got into the liquor store and things soon ran out of control. The
ship's corporal died, bludgeoned to death in the hold; another
dozen, known captain's favorites or those suspected of being
informers, were killed. Marcoyn had led the blood-maddened
crewmen on their hunt for enemies, had hung the remaining
lieutenants and a fourteen-year-old midshipman, Sempter, from
the mizzen shrouds, and there garroted them one by one. Derec
had stood by underneath, watching the starting eyes and kicking
heels, helpless to prevent it—he was the ship's sailing master,
another officer, and if he'd objected he would have danced in
the shrouds with the others.

After the crew had sobered, Derec had been able to reassert
his authority. Levett, who had hidden during the mutiny, had
lent supernatural influence to Derec's command. Now Derec
was captain, and had chosen his officers from among the bo-
sun's and master's mates. Marcoyn, who was illiterate and
could not navigate, had been given the marines, whose morale
and efficiency he was in the process of ruining with a brutality
and capriciousness as hardened as that of Captain Lord Fors.

"You have done as well as you could, Captain," Levett
said. "But now that you possess the royal favor, can you not
do without me?"

Derec looked up at him. "Not yet, wizard. You are the best windspeller I know."

Levett was silent for a time, then shrugged. "Very well. Let us go about our lessons, then."

Derec reached inside his shirt for his amulet of Thurn Bel. The wizard seated himself. "Clear your mind, Captain," he said, "and summon your power. We shall try again."

Drained, his lesson over, Derec stepped onto the poop and nodded briskly to Random, the officer of the watch. Moaning through the rigging and rattling the windsails was the fitful wind that he had, at great effort, succeeded in summoning. Not much to show for three hours' effort.

He stepped to the stern and gazed over the taffrail at the lights of Ka Zhir. His eyes moved to the cliffs above, where his apartment and his harlot waited in Jeng's palace. She would be disappointed tonight, he thought; the wizardry had exhausted him.

Time to call his barge and head ashore. The order poised on his lips, he turned to head back for the poop companion. He froze in his tracks, terror lurching in his heart.

Dark forms dangled from the mizzen shrouds, their legs stirring in the wind. Tongues protruded from blackened lips. Pale eyes rolled toward Derec, glowing with silent accusation.

Wrenching his eyes from the sight, Derec looked at Random, at the other men on deck. They were carrying on as normal. The ghosts were invisible to them.

Derec looked again at the dead and stared in horror at young Sempter, the boy swinging from the shrouds with the garrote still knotted about his neck.

The dead had risen, risen to curse him.

He was doomed.

Drums and cymbals beat time as Derec's rowing squadron backed gracefully onto the shelving pebble beach of Ka Zhir's Outer Harbor. *Birdwing*, a damaged galleass in tow, dipped its ensign to its nominal Zhir admiral. The galleass had lost its rudder in an autumn storm, had broached-to and been pounded before the rowers got it under way again. *Birdwing* was continuing to the Inner Harbor, to deliver its crippled charge to the Royal Dockyard.

"Keep the Speckled Tower right abeam 'til the octagonal tower comes in line," the Zhir pilot said. "Then alter course three points to larboard to clear the New Mole."

"Aye aye, sir," said the timoneer.

The sound of anchors splashing echoed over the bay, followed by the roar of cable. The squadron's three prizes, all round-bowed merchantmen, had just come to rest. Derec, looking out over the taffrail, saw the crippled galleass slew sideways in a gust, then come to a sharp check at the end of the hawser. *Birdwing* gave a brief lurch as the cripple's weight came onto the line.

The bonaventure flapped overhead as *Birdwing* turned gracefully to larboard. A ghastly stench passed over the quarterdeck, and Derec hawked and spat. Ka Zhir used slaves in some of their ships, and they were chained to the benches and lay in their own filth—the smell was incredible. Derec turned away from the galleass and faced forward, his eyes automatically giving a guilty glance to the mizzen shrouds. His mind eased as he saw the clear, tarred black hawser cutting through the bright blue tropical sky.

Over his voyages of the last six months, the ghosts had returned many times, every few days, sometimes in broad daylight. Usually Derec saw them hanging in the mizzen rigging, but on occasion he'd see them elsewhere: Lt. Varga, his wounds pouring blood, his hair twined with seaweed as he watched Derec from amid the crew as the hands witnessed punishment; the ship's corporal, his skull beaten in, sitting on the main crosstrees and laughing through broken teeth as the ship went through gun drill; and once, most horribly, Derec had entered his cabin at dinnertime only to find Midshipman Sempter sitting at his place, gazing at him over his meal, his mouth working silently as he tried to speak past the garrote. Derec's steward had watched in amazement as the captain bolted the room, then returned later, sweating and trembling, to find the ghost gone.

Nothing untoward had ever happened: Derec's luck on his voyages had been good. Admiral Zhi-Feng, Derec's nominal superior, was an intelligent man, and on Prince Jeng's orders had diffidently followed Derec's advice; he was learning quickly, and had recommended that *Birdwing*'s lines be taken by draftsmen so that an entire squadron of race-built galleons might rise on the Royal Dockyard's stocks. Five galleons were a-building and would be ready by spring. Derec had fought three engagements with Liavekan squadrons and won them all, capturing two galleasses, four galleys, and a number of smaller craft; he had sent in over forty merchant ships as prizes. Corrupt and slow though Ka Zhir's prize courts were, they had made Derec a wealthy man: the strongbox he kept beneath the planks in his sleeping cabin was crammed with gold and jewels. Prince Jeng's War was proving successful, much to the discomfort of Liavek. With an entire squadron of galleons, Derec had no doubt the Liavekan navy would be swept from the seas.

Derec glanced up at the royal palace, the white walls on the tall brown cliffs, and frowned at the sight of the flag that flapped from its staff. Something was wrong there. He stepped to the rack, took a glass, and trained it on the flag. The Royal Standard leaped into view. Derec took a breath.

So King Thelm was back, having presumably recovered from his illness. Jeng would no longer be Regent; absolute power had now passed to his father. He wondered at the alteration's implication for himself, for *Birdwing*, and decided there would be little change. Thelm might negotiate an end to the war, but still *Birdwing* and Derec had proven themselves over and over again: Thelm wouldn't throw away such a strategic asset.

''Bel's sandals!'' SuKrone's curse brought Derec's eyes forward. Amazement crackled in his mind.

Birdwing had rounded the fortification at the end of the New Mole, and the entire Inner Harbor was opened to view. The harbor was full of the tall masts and dark rigging of a northern fleet, the huge round-bellied caravels that brought metals, pitch, and turpentine to Ka Zhir every autumn, returning with sugar, kaf, and spices; and riding to anchor were northern warships, three high-charged galleons and one leaner, lower shape, a race-built galleon like *Birdwing*, but longer, showing thirty gunports each side.

Floating above each ship was a green ensign with two gold crowns, the flag of Derec's homeland.

They had come early this year, and caught Derec unprepared.

The scent of death swept over the poop. It was just the smell of the galleass, Derec thought; but still his spine turned chill.

''What do we *do*, Captain?'' Marcoyn's mad eyes were wild. Drunkenly, he shook his fist in Derec's face. ''What the piss do we *do*? They're going to have us kicking in the rigging by nightfall!''

Birdwing was still moving toward the Inner Harbor, a party of men standing in the forecastle ready to drop the best bower. Derec was looking thoughtfully over the rail. One of the big galleons—Derec recognized the *Sea Troll*—had storm damage: one topmast was gone. The *Double Crowns* was missing its castles: they had presumably been razored in an effort to make it as light and handy as *Birdwing*. *Monarch*, the other high-charged galleon, stood closest, towering over every ship in harbor and carrying eighty guns. But it was the other race-built ship that had an admiral's red pennant flying from its maintruck, and it was to this ship that Derec's eyes turned. *Torn II*, he thought: so they had built her, and sent her here to find her precursor.

"Captain! Answer, damn you!'' Marcoyn staggered, not from the heave of the deck but from his liquor.

Derec turned his eyes on the man and tried to control the raging hatred he felt. "We will wait, Mr. Marcoyn,'' he said.

"You've got to *do* something!'' Marcoyn raged. "You know Prince Jeng! *Talk* to him!''

Derec looked at Marcoyn for a long moment. Marcoyn dropped his unfocused eyes, then his fist.

"We fight under the flag of Ka Zhir,'' Derec said, indicating the ensign flying overhead. "We have Zhir protection. The trading fleet is here, aye, but it's under the two hundred guns of Fort Shzafakh and another two hundred on the mainland. They *daren't* attack us, Marcoyn. Not openly.''

Marcoyn chewed his nether lip as he thought this over. "Very well, SuPashto,'' he said.

Derec stiffened. "*Captain* SuPashto, if you please, Mr. Marcoyn.''

Marcoyn's eyes blazed dull hatred. "*Captain*,'' he spat. He saluted and turned away.

The other crewmen, the small, dark Zhir standing beside the tall, fair Farlanders, had watched the confrontation, trying hard to conceal their rising fear. Derec's quiet tones had seemed to calm them. He stepped forward to the break in the poop.

"They daren't touch us, boys!'' he shouted. "Not openly. But there will be Two Kingdoms men ashore on leave, and for now we'll have no shore parties. When we *must* send parties ashore, we will go armed and in large groups. Now,'' he ventured a ragged grin, ''let's show them what we've learned. As soon as our anchor's down, I want those sails harbor-furled, without a dead man in 'em; I want our old chafing-gear down; and I'll have some parties detailed to renew our gilding. Mr. Facer, see to it.''

''Yes, sir.''

Derec nodded curtly and stepped to the weather rail. He watched the northern fleet grow closer.

The admiral's summons came at sunset. Derec was half expecting it; he'd seen Zhi-Feng's barge take him ashore to his quarters in the Lower Town. Derec put on his best clothes, strapped on his rapier, and thrust a pair of pistols in his belt. He called for his gig and had himself rowed to the admiral's apartments.

The admiral was dressed in a gorgeous silk robe, and his hair and beard had been curled and perfumed. Gemstones clustered on his fingers. He drank wine from a crystal goblet as big as his head. His belt had scales of gold.

Derec scarcely noted this magnificence, his attention instead riveted on the admiral's other visitor, a portly man plainly dressed. He fell to his knees and raised his palms to his forehead.

''Rise, Captain,'' said Prince Jeng. ''Forgive this melodrama, but I thought it best not to let anyone know we had met.'' He sat in a heavy cushioned chair, eating red licorice. Derec rose. Jeng looked at him and frowned.

''Problems are besetting the two of us, Captain SuPashto,'' he said. ''The same problems, actually. My father, and the trading fleet.''

''I trust in your guidance, Highness.''

Jeng seemed amused. ''That's more than *I* can say, Captain. Neither I nor anyone else really expected His Encompassing Wisdom to recover; and I'm afraid the old man's found my regency a bit . . . premature . . . in diverting from his policies. He didn't want a naval war with Liavek in his old age, and now he's got one, and if the war hadn't been so successful, half the Council would have got the chop.'' Jeng grimly raised the edge of his hand to his throat. ''But since we're winning,'' he added, ''he's not sure what to do. At this point I think we'll fight on, so long as we stay ahead.'' He picked up a stick of licorice and pointed it at Derec like a royal scepter. ''That makes you valuable to him, and so you may thank your victories for the fact that you and Zhi-Feng haven't been beheaded on your own quarterdecks.''

''I owe my victories to your kindness and support,'' Derec said. ''May Thung preserve Your Highness.''

''Thank you for your concern, SuPashto, but I doubt I'm in real danger,'' Jeng said. ''I'm the only heir the old man's got left. The first went mad, the second died trying to invest his luck, the third played a losing game with His Scarlet Eminence and got his neck severed for losing . . . there's no one left but me. The worst that will happen to me, I think, is exile to an island. It's everyone around me who'll lose his head.'' He smiled. ''His Encompassing Wisdom might want to perpetrate a massacre just to show everyone he's back.''

Zhi-Feng looked a little green. ''Gods keep us from harm,'' he murmured.

Jeng chewed meditatively on his licorice wand. ''The problem presented by my shining and beloved ancestor, may Thung preserve him, may be finessed,'' he said. ''The problem of your trading fleet is not so easily dealt with. Briefly, they want you dead.''

''I expect no less, Highness.''

''They have demanded that you and your ship be turned over to them. This demand has thus far been refused. You are too valuable to the war effort.''

Derec felt his tension ease. ''I thank Your Highness.''

Jeng's eyebrows rose. ''*I* had little to do with it, Captain. His Encompassing Wisdom cares little for my counsel these days. We may thank the old man's common sense for that— he's not going to throw away the war's biggest asset, not without some thought, anyway. No, the problem is that your northern admiral is proving damnably clever.''

''May I ask which admiral, Your Highness?''

''I have heard you speak of him. One Captain-General Collerne.''

A cold wind touched Derec's spine. For the first time in this interview he felt fear. ''Aye,'' he said. ''A clever man indeed.''

''You know him well?''

''My first captain. Brilliant. He designed *Birdwing* and

taught me everything I've learned about the sea. He got me my master's warrant. He's the best sailor I know.''

Jeng looked at Derec coldly. "I'd advise you to leave off this admiration and learn to hate him, Captain SuPashto. He wants your hide, and he won't leave the Sea of Luck without it.''

Yes, Derec thought, that was Collerne. Brilliant, unforgiving, a demon for discipline. He would not countenance mutiny, not even against the evil man who had supplanted him in his longed-for command.

"I must trust to Your Highness's protection," Derec said simply.

Jeng's eyes were shards of ice. "My protection is worth little. Let me tell you what your damned captain-general did. Once he realized we wouldn't give you up because of your value to the war, he offered to fight in your place. In exchange for you and the other ringleaders, he's offered us his two best ships, *Torn II* and *Double Crowns*, to fight under our license and flag for the next year. Collerne himself has offered to command them.'' Jeng sucked his licorice wand. "The implication, I believe, is that if we refuse him, he'll offer his ships to Liavek instead.''

Derec's mouth turned dry. "Can he do that, Your Highness? Does his commission extend that far?''

"If it doesn't, he's taking a remarkable amount of initiative. The fact is, he's made the offer, and the King's considering it.''

"Highness," the admiral said. There was sweat on his perfumed brow. "We—Captain SuPashto and I—we have experience in this war. We've fought together for six months. Our crews are well drilled and every man is worth three of this Collerne's.''

Jeng looked bleak. "I shall attempt to have some friends on the Council point this out to His Encompassing Wisdom. But in the meantime I'll try to get you both out of the harbor. If Collerne can't find you, he can't kill you.''

"Very well, Your Highness," said Zhi-Feng. He looked somewhat less anxious.

"Your fleet is ready?''

"We need only take on water," Derec said. "*Birdwing* has six months' provision. The rowing fleet carries victuals only for six weeks, but we can take food from captured ships if necessary. Or buy it ashore.''

"I will have water-lighters alongside at dawn,'' Jeng said. He threw down his licorice and straightened. ''I'll try to . . . persuade the harbor master to send you a pilot. If he's not aboard by nightfall, warp your way out the back channel. I'm afraid now the New Mole's completed, the chain bars the main channel at sunset, so you can't escape that way.''

"Your Highness is wise.'' The admiral bowed.

Jeng's face turned curious. He looked at Derec. ''How do they treat mutineers in your navy, SuPashto?'' he asked.

"They are tied to the mast of a small boat,'' Derec said, ''rowed to each ship in the squadron and flogged in view of each ship's company. Then they are taken to the admiral's ship, hung from the mizzen shrouds, and disemboweled. Before they can die they are garroted. Then their bodies are preserved with salt and hung in an iron cage 'til they weather away.''

"That sounds most unpleasant,'' Jeng said mildly. ''Were I you, I would provide myself with poison. When the time comes, you can cheat your countrymen out of some of their fun.'' He shrugged. ''Life is full of experiences, my philosophers tell me, but I think I can attest that some are best avoided.''

Desolation stirred in Derec like a rising autumn gale. ''I will follow your advice in all things, Highness,'' he said.

When he returned to the ship, Derec didn't look up. He knew the ghosts were there, dark shadows that smiled at his approaching doom.

The water-lighters arrived just before dawn, and just afterward a messenger from the palace. *Birdwing* was to remain at anchor in the Inner Harbor until the complication with the Two Kingdoms fleet was resolved. If the galleon moved, she would be fired on by every gun on Great Kraken Island.

There was a hush on the *Birdwing* after that. Derec bought fresh food and wine from lighters offering wares alongside— he never let the hucksters aboard, fearing Two Kingdoms agents—and he kept the crew at their tasks, brightening the ship's paint and overhauling the running rigging; but the men were subdued, expectant. Dark shapes hung in the shrouds, filling the air with the stench of death. Red stains bubbled silently on the white holystoned planks. Derec kept his eyes fixed firmly on the horizon and sent the wizard ashore to buy poison. Levett returned with a vial of something he said was strong enough to kill half the crew.

On the evening of the second day, the summons from court arrived. Derec was ready. He spoke briefly with his officers concerning what was to be done after he left, put on his best clothing, and dropped two small pistols in his pockets.

With an escort of the Zhir Guard, quaintly old-fashioned in their ancient plumed helmets, he was rowed to the quay, then taken in a palankeen up the steep cliffs to the palace. There were new heads above the gate, illuminated by torches: a pair of the Council had died just that afternoon. The wall beneath them was stained with red. Local witches clustered beneath, hoping to catch the last of the ruddy drops in order to make their potions. A chamberlain took Derec through the halls to an anteroom.

"Wait within," the chamberlain said, raising his palms to his forehead. "His Everlasting and All-Encompassing Wisdom will grant you audience as soon as the Council meeting has concluded."

"May Thung protect His Majesty," Derec answered. He turned to the door.

"I shall send refreshment," the chamberlain said. Derec opened the door, stepped inside, and froze.

Glowing eyes turned their cold light on him. The ghosts were there, Varga with blood and seawater dripping from his clothes, the corporal with brains spattered over his clothing, the others with blackened faces and starting eyes, the garrotes twisted about their necks. Terror poured down Derec's spine.

Young Sempter stood before Derec, five paces away. His brass-buttoned jacket, too big for him, hung limply on his boyish frame. His feet, the feet that had kicked their shoes off as he died, were bare. There was a hole in one stocking. Sempter's mouth worked in his beardless face, and he took a step forward. Derec shrank back. The boy took a step, and another. His pale hand came up, and it closed around Derec's amulet of Thurn Bel. He tugged, and the thong cut into Derec's neck like a garrote. Derec smelled death on the boy's breath. The boy tugged again, and the amulet came free.

"Take him," Sempter said, and smiled as he stepped back.

Strong hands closed on Derec's arms. His pistols and his vial of poison were pulled from his pockets. His rapier was drawn from its sheath.

The image of Sempter twisted like that in a distorting mirror, faded, became that of Levett. The others were Zhir Guard. Their officer was holding Derec's sword.

Levett held up the amulet of Thurn Bell. "Never let another mage know where you keep your power, Captain," he said. He pocketed the amulet. "The rest of his men will surrender easily enough. They're fools or boys, all of them."

Derec's mind whirled as cuffs were fastened before him on his wrists. A chain was passed from the shackles between Derec's legs. The Guards officer unfolded a scroll and began to read.

"By order of King Thelm and the Council, Captain Derec SuPashto is placed under arrest. The Royal Authority is shocked"—she was remarkably straight-faced in conveying the King's surprise—"to discover that Derec SuPashto is a mutineer and rebel. He is commanded to the Tiles Prison under close guard, until he can be turned over to Two Kingdoms justice." She rolled up the scroll and placed it in her pocket. Her face was expressionless. "Take the prisoner away."

Derec looked at Levett. Mist seemed to fill his mind. "There were never any ghosts," he said dully.

Levett looked at him. "Illusions only," he said.

The man behind Derec tugged on the chain. Derec ignored it. "You planned this," Derec said. "All along."

"Something like it." Levett looked at him from three paces away, the distance beyond which Derec could not manipulate any power stored in the amulet. "I regret this, Captain. Necessity compelled me, as it compelled you during the mutiny. I want to return to our homeland and to live in peace with my family. Collerne can guarantee that, and you can't."

The guard, impatient, tugged hard on Derec's chain. Pain shot through Derec's groin. He bent over, tears coming to his eyes.

"This way," the guard said. Stumbling, Derec let himself be dragged backward out of the room. A push sent him staggering forward. With five of the Guard and Levett, he was marched from the palace, beneath the dripping heads of traitors and into the night.

No palankeen waited: he would walk down the long switch-back path to the Lower Town, then through town to the prison. The cool night breeze revived him. The officer lit a torch and gave it to one of her men. The party was silent save for the clink of the guards' chain coifs as they walked.

The Lower Town was growing near, tall buildings shuttered against the violence of the streets. Anyone with sense went armed here, and in company. Derec began to murmur under his breath. The party passed into the shadows of the crowded buildings. The street lamps were out, smashed by vandals. Derec's heart beat like a galley's kettledrum.

A pike lunged from an alley and took the Guards officer in the side. A dark body of men boiled from the darkness. The shackles dropped from Derec's wrists, and he lunged for the guard to his right, drew the main gauche from the man's belt, and slid it up under the chain coif to cut the astonished man's throat. Feet pounded the cobbles. Steel thudded into flesh. The torch fell and went out. Derec spun, seeing in the starlight the stunned look on the guard who was suddenly holding an empty chain where once a prisoner had been. The dagger took him in the heart, and he died without a sound.

A dark figure reeled back: Levett, already dead from a rapier thrust through both lungs. Marcoyn's bulk followed him, boarding axe raised high; and then the axe came down. Derec turned away at the sound of the wizard's head being crushed. Facer stepped out of the darkness, his face sunburned beneath his leather-and-iron cap, his sword bloody.

"Are you well, Captain?"

"Aye. Good work. Drag the bodies into the alleys where the City Runners won't find them."

"Fucking traitor." There were more thudding sounds as Marcoyn drove the axe into Levett again and again. Finally the big man drew back, grinning as he wiped a spatter of blood from his face. Liquor was on his breath.

"Got to make sure a wizard's dead," he grunted. "They're tricky."

"Best to be certain," Derec said, his mind awhirl. He'd posted the men here and knew what was coming, but the fight had been so swift and violent that he needed a moment to take his bearings. He looked at the dead wizard and saw, in the starlight, the amulet of Thurn Bel lying in the dust of the alleyway. He bent and picked it up. *Never let another mage know where you keep your power*, Levett had said; and Derec had always followed this prescription, though Levett never knew it. He'd invested his power in one of his brass earrings, one so old and valueless that no captor looting valuables would ever be tempted to tear it from his ear.

The bodies were dragged into the alley, piled carelessly atop one another. Wind ruffled Derec's graying hair: somewhere in the melee, he'd lost his cap. "To the ship, Captain?" Facer asked. He held out Derec's sword and the Guards officer's brace of wheellock pistols.

Derec passed the sword belt over his shoulder and rammed the pistols in his waistband. "Not yet," he said. "We have another errand first." He grinned at Facer's anxiety. "We have to wait an hour for the tide in any case, Lieutenant."

"Yes, sir." Doubtfully.

He led them through the empty streets of the Lower Town. Even the taverns were shut. Working people lived here, dockworkers and warehousemen: they didn't roister long into the night. Derec searched for one narrow apartment, found it, knocked on the door.

"Who is it?" A young, foreign voice.

"Captain SuPashto of the *Birdwing*."

"A moment."

The Tichenese wizard, Tevvik, opened the door, a lamp in his hand. His long hair was coiled on his head, held in place by a pin in the shape of a blue chipmunk. He recognized Derec and smiled. "An unexpected pleasure, Captain," he said. His Zhir was awkward.

"We're sailing for Liavek immediately. You're to accompany us."

Tevvik looked surprised. "I'm to be exchanged?"

"Something like that."

Tevvik thought about this for a moment, and shrugged. "I think I'd rather stay, Captain. I've developed a profitable business here."

From over his shoulder, Derec heard Marcoyn's growl. Derec was tempted to echo it. Instead he decided to be frank. "We're escaping arrest," he said. "You're accompanying us because you're a water wizard."

Tevvik's eyes widened. "You mean I'm being *abducted*?" He seemed delighted by the news.

"Aye. You are."

The wizard laughed. "That puts a different complexion on matters, Captain. Of course I'll accompany you. Do I have time to fetch my gear?"

"I'm afraid not."

Tevvik shrugged, then blew out his lamp. "As you like, Captain."

The waterfront district was a little more lively: music rang from taverns, whores paraded the streets, and drunken sailors staggered in alleyways looking to be relieved of their money. Derec and his party moved purposefully to the quay, then took the waiting barge to the galleon.

"Everything's prepared, Captain," Facer said. "We've cleared for action and the men are at quarters. The yards are slung with chains, the cable's ready to slip, the sails can be sheeted home in an instant, and we aren't showing any lights."

"Has the other party found our pilot?"

"SuKrone's got her under guard in the gunroom."

"Very good."

The boatmen tossed oars and Derec jumped for the entry port. He stepped onto the maindeck and sensed rather than saw his crew massed beneath the stars. He mounted the poop, then turned to face them. "We're running for Liavek, men," he said. "I have reason to believe they will welcome us."

There was a stirring ended swiftly by the petty officers' voices calling for silence.

"Those of you who were slaves," Derec said, "are now free."

Now there was an excited chattering that took the officers some time to quiet. Derec held up a hand.

"You may have to fight to keep that freedom, and that within the hour. Now—quietly—go to your stations. No drums, no noise. Facer, fetch me the pilot."

Derec leaned against the poop rail, pulled the big horse pistols from his waistband, and carefully wound the spring-driven locks. He was aware of the Tichenese wizard standing by, watching him. "Do you know weather magic, Wizard?"

"Some. It is not my specialty."

"What is?"

"Fireworks. Explosions. Illusion."

"Can you make *Birdwing* look like something else?"

"Your ship is a little large for that. Perhaps I could cloak it in darkness. The darkness will not be absolute, but it may make its outlines less clear."

"Very well. Do so."

Facer and SuKrone pushed the pilot up the poop ladder. She was a small, dark woman, her head wrapped in a kind of turban. She was dressed in the house robe she'd been wearing when SuKrone's men had kidnapped her. Derec pointed one of his pistols at her, and he heard her intake of breath.

"Take us out by the back channel," he said coldly. "If you fail me, I will shoot you twice in the belly. Follow my instructions, and I'll put you over the side in a small boat once we're clear."

The pilot bowed, raising her palms to her forehead. "I understand, Your Excellency. But we must await the tide."

"Half an hour."

"Thereabouts, yes."

"Do not fail me." He gestured with the pistol. "Stand over there."

"Your obedient servant, Excellency."

"Wizard, Facer, come with me." Derec stepped forward off the poop, along the gangway, climbed the fo'c'sle. The land breeze brought the sound of music and laughter from the town. Derec looked to starboard, where the twisting back channel between Great Kraken Island and the mainland was invisible in the darkness. Glowing softly in the night, masthead riding lights stood out against the black.

"There's our problem," he said. "*Double Crowns* is moored right near the entrance to the passage. We'll have to pass within half a cable."

Facer pursed his lips, blew air hesitantly. "They've lookouts set for us, I'm sure. They know we want to run. And if they give the alarm, Shzafakh's bastions will blow us to bits."

"My darkness won't cover us *that* well, Captain," the wizard said. He was speaking easily in Derec's own language, and with a native accent: apparently he'd spent time in the Two Kingdoms.

"We can't fire on them without raising an alarm," Derec mused. "We can't run aboard them without calling attention to ourselves.'' He shook his head. "We'll just have to run past and hope for a miracle.''

"Captain . . .'' Tevvik's tone was meditative. "If we can't pass without being noticed, perhaps we can make people notice something other than ourselves.''

"What d'ye mean, wizard?''

"Perhaps I can cause an explosion aboard *Double Crowns*. Then maybe the gunners in Shzafakh will think we're running from a fire, not for freedom.''

Derec scowled. "The magazine is protected against spells.''

"I'm sure. But powder in the open is not.''

"They would not have cartridges in the open—it's all held in the magazine 'til needed. Don't waste my time with these notions, wizard.''

"I was suggesting a boat full of powder nestled under that ship's stern. I can make *that* go off well enough.''

Astonishment tingled in Derec's nerves. He tried not to show it; instead he stroked his chin and frowned. "With a little sorcerous wind to push it where it's needed, aye,'' he said. He pretended to consider. "Very well, wizard,'' he said. "We'll do it. Facer, fetch the gunner.''

Tevvik smiled. "I wish you wouldn't use the word 'wizard' that way, Captain. The word's not a curse.''

Derec looked at him. "That's a matter of opinion, Mr. Tevvik.''

He led the Tichenese back to the quarterdeck and gave the orders for men to file to the magazine and bring up ten casks of powder. "Barefoot only, mind,'' he said. "No hobnails to strike a spark. Belts and weapons are to be laid aside. Scarves tied over their ears so their earrings won't strike a spark.'' He drew his pistols and pointed them at Tevvik.

"Don't set them off when they're alongside,'' he said, "or I'll serve you as I'd serve the pilot.''

The wizard raised his hands and grinned. "I have no intention of blowing myself up, Captain.''

"Maintain those intentions,'' Derec said, "and we'll have no trouble.''

The barge was loaded with powder, and canvas thrown over the barrels to avoid getting them wet. The boat's small mast was raised, its lateen set, its tiller lashed. The boat was warped astern and Derec concentrated, summoning his power, keeping

it ready. A small wind to blow his thirty-foot barge was fully
within his capabilities.

"Tide's turning, Captain."

"Very well. Prepare to slip the cable and sheet home."

"Aye aye, sir."

There was a murmur of bare feet as men took their stations.
Derec took a careful breath. "Sheet home the main tops'l. Set
the spritsail and bonaventure."

The heavy canvas topsail fell with a rumble, then rumbled
again as it filled with wind. *Birdwing* tilted, surged, came alive.
Water chuckled under the counter.

"Slip the cable."

The cable murmured from the hawsehole, then there was a
splash as its bitter end fell into the sea. A pity, Derec thought,
to lose the best bower anchor.

"Helm answers, sir," said the steersman.

"Larboard two points. There. Amidships."

Derec glanced over the stern, saw phosphorescence glinting
from the bone in the teeth of the powder boat.

Birdwing was barely moving. The back channel was dangerous and twisting; he needed maneuverability there, not
speed.

"Pilot," he said. The woman stepped forward.

"Sir."

"Take command. No shouting, now. Pass your orders quietly."

"Yes, sir."

The pistols were growing heavy in Derec's hands. He ignored
the tension in his arms and stepped to the weather rail, peering
for sight of *Double Crowns*. The masthead lights were growing
nearer. Five cables. Four. Three. He summoned his power.

"Cast off the boat."

Derec's heart leaped to his throat as the boat lurched wildly
to the first puff of wind and threatened to capsize, but the barge
steadied onto its course, passing to weather of *Birdwing*. He
guided the boat with little tugs of his mind, aimed it toward
Double Crowns.

Two cables. Now one, and from across the water a shout.
More shouts. The barge thudded against the razee galleon's
tumblehome near the stern. A drum began beating. Alarm
pulsed in Derec: on this still night, that drum would be heard

all over town. Derec steeled his mind to the necessity of what was to come.

"Give us fire, wizard," he said.

"Your obedient servant." Tevvik pursed his lips in concentration and made an elegant gesture with his hand. Derec remembered at the last second to close his eyes and preserve his night vision.

Even through closed lids he saw the yellow flash. A burst of hot wind gusted through his hair. He could hear shouts, screams, and, from his own ship, gasps of awe. He opened his eyes.

Double Crowns seemed unchanged, but he could hear the sound of water pouring like a river into her hold. The drum was silenced; in its place were cries of alarm. As Derec watched, the razee began to list. Crewmen poured from the hatches in a storm of pounding feet. The galleon's list grew more pronounced; Derec could hear things rolling across the deck, fetching up against the bulwarks. Then came a sound that was a seaman's nightmare, a noise that half paralyzed Derec with fear—the rumble of a gun broken loose, roaring across the tilting deck like a blind, maddened bull before it punched clean through the ship's side, making another hole through which the sea could enter.

He couldn't stand to watch anymore. He moved to the other side of the poop, but the sounds still pursued him, more guns breaking free, timbers rending, men screaming, the desperate splashing of drowning crewmen. Then, mercifully, *Birdwing* was past, heeled to the wind, and entering the channel.

The pilot negotiated two turns before the first challenge came from one of Fort Shzafakh's bastions. The island rose steeply here, and *Birdwing* ghosted with its sails luffing for lack of wind. The fort was perched right overhead—from its walls the garrison could as easily drop cannonballs on *Birdwing* as fire them from cannon.

"Hoy, there! What ship is that!"

Derec was ready. He cupped his hands and shouted upward in his accented Zhir. "Two Kingdoms ship *Sea Troll*!" he roared. "A warship blew up in harbor and started fires on other ships! We're trying to run clear!"

"Holy Thung! So that's what we heard." There was an awed pause. "Good luck, there."

"Much obliged."

Birdwing ghosted on. Derec could see grins on the faces of his officers, on the wizard. In his mind he could only hear the sounds of *Double Crowns* filling with water, men dying and timbers rending. He barely noticed when the channel opened up and ahead lay the dark and empty sea.

An hour after dawn the land breeze died. The pilot had been put ashore long since, and even the old cone of Great Kraken Island was below the horizon: *Birdwing* was running northwest along the coast in the clear, broad, shallow channel between the mainland and Ka Zhir's stretch of low boundary islands. Winds were often uncertain in the morning, particularly near the coast and especially during the transition between the nightly land breeze and the daytime sea breeze: there was nothing unusual about it. Derec dropped the second bower anchor and let the galleon swing to and fro in the little puffs that remained. The crew drowsed at their stations. Fretfully Derec looked southward. *Sea Troll*, he thought, was damaged: it could not pursue without raising a new main-topmast. But *Monarch* and the new race-built ship were fully seaworthy. Were they becalmed as well? He suspected not. Derec looked at the Tichenese.

"Master Tevvik, do you think we can whistle up a wind between the two of us?"

The wizard spread his hands. "I am willing to try, Captain. I am not an expert."

Derec called for a pot of kaf, ordered breakfast for the crew, and the two went to his day cabin. The partitions separating the cabin from the maindeck had been broken down when *Birdwing* was cleared for action, providing a long, unbroken row of guns from the stern windows to the bow, and Derec's table was hastily brought up from the orlop, and blankets to screen him from the curious eyes of the crew.

"You're planning on privateering for Liavek now, I take it?" the wizard asked. "There will be a Two Kingdoms fleet in harbor, you know."

"I'll find a small harbor somewhere along the coast. Come in under a flag of truce, negotiate with the Levar's government."

"I can speak for you." Derec looked up in surprise. The

wizard smiled again. "I know a man named Pitullio—he worked for His Scarlet Eminence."

"I thank you," Derec said. "I'll consider that."

For two and a half hours he and the wizard tried to raise a wind, preferably a strong westerly that *Birdwing* could tack into and *Monarch*, the old-fashioned high-charged galleon, could not. The puffs continued, the ship dancing at the end of its cable, sails slatting.

"Captain." Facer's voice. "The lookouts see a squall coming up from the south."

Derec sighed. He could feel sweat dotting his brow: he had been concentrating hard. The wizard looked at him with amused eyes, grin white in his dark face.

"It's not *our* wind," Tevvik said, "but I hope it will do."

Derec rose wordlessly and pushed aside the curtain. His body was a mass of knots. "Ready a party at the capstan," he ordered. "I don't want to lose another anchor." He climbed to the poop.

It was a black squall, right enough, coming up from the south with deliberate speed. Ten minutes of stiff wind, at least, and with luck the squall might carry *Birdwing* with it for hours, right into the stronger ocean breezes. Derec had the second bower broken out. The galleon drifted, waiting for the squall.

Derec looked into the darkness, hoping to gauge its strength, and his heart sank.

Right in the center of the squall, he saw, were two ships. He didn't need his glass to know they were *Monarch* and *Torn II*, driving after him on a sorcerous breeze. Perhaps their wizards had even been responsible for his being becalmed.

"Quarters, gentlemen," he said. "We are being pursued. Have my steward fetch my armor, and send the wizard to the orlop."

He stopped himself, just in time, from glancing up into the mizzen shrouds. The ghosts of his slaughtered countrymen, he knew, had been an illusion.

But now, more than ever, he felt their gaze on the back of his head.

They were coming down together, Derec saw, straight down the eight-mile slot between the mainland and the sandy barrier isles. *Monarch* was to starboard of the race-built ship, three or four cables apart. There was a black line drawn in the azure sea a mile before them where the squall was pushing up a wave.

"We'll try to outrun them," Derec said. "We may prove their match in speed." He tried to sound confident, but he knew his assurances were hollow: the conditions were ideal for *Monarch*, booming straight downwind with her baggy sails full of sorcery. "If we lose the race," Derec went on, "I'll try to get the weather gage. If we're to windward, *Monarch* at least will be out of the fight."

A sigh of wind ruffled *Birdwing*'s sails. The ship stirred on the water. The sails filled, then died again. Derec strapped on his armor and watched as the darkness approached.

And then the squall hit, and the sun went dark. The sails boomed like thunder as they flogged massively in the air; the ship tilted; rain spattered Derec's breastplate. Then the sails were sheeted home, the yards braced—the helm answered, and *Birdwing* was racing straight downwind, a white bone in its teeth, sails as taut as the belly of a woman heavy with child. Magic crackled in Derec's awareness, a seething chaos of storm and wind. Desperately he looked astern.

Monarch seemed huge, castles towering over its leaner consort, its masts bending like a coachwhip in the force of the wind. Derec gauged its speed, and a cold welling of despair filled him. *Birdwing* seemed to be maintaining its lead over *Torn II*, but *Monarch* was surging ahead as studding sails blossomed on its yards. *Birdwing*'s own studding sails were useless in this wind; the stuns'l booms would snap like toothpicks.

Derec stiffened at the sound of a gun: the big ship was trying its chasers. *Monarch* was pitching too much in this following sea, and Derec never saw the fall of shot.

Yard by yard the great ship gained, its black hull perched atop a boil of white water. Derec hoped for a miracle, and none came. Hollow anguish filled him.

"Take in the t'gallants," he ordered. "We will await them." Diligently he fought down despair. "Don't send down the t'gallantyards," he said. "We may yet be able to show them our heels."

Monarch's stuns'ls began coming in as they perceived De-

rec's shortening sail. The maneuver was not done well, and
sheets began to fly, spilling wind from sails, a last-ditch method
of slowing *Monarch* so that it would not overshoot its target.

Derec watched nervously, gnawing his lip, trying to summon
his power and weave a defensive net around his ship. He could
feel Tevvik's energies joining his, strengthening his shields.
Another gust of rain spattered the deck; gun captains shielded
their matches with their bodies. *Monarch* looked as if it was
coming up on *Birdwing*'s larboard side, but that might be a
feint. Would the huge ship alter course at the last minute and
try for a raking shot across *Birdwing*'s stern? If so, Derec had
to be ready to turn with her. Plans flickered through Derec's
mind as he gauged possible enemy moves and his own re-
sponses.

"Load the guns. Roundshot and grape. Run out the larboard
battery." Maybe the guns running out would prod *Monarch*'s
captain into making his move.

But no. The man seemed eager to get to grips, and disdained
maneuver. He had almost thirty guns more than Derec; he could
afford to let them do his thinking for him. The black ship came
closer, its little scraplike sprit topsail drawing even with *Birdwing*'s stern. Derec could hear officers' bellowed commands
as they struggled to reduce sail.

Anxiety filled Derec as the ship rumbled to the sound of gun
trucks running out. *Monarch* was pulling up within fifty yards.
Torn II was eclipsed behind the big ship, but now that *Birdwing*
had shortened sail he could expect her shortly. He glanced
again at the men, seeing the gun captains crouched over the
guns with their slow matches, the officers pacing the deck with
rapiers drawn, ready to run through any crewman who left his
station. "No firing 'til my order!" Derec bellowed. "There
may be a few premature shots—ignore them!" And then in-
spiration struck. He turned to one of Marcoyn's marines, a
blond man sighting down the length of a swivel gun set aft of
the mizzen shrouds. "Blow on your match, man," Derec said.
"I'm going to try a little trick."

The marine looked at him uncertainly, then grinned through
his curling blond beard, leaned forward over his matchlock,
and blew. The match brightened redly. "You other marines,
stand ready," Derec said. He looked at the black ship, and
fear shivered down his spine as he saw himself looking straight

into the muzzle of a demicannon. Each enemy gunport had been decorated with the snarling brass head of a leopard: now guns were running out the beasts' mouths. *Monarch*'s foremast was even with *Birdwing*'s mizzen. Derec waited, his pulse beating in his ears, as *Monarch* crawled forward with glacial speed.

"Pick your target," Derec told the marine. "Steady now! Fire."

The four-pound mankiller barked and the air filled with a peculiar whirring noise as grapeshot and a handful of scrap iron flew toward the enemy. "Fire the murderers!" Derec spat. "Now!"

Another three minions banged out, and then there was a massive answering roar as every enemy gun went off, flinging their iron toward *Birdwing*. The smaller ship shuddered as balls slammed home. Derec took an involuntary step backward at the awesome volume of fire, but then he began to laugh. He'd tricked *Monarch* into firing prematurely, before all her guns bore. They'd wasted their first and most valuable broadside, half the shot going into the sea.

"Reload, you men! Helmsman, larboard a point!" Derec cupped his hands to carry down the ship's well to the gundeck below. "Fire on my command! Ready, boys!" *Birdwing* began a gentle curve toward the giant ship.

"Fire!" The deck lurched as the big guns went off, the long fifteen-foot maindeck culverins leaping inboard on their carriages. Derec could hear crashing from the enemy ship as iron smashed through timbers. "Reload!" Derec shrieked. "Fire at will! Helmsman, starboard a point!"

Enemy guns began crashing. Derec saw a piece of bulwark dissolve on the maindeck and turn to a storm of white fifteen-inch splinters that mowed down half a dozen men. Shot wailed overhead or thudded into planking. Musketry twittered over Derec's head: the enemy castles were full of marines firing down onto *Birdwing*'s decks. The smaller ship's guns replied. For the first time Derec felt a magic probe against his defenses; he sensed Tevvik parrying the strike. There was a crash, a deadly whirl of splinters, and the yellow-bearded marine was flung across the deck like a sack, ending up against the starboard rail, head crushed by a grapeshot. Derec, still in his haze of concentration, absently sent a man from the starboard side to service the gun.

Guns boomed, spewing powder smoke. *Birdwing*'s practiced crews were loading and firing well. Derec smiled; but then his ship rocked to a storm of fire and his heart lurched. His crews were faster in loading and firing, but still the enemy weight was overwhelming. Derec's smaller vessel couldn't stand this pounding for long. He gnawed his lip as he peered at the enemy through the murk. His next move depended on their not seeing him clearly.

The deck jarred as half a dozen gundeck demicannon went off nearly together. Smoke blossomed between the ships, and at once Derec ran for the break in the poop.

"Sailtrimmers, cast off all tacks and sheets!" he roared. "Gun crews shift to the starboard broadside! Smartly, now!" He could see crewmen's bewildered heads swiveling wildly: man the *starboard* guns? Had *Torn II* run up to starboard and caught them between two fires?

"Cast off all sheets! *Fly'em!* Run out the starboard battery!"

Topsails boomed as the great sails spilled wind. *Birdwing*'s purposeful driving slowed as if stopped by a giant hand. The flogging canvas roared louder than the guns. The galleon staggered in the sea, the black ship pulling ahead. Frantically Derec gauged his ship's motion.

"Hard a-larboard, Sandor! Smartly, there!"

Losing momentum, *Birdwing* rounded onto its new tack. A rumble sounded from the gundeck as the demicannon began thrusting from the ports. "Sheet home! Sailtrimmers to the braces! Brace her up sharp, there!"

There; he'd done it: checked his speed and swung across the black ship's stern. He could see the big stern windows, the heraldric quarterings of the Two Kingdoms painted on the flat surface of the raised poop, officers in armor running frantically atop the castle, arms waving. . . .

"Fire as you bear! Make it count, boys!"

Birdwing trembled as the first culverin spat fire. The whole broadside followed, gun by gun, and Derec exulted as he saw the enemy's stern dissolve in a chaos of splinters and roundshot, a great gilt lantern tumbling into the sea, the white triangle of the bonaventure dancing as grape pockmarked the canvas. . . . He'd raked her, firing his whole broadside the length of the ship without the enemy being able to reply with a single shot. Derec laughed aloud. "We've got upwind of them!" he shouted. "They'll not catch us now!"

"Holy Thung! Look ahead!" Random's young voice was frantic. Derec ran to the weather rail and peered out.

Torn II was bearing down on them, bow to bow, within a cable's distance. She'd been trying to weather *Monarch* so as to attack *Birdwing* from her unengaged side, and now the two race-built ships were on a collision course.

"Hands to the braces! Stations for tacking! Starboard guns load doubleshot and grape! Put the helm down!"

Birdwing, barely under way again, staggered into the wind. Canvas slatted wildly. *Torn II* was bearing down on her beam, its royal figurehead glowering, waving a bright commanding sword.

"Fire as you bear!" Derec pounded the rail with a bleeding fist. "Run out and fire!"

The marines' murderers spat their little balls and scrap iron. Then a demicannon boomed, and another, then several of the long maindeck culverins. *Birdwing* hung in the eye of the wind, all forward momentum lost, the gale beating against her sails, driving her backward. More guns went off. *Torn*'s spritsail danced as a roundshot struck it. Captain-General Collerne was curving gently downwind, about to cross *Birdwing*'s stern at point-blank range.

"Starboard your helm! Help her fall off!"

Too late. Captain-General Collerne's scarlet masthead pennant coiled over the waves like a serpent threatening to strike. "Lie down!" Derec shouted. "Everyone lie down!"

He flung himself to the planks as the world began to come apart at the seams. The ship staggered like a toy struck by a child's hand as an entire rippling broadside smashed the length of *Birdwing*'s hull. Gunsmoke gushed over the quarterdeck. The taffrail dissolved. The bonaventure mizzen collapsed, draping the poop in pockmarked canvas. Yards of sliced rigging coiled down on the deck. Below there was a metallic gong as a cannon was turned over on its shrieking crew.

Then there was a stunned silence: *Torn* had passed by. Through the clouds of gunsmoke Derec could see Marcoyn standing, legs apart, on the fo'c'sle, sword brandished at the enemy, an incoherent, lunatic bellow of rage rising from his throat. "What a madman," Derec muttered, his ears ringing, and then he got to his feet.

"Brace the spritsail to larboard!" he called. "Clear that wreckage!" The tattered remains of the bonaventure were turning red: there were bodies underneath. As the canvas was pulled up, Derec saw one of them was Facer, the sunburned man cut in half by his homeland's iron. Derec turned away. He would pray for the man later.

Slowly *Birdwing* paid off onto the larboard tack. The sails filled and the galleon lost sternway. Water began to chuckle along the strakes as the ship slowly forged ahead. Canvas boomed as *Torn II*, astern, began to come about. Derec looked anxiously over the shattered taffrail.

Monarch was only now lumbering into the wind: she was almost a mile away and had no hope of returning to the fight unless the wind shifted to give her the weather gage once again. But *Torn II* was the ship that had worried Derec all along, and she was right at hand, completing her tack, moving onto the same course as *Birdwing*. If she was faster sailing upwind, she could overhaul the fugitive ship. Derec gave a worried glance at the set of his sails.

"Keep her full, Sandor. Let her go through the water."

"Full an' bye, sir."

"Set the t'gallants." He was suddenly glad he hadn't sent down the topgallant yards.

"Aye aye, sir."

"All hands to knot and splice."

The topgallants rumbled as they were smoothly sheeted home. *Birdwing* heeled to starboard, foam spattering over the fo'c'sle like handfuls of dark jewels tossed by the spirits of the sea. She was drawing ahead, fast as a witch as she drove through the black gale. Water drizzled from the sky, washing Facer's blood from the planks. The water tasted sweet on Derec's tongue, washed away the powder that streaked his face.

Torn's topgallant yards were rising aloft, a swarm of men dark on her rigging. *Birdwing* made the most of her temporary advantage; she'd gained over a mile on her adversary before *Torn*'s topgallant bloomed and the larger ship began to race in earnest.

Derec felt his heart throbbing as he slitted his eyes to look astern, judging the ships' relative motion. *Birdwing* had lost its bonaventure: would that subtract from the ship's speed? He continued staring astern. His face began to split in a smile.

"We're pulling ahead!" he roared. "We've got the heels of her, by Thurn Bel!"

A low cheer began to rise from the crew, then, as the word passed, it grew deafening. *Birdwing* was going to make its escape. Nothing could stop her now.

Two miles later, as *Birdwing* neared a half-mile-wide channel between a pair of boundary isles, the wind died away entirely.

The sails fell slack, booming softly as the ship rocked on the waves.

From astern, traveling clearly from the two enemy vessels, Derec could hear the sound of cheering.

"Sway out the longboat! Ready to lower the second bower! We'll kedge her!"

The words snapped from Derec's mouth before the enemy cheering had quite ended. There was a rush of feet as the crew obeyed. Derec wanted to keep them busy, not occupied with thinking about their predicament.

"Send a party below to splice every anchor cable together. Fetch the wizard. A party to the capstan. Bring up the tackles and the spare t'gallant yards. We're going to jury a bonaventure. SuKrone, help me out of this damned armor."

One of the two longboats was swung out and set in the water. Carefully, the remaining bower anchor was lowered into it, and the boat moved under oars to the full length of the spliced anchor cables. Then the anchor was pitched overboard into the shallow sea and crewmen began stamping around the capstan, dragging the ship forward by main force until it rested over its anchor.

Tevvik appeared on deck to Derec's summons. He looked haggard.

"Hot work, Captain," he said. "Their wizards are good."

"I felt only one assault."

"Good. That means I was keeping them off."

"We're going to need wind."

Tevvik seemed dead with weariness. "Aye, Captain. I'll try."

"I'll work with you. Stand by the rail; I'll be with you in a moment."

The sound of clattering capstan pawls echoed from astern. *Torn* and *Monarch* were kedging as well.

"Up and down, sir." *Birdwing* was resting over its anchor.

"Bring her up smartly."

"Aye aye."

Birdwing lurched as the anchor broke free of the bottom. Derec moved toward the poop ladder, then frowned as he saw the two stream anchors lashed to the main chains. A shame, Derec considered, that so much time was wasted getting the anchor up, then rowing it out again. Capstan pawls whirred in accompaniment to Derec's thoughts.

"Swing out the other longboat," he said. "We'll put one of the stream anchors on the other end of the cable. Have one anchor going out while the other's coming in." He grinned at SuKrone's startled expression. "See to it, man!"

"Sir."

Crewmen rushed to the remaining longboat. Derec walked to where the Tichenese was waiting, propped against the lee rail where he'd be out of the way.

"We shall try to bring a wind, wizard," Derec said. "A westerly, as before. Ready?"

"I'll do what I can."

Wearily Derec summoned his power, matched it to the wizard's, and called the elements for a wind. Meanwhile a spare topgallant mast was dropped in place of the broken bonaventure mizzen, a lateen yard hoisted to its top, a new bonaventure set that hung uselessly in the windless air. Derec and Tevvik moved into its shade. Capstan pawls clattered, drawing the race-built ship forward, through the channel between barrier islands, the two longboats plying back and forth with their anchors. The pursuers were using only one anchor at a time and were falling behind. The water began to deepen, turn a profounder blue. *Torn II* crawled through the island passage. *Monarch*'s topgallant masts loomed above the nearer island.

The heat of the noon sun augured a hot afternoon. Pitch bubbled up between the deck seams and stuck to crewmen's feet. Weary sailors were relieved at the capstan and fed.

"Deck, there! Captain! Right ahead! *See what's happening!*"

Derec glanced up from his summoning, and his heart lurched as he saw the wind itself appear, visible as a dim swirling above the water; and then the sea itself rose, a wall of curling white foam. Desperate energy filled him.

"Clew up the t'gallants! Close the gunports! Call the boats back! Clew up the fores'l!"

The sea was coming with a growing hiss, a furious rank of white horsemen galloping over an azure plain. Tevvik looked at the wave with a dazed expression. "It's all coming at once," he said. "It's been building out there, everything we've been summoning since dawn, and now it's all on us at once."

"Helmsman! A point to starboard! Use what way you can!"

Sails were clewed up in a squeal of blocks. The entry port filled with frantic sailors as one of the boats came alongside. There was a cry of wind in the rigging, an anticipation of what was to come. Derec ran to the mizzen shrouds and wrapped his arm around a stout eight-inch tarred line. He looked at Tevvik.

"I suggest you do likewise, wizard."

And then the summoning was on them. The bow rose to the surge of white water and suddenly the air was full of spray as the frothing sea boiled around the ship. Canvas crashed as it filled with wind, bearing *Birdwing* back 'til suddenly she came up short at the end of her anchor cable, and with a plank-starting shudder the galleon was brought up short, burying her beak in foam, a wave sweeping the decks fore and aft, carrying crewmen and capstan bars and everything not lashed down in a frantic, clawing spill for the stern. . . . Derec closed his eyes and mouth and tried to hang on, his shoulders aching as the water tore at his clothing and body. His mind still registered what was happening to the ship, the jarring and checking that meant the anchor was dragging, the demon shriek of wind in the rigging, the thrumming tautness of the shroud around which Derec wrapped his arms. . . .

Just as suddenly, the white water was gone, past. A strong sea breeze hummed in the rigging. Half-drowned crewmen lay on the planks like scattered driftwood, gasping for air. Exultation filled Derec.

"Hands to the capstan! Prepare to set the fores'l and t'gallants! Lively, there, lively—we've got a wind!"

The stunned survivors raised a feeble cheer and dragged

wearily to their work. The other longboat—miraculously it had survived, bobbing on the wave like a twig—picked up a few swimmers who had been carried overboard, then came to the entry port in a mad thrash of oars. Wind whipping his hair, Derec gazed astern to see the wall of white as it drove toward his enemies.

Torn II had seen it coming and had had time to prepare. Her boats were in, her anchor catted home; and Derec suppressed a surge of admiration for the proud way her head tossed to the wave, the clean manner in which she cut the water and kept her head to the wind. Then the wave was past, and she began setting sails. Derec's gaze shifted to *Monarch*. The wave was almost on her.

She hadn't seen it coming; that much was clear. She'd just kedged clear of the southern tip of the island, and the white water was within two cables' lengths before *Monarch* was aware of it. Suddenly there was frantic movement on her decks, sails drawing up, the boats thrashing water; but the white water hit her broadside, driving her over. She staggered once, then was gone, only wreckage and the tips of her masts visible on the rushing water. Derec blinked: it had happened so fast he could scarce believe the sight of it. He looked again. His eyes had spoken truly: *Monarch* was gone.

"Thurn Bel protect them," Derec said, awed, reaching automatically for his amulet and finding nothing. He knew precisely what had happened. The gunports had been open on this hot afternoon, and the wind and water had pushed her lower ports under; she'd filled and gone down in seconds. Six hundred men, their lives snuffed out in an instant. Derec shook his head, sorrow filling him. Why was he fated to kill his countrymen so?

"The sea trolls will feed well tonight," Tevvik said solemnly. His hairpins had been torn from his head, and his long dark hair hung dripping to his shoulders.

SuKrone's voice broke into Derec's reverie. "Cable's up and down, sir."

"Break the anchor free. Lay her on the larboard tack."

The anchor came free with a lurch, the yards were braced round, the birdwing sails set and filled with wind. *Birdwing* heeled gracefully in the stiff ocean breeze.

"This isn't over yet," Derec said as he watched *Torn II*

flying after them. "The captain-general's lost two ships, half his squadron, with nothing to show for it. He's got to bring us back or he's done for. He'll never have another command."

"We're faster than he on this tack."

"That won't end it. He'll spend the rest of his life in the Sea of Luck if he has to."

"Let us hope," Tevvik said, his eyes hardening, "he will not live long."

Derec shook his head: he couldn't wish Collerne dead, not Collerne who had been such a friend to him, who had raised him to the highest rank to which a non-noble could aspire.

The brisk wind carried *Birdwing* smartly over the water, the bow rising to each ocean wave. But then the wind dropped little by little and *Torn II* began closing the distance, her red admiral's pennant snapping in the breeze like a striking serpent. *Birdwing* was only faster in stiffer winds: *Torn* had the advantage here. Derec's heart sank.

"We shall have to fight, then. Gun captains to draw their cartridges and replace them with fresh—they may have got wet. All hands check their powder."

Derec donned his cuirass—the helmet had been washed overboard—and reloaded his pistols. Tevvik returned to the safety of the orlop. There was no cheer among the crew as they went to their tasks, only a kind of grim despair.

They had labored all day, escaped death so many times. Were they cursed, to be so forced into yet another struggle?

"Stations for tacking," Derec said. "We'll see how badly the captain-general wants to fight us." He could still not bring himself to speak of the man disrespectfully.

Birdwing came across the wind easily. "Ease her a bit," Derec ordered. "Keep her full." He ordered the guns loaded with roundshot and gauged his distance carefully. "Back the main tops'l," he said finally. "Run out the larboard battery." He was going to give Collerne a hard choice. "Ready, boys!" he called. "Aim carefully, now!" The ship's motion altered as the main topsail backed, as the ship's speed checked and its corkscrew shudder ended. Carefully Derec gauged the ship's motion. Tops'l aback, *Birdwing* was a far steadier platform.

"Fire!" The deck shuddered to the salvo. White feathers leaped from the sea around *Torn*. "Fill the tops'l! Reload and run out! Helm down!"

Derec looked at the other race-built ship, eyes narrowing. His maindeck culverins, longer though with a smaller bore than the demicannon on the gundeck, were ideal at this range. He would claw to windward, fall off, fire, then claw to windward again while his crews reloaded: he was going to punish *Torn II* mercilessly on the approach, make her pay for every fathom gained. The enemy couldn't reply, not without luffing out of the wind to present her broadside.

Collerne had two choices now, Derec knew. He could continue beating toward *Birdwing*, paying for every inch with lives, or he could luff and open the battle at this range. The battle wouldn't be decisive at a half mile's distance—the two ships would fire off their ammunition at this range, fail to do mortal damage, and that would be the end of it. Derec prayed Collerne would choose the latter outcome.

"Back the main tops'l! Run out!"

Another broadside crashed out. "Fill the tops'l! Load! Helm down!"

Luff, Derec thought fiercely as he looked at the enemy. Luff, damn you.

The enemy were determined to stand Derec's fire. His heart sank at the thought of killing more of his countrymen.

Having no choice, he did what he must. He fired another broadside, tacked, fired the larboard guns. *Torn*'s bow chasers replied, pitching a ball at *Birdwing* every few minutes; but *Torn II* had to be taking punishment as she came into the culverins' ideal range. Her sails were as pitted by shot holes as the cheeks of a whore with the Great Pox.

Five hundred yards. "Fire!" He could hear the sound of shot striking home. Four hundred. "*Fire!*" Three. "*Fire!*"

The wind blew the ocean clear of smoke. Derec stared to leeward, hoping to see a mast fall, a sail flog itself to bits, anything that might allow him to slip away. Nothing. Reluctantly he gave the orders.

"Fill the mains'l. Clew up the t'gallants. We'll give the captain-general the fight he's come for."

The guns lashed out once more and then *Torn* luffed elegantly, the bronze guns running out the square ports, two lines of teeth that shone in the bright southern sun. There were gaps in the rows of teeth; two ports beaten into one, another empty

port where a gun may have been disabled. Derec's breath
caught in his throat.

Fire lapped the surface of the ocean. *Torn*'s crew had waited
hours for this and it seemed as if every shot struck home, a
rapid series of crashes and shudders that rocked the deck beneath Derec's feet. There was a cry as a half dozen of Marcoyn's marines were scattered in red ruin over the fo'c'sle,
then a shriek, sounding like the very sky being torn asunder,
as a ball passed right over Derec's head to puncture the mizzen
lateen. He was too startled to duck.

Birdwing's guns gave their answering roars. Derec gave the
command to fire at will. He could sense the magic shields
Tevvik wove about the ship; felt a probe, felt it easily rebuffed.
There was only one enemy wizard now; he was as tired as
everyone else. The range narrowed and the marines' murderers
began to bark. Gunfire was continuous, a never-ending thunder.
A musket ball gouged wood from the mizzen above Derec's
head; he began to pace in hope of discouraging marksmen.

Derec's ship seemed to be pulling ahead as the range narrowed and *Birdwing* stole *Torn*'s wind. Derec didn't want that,
not yet; he had the foretops'l laid aback, allowed *Torn* to forge
ahead slightly, then filled the sail and resumed his course.

Fifty yards: here they would hammer it out, guns double-
shotted with a round of grape choked down each barrel for
good measure. A maindeck culverin tipped onto its crew, its
carriage wrecked by a ball. There was a crash, a massive rumble
followed by a human shriek. Derec stared: the main topgallant
had been shot away and come roaring down, a tangle of rigging
and canvas and broken timber. Marcoyn already had a party
hacking at the wreckage and tossing it overboard. Derec
clenched his teeth and waited. Thunder smote his ears. Gunpowder coated his tongue in layers, like dust on a dead man.

The wreckage was clear: good. The enemy was falling a bit
behind. "Set the fore t'gallant!" Derec roared; the seamen
gave him puzzled glances, and he repeated the order.

Canvas boomed as the topgallant was sheeted home; Derec
could feel the surge of speed, the lift it gave his nimble ship.
He peered over the bulwark, squinting through the smoke that
masked the enemy. With his added speed, he'd try to cross
her bows and let her run aboard: he'd have his every gun able
to rake down the enemy's length with scarce a chance of reply.

"Put up the helm!" A musket ball whirred overhead; two quarterdeck murderers barked in reply. The marines were cursing without cease as they loaded and fired, a constant drone of obscenity. Derec wondered where they found the energy.

Birdwing curved downwind like a bird descending on its prey, Derec staring anxiously at the enemy. He felt his heart sink: the blue sky between the enemy's masts was widening. Collerne had been ready for him, and was matching *Birdwing*'s turn with his own.

"Helm hard to weather!" Frantic energy pulsed through Derec. "Hands to the larboard guns! Run 'em out! Braces, there! Brace her around!"

If he made his turn quick enough, he might be able to slide across Collerne's stern and deliver a raking shot with his fresh larboard broadside, a stroke as devastating as that which *Torn* had fired into *Birdwing*'s stern that morning.

Sails boomed and slatted overhead. The firing trailed off as the guns no longer bore. Derec ran frantically for the larboard rail and saw, too late, a tantalizing glimpse of *Torn*'s stern, a glimpse lasting only a few seconds before it slid away. Derec beat a fist on the rail. The maneuver hadn't worked at all— Collerne had anticipated everything. The ships had just changed places, larboard tack to starboard, like dancers at a ball. And *Torn* was firing with a new broadside now, not the one he'd punished for the last few hours.

"Luff her! Gun crews, fire as you bear!" He'd get in one unopposed broadside, at least.

The unused broadside blasted away into *Torn*'s starboard quarter. Derec could see splinters flying like puffs of smoke. He filled his sails and surged on.

Now they were yardarm to yardarm again, the guns hammering at point-blank range. The crews were weary, taking casualties, and the rate of fire had slowed: the deadly iron thunderstorm was blowing itself out. A whirring charge of grape caught SuKrone in the side and flung him to weather like a doll, already dead; a musket ball whanged off Derec's breastplate and made him take a step back, his heart suddenly thundering in panic. Frantically he began pacing, his feet slipping in pools of blood.

Who was winning? *Torn* had been hard hit, but her weight of armament was superior; she had a larger crew, having prob-

ably taken men off the damaged *Sea Troll*; and Derec was
forced to admit she had the better captain. *Birdwing* had been
hit hard in the first fight, and her crew were exhausted. Everywhere he looked Derec saw blood, death, smoke, and ruin.

He'd try his trick one more time, Derec thought. He couldn't
think of anything else. If it didn't work, he'd just fight it out
toe to toe until there was nothing left to fight with. He wouldn't
surrender. If *Birdwing* lost, he'd take one of his stolen pistols
and blow his own brains out.

Birdwing was forging ahead, the topgallant still set. Very
well. He'd try to do it better.

"Hands to tacks and sheets! Hands to the braces! Ready,
there? Helm to weather!"

Birdwing lurched as the rudder bit the water. Bullets twittered
overhead. The enemy wizard made some kind of strike, and
Derec felt it deep in his awareness; his mind lanced out and
parried. He could sense Tevvik there, feel a part of the foreigner's mind merge with his own.

If you ever do anything, he begged, *do it now*.

The answer came. *Very well*.

Derec looked up again, saw the blue space between the
enemy's masts increasing. Damn: he'd been anticipated *again*.

"Hard a-weather! Sheets, there! Man the starboard guns!"

They were dancing round again, just changing places. The
bonaventure and mizzen lateen boomed as the wind slammed
them across the deck. Derec saw the enemy stern and knew
he could never cross it, knew it for certain—and then there
was a yellow flash, *Torn*'s windows blowing out in rainbow
splinters, bright light winking from each gunpoint along the
maindeck. Guns boomed, firing at empty sea. Derec's mouth
dropped as he saw an enemy marine, standing with his firelock
in the mizzen chains, suddenly fling his arms back as each of
the powder flasks he carried across his chest went off, little
dots of fire that knocked him into the shrouds . . .

Tevvik, Derec thought. He specialized in fireworks. But now
Derec was screaming, his throat a raw agony.

"Fire as you bear!" *Birdwing* was going to win the race:
the maindeck explosion had paralyzed the enemy, possibly
blown the helmsmen away from the whipstaff.

The guns went off, flinging hundreds of pounds of metal
into the helpless ship's stern. *Torn* wallowed, the wind pushing

her away. Derec could hear her crewmen screaming for water buckets. Tevvik must have set off a pile of cartridges on the maindeck, spreading fire, making guns go off prematurely while their crews were still ramming shots home. . . .

Birdwing followed, firing shot after shot; *Torn*'s crew was desperately fighting fires and could not reply. Derec sensed a new energy in his gunners; they were firing faster than they had since the enemy's approach. They knew this was victory and wanted to hasten it.

"Captain." It was one of the surgeon's assistants, a boy in a bloody apron. Derec glared at him.

"What is it?"

"The wizard's unconscious, sir. The Liavekan, what's-his-name. He just yelled something in his heathen tongue and collapsed. Surgeon thought you'd need to know."

Derec put his hand on the boy's arm. "Compliments to the surgeon. Thank you, boy."

The guns roared on. *Torn* got her fires under control, but the explosion had devastated the crew: they didn't have the heart to continue. When all the gun crews dribbled away, heading for the hatches, the officers conceded the inevitable and hauled down their colors. *Birdwing* came alongside to take possession.

Collerne, leading his surviving officers, surrendered in person, a tall, white-haired man in beautifully crafted muscled armor, a splinter wound on one cheek, both hands blackened where he'd beat at the fire. Derec looked into the man's eyes, hoping to see some sign of friendship, of understanding for what Derec had had to do. There was nothing there, no understanding, no friendship, not even hate. Derec took his patron's sword wordlessly.

"We've done it, SuPashto! Beaten 'em!" Marcoyn was by Derec's side now, his pale, unfocused eyes burning fire. "We're *free*!" Marcoyn saw Collerne standing mute by the poop rail; he turned to the captain-general, stared at him for a long moment, then deliberately spat in his face.

"Free, d'ye hear, Collerne?" he roared. "You thought you'd strangle us all, but now I'll throttle you myself. And now I'll be captain of your ship as well."

The spittle hung on Collerne's face. He said nothing, but his deep gray eyes turned to Derec, and Derec's blood turned chill.

Derec put a hand on Marcoyn's armored shoulder. "He's worth more in ransom alive," he said. "You and your people take possession of the other ship."

Marcoyn considered this, the taunting grin still on his face. "Aye," he said. "Maybe I'd like their money more than their lives." He gave a laugh. "I'll have to give it some thought. While I enjoy my new cabin on my new ship."

He turned to his men and roared orders. There were cheers from the marines as they swarmed aboard *Torn II* and began looting the enemy survivors. Collerne's eyes turned away from Derec. There was no gratitude there, just an emptiness as deep as the ocean. Despair filled Derec. The rapier in his hand felt as heavy as a lead weight.

"Go to my cabin, Captain-General," he said. "Wait for me there. I'll send the surgeon to tend to your hands." In silence, Collerne obeyed. Derec sent the other officers below to the cable tier and had them put under guard.

Suddenly Derec was aware of Tevvik standing by the break of the poop. How long had the wizard been there? His face showed strain and exhaustion, but he'd heard everything; his hooded expression demonstrated that well enough.

Derec glanced up at the mizzen shrouds. There wasn't room any longer for all the countrymen he'd killed; the ghosts, he thought, would have to stand in line.

It wasn't over yet, Derec knew. The Two Kingdoms trading fleets came to the Sea of Luck every year, and sailors had long memories. Squadrons would hunt for *Birdwing*, and even if Derec received the protection of one of the cities, there would still be kidnappers and assassins. No end to this killing, Derec thought, not until I'm dead. Will the gods forgive me, he wondered, for not killing myself and ending this slaughter?

The two race-built ships spun in the wind, locked together like weary prizefighters leaning against each other for support. Wreckage and bodies bobbed in the water. From *Torn II* came a smell of burning.

Derec realized he was the only man remaining who could navigate. He ordered his charts to be brought up from the safety of the hold.

"Secure the guns," he said. "I'll chart a course north, to Liavek."

● ● ●

The sea was kind that night; a moderate wind, a moderate swell. The two ships traveled under easy sail and echoed to the sound of repairs.

Near staggering with weariness, Derec paced *Birdwing*'s weather rail. Collerne still waited in Derec's cabin. Marcoyn was probably drunk and unconscious in the admiral's cabin aboard *Torn*. Only Derec was without a place to sleep.

There was a tread on the poop companion, and Derec saw Tevvik approaching him.

"You have recovered?" Derec asked. His tongue was thick. No matter how much kaf he consumed his mouth still tasted of powder.

"Somewhat." The wizard's voice was as weary as his own. "May I join you, Captain?"

"If you like." Exhaustion danced in Derec's brain. He swayed, put a hand on the bulwark to steady himself.

Tevvik's voice was soft. "You will have to make a choice, Captain," he said.

"Not now, wizard."

"Soon, Captain."

Derec said nothing. Tevvik stepped closer, pitched his voice low. "If Marcoyn gets his way, you will all die. His Scarlet Eminence won't make a deal with a butcher."

"This is my affair, wizard. None of yours."

"Only the thought of ransom kept him from another massacre. What will happen when he realizes the ransom will never come? Liavek isn't at war with the Two Kingdoms—their prize courts will never permit you to ransom a neutral. When Marcoyn thinks things through, there will be trouble." Tevvik's easy smile gleamed in his dark face. "I can deal with Marcoyn, Captain. He will have gone overboard while drunk, and that's all anyone will ever know."

Derec glared at the foreigner and clenched his fists. "I'll have my own discipline on my own ship," he grated. "I don't need wizard's tricks, and I won't be a party to conspiracies."

"It's far too late for that, Captain."

Derec jerked as if stung. "It's not too late to stop."

"Events generate their own momentum. You of all people should know that." He leaned closer, put a hand on Derec's shoulder. "Marcoyn's marines have the firelocks, Captain. He has possession of one ship already, and he can take yours anytime he wants.''

"He needs me. The man can't navigate."

"Once he turns pirate, he can capture all the navigators he needs."

"I can deal with him, wizard!" Derec's voice roared out over the still ship. Tevvik took a step back from the force of his rage.

His mind ablaze, Derec stormed down the poop ladder, past the startled helmsman, and down the passage that led to his cabin. The guard at the door straightened in surprise as Derec flung open the door.

Collerne looked up. He was out of his armor and seated in one of Derec's chairs, trying to read a Zhir book on navigation with his bandaged hands. Derec hesitated before the man's depthless gaze.

"I want you off my ship, Captain-General," he said.

Collerne's eyes flickered. "Why is that, Mr. SuPashto?" He spoke formally, without expression.

"I'm going to put you and your officers in a boat and let you make your way to Gold Harbor. You'll have food and water for the trip. A backstaff so you can find your latitude."

With a careful gesture, Collerne closed his book and held it between bandaged hands. "You are running for Liavek, are you not? Can you not let us off there?"

Derec looked at him. "It's for your safety, Captain-General."

Collerne took a moment to absorb this. "Very well, Mr. SuPashto. I understand that you might have difficulty controlling your people now that they've had a taste of rebellion."

Suddenly Derec hated the man, hated his superiority, the cold, relentless precision of his intelligence. "You would have strangled and eviscerated every man on this ship!" he said.

Collerne's voice was soft. "That was my duty, Mr. Su-Pashto," he said. "Not my pleasure. That's the difference between me and your Mr. Marcoyn."

"Marcoyn had a good teacher," Derec said. "His name was Captain Lord Fors. Marcoyn's an amateur in cruelty compared to him."

Collerne stiffened. Mean satisfaction trickled into Derec's mind; he'd got a reaction from the man at last. He wondered if it was because he'd scored a point or simply had the bad taste to criticize one officer in front of another.

"The only order I've ever had questioned," Derec said, "is the one that would prevent my people doing to you what you fully intended to do to them. Now"—he nodded—"you will follow me, Captain-General, and from this point onward you will address me as captain. Maybe I wasn't born to the rank, but I think I've earned it."

Collerne said nothing, just rose from his chair and followed. Perhaps, Derec thought, he would say nothing at all rather than have to call Derec by his stolen title. Derec collected the rest of the officers in the cable tier and then climbed to the main-deck. *Birdwing*'s remaining small boat had been warped astern after the fight, and Derec had it brought alongside. He put a stock of food and water aboard, made certain the boat had mast, cordage, sail, and backstaff, then sent the prisoners into it. Collerne was last. The captain-general turned in the entry port, prepared to lower himself to the boat, curled his fingers around the safety line. His bandaged hand slipped uselessly, and Collerne gave a gasp of pain as he began to topple backward into the boat.

Derec leaned out and took the captain-general's arm, steadying him. Collerne looked at him with dark, fathomless eyes.

"I acted to preserve the ship, Captain-General," Derec said. "There was no other way. *Birdwing* was your dream, and it is alive, thanks to me."

Collerne's face hardened. He turned away, and with Derec's assistance lowered himself into the boat.

"Cast off," said Derec. He stepped up to the poop and watched the fragment of darkness as it fell astern, as it vanished among the gentle swells of the Sea of Luck.

He'd said what he'd had to, Derec thought. If Collerne refused to understand, that was naught to do with Derec.

"What now, Captain?" Tevvik's voice. Derec turned to the wizard.

"Sleep," he said. "I'll deal with Marcoyn in the morning."

Derec rose at dawn. He wound his two pistols and put them in his belt, then reached for his sword. He stepped on deck, scanned the horizon, found it empty save for *Torn II* riding two miles off the starboard quarter. He brought *Birdwing* alongside, shouted at the other ship to heave to, then backed *Birdwing*'s main topsail and brought her to rest a hundred yards from the other ship. He armed a party of *Birdwing*'s sailors and had them ready at the entry port. Derec told *Torn*'s lookout to give Mr. Marcoyn his compliments and ask him to come aboard *Birdwing*.

Out of the corner of his eye, Derec saw Tevvik mounting the poop ladder. The Tichenese seemed unusually subdued; his expression was hooded, his grin absent entirely.

Marcoyn arrived with a party of half a dozen marines, all dressed grandly in plundered clothing and armor. The big man looked savage; he was probably hung over. A brace of pistols had been shoved into his bright embroidered sash.

Derec could feel tension knotting his muscles. He tried to keep his voice light. "I need you to resume your duties aboard *Birdwing*, Mr. Marcoyn," Derec told him. "I'm sending Sandor to take charge of the prize."

There was a pause while Marcoyn absorbed this. He gave an incredulous laugh. "Th' piss you will," he said. "The prize is mine!"

Derec's nerves shrieked. Ignoring the sharp scent of liquor on Marcoyn's breath, he stepped closer to the big man. His voice cracked like a whip. "By whose authority? I'm captain here."

Marcoyn stood his ground. His strange pale eyes were focused a thousand yards away.

"The prize is mine!" he barked. "I'm in charge of the sojers here!"

Hot anger roared from Derec's mouth like fire from a cannon. "And *I* am in charge of *you*!" he shouted. He thrust his face within inches of Marcoyn's. "*Birdwing* is mine! The prize is mine! And *you* and your sojers are mine to command! D'you dispute that, Marcoyn?"

Do it, Marcoyn, he thought. Defy me and I'll pistol your brains out the back of your head.

Marcoyn seemed dazed. He glanced over the poop, his hands flexing near his weapons. Derec felt triumph racing through his veins. If Marcoyn made a move he was dead. Derec had never been more certain of anything in his life.

Marcoyn hesitated. He took a step back.

"Whatever you say, Captain," he said.

Readiness still poised in Derec. Marcoyn was not safe yet, not by any means. "You are dismissed, Marcoyn," Derec said. "I'd advise you to get some sleep."

"Aye aye, sir." The words were mumbled. Marcoyn raised his helmet in a sketchy salute, then turned away and was lost.

Tension poured from Derec like an ebbing tide. He watched the burly marine descend the poop ladder, then head for his cabin. He looked at Marcoyn's marines.

"Return your firelocks to the arms locker," he said. "Then report to Randem's repair party."

"Sir."

Derec sent Sandor and some of the armed sailors to the *Torn*, then looked up at the sails. "Hands to the main braces," he said. "Set the main tops'l. Steer nor'nor'west."

Men tailed onto the braces, fighting the wind as they heaved the big mainyards around. Canvas boomed as it filled, as *Birdwing* paid off and began to come around, a bone growing in its teeth.

Relief sang in Derec's mind. He had managed it somehow, managed not to have to become Marcoyn in order to defeat him.

"Well done, sir." Tevvik's voice came quietly in Derec's ear. "But you should have let me handle him. Marcoyn's still a danger."

"To no one but himself." Flatly.

"I disagree, Captain. What will happen when he discovers you've set Collerne and the others free?"

"Nothing will happen. He will drink and mutter and that will be the end of it."

"I pray you are right, Captain."

Derec looked at him. "I won't have a man killed because he *might* be a problem later. That was Lord Fors's way, and Marcoyn's way, and I'll have none of it."

Tevvik shook his head and offered no answer. Derec glanced aloft to check the set of the sails.

Suddenly he felt his heart ease. He was free.

No more mutinies, he thought.

Birdwing heeled to a gust, then rose and settled into its path, forging ahead through a bright tropical dawn.

As Bright as New Coppers

by Bradley Denton

When two coins are minted
from wild luck in Rain,
the forces shall rage
and cause great ones pain.
—The Book of the Twin Forces

DRAINED AND SWEATING, Mardis slipped her silver bracelet over her wrist and stumbled out of the bedroom. Investiture hadn't been as terrifying as it had been the year before, but it had been even more tiring because of the unusually hot weather. She felt as though she had spent the morning inside a brick oven.

Thardik, the wizard who had trained her, was still sitting in his own chalked circle on the floor of the front room. "It's done," Mardis told him. "My luck's invested for another year." She held up her hands and murmured a phrase, sending miniature bolts of blue lightning crackling from her fingertips for a few seconds. It was a trick that she'd been practicing every evening during the few minutes that her birth-moment magic was available, but it had never been so impressive as this. "And it works, too. Mere words cannot express my apathy."

Thardik, grunting in discomfort, uncrossed his legs. "Gods, that feels good. My legs have been cramped for the past hour.

64

I was afraid I couldn't keep the magic-suppression spell in f-force if I stretched.''

Mardis glanced at the sandglass on the mantelpiece. "At least you didn't have to restrain my wild luck from its mischief as long as you did last year. We've only been at it two hours. That must be some kind of record."

Thardik nodded. "No doubt. Nevertheless, I suggest you spend your remaining birth hours resting from the ritual." He paused. "You are a magician of a rare sort, Mardis. It won't take you long to earn the levars you need to erase the b-bakery's debt." He tried to stand and fell back with a thump.

Mardis grasped his wrists and managed to pull him to his feet. "I only wish there were some other way," she said. "I really don't want to be a wizard."

Thardik flexed his knees, and they popped. "We do what we must in this world," he said. "I wished to be a wizard as powerful as you with your wild luck will be, but I am not— so I count myself lucky that I can levitate s-stones. My declining years, at least, will not be spent in poverty, and when I am gone, you can take your twins to the railroad's Central Station and tell them that your teacher Thardik helped to b-build it."

"Speaking of poverty," Mardis said, wiping sweat from her face with her blouse sleeve, "you needn't worry about the cost of the gold dust you had to buy for the suppression spell. I'll go with you to the Station tomorrow to see whether they'll hire me as well, and you can have my first month's wages."

Thardik scratched his head between two of its various tufts of white hair. "My child, if you, with your skills, settle for railroad wages, you are a fool. Besides, the gold I sprinkled around the house is a birthday gift."

Mardis embraced him. "Thanks, but I'm going to pay for it anyway," she said. "Still, I suppose I *should* try to find more wizardlike employment than the railroad. Otherwise, Karel and I will be in debt until the next Levar." She sighed as she released Thardik from the embrace. "It's time to stop whining, in any case. Like it or not, Karel's father died and left the bakery in debt, and I gave birth to two new mouths to feed when we expected only one." She passed a hand over her damp, tangled hair. "I don't like magic, but the sad truth is that it pays better than crisp-buns."

"You would have had to invest your wild luck anyway because of what it would do to you if you became pregnant again," Thardik said. "Failing to perform investiture could c-cost you your life."

Mardis shrugged and then winced as she felt a twinge in her shoulder. "I know, but that isn't my only concern anymore. If it were, I would've invested my luck in a sweet roll and let Karel eat it, as I did last year."

Thardik's eyes grew as big as ten-levar pieces. "So that's what happened. No wonder you didn't turn to magic as soon as your troubles started—you *couldn't*. Rashell thought you were just being s-stubborn."

Mardis crossed the room to the worn camel-hair couch that she and Karel had bought secondhand at the Two-Copper Bazaar. "Well," she said, flopping down on her back, "you can tell Mother that she's finally got her wish; I'm a wizard. This time, I invested my luck in my—"

Thardik clapped his hands over his ears and headed for the door. "I don't want to know," he said. "I'd blurt it to somebody, and *then* you'd be in a fix."

Mardis yawned. "Good point. Liavekan magicians are competitive enough that one of them might steal my luck piece to keep me from stealing clients."

"I know some who would do it just for the f-fun of it," Thardik said. He opened the door, letting in a bright wash of midmorning sunshine. "Since it's Luckday and I don't have to work, I think I will indeed visit your mother and tell her that your investiture was successful. She'll worry otherwise."

Mardis chuckled sleepily. "If I know my twins, Mother won't have had a spare moment to spend on worry."

"Shall I have her bring them back here?"

Mardis shook her head. "She's keeping them the rest of the day. I can only lie here an hour, and then I've got to get to the bakery. Karel will worry too, though I told him not to when I shoved him out this morning. And he'll need my help with the Luckday bread-baking, because poor Brenn isn't much use. She just hasn't cared about the business since Delfor died."

Thardik nodded in sympathy, then asked, "Do you have any message for your mother, other than the happy news of your investiture?"

Mardis yawned again. "No. Just kiss Larren and Asriel for

me, and don't be surprised if they try to pull out what's left of your hair. Karel's not joking when he called them little bandits.''

The old wizard smiled. ''If I am foolish enough to let a four-month-old babe tangle his or her little fingers in my hair, I deserve my fate.'' He pressed his right palm to his forehead. ''Farewell, Mardis. I shall take your blessings to your son and daughter, whose faces shine as bright as new coppers in the light of the summer s-sun.''

Mardis groaned. ''I asked you to kiss them, not drool over them.''

Thardik stepped outside. ''I shall try to remember the difference,'' he said, closing the door behind him.

Mardis folded her hands on her abdomen and grimaced as she felt the excess fat there. She had still not lost all of the weight she had gained during pregnancy. She had always associated getting fat with growing old—because her stocky mother, Rashell, had always seemed incredibly old to her—and thus she had the unpleasant feeling that she, at the age of nineteen, was getting old herself. Only a year ago, she had been a child; now she had two children of her own, a failing bakery, a husband whose spirits seemed to sink daily . . . and a layer of flab around her hips and middle.

She wondered if Larren and Asriel would grow up seeing her in the same way that she had seen Rashell—as a broad-bodied worrier who couldn't be happy. Would they never see her as she would always see herself—as the slim, laughing girl she had been the year before, holding her braids like handles as she teased Karel about the bracelet he had just given her?

She raised her right arm to gaze at the intricately engraved silver band that had been Karel's wedding gift and that was now the vessel of her wild luck. Almost white against her dark arm, it was a delicate, beautiful piece of work . . . but it seemed less bright than it had been last year. She still cherished it, but it was ever-so-slightly tarnished now, and even if it were polished, it would never be quite the same—it would never be *new*—again.

Just as Mardis would never be a slim, laughing girl again. No doubt she would laugh again, and perhaps even lose the weight she had gained, but . . .

Things would get better. They had to. She loved Karel, and
knew that he would not be so melancholy once they paid their
debts. He had lost every aspect of the child on the day that his
father had died six months earlier, but his delightful humor
was still there, just under the surface. He was only twenty, and
he couldn't stay sad forever.

And then, of course, there were the twins.

Mardis's labor had been difficult, and the only way she had
been able to stand it had been to focus on the likelihood that
her baby would have the same birth moment that Mardis herself
did—but then the whole thing had ended with an agonizing
contraction a half hour *before* her own birth moment, and the
one baby she had expected had immediately been followed by
another. The midwife, shocked, had looked up at her and said,
"You don't have any more surprises for me, do you, dearie?"
Mardis had longed for the strength to kick her.

As for the babies themselves . . . More temperamental, trou-
blesome children, she was sure, had never been born in either
Liavek or the Empire of Tichen. (Ka Zhir, maybe.) When
Larren was happy, Asriel was cranky; and when Asriel laughed,
Larren screamed. It was impossible to keep them both pacified,
and Mardis was only too glad to let Rashell watch them for
several hours each day while she herself worked at the bakery.

Despite all that, though, Thardik was right—their faces *did*
shine like new coppers, and there was no perfection like the
perfection of their tiny fingers and toes. Larren, the boy, already
had a shock of gleaming black hair that was exactly like Karel's;
and Asriel, the girl, had deep, dark eyes that Karel swore were
duplicates of Mardis's own. And even as Mardis and Karel
commented on these features, they would notice that Larren's
eyes, though less dark than Asriel's, were a lovely hazel color
with small flecks of green and gold; and that Asriel's hair,
though less dark and thick than Larren's, was as soft and fine
as spun silk.

Strangers often said, with wonder and admiration in their
voices, that the infants looked precisely alike . . . a remark that
Mardis always assumed meant that both babies were excep-
tionally beautiful. Karel called them little bandits because they
stole hearts.

As Mardis gazed at her luck piece, she realized that while
she had lost some precious things, she had gained others. For

better *and* worse, she had traded her childhood to become a baker, a spouse, and a mother.

And now, she reminded herself in resignation, she had become a wizard as well.

The silver bracelet felt hot on her wrist.

Mardis awoke with her bare forearms and calves sticking to the couch. For a moment she thought, groggily, that she had dreamed the sound of knocking, but then it came again. Someone was at the door.

As she sat up, she discovered that her body ached all over. Investiture had taken more out of her than she'd realized, and now all she wanted in the world was to be left asleep. The sandglass on the hearth indicated, though, that it was almost midday, and time to go to the bakery.

It would be impossible to fall asleep again, anyway. Whoever was at the door was using something other than knuckles and seemed willing to keep knocking until the door wore away to splinters.

Mardis's white cotton blouse and calf-length pants clung to her skin as she stood, and she pulled them free, shuddering at the sound the damp cloth made. The day was getting hotter by the moment. She looked down at the couch and saw a huge dark patch in the shape of her torso.

After pulling on well-worn shoes, she went to the door. "I'm coming, I'm coming," she said, her voice a sleep-thickened croak. "Gods, give it a rest." The rapping continued.

Angrily, she unlatched the door and jerked it open. "What's so damned—"

Mardis's words died in her mouth as she saw the stranger standing outside her door: a short, pretty woman who looked no older than Mardis herself and who was perhaps even younger, with dark blond hair and eyes of a startling blue. Even more startling than her eyes, though, was the fact that over her tight, mid-thigh-length tunic and knee-high boots, she wore the red robes of a priest of the Faith of the Twin Forces.

"Oh, I'm so glad!" the priest said, tossing away a small stone. Her voice was high-pitched, like that of a little girl. "I was afraid for a moment that no one was home!" She brushed past Mardis and entered the house.

Mardis, almost overcome by surprise and by the heavy scent

of the priest's exotic perfume, said, "I—I'm afraid you must
have the wrong house, your . . . um, your . . ." What was it the
Red priests liked to be called? Mardis felt thick-headed and
confused.

The blond woman reached the center of the room, where
Thardik's circle was still chalked on the floor, and then turned,
smiling coyly, to face Mardis. "I'm a margrave. You may call
me 'Your Grace.' "

Mardis didn't move from the doorway. "Well, ah, Your
Grace," she said hesitantly, "no one here belongs to your—
I mean, no one here is too religious, but we lean toward the
Way of Herself, so . . ." She held the door open wider, silently
inviting the priest to leave.

The smaller woman's expression became a pout. "Isn't this
the home of Karel, the baker's son? I think his father's name
was Delfor, his mother's name is Brell."

Mardis's clothes were sticking to her skin again, but she felt
far too self-conscious to allow herself to pull them free. "His
mother's name is Brenn," she said. "His father died of illness
six months ago."

The priest sighed. "Yes, I know, the poor man. That's why
I'm here, you see—I want to offer my condolences to my"—
she blushed—"old friend on the loss of his father."

Mardis stared at the flush on the young woman's cheeks and
became even more aware of her own sweat, rumpled clothes,
and disarrayed hair . . . and of how utterly perfect and pretty
the priest looked in comparison. "I can't imagine how you
know Karel," she said stiffly, "but in any case, six months is
a long time to wait before offering condolences."

The pout became exaggerated. "Oh, dear. Please, please—
shut the door, and I'll explain."

Mardis opened the door wider still. "I don't even know your
name," she said.

The priest's eyes flashed. "I am the Margrave of Narnitalo.
As I said, you may call me 'Your Grace.' " She crossed the
room to the camel-hair couch and sat down with one bare knee
crossed over the other, her robes spread about her like an open
tent.

Mardis shut the door. "Very well, Your Grace," she said,
crossing her arms. "Explain."

The priest's hands cupped her knee. "I've been cloistered

in the temple, instructing the initiates. Why else would I wait so long before visiting? I didn't hear about poor Delfor until after we ordained the new priests two days ago." She rubbed her knee. "Now, please, is Karel home? Surely he's not working on a Luckday, is he? Especially such a hot one!" A sour look crossed her face. "Hot days always make me feel sticky. I *hate* feeling sticky."

Mardis was becoming increasingly suspicious of this overly pretty, Farlandish-looking woman. "Karel *is* working on a Luckday," she said. "And I hope you'll forgive me for saying so, but you don't look old enough to be more than an initiate yourself. Your Grace."

The other's eyes flashed again, but then she gave Mardis a dazzling smile. "Not every high priest—that's what *I* am—is as old as His Scarlet Eminence. Many of us are ordained quite young. Karel would be a priest himself if he hadn't changed his mind."

Mardis felt as though she had been struck with a hammer. "That's—that's nonsense."

The priest tossed her head so that her shining hair all spilled to one side. "It is *not*," she said haughtily. "How else would a margrave meet and, um, get to know a baker's son? We were initiates together. Karel only stayed a year, though; he left when he was fifteen. I would have thought that a sister, or cousin, or whatever you are, would know all that." She sighed and licked her lips. "I've really missed him."

Mardis's head was buzzing, and in her dizziness the only thing she could be sure of was that she hated the pretty Red priest. "I'm not his cousin," she said, hearing her own voice as a disembodied noise. "We're married. We have two children."

The priest stood, her blue eyes wide and gleaming. "Why, that's wonderful," she said, rushing across the room with her scarlet robes billowing. As she embraced Mardis, the robes surrounded them both.

Mardis felt as though she were being suffocated, and then as though the robes were trying to devour her.

"I thought he'd never get over me," the priest said, hugging Mardis tightly. "I'm so glad he found someone!"

Mardis wanted to hit the priest in the mouth, but she couldn't get free of the embrace or the robes. The wild thought occurred to her that none of this was really happening, that she was lying on the couch and dreaming. But then she felt small, soft hands slide down her sweat-slicked arms, and she knew that it wasn't so.

"You're so *lucky*," the priest whispered, and swirled away in a blur of scarlet. The door opened and closed so quickly that Mardis would not have been aware of it had it not been for the blaze of sunlight that blinded her for an instant, and then was gone.

She stumbled across the room to the couch and sat down heavily. For the first time, she felt that she did not know her husband at all—did not, in fact, even know herself. She wished that the twins were there so that she could touch them and feel their reality.

She rubbed her arms and wrists. Despite the heat, she felt chilled from the touch of the priest's hands on her skin. Could Karel really have known that woman? Could he really have—

Mardis's thoughts froze as her left hand rubbed her right wrist. Then, feeling dead inside, she lifted her right arm.

Her silver bracelet, and her luck, were gone.

Mardis ran up and down the dusty street in a panic, searching each alley and doorway, but the blue-eyed Red priest—if that was what she really was—had vanished like smoke. A few neighbors had seen her approaching Mardis's house, but no one had seen her leave.

Finally, breathing hard with fatigue and rage, Mardis headed toward Merchant's Way and the bakery. If Karel really did know the blond woman, maybe he would also know how to find her. Later, he would have some explaining to do, but for now the only thing that mattered was that her luck piece had been stolen.

She entered the bakery through the back entrance, slamming the door against the wall, and found Karel brushing melted butter over hot loaves. He glanced up at the noise, and Mardis saw that he looked as handsome as ever despite the heat. It made her even angrier.

"Mardie!" he exclaimed as she strode toward him. "I thought you'd have to stay home the rest of the—" His expression became one of fear. "Wasn't your ritual successful? Weren't you able to—"

She cut him off. "Yes, I did it. Of course I did." She crossed the kitchen toward the door that led to the bakery's public room. "Is Brenn here?"

Karel resumed buttering the loaves. "There weren't any customers, so I sent her home."

Mardis turned back toward him. "Good. I don't want her to hear this. The way she's been, it could kill her."

Karel dropped the brush into the butter bowl and came to Mardis, putting his hands on her shoulders. "Gods, Mardie, what is it?"

For the first time, she saw that he was getting worry lines around his eyes. Her anger softened slightly; what had happened wasn't his fault. At least, she didn't think it was. "My bracelet's been stolen," she said miserably.

Karel looked stunned. "The one I gave you?"

"The thief pulled it off before I knew what was happening." Mardis struck Karel's chest with both fists. "Damn it! I *let* her do it!"

Karel drew back and rubbed his chest. "Don't take it out on me. Look, if the thief was that close, you must've gotten a good look at her. We'll go down the street to the City Guard post, and chances are they'll know who it is."

Despite herself, Mardis had to blink away tears. She felt as though something inside her were being shredded to pieces. "You don't understand," she said tremulously. "I used the bracelet for investiture. It was the only thing I could think of, the only thing I cared about enough—She stole my *luck*, Karel!"

Karel closed his eyes. "Rikiki's nuts," he breathed.

Mardis leaned on the bread table and almost let herself slump to the floor. "I don't know what to do," she said.

Karel pulled her upright. "We do the same thing. We go to the City Guard. The thief couldn't have known she was stealing a luck piece, and if we don't tell anyone, she won't find out." He steered her toward the rear door. "Come on. Tell me what she looked like while we walk. It'll keep your memory fresh."

"She was dressed as a Red priest," Mardis said. "She said she knew you."

Karel stopped, looking as though he had seen something that he feared would turn him to stone. "This—this happened on the street?" he asked.

Mardis felt her anger returning. Karel *did* know the thief. "No. She came into the house before I could think to keep her out."

"Describe her." His voice was a whisper now.

Mardis crossed her arms. "Short. A little pale. Blue eyes, light hair. She claimed to be a margrave, although I've never heard of a margrave stealing bracelets."

Now it was Karel who leaned on the bread table as though he might fall. "I know her," he said. "The Margrave of Narnitalo. She and I were initiates together. I was going to be a Red priest."

"So she told me," Mardis said bitterly. "Apparently thieves aren't necessarily liars, and husbands aren't necessarily what they show their wives."

Karel lowered his head. "I thought of telling you about my Red period a thousand different times, especially in the first year after we met, but . . . I was afraid that if I did, I'd also have to tell you about Narni. I wasn't sure you would understand."

"You were right. I don't."

He looked up at her, his eyes pleading. "Mardie, I was only fourteen, and she was sixteen. At least, that's what she said. I entered the Temple as a stupid act of rebellion against my parents, and while I was there, I . . ."

"Made love to a margrave."

"I was *fourteen*!" Karel shouted. "I didn't have any sense! And when I finally did, I ran away from the Temple and away from *her*! She tried to force me back, and when that didn't work she spied on me for months to find ways to punish me. She was the most manipulative, cruel little—" He stopped, and then, in a quieter voice, said, "I would have told you all about it a long time ago, but I didn't want you to know that I had ever been such a fool."

Mardis's anger did not weaken, but its focus shifted away from Karel. "I'll forgive you for the things you did before we met," she said, going to him. "Right now, though, all that matters is that this damned priest—"

"Narni," Karel said.

Mardis clenched her teeth. The thief's nickname was irrelevant. "All that matters," she said furiously, "is that she's got my luck piece—assuming that she's the same priest you knew then.''

''No one else fits your description,'' Karel said, ''and no one else would do what she did to you.''

''But *why* did she do it?'' Mardis asked. ''Just to torment the wife of an old lover?''

Karel shook his head. ''That might be enough for her, but I think it's something else.'' He hesitated. ''Ever since the twins were born, I've had a feeling . . . If I'd had any idea that she'd steal your luck, Mardie, I would have moved us as far from Liavek as I could.''

''I wouldn't have gone,'' Mardis said sharply. ''Liavek's my home, and I'll never leave.'' Then she realized what else he had said. ''And what have the twins got to do with this?''

Karel stood up straight. ''There's a prophecy in *The Book of the Twin Forces*. It's a little vague, like all prophecies, but it predicts that a woman whose luck is wild will give birth to twins who will grow up to be of great power. These twins will either strengthen or destroy the Faith—or perhaps Liavek itself. And since they may choose either path, they're thought to embody both 'good' and 'evil,' which will switch from one child to the other until they agree on a balance that pleases them.''

Mardis stared at him. ''Why didn't you say something before this?''

He looked away. ''Because it's only a superstition. Besides, the only way the high priests could have found out about *our* twins would be if Narni was still spying on me after all this time, and I didn't want to believe that.''

Mardis felt panic beginning to well up in her again. ''Karel, did you think that if the Red priests did find out about the twins, and about my luck, that *they* would think it was only a superstition?''

''I just . . . I don't know,'' Karel said.

Mardis wanted to hit him again, but restrained herself. ''All right, then; we'll worry about that as soon as we can. Right now, I need my luck piece, and since the City Guard isn't likely to believe that a high priest and margrave is a thief, we'll have to regain it ourselves. Any ideas?''

Karel seemed to gaze at something far away. ''There might

be a way,'' he said. ''She must have known that you'd describe her to me, so—''

The sentence remained unfinished. The door to the public room flew open, and Thardik burst in, dragging a disheveled, glassy-eyed Rashell with him.

''Th-the t-t-t—'' Thardik cried, stuttering so badly that he couldn't get his second word out.

Mardis hurried to them and took the burden of her mother's weight from the wizard. ''What in the name of—'' she began, but stopped as she saw who was missing. ''The twins!'' she shouted. ''Mother, where are the twins?''

Rashell's glazed expression vanished and was replaced by one of terror. ''They took them!'' she shrieked. ''Five men came in and took them!''

Mardis was unable to comprehend what had happened until Karel grasped her arm. When she turned toward him, his face looked as though it had been carved from stone.

''I know who they are—who they *must* be,'' he said. Again he seemed to gaze at something far away. ''The soldiers of the Faith. The Scarlet Guard.'' His eyes closed. ''The Red priests have our children.''

Mardis was already in the alley behind the bakery before Karel caught her and dragged her back inside. She felt as though she were on fire, and only one thought seared through her: *I have to get them back I have to get them back I have to get them back . . .*

Distantly, then, as though it were a shout from across the city, she heard Karel's voice. ''They're all right,'' he insisted. ''Larren and Asriel are *all right*.''

''How do you know?'' she managed to ask. A mist fell away from her eyes, and she saw Thardik and Rashell looking at her worriedly.

Karel's grip relaxed slightly. ''The Red priests don't want to hurt them, Mardie. If they were certain that the twins posed a danger to the Faith, then . . .'' He turned Mardis so that she faced him. ''I know how these people work. If they wanted—'' He took a deep breath. ''If they wanted our babies dead, we would have found them dead in their cradles. Instead, Narni had the Scarlet Guard kidnap them.'' His eyes seemed to grow darker. ''She had to realize that I'd figure all this out.

Either she wants to see what we'll do—or what *you'll* do, Mardie—or she did it this way simply because she enjoys being cruel.''

Mardis bit her lower lip. ''In other words, the most powerful people in Liavek have taken our children, and we can't do anything about it.''

Karel shook his head. ''We should tell the City Guard that the twins are missing . . . but since we don't have the proof we'd need to accuse Narni or the Scarlet Guard, I'm afraid that if Larren and Asriel are to be returned to us, I'm going to have to arrange it myself.'' He made a noise of bitter disgust through his nose. ''Narni will be expecting me, no doubt.''

''W-would someone p-please explain what's happening?'' Thardik asked piteously.

Mardis allowed Karel to put an arm around her shoulders and take her back to the center of the kitchen. Then, together, they told Rashell and Thardik of the prophecy and of the theft of Mardis's bracelet.

''The priest must have stolen my luckpiece to keep me from retaliating magically once I discovered that the twins had been kidnapped,'' Mardis said, sitting on a stool Karel had brought for her. It was agony to remain still, but she had decided that her husband was right; she would have no chance of getting Larren and Asriel back if she wasn't thinking clearly. ''But if that was her only reason, I don't know why she just didn't have me killed.''

''She's being cautious because of the prophecy,'' Karel said. ''If you were murdered, the twins might find out later and take revenge. But with a bit of spying, she could discover your birth hours. She'd know the time was close when Thardik purchased the gold dust. Then, once you began your ritual, all she had to do was peek through the bedroom window to see your luck piece. After Thardik left, she took advantage of your fatigue to steal it. That way, she could neutralize you without killing you.''

''So she may think now,'' Mardis said grimly, ''but she'll surely decide to murder both you and me when we try to spoil her plans. After all, Larren and Asriel are just babies; if we don't get them back, they won't even remember us, let alone take revenge for our deaths.''

Rashell spoke fiercely. ''Those Red thieves have more than

you and Karel to deal with, daughter. They have *me* as well."

Thardik linked his right arm with Rashell's. "I m-may not b-be much of a wizard," he said, "but I am n-no coward. I've become skilled at c-cutting and levitating stone, and I'll raze the R-Red T-Temple and throw the pieces into the sky if that's what it t-takes."

Mardis rose and hugged them both. "I suspect that the Temple is guarded with counterspells against that sort of thing," she said. "But I do want your help, because the only magic I have now is birth-moment magic."

"What's that?" Karel asked, frowning. He had never studied magic and knew almost nothing of how it worked.

"It's a bit of luck that can be used each day during one's actual birth moment," Mardis answered. "But it's weak, and mine will only be with me briefly at ninth hour. I've been practicing with it every day since I decided I'd have to be a wizard, but I doubt that I'm good enough to take on the Scarlet Guard. Thardik's skills may be all we have when we enter the Temple."

" 'We' aren't entering," Karel said. "I'm going in alone."

Mardis's eyes flashed. "Not without me, you're not."

He gave her a weak smile. "I have to, Mardie. I think I can enter the Temple without being spotted, and I know where Narni's chambers are, so I can catch her off-guard."

"And then what will you do?" Rashell demanded.

"Whatever it takes to discover where my children are and how I might get them back safely."

Mardis put a hand under Karel's chin and raised his head so that his eyes locked with hers. "So why can't I go with you?" she asked.

He shrugged. "Because when I was an initiate, I only managed to steal one set of scarlet robes."

Dusk would be falling soon. Mardis, Thardik, and Rashell sat on one of the semicircular stone benches surrounding the Fountain of the Three Temples, pretending to be just three more relaxed Liavekans watching the last red gleams of sunlight sparkle amid the streams of cascading water. The mist that surrounded them like a fog only made the evening hotter and more horrible as far as Mardis was concerned. There was no breeze; the air was as dead as the dust in the streets.

For the hundredth time, Mardis was unable to keep herself from glancing up at the clock set into the fountain's center spire. It was a few minutes past seventh hour.

"Damn," she whispered, looking over her shoulder across the cobblestoned common. Two members of the Scarlet Guard stood on either side of the Red Temple's perpetually open main entrance like a pair of vermilion statues. "It's been two hours. I'm going after him." She began to stand.

Thardik put his hand on her arm and pulled her back down. "Those two at the d-door might ask you your b-business, and what would you s-say?"

Rashell put her head in her hands. "Karel's been caught. Oh, why didn't he go to the east entrance as I told him? There aren't so many eyes watching that one."

"N-no, but that would have t-taken him right past the b-beadle," Thardik said, "and then he would have b-been nabbed for certain. Really, I d-don't think those two guards even glanced at him, and once he was p-past them, who would have s-stopped him?"

"The Margrave of Narnitalo," Mardis growled, turning back to face the fountain again. *She's probably making him bed her as payment in advance for letting him see the twins. And when she's through, she'll laugh at him for believing that she meant to keep the bargain.*

Rashell began sobbing, as she had done every few minutes throughout the afternoon. "If I had fought, or if I had scooped up the babies and run—"

Mardis rubbed her mother's neck. "Don't be ridiculous. What could you have possibly done against five men?" She paused, afraid of how Rashell would react to what she had to say next. "I really think you should go home, Mother. Thardik has to stay because we may need magic, but . . ."

Rashell looked up angrily, her mood changing as rapidly as the fountain's water fell to the pool. "But I'm useless, is that it? Well, we'll see about that if it comes down to a fight!" She reached into a pocket of her smock and pulled out a serrated bread knife. "I borrowed this from your bakery."

"P-put that away!" Thardik said, looking around in terror at the numerous strolling citizens. "Someone might s-see!"

Rashell returned the knife to her pocket. "I won't sit at home while my grandchildren are in danger,'' she said grimly. ''So don't count me out, daughter.''

Mardis met her mother's firm gaze. ''All right,'' she said softly. ''I won't.''

Thardik grasped her wrist. ''Look!'' he whispered.

Mardis turned and saw two figures in priests' robes emerge from the Red Temple's main entrance. One was short and fair; the other tall and dark: Narni and Karel. As they came down the steps together, a scarlet-trimmed black carriage drawn by a single horse appeared around the Temple's southeast corner. It stopped at the foot of the steps, and Narni and Karel climbed inside. Immediately, the driver snapped the reins, and the horse started toward the Levar's Way at a fast trot.

Mardis jumped to her feet. ''Asriel and Larren weren't with them,'' she said worriedly, stepping away from the bench.

''M-maybe that's where they're g-going,'' Thardik said, joining her. ''To the t-twins.''

Rashell stood as well. ''At least Karel doesn't seem to be a prisoner.''

''At least,'' Mardis muttered, and then began running so as not to lose sight of the carriage. Somehow, the fact that Narni had not had Karel seized made her more rather than less anxious.

The black-and-scarlet carriage reached the Levar's Way and began heading south, leaving the slower traffic of camels and carts behind. For an instant, Mardis felt a stab of panic as she realized that she would have no hope of keeping it in sight while on foot, but then she saw two ugly contraptions, pedicabs, parked beside each other between the Levar's Way and the Gold Temple ruins. Their drivers were lounging in their seats, passing a flask back and forth.

Mardis clambered into the passenger seat of the cab closer to the street, leaned forward, and slapped the driver on the shoulder. ''Follow that carriage!'' she cried, pointing.

The muscular woman in the driver's seat looked back sardonically. ''I've only been pedaling this thing two weeks, and already I can't count the number of times I've heard that. Except it's usually 'Follow that camel!' Well, sorry, mistress, but not tonight. I'm off duty.''

''I'll give you a levar!'' The carriage had all but disappeared around the curve of the Way.

The driver scratched her jaw. "Well . . . all right," she said. "But only if you help pedal."

Mardis put her feet on the wooden passenger pedals and began pumping. The contraption moved sluggishly at first, giving Mardis time to hear Thardik and Rashell enter the second vehicle and tell its driver to "Follow that cab!"

Then, as the pedicab entered traffic, Mardis's driver began pedaling furiously. The cab shot forward after the carriage, and Mardis could only hope that her companions, who possessed her only weapons, would be able to keep up.

Regardless, though, she couldn't wait. She had to keep Karel in sight so that she could be with him when he found their son and daughter.

The black-and-scarlet carriage sped far across the city to the docks, and the sky was dark by the time it finally stopped before a weathered, sagging warehouse on a narrow street that Mardis did not recognize. From the mingled smells of dead fish and seaweed, though, she knew that it was close to the bay. Her pedicab was trailing the carriage by a good distance, and she was just able to see Narni and Karel emerge. Narni was carrying a glowing lantern.

Mardis stopped pedaling and stared at the warehouse, wishing that she could see through its walls. *Are you in there, Asriel? Do you know I'm coming for you, Larren? Why can't I feel your presence if we're this close?*

She shook herself. Already her cab was closer to the warehouse than she would have liked. The street, probably bustling by day, was almost empty of traffic now, and she was afraid that Narni might spot her. "Stop here," she said.

Wheezing, the driver steered the vehicle to the edge of the street and pulled back the hand brake. The cab lurched as it stopped, and Mardis nearly cracked her head on the back of the driver's seat.

"One levar, as agreed," the driver croaked, slumping over the steering bars. "Although if I'd known I'd have to work so hard for it, I'd've thought twice."

Mardis stepped out and handed over all three of the silver coins she'd grabbed from the bakery's cashbox. "The extra half-levar is for your trouble," she said, "and I'd appreciate it if you wouldn't tell anyone about following the carriage. I'm planning a surprise.'' She looked up as she spoke and saw that the carriage was continuing down the dirty street. Narni had opened a door and was entering the warehouse; Karel was following.

The pedicab driver accepted Mardis's coins with a weary grin. ''Mistress, for an extra half-levar, I'll be happy to forget that I ever picked you up at all.'' She began pedaling again and left Mardis standing alone in the street.

As the carriage and then the pedicab disappeared, Mardis realized that she was standing in a shaft of yellow light from a window in the nearest building. Quickly she moved into the shadows, wishing that she'd had enough sense to tell the driver to stop in the dark.

She had no sooner stepped out of the light when she heard a loud clatter, and Rashell and Thardik's cab appeared. It was slowing, both sets of pedals clacking around and around from sheer momentum, and stopped as it reached the shaft of light.

''I'm sorry,'' the driver said, panting. ''We've lost them. It's too hot, and you didn't help me pedal enough.''

Mardis stepped into the light and hissed. Thardik and Rashell saw her, but their driver, wiping sweat from his eyes, did not. Mardis returned to the shadows.

Stiffly, Rashell climbed out of the cab and turned to help Thardik. ''Very well, young man,'' she said sternly. ''But don't expect to grow rich running your business this way.''

The driver made a rude gesture and pedaled away, groaning. Thardik and Rashell, waddling as if their joints had fused, moved through the yellow light to where Mardis waited.

Mardis pointed at the ramshackle warehouse. ''The priest took Karel in there.''

''So what do we do n-now?'' Thardik asked.

Mardis hesitated, biting her lip. ''I'll enter first,'' she said uncertainly. ''Thardik, you follow a few seconds later, but stay well behind me so that you're not seen. I'll make a racket to get the priest's attention, and when she confronts me, I'll pretend that I still have my luck. I'll threaten to cave in the roof if she doesn't do as I say.''

''She won't b-believe you,'' Thardik said nervously.

''She will if you tear down a chunk of the ceiling and keep it hovering over her head,'' Mardis said. ''You do that sort of thing at the Station all the time, don't you? Cut things apart and levitate the pieces?''

Even in the poor light, Mardis saw the old wizard's expression of pleased surprise. "Why, yes," he said. "I *d-do*, don't I?''

Mardis nodded. "And if the priest doesn't see you, she'll think she stole the wrong item from me—which could mean that she and her cronies will be intimidated enough for us to get the twins back without a fight."

"And what am *I* to do?" Rashell said angrily.

Mardis faced her. "I want you to wait just outside the entrance—gods, I hope it isn't guarded; I haven't seen anyone—and be ready to come if I shout for you. If Larren and Asriel are inside and my bluff doesn't work, you need to get them out while Thardik, Karel, and I keep the priest and whoever else is in there occupied."

"G-good p-plan," Thardik said.

Mardis started down the street toward the warehouse. It was probably a terrible plan, but she couldn't take any more time with it. She had to know what had happened to her babies.

Mardis listened at the door where Narni and Karel had entered, but she heard nothing. Nor could she see any light through the cracks. Taking a deep breath, she pressed on the spring-latch and found it locked.

"Let me," Rashell murmured, pushing Mardis aside. She pulled out the serrated knife and slid it between the door and the jamb.

"S-something's wrong," Thardik whispered from several paces behind them.

Mardis glanced back at him. "It's just a spring-latch. Mother should be able to open it."

"N-not that." Even though his voice was only a whisper, Mardis could hear him beginning to panic. "I c-can't come any c-closer. There's some k-kind of spell here to k-keep out wizards."

"How could a spell know who's a wizard and who isn't?"

"It c-could be a barrier against luck v-vessels." Thardik reached into a pocket and withdrew a small object, which he placed on the ground. Then he stepped forward. "That's it, all r-right."

Before Mardis could absorb the implications of that, the latch popped open, and the door squeaked inward on ancient hinges. Rashell flourished her knife before putting it away. "I should have been a burglar, like your father," she whispered. "May Rikiki nibble his rotten soul."

"He may nibble us all before this is over," Mardis muttered, and then pointed at Thardik's luck piece. "Do you suppose we could get it inside if *I* carried it?"

Thardik held his hands palms upward and shrugged.

Mardis stepped past him and bent to pick up the object. It was smooth and warm in her hand, and she recognized the shape immediately. "An acorn?" she said aloud, surprised.

"I thought it m-might help me become a mighty oak," Thardik said. "It d-didn't work too well."

Mardis pocketed the nut and stepped back past the point where the old wizard had been stopped. "I thought so," she whispered. "With me, it's just an acorn. Stay at least three paces away until we're inside, Thardik; the barrier spell is probably in effect right up to the doorway. Once we're in, I'll pass this back to you. Except for that, the plan stays the same."

Thardik moved well clear of the doorway so that Mardis could enter, and Rashell squeezed her daughter's arm as she came close. "I'm here," the older woman murmured. "Remember that."

Mardis squeezed Rashell's arm in response and then stepped toward the dark, half-open doorway. Her mouth felt as though she had just eaten dry sand.

As she began to slip inside, a high-pitched wail emanated from far back in the warehouse.

Mardis froze. *Larren! That's Larren!*

Then all fear was forgotten, and she plunged into the waiting blackness.

Mardis slipped on sawdust and collided with the walls of a narrow passageway as she ran, blind, toward the sound of her baby's cry. It was like trying to sprint while trapped in the black glue of a nightmare.

She knew that she had left the passageway and entered a cavernous room when the cry began to echo and she saw the dim glow of a cloth-covered lantern several paces to her left. She changed direction and headed for the light.

"Now!" a voice cried, and Mardis was jerked to a halt as she was seized from either side. Too late, she remembered that she was to have passed the acorn luck piece back to Thardik as soon as they had entered the building.

The cloth was removed from the lantern, and Mardis, blinking at the sudden brightness, saw Narni and Karel standing before a small wooden table. With them were four uniformed members of the Scarlet Guard—two of whom held Karel, and another of whom was pressing the flat of his sword to Karel's mouth. On the table, beside a sandglass, stood a large wicker basket containing a squirming shape that had to be Larren. She could not see Asriel, but was certain she was there. If Larren was upset, Asriel was sure to be content.

Mardis strained toward the table, but was held fast by two Scarlet Guards. She stamped on the foot of the one on her right, but it had no effect.

"Is her companion with us as well?" Narni called, holding her lantern higher.

"Here," a rough voice answered, and two more guards dragged Thardik abreast of those who held Mardis. The old wizard's face was as red as hot coals.

"I'm sorry," Mardis said, speaking loudly to be heard over the baby's cries. "I didn't think too well."

Thardik blinked, looking like an old, tufted owl. "It d-doesn't matter, child," he said. "Considering the odds, we c-came *close enough.*"

Mardis noted the emphasis he gave his last two words and then mentally measured the distance between them. Was Thardik within three paces of the acorn in her pocket? It looked a bit far to her, but . . .

"More light!" Narni commanded, handing the lantern to her one unoccupied soldier, who placed it on the table. The two guards holding Karel released him, then turned and strode in opposite directions to light lanterns that hung from wooden support columns.

As the lanterns flickered to life, Mardis saw that she was in a huge sawdust-floored chamber, the illuminated portion of which was empty save for the table and a chopping block at the foot of one of the support columns. Atop the chopping block lay a slim, gleaming circle of metal: Mardis's silver bracelet. The enormous soldier who had lit the lantern above it remained standing there, his arms folded over his chest. The other guard returned to stand with Narni.

"Did anyone besides the old fat-sack come in with her?" Narni asked sharply.

One of the guards holding Thardik answered. "No, Your Grace. The hall was empty but for this one. Shall I search outside?"

Narni pursed her lips for a moment and then said, "Don't bother. The barrier spell will stop wizards, and the only others who might have come are the grandmothers. We have nothing to fear from *them*—and they aren't here anyway, are they, love?" She looked up at Karel as her guard lowered the sword from Karel's mouth to his throat.

Karel's expression was blank. "No," he said. "As I told you, I asked my mother to care for Rashell, who was hysterical."

Narni gestured at Mardis and Thardik. "You also told me that you slipped away from these two. But it seems that they followed you, doesn't it?"

"So it seems."

Narni reached up and chucked him under the chin. "You wouldn't lie to an old lover, would you, sweet?"

Karel pushed her hand away, ignoring the snarl of the guard who held the sword at his throat. "I know better than to try to match a professional at her trade."

Mardis felt that she loved him more at that moment than ever before.

Narni stuck out her lower lip in the same pout that Mardis had seen that afternoon. "Now you're trying to make me feel bad," the priest said in her little-girl voice. "I don't like that." The pout disappeared as quickly as it had come. "Besides, dear heart, you *have* tried to match me. You came to my chambers hoping to convince me to return your brats, but you wouldn't even hop into bed. That showed a lack of willingness to bargain, if you ask me."

Karel didn't even look at her. "You brought me here anyway."

Narni waggled her finger. "But not to hand them over to you, my first and truest love. Within the hour, they'll be taken aboard a ship that will carry them to Gold Harbor, where they'll be cared for by parents of my choosing. If these are indeed the twins of the 'two coins' prophecy, they must be raised within strict ideological guidelines—and it's best that their home be some distance from Liavek. Neither the Zhir nor the Tichenese will expect their conquerors to come from a city committed to neutrality.''

Larren's wails grew shriller, and unusually, Asriel joined him in his screams.

Mardis strained against her guards again. "You'll take them nowhere!" she cried. "They're our children, and they're *staying* ours."

Narni looked exasperated. "They'll accept whoever we choose to raise them. They won't know the difference."

"We'll come after them," Mardis said.

The babies' wails subsided.

Narni sighed. "I was afraid of that. That's why I had to arrange things so that Karel would come to me—because I could then bring him here, and you would follow. That's the only way I can do what I must without anyone else knowing about it." She snapped her fingers, and two guards seized Karel again. "A few citizens may have seen me or my servants about our business with you and your mother earlier today, but there will be nothing to link the Faith of the Twin Forces to what will be found here tomorrow. As for the grandmothers—well, even if they were to learn where the twins will be living, they wouldn't survive the sea voyage there. I'd have to see to it."

Karel struggled against his captors now, but had no better luck than Mardis. "Damn me for an idiot," he growled through clenched teeth.

Narni stood on tiptoe and kissed his lips. "Of course, sweet. I hereby damn you for an idiot."

"If you want us dead," Mardis said bitterly, "why not just kill us instead of baiting us like this?"

Narni pirouetted with a flourish of scarlet robes. "Because I love my work!" she sang.

"P-perhaps," Thardik said, sounding as if he was fighting to suppress his terror. "B-but you also have to know whether you succeeded in stealing Mardis's t-true luck piece, so I will t-tell you: She knew you were spying on her, and she p-placed the bracelet so you would *think* it was her v-vessel." He raised his voice in defiance. "That means that if you t-try to harm us, your whole scheme will be torn apart in a whirlwind of wild m-magic.'' He looked at Mardis. ''Child, the p-priest thinks that if she provokes you, and you do nothing, that must m-mean that you are without power. Only then will she feel safe in c-cutting our throats.''

Narni giggled. ''Don't be silly, Master Fat-Sack. This place is surrounded by a spell that would keep out her luck piece anyway. And as for birth-moment magic—'' She glanced at the sandglass. ''We'll be finished here before she can use that. I know her birth moment too, you see.''

''A barrier spell created with ordinary magic may have d-difficulty against wild luck,'' Thardik said, sounding braver. ''Mardis, I suggest a demonstration. Then maybe this spoiled girl will s-stop annoying us.'' His eyes met Mardis's with a look that said he was ready to try the spell they had agreed upon.

''Very well,'' Mardis said. *Let him be close enough*, she prayed to all of the gods in general. *Please, let him be close enough.* She tilted her head back until she was looking straight up. A rumbling noise filled the air, and dust fell from the high ceiling.

''Cut the bracelet!'' Narni cried.

Mardis snapped her head down and saw that the guard beside the chopping block had drawn his sword and was raising it high.

''No!'' she shouted, and only then realized what she had done.

Narni laughed humorlessly. ''Move Master Fat-Sack farther away from her,'' she said. ''She's got his luck piece. A bit of monkey dung, no doubt.''

The guards did as the priest commanded, and the rumbling ceased. Mardis couldn't suppress the miserable thought that anyone as stupid as she *deserved* to die.

The guard by the chopping block, still holding his sword high, looked at Narni with questioning eyes.

''Well, go ahead,'' the high priest said impatiently. ''Once it's broken, we'll *know* she can't hurt us.''

The sword flashed downward. Simultaneously, a smaller flash shot across the chamber and struck the big man on the wrist before glancing off the support column and falling to the sawdust. The guard, crying out in pain, buried the edge of his sword in the chopping block, missing the bracelet entirely.

Then, as he stared at his bleeding wrist, Rashell charged out of the passageway and across the chamber, ramming her head into his ribs. He fell to the floor with the heavy woman on top of him.

Mardis felt her own captors' grips slacken as their instincts told them to help their comrade, and she drove her elbows into their bellies. Then, wrenching free, she sprinted toward the chopping block.

Rashell clambered to her feet and snatched up the bracelet, holding it high and shouting, "I have it, daughter, I have it!" over Narni's cry of frustration.

Mardis could sense that two guards were close behind her, but all she had to do was get within three paces of the bracelet, and then—

The guard on the floor rolled into Rashell's legs, tripping her, and in an instant he was straddling her with a dagger at her throat.

"Stop or she dies!" he shouted. He sounded as though he hoped Mardis would *not* stop.

Mardis halted, at least five paces from her goal, and her pursuers grasped her arms. Larren and Asriel began crying anew.

Narni hurried across the room with her one unoccupied guard and leaned down to pluck the bracelet from Rashell's grasp. Then she turned and glared at Mardis.

"Why couldn't you have just stayed home?" the priest said. "Then I would've known for certain that I had your magic and that you wouldn't be a problem. When Karel came to see me, I could've had some fun and then let him go. But since you *didn't* stay home, I had to find out whether you still had your luck, and now that I see what a nuisance you're going to be, I . . ." She scuffed her boot on the floor, raising a small cloud of sawdust. "I don't have any choice. If I should release you, knowing that you'd be a threat . . ."

Mardis, feeling numb, looked back at the sandglass. If only her birth moment weren't still a half hour away, then she could at least try to do something, *anything*—

Narni pocketed the bracelet and waved at her guards. "All right," she said, her voice quavering. "Do it." She covered her eyes with both hands and fled into the darkness beyond the support column.

Abruptly, the twins stopped crying.

Mardis, her eyes darting wildly in a desperate search for an escape, saw everything happen at once:

The guard holding the sword at Karel's throat drew back to strike.

The guard on Thardik's left looped a cord around the wizard's neck and began to pull it tight.

The bleeding guard raised his dagger and drove it toward Rashell's heart.

Mardis felt a pistol barrel pressing into her side.

And then . . .

The sword crumbled to powder.

The cord snapped.

The dagger turned into a lizard and scurried up its wielder's sleeve.

The pistol became a stick of soft dough.

For a moment the Scarlet Guards stared, dumbfounded, at the things that had been their weapons, and then they released their prisoners and fell to their hands and knees, snuffling in the sawdust and grunting like pigs.

Narni ran backward out of the darkness and collided with the chopping block, and the sword that was stuck there became an enormous black snake that coiled around her torso. Her robes melted into a gelatinous red substance that flowed about her as if alive and coated her from head to foot. "Eeeeewww!" she squealed, covering her face again. *"Eeeeeewwww!"*

Then the priest rose from the floor, flipped upside-down, and swooped up until her feet touched the high ceiling. She swayed there, still shrieking, while Mardis stared up in astonishment.

Rashell and Thardik joined Mardis, and they, too, gazed up at the priest. "This c-could get us into b-big trouble," Thardik whispered.

Then Karel joined them as well, carrying the basket that held the twins. Mardis, instantly oblivious to the priest and her soldiers, looked down at her children and was amazed to see that both were gurgling happily.

"Look at them," she said, stroking their perfect little arms and cheeks. "Thardik, how could you have said that their faces are as bright as new coppers? They're at least as bright as gold levars, and more beautiful.''

"That's from our side of the family," Rashell said.

"Could we p-please get out of here?" Thardik asked, glancing up at the quivering Narni, whose squeals had become whimpers. He sidestepped to avoid a falling dollop of red goo. "I'm starting to feel a little s-sick.''

Karel leaned close to Mardis. "Uh, I don't know just what's happened here," he said in a low voice, "but if we leave things like this, we'll have to flee Liavek, and even then we'll never be safe. Narni may have failed, but sooner or later, His Scarlet Eminence or some other high priest will find us.''

Reluctantly, Mardis looked up from Larren and Asriel. "Your Grace," she shouted to the dangling Narni. "I hope you and your fellow priests will see now that wild luck cannot be suppressed, and that children should not be separated from their parents. However, I'll make you a bargain: I'll undo all that I've done here and will raise my twins with the utmost respect for Liavek, for the Red Faith, and for the Levar and her Regent—although I will *not* require them to subscribe to the Red Faith or to any other. I will swear to all of this, provided that *you* swear, as a representative of His Scarlet Eminence and on your life, that neither you nor any other agents of the Faith of the Twin Forces will ever again interfere in any way with the lives of these twins or with the lives of any of their friends or family.''

Narni's squirming subsided slightly, and even in her obvious distress, she spoke coldly. "And just what will you do if I refuse your bargain, Karel's chubby wife?''

Mardis gritted her teeth and took a deep breath. "I'll leave you here and burn this place. Furthermore, when my twins have gained their full powers, I'll have them destroy your Temple and Faith.'' It was a massive bluff, but she didn't think that Narni would doubt her . . . especially since the priest had a snake coiled about her waist, was coated with red slime, and was hanging upside-down from the ceiling.

"If I accept your terms," Narni said, "what guarantee do I have that you won't go back on your word?''

"If I break my part," Mardis answered, "the agreement will

become void, and you and the other priests will be free to do as you like.''

A long silence followed, but at last Narni swore, on her Faith and her life, that she accepted Mardis's terms.

''Thank you, Your Grace,'' Mardis said. ''Now, before I begin to fulfill my part of the bargain, I have a request: That bracelet was my husband's wedding gift, and I would like it returned.''

Narni dropped the slime-coated silver band, and Mardis caught it. Immediately, the close proximity of her invested luck filled her with an intense feeling of well-being, and when she slipped the bracelet onto her wrist, she felt better still. She wiped off the slime with her sleeve.

''All right, I've done it,'' Narni said. ''We've got a bargain, so let me down and get this *snake* off me. *Eeeewwww*, he's *licking* me, get him *off*!''

''Of course, Your Grace,'' Mardis said dryly, and then she nudged Thardik and whispered, ''Go ahead.''

Thardik gazed at her with a confused expression. ''W-what?'' he asked.

Mardis chuckled. She might have known that Thardik wouldn't be able to undo his own work. Now that she had her wild luck back, though, she might be able to reverse another wizard's conjuring. . . .

In another minute, all eight soldiers were on their feet, and Narni, her robes restored and the snake only a sword in the sawdust, stood before Mardis, glaring with fury and frustration.

''Do you have any idea what my Temple will do when I report all of this?'' the priest cried. She looked down at the sword on the floor. ''I ought to—''

Mardis held up her hands, fingers spread, and sent streaks of blue lightning crackling out to whip around Narni. They returned to her and disappeared with a snap.

''What you ought to do is stay clear of me,'' Mardis said. ''A bargain is a bargain. As for your fellow priests, you can tell them that you were able to eliminate the danger of the prophecy without taking lives or kidnapping the twins from their rightful home. You opted for a balanced path instead of one of violence. As I understand it, that should be exactly in accordance with your Faith.''

Narni rolled her eyes. ''A lot you know about the Faith of

the Twin Forces, baker,'' she said, and then gestured to her soldiers and started toward the passageway.

She paused beside Karel. ''You know why I've kept track of you, don't you?'' she said in a tiny voice. ''You really were my first love.''

Karel shook his head. ''No, Narni. *You* were.''

The high priest sniffed and stalked out, her Scarlet Guards trailing her in a tight pack as if they couldn't wait to be out on the street.

Mardis, her mother, her husband, her children, and her oldest friend were left alone in the warehouse. The four adults stood looking at one another for a long moment, and then they burst into laughter, finally releasing the tension that had gripped them all day. Asriel, startled by the sudden noise, began to wail again, but Larren continued to gurgle.

''Thardik, I didn't know you had that much magic in you,'' Mardis said between chortles, clapping him on the shoulder. ''I was afraid for a moment that Her Grace would be stuck up there until Liavek crumbled into the sea, simply because you couldn't reverse your own spell!''

Thardik blinked. ''Me? I was too far from my acorn to do a thing. I thought *you* did it all with birth-moment m-magic.''

Mardis stopped laughing.

Rashell, looking at the sandglass on the table, said, ''Why, she couldn't have. Her birth moment is still several minutes away.''

''And I was even farther from my luck piece than Thardik was from his,'' Mardis added.

Karel set the basket on the floor and rubbed his forehead. ''Now, wait—If Thardik didn't create any of that chaos, and *you* didn't...''

Mardis glanced at the sandglass, which confirmed what she already knew. ''Larren and Asriel were born a quarter of an hour ago on the thirteenth day of Rain,'' she murmured, and then stared down at her wailing daughter and laughing son.

She heard Karel swallow hard.

''Precocious little bandits, aren't they?'' he said.

FESTIVAL WEEK

The Grand Festival: Sestina

by John M. Ford

This week, unlike all others, has six days.
The first prefigures four forthcoming years,
And, since no one plays lightly with one's luck,
The usual advice is: sleep all night,
The morning after, walk soft on the streets,
Do nothing that you would not gladly do.

People get born all over. Though they do,
The Liavekans bundle up those days
And hold one party up and down the streets
Whatever be one's origin or years;
A birthday ball from morning until night,
A universal fib to guard one's luck.

Religion, as the paradigm of luck,
Is something lucky people tend to do;
And so, until descend the shades of night
The faithful strut their ways. Then full-of-days
Give pageant over to the young in years:
And something much, much older walks the streets.

The hawker's hurlyburly crowds the streets:
They'll sell you lamps and lagers, larks and luck,
They'll swear the prices are the best in years

(As at no other time they ever do)
Perhaps you'll see (for these are run-mad days)
A wealthy man turn beggar in the night.

Tonight will be the very longest night.
There will be such commotion in the streets
The echoes may not die away for days;
So have another drink, and trust to luck
You'll find your way back home, and when you do,
Proclaim you haven't been so sick in years. . . .

Past crazy days there follow sober years.
And in the day that follows that long night,
One finds some more constructive thing to do:
Repair the damage, sweep the littered streets,
Do something kind for those with lesser luck,
Breathe deep and brace up for the brave new days.

But now those years are dancing in the streets,
A week-long night's dream full of life and luck
And all we yet shall do. These are the days.

Divination Day: Invocation

by John M. Ford

So many minutes make one day as days fill out four years
And as such correspondences beguile the human mind
One day is cast (that never on the calendar appears)
The image of the fifteen hundred following in fine

The empty little hours are when the sweetest dreams occur
The love that sweats for your desires, the power desire
    employs
Until the senseless pleasures pop as though they never
    were
And hands crush pillows clutching at what light of day
    destroys

The morning shines with prospects, brooks no limit to your
    powers
And soon you will be working—but not prematurely soon
The waiting work soon swells to jam the ever-dwindling
    hours
Until procrastination meets the headsman's stroke of noon

The afternoon dissolves into a swirl of things undone
You beg the rushing minutes what they cannot stop to give
You cannot reef the sails of time nor anchor-chain the sun
You cannot live two lives or catch your teardrops in a
    sieve

The moon and stars illuminate the counsels of the night
A cool black velvet respite from the rages of the sun
Consider what you've done this far, consider what you
    might
Consider that the night will end and all things shall be
    done

A handful of the desert trickles timewise through a glass
And empty fingers stroke the sand to feel out what comes
    next
The juggler's trick with moments is to catch them as they
    pass
And live the years as more than just a gloss upon the text

A Hot Night at Cheeky's

by Steven Brust

THE SIGN OUTSIDE the inn showed the south end of a mule heading north. The place was called Cheeky's, after the owner, Cheeky, whose name was Mariel. It was in Old Town, or, rather, just outside it, its door looking onto Rat's Alley near the Soldier's Gate. Its single story pushed up against Farrier's Way as if it was about to step onto the street and be swept straight to the docks and thence to the sea.

The main room was rather long, with the bar running its entire length to the left of the door. It was dark most of the time. Beyond this room was a door that, presumably, led back to Cheeky's living quarters. In fact, it didn't. It led back to a small, private bar, and a private meeting room, but the only people who knew of this were the staff and those few who received notes that said, "Go back through the door, help yourself at the private bar, and wait in the meeting room." Such notes were not common.

Cheeky's clientele included a fair share of sailors, a few day-laborers, some merchants, and more than a few of the older and prouder—if not richer—representatives of Liavekan society. It didn't have the best pot-boil in Liavek; it didn't have the worst. The home-brew ale was fine, the choice of wines good enough, the whiskey and brandy not very overpriced. There were occasional fights, but not too many nor too bad. The bouncers' names were Tsep and Vejed, and the wizard's name was Ried. Ried wasn't officially associated with the inn, but he hung around a lot because he was a good friend of the owner, Mariel, whose name was Cheeky.

The first to arrive that evening was a man built something like a Redshore Retriever. He had the big barrel chest, the powerful legs, and the same sad eyes as the dog, and it would not be hard to believe that beneath them was as keen a nose. His name was Rye. He left his footcab in the street outside Cheeky's and went in. It was Divination Day. The three-quarters bell had rung a few minutes before. Twilight was rearing its indefinite head.

Rye walked back past the stage, where a musician was begging a cittern to come to tune with itself. Rye spoke briefly to Vejed and showed him a small slip of paper. Vejed shrugged and pointed to the back. Rye went back until he came to the private bar. A lithe woman of perhaps six or seven and twenty, with olive skin, a very thin face, and hair so straight it looked dead, glanced at him and said, "The room at the end of the hall. I'll be right there," and went back to studying the camel-racing predictions in the *Crier*.

Rye, somewhat hesitantly, helped himself to an ale and took it back to the room Cheeky had indicated. There was a single table there, with six chairs. He walked to the far end and sat down.

Presently, Cheeky came through the curtained doorway and sat across from him. She held a tall glass of dark tea with a large piece of ice floating in it. She took small sips, swallowing with relish.

"I'm Cheeky," she said.

"Rye. You sent the message?"

"Yes. It was the only way I could think to make contact with others."

"Others? Then there will be others showing up?"

"I hope so."

"You have something?"

"Yes, but I'll need help."

Rye grunted. "I had not thought you sent for me out of charity." At that point, a short woman in a shapeless cloak entered, holding a glass of pale wine. She had an attractive V-shaped face and amazing blue eyes, and when she pulled the hood back her hair was the startling light color of the Farlands.

"I'm the Margrave of Narnitalo," she said, sitting down next to Rye.

"Cheeky. I own this place."

"Rye. Good day, Narni."

She started. "You know me?"

"I've seen you many times at your Temple. I pull—pulled a footcab. I had no idea you worked for Dashif, though."

"Oh." She bit her lip. "Did you work for him, then?"

"I spied for him, especially along Wizard's Row. I also ran errands. I don't know how they found out about me."

Cheeky spoke up. "They've broken His Scarlet Eminence's codes, and Dashif's. They know all of us by now except me, and I doubt that I can last long. That's why I've brought us together. I hope they don't know all of his means of getting messages to his agents. If they do, Arenride, or one of his men, is liable to show up."

Narni shuddered. Rye made no response.

The curtain parted again, and an old woman entered, nodded to those assembled, and sat down next to Cheeky, across from Narni. She sipped from a steaming cup of kaf.

Narni studied her and frowned. "Aren't you Myglynn? Didn't you clean the Levar's chambers at the palace?"

"Indeed, mum, I am."

"I had no idea—"

"Ah," said Rye. "I've heard of you. I've carried messages all over the city that originated with things you've discovered. I'm Rye."

"Narni."

"Cheeky."

"How are you getting along?" asked Narni.

"Not well. I've been discovered by Arenride, and I've been in hiding for a week. He wants to arrest all of Dashif's agents, and I'm too old for prison, and I don't know how to get out of the city."

Narni nodded. "Nor I. I've tried. They killed Bilthor when he tried to sneak out one of the secret ways, and they almost caught Gerin at Drinker's Gate."

"Almost?" said Rye. "He escaped?"

"So I've heard. He led them a merry chase through Old Town, but—"

"And a merry chase it was indeed," said a tall, very dark-skinned gentleman in a yellow silk dress robe and gold-laced sandals, who carried a walking stick in one hand and a brandy snifter in the other.

Cheeky said, "You are Gerin?"

"I am."

"Yes," said Myglynn, slowly. "I've seen you around the palace, haven't I?"

"Quite, madam," said Gerin. He sat down next to her and addressed the woman at the opposite end of the table, "You, I know, are Cheeky, our gracious host. These others I'm afraid I don't know."

"Narni."

"Myglynn."

"Rye. I've heard of you. I believe you were involved in blackmail for Dashif?"

Gerin sniffed. "I should prefer to say that I gathered information from those not disposed to give it—"

"That's what I did, too," said Narni, her odd blue eyes twinkling.

"—and that I did these things for the good of the city."

"The city," said Myglynn, her gnarled hands clenching, "no longer appreciates our actions."

"Well, certainly the Three Sisters don't."

"I wonder," said Rye slowly, "which one actually wants us imprisoned. It must be one of them; Arenride wouldn't go after us on his own, you know, and I doubt the Levar cares."

"Probably Geth Dys," said Narni, who always followed politics closely. "His whole church has hated Dashif for a long time. Something about a message they were trying to send the Levar that he intercepted."

"Yes," said Rye slowly. "I think I heard something of that." He sighed. "Well, there are worse people to be facing than Arenride. He's honest."

"Does it matter?" said Narni. Rye shrugged.

The curtain moved once more, and a plump, middle-aged woman came in. She carried a small glass of whiskey with water and sat somewhat hesitantly next to Myglynn, across from Gerin. Myglynn smiled and said, "Teci, aren't you?"

"Why, yes, how do you know?"

"I've bought peaches from you, many times."

"I'm sorry. There are so many—"

Gerin said, "You worked in the market, didn't you? Amassing information?"

Cheeky said, "Yes, I recognize the name. You were Dashif's first choice for everything that happened anywhere near the market, or among the merchants, or—"

"Oh, posh," she said, blushing. "I just listened to gossip and passed it on to him."

"And," said Gerin, "occasionally put out a word or two that he wanted spread?"

"Well, maybe. But who are all of you? I got a message from the bird, which I didn't think anyone knew about, but—"

"I sent the message," said Cheeky.

"Very well, and I certainly recognize you, dear, and I love this place. And of course, I've seen the Margrave of Narnitalo in the market. I remember her the day of the Massacre, talking to those two nice young—"

"There is no need to discuss it," said Narni.

"All right, dear. But I don't know the rest of you."

"I am Gerin."

"Rye."

"Myglynn."

Cheeky cleared her throat. "Well, then, since we—"

The curtain moved once more, and a large man entered. Very large, the sort of man who must be careful with his hands lest he crush anything he takes into them. His skin was pure ebony, his robes were white, and well, if not finely, made. His hand dwarfed a large goblet of water.

Cheeky said, "Ynnd i'Drssail. I've seen you in here with your men and heard you called by name many times, but, by the Daughter, I had no idea you were one of Dashif's."

"Ah ha," said Myglynn. "So this is the Caravaneer. Sir, I've heard the late Count speak of you highly."

The one called Ynnd looked at all of them, his eyes narrowing. Then he said, "You, Rye, I know, but I do not know what you are doing here."

"I worked for Dashif, as, I'm certain, did you."

"Dashif. Yes." He pronounced the name oddly, with the accent on the second syllable. He shrugged. "I am a trader. I sold him information for money. I'd have done as much for anyone. Now I find that this has made me a criminal, and I am hunted and unable to leave the city. I do not understand why."

"That," said Cheeky, "is why we're here."

"I do not know most of you."

"Call me Cheeky. This is my establishment." He bowed his head. "We seem," she went on, "to be short one chair. If you would move to the back and wait, good sir, I will fetch another."

Ynnd moved to the back of the room as she'd asked, then said, "How may I trust all of you, when goodman Rye is the only one of you I've seen, and I did not know he was one of Dashif's trusted men?" He spread his palms.

Gerin shrugged. "My dear sir, how may any of us trust any of us? We all know for whom we worked; it was hardly an occupation to inspire trust, was it? But there you have it. I am Gerin."

"I am Myglynn."

"Teci."

"I'm the—mmm, just call me Narni."

Ynnd frowned. "I have heard of you. Dashif spoke your name once, as the one to whom I was to have a certain note sent, concerning a Zhir emissary."

"Oh, that came from you?"

"Indeed."

He bowed to them, his fists before him. "The bird reached me," he said, "when I had never thought to see it, yet I feared at first to answer it."

"I was pretty scared, too," said Teci. "But what else could we do? Every day, I heard of someone else being captured and put in prison, or even killed. We have to do something. Where the devil is Cheeky, anyway?"

Narni said, "I hope she has—well, here she is."

Cheeky returned, carrying a chair. She frowned, looking at the rather cramped room. Gerin stood and said, "Allow me to assist you."

"Thank you, Gerin, but perhaps it would be easier to simply rotate a chair down, rather than passing it over everyone's head. I'd hate to have anyone damaged."

When this was done and everyone was at last seated, Myglynn sipped at her kaf and addressed Cheeky. "We need to know—"

"Ah. Of course. Why I've called you here. It is very simple. I have a boat, which is large enough to brave the Sea of Luck, but quite likely small enough to escape detection. That is hard, you know. The harbor is lousy with naval vessels."

Ynnd's eyes narrowed. "All of that is not for us, is it?"

"I don't think so," said Narni. "I think the Three Sisters are worried about the Zhir."

Rye said, "You'll need help handling this boat? I warn you, I'm no sailor."

"I am," said Cheeky. "Unskilled hands will be fine. I only need three or four of you to help with the boat, but I will turn no one away"—she smiled here at Myglynn—"and the boat is large enough for passengers. Food is prepared; I only wanted to find three or four who could help and would under no circumstances turn me in. That was why I found all of you, who are in the same predicament."

Ynnd nodded slowly. "I have never been on the sea, yet I think I can do what is needed. I will help you."

Myglynn frowned. "I can hardly help steer a boat. I am thankful that you will allow me to escape with you, but why did you ask me?"

Cheeky shook her head. "You don't understand. The birds were set up by Dashif as a means to reach as many of his agents as he could in case of some dire need. They fly about, and anyone recognizing their flying pattern signals them in the proper way, as all of you did, and then they are able to take the message. I had no idea to whom the messages would go. I merely hoped that Arenride hadn't learned of the method, so they would only go where they ought to."

"Is there any way to know if they have?" asked Rye.

"Indeed yes. The birds return, and either the message has been properly acknowledged, or not. An agent of Arenride might be able to read the message, but I doubt he would know how to return it to its sender."

Narni nodded. "So you were able to know, if not exactly who, then how many of us were going to show up."

"That is correct," she said cheerfully. "There were five acknowledgments. Therefore, there were five messages received by agents of Dashif."

"But, good heavens," said Gerin. "Then one of us—"

"Exactly," said Cheeky, still smiling. "One of you is in

the service of the Regents, and is only here to betray the rest of us. Would anyone care for another drink?''

After a moment's silence, Gerin took a sip of his brandy and said, ''Charming.''

Narni said, ''I am not unarmed.'' ·

''Nor am I,'' said Rye.

''I am,'' said Gerin. ''Completely unarmed.'' He smiled as he said it, and his eyebrows twitched.

Ynnd flexed his powerful hands and said nothing.

Teci said, ''What shall we do? Are they going to come in and arrest us all?''

Cheeky shook her head. ''I doubt it. Not before they find out what we're up to. They're probably hoping to find and catch a few more of us.''

''But Arenride,'' continued the fruit-vendor. ''His agents may be outside.''

''Oh, I'm sure they are,'' said Cheeky. ''But they don't know where we're going, and I certainly don't intend to leave by the front door.''

''Then how?'' asked Rye, coolly.

''We shall see,'' said Cheeky.

''With all due respect,'' said Gerin. ''Needn't we come up with some method of determining which one of us is working for the Sisters?''

''Why?'' asked Cheeky. ''We are now waiting for the tide to be in, which shouldn't be much longer. Then we, as a unit, will leave here by a secret exit and go down to the boat. If any of our party attempts to leave, or to signal anyone, we shall kill him. We are, after all, six to one. Then we will set sail, and eventually achieve freedom, and then go our separate ways. At this time, Arenride's agent will be free to return to his master.''

Rye smiled and nodded, as if he appreciated the humor of her plan.

Teci shuddered. ''I'm scared,'' she said.

''I'm afraid,'' said Rye, ''that we cannot allow you to leave.''

Her eyes grew wide, as if it had never occurred to her that someone might think that *she* worked for the Regents.

''What we need,'' said Gerin, ''is for Rikiki to appear, as

he is supposed to have done for the slaves in Gold Harbor, and part the Sea of Luck again.''

Cheeky shrugged. ''That shouldn't be necessary. Besides, we are going *to* Gold Harbor, not escaping it.''

Myglynn said, ''I wish there were a way to know which of us—'' She stopped as if she couldn't bring herself to say it. For a moment she looked very uncomfortable; her breathing quickened and she held her hand to her chest. The others looked at her, worried, but at last she smiled and shook her head. ''I don't know what that was,'' she said weakly, ''but I didn't like it.'' Then, as if embarrassed, she dropped her eyes to her lap. Her coffee was almost gone.

Narni suddenly said, ''Mightn't the agent have a magical means of signaling for help?''

''Possibly,'' said Cheeky. ''But while I was out of the room getting the chair, I had Ried, my magician friend, raise a quick but effective spell to prevent any such communication. We will all be gone by the time it fails. And, I'm sorry to say, so will this tavern.'' She sighed.

''What do you mean?'' said Teci, hoarsely.

''I mean,'' said Cheeky, ''that as we leave, the tavern will be quickly evacuated, and Ried, to whom I have just given a large sum of money, will blow the place to bits. This will help cover our escape, as the authorities will believe that we have all died, perhaps in a struggle with their agent.''

This time Ynnd laughed aloud. ''Was this planned from the beginning?''

''Hardly. I arranged it when I went out for the chair.''

Still sitting, Ynnd bowed very low, as one who acknowledges a well-placed stroke. Upon raising his head, he came fully to his feet, a knife in his hand that was as long as a normal man's forearm. There were gasps from around the room, but no one moved. ''You!'' said Narni. ''But—''

''No. I am not a traitor. But I will share no boat with an enemy. I will learn now who he is, and he will die.''

''Just exactly how,'' said Narni coldly, ''are you going to learn that?''

He frowned. ''It cannot be the lady who has called us here, for she would not have told us of the spy, she would only have the guards waiting to arrest us. That leaves six. I know it is not me—''

"But I don't know that," said Rye, and he was suddenly holding a small, compact wheellock pistol. Before anyone could move he had wound it, and the barrel was fixed at Ynnd's head. They glared at each other, scant inches apart, Ynnd towering over the shorter man, but the pistol looking very large, indeed.

"So, it is you," said Ynnd, growling. He didn't drop his knife, merely stared, his dark eyes burning.

"*I* think it's *you*."

Myglynn shuddered, clenched her fists, and seemed to try to draw into herself. Narni turned pale. Gerin and Cheeky sat, apparently unmoved. Teci said shrilly, "This is stupid. Rye, put that thing away before it goes off. And you, Ynnd, stop waving that around or you'll cut someone. If anyone has any good ideas on how to find out which one of us—" She stopped suddenly, and stared hard at Cheeky.

"What is it?" said Ynnd.

Teci shook her head. "I have to think." She closed her eyes for a moment, during which time Rye and Ynnd continued to face each other down, neither of them moving. Teci opened her eyes again and stared hard at Cheeky. "You've taken care of everything, haven't you?"

"Yes," said Cheeky, "except the problem of convincing all of you that I have."

"I'm convinced, dear," said Teci. "Is the tide in by now?"

"I think it is."

"Then give the signal and let's go."

Cheeky nodded, stood, and stuck her head past the curtain for a moment, then returned and nodded again. The wall directly behind Ynnd opened, revealing a ladder to what had to be an underground path. Still, Ynnd and Rye didn't move.

Teci said, "Do you both agree that two of us aren't likely to be agents of Arenride?"

Ynnd nodded grudgingly, but Rye said, "Why not?"

"Oh, come now," said Narni. "At this rate we'll all be working for the Three Sisters except you."

"Very well, then," said Rye. "What of it?"

"Well," continued Teci, "I say that it is neither of you."

"As do I," said Cheeky.

"Is that enough?" said Narni. "Can we leave?"

"How do you know?" said Rye.

"The building is being evacuated," said Cheeky calmly. "In just a few minutes, it will blow up. Shall we leave?"

Rye growled, lowered his pistol, and let the lock unwind. Ynnd put his knife away, then turned and took the ladder down. Rye followed him, then Narni. At that point, there was a sudden cry. "Excuse me, but I seem unable to move from this chair."

Cheeky turned. "It's not your fault, my dear Arenride. It's the nature of the chair."

The one who had been called Gerin relaxed. "Ah. You recognized me, then."

"No, deduced it. I'm afraid I haven't time to talk now, however. I'm sorry."

She quickly vanished down the ladder, followed by Myglynn, who moved very fast for all her age. Teci was last, and when the fruit-vendor reached the bottom, Cheeky pulled a rope and the door closed above them.

"This way," she said. "Quickly," and they set off down a long, low, sloping dirt hallway. They had only gone a few score of feet when they were rocked by an explosion above and behind them. There was hardly a pause. Narni and Rye both squeezed Cheeky's shoulder as they made their crouching way toward the waterfront. Other than that, there was no mention of the tears Cheeky shed for the tavern that had meant so much to her for so many years.

The friendly tide took the dinghy out as the last rays of the sun turned the water to blood. The oars, wielded by Ynnd on one side and Teci and Rye on the other, made almost no noise. Cheeky stared forward, on the constant lookout for other ships, ships that might contain those with orders to detain and arrest renegades from the late Count Dashif's private network of informants, spies, and blackmailers.

When, after a long time, they reached the small, single-masted skiff in which they hoped to cross the Sea of Luck, they raised sail, and Cheeky directed them away from Liavek and toward safety. They didn't breathe easily until they could no longer see the lights of the harbor.

"You knew who it was when you first left the room, didn't you?" said Narni.

Cheeky nodded. And turned to Teci. "You duplicated my reasoning?"

"Yes."

"What reasoning?" said Narni. "I'm curious."

"As am I," said Ynnd, "though not as curious as I am relieved."

"Not as relieved as I am," said Rye.

"Oh," said Teci, "I've always been good at listening to people's stories and putting things together, especially when you get three sides of a story and have to figure out what really happened. Although, I don't know how Cheeky figured it out."

"I'm not Cheeky anymore," she said. "Call me Mariel."

"All right, Mariel," said Narni. "What happened?"

"To be honest, I wasn't certain even when I arranged for the magicked chair and contrived for Arenride to sit in it. I *thought* I had it figured out, but I was going to go ahead with my initial plan anyway, because I wasn't sure I was right, until I saw Teci figure it out."

"Well?" said Myglynn.

"Nothing magical," said Mariel. "I had to assume there was only one, because if there were two of them, well, we'd never get out of there alive. So with a little figuring, which I started doing as soon as Ynnd walked in, it wasn't too hard. There were only seven of us, and I knew it wasn't me. I recognized Ynnd, and although I didn't know what she looked like, I'd heard of Teci. Myglynn identified Teci, so that eliminated her. Myglynn had also heard that Ynnd worked for Dashif, so I knew he wasn't it, as long as I could be sure it wasn't you, Myglynn."

The woman looked up and squinted. "And how did you know it wasn't me?"

"Narni recognized you, and Rye knew you worked for Dashif."

"But," said Narni, "if either of us—"

"You," Mariel told Narni, "were vouched for by Rye and Ynnd, as I recall from my listening post while I was outside. And Rye was vouched for by Ynnd."

Ynnd nodded slowly. "So Gerin was the only one no one knew."

Rye shook his head. "I'd heard of him, and so had Narni, and, Myglynn, didn't you say you'd seen him around the palace?"

Myglynn nodded, looking puzzled.

"I knew that," said Mariel. "That was why I was worried. But you only said you'd seen him around, not that you knew him by name. So I thought, what if Gerin *was* captured at Drinker's Gate, and Arenride had rumors spread that he had escaped, hoping for just such a chance as this? It isn't unlikely that Arenride was seen around the palace, yet he wasn't there so much that any of us would have been likely to recognize him, especially without his beard."

Teci nodded. "Those were my thoughts, as well."

"It is good you had them."

"But," said Rye, "how could you be sure that it wasn't an agent who used to work for Dashif who was now working for Arenride, maybe in exchange for his freedom?"

Teci shrugged. "I worried about that, but—"

"No, you missed that part of the conversation. You, Rye, solved that for me yourself."

"I did?"

"Yes. You and Narni established who was after Dashif and why. The White priests don't want *any* of us left. Arenride wouldn't use a man, and then let him be jailed; he'd insist on guarantees Geth Dys wouldn't give."

"That's it," said Teci. "It had to be an agent who didn't work for Dashif, which meant it had to be the one who called himself Gerin."

"It's a shame about Arenride," said Narni. "He was, after all, honest."

Teci said, "Don't feel bad, dear. I let him go."

"You *what*?"

"He was such a nice young man. I *do* hope he made it out in time."

"But then he'll send—"

"No, I asked him not to."

Ynnd shook his head. Rye groaned. Narni looked at Cheeky, who said, "I was hoping she would. Remember, we might want to return someday. I think having spared Arenride's life will count for something, don't you?"

"If we make it out in the first place," Narni sighed. "I wasn't made for this life. I wasn't. Really. If we get out of this, I'll . . ." Her voice trailed off, as if she either didn't know what she wanted to do, or wouldn't give it voice.

Silence fell, and the six of them stared ahead, uneasily.

Birth Day: Sonnet

by John M. Ford

I do not know the day that you were born,
Nor know you mine. Our local mystery
Proclaims that when the hidden time's outworn,
Then luck's tied off like birth-cord. Therefore we
Knit all our birthdays into one, and dance
(Hands held) around the edges of the thing:
You guess that mine's in summer. (Not a chance.)
While I suppose that yours is in the spring.
The years will never wear the puzzle out,
For who can live to hope to see the day
When earth unravels birth? Confirm the doubt,
The end we cannot reach; and those who say
Those dates are both well known, and all of this
Pretense, do not know what a secret is.

A Prudent Obedience

by Kara Dalkey

THERE IS, WITHIN the miracle that is a gossamer wattletree seed, a structure—a support so fine that it is invisible—that enables the life within To Be. There is, within the miracle that is the city of Liavek, a structure—one among the many, unacknowledged—that enables life in the city To Be. There is, within the miracle that is a work of art, a structure—even if only suggested by its negative, or its absence—that enables its beauty To Be. There is, within the miracle that is the universe . . . but that need not be said, for without structure, the universe Would Not Be.

A cool sea breeze ruffled the colorful clothing of the people lining the streets of Liavek. Festival Week in this liveliest of cities on the Sea of Luck was like no other time and place in the world. Maljun Nivelo, aging servingman to the renowned and somewhat infamous art advisor Aritoli ola Silba, regarded these festivities with both gratitude and annoyance.

From the Levar's Park, in a spiral fashion around the city, the Procession of Faiths was making its way. To one such as Maljun, whose faith was not represented in the procession, the event was a nuisance. It seemed designed to interfere with traffic in the maximum number of places on the maximum number of streets. Holidays were, in general, a nuisance to those of Maljun's profession. The necessary goods and services tended to become unavailable, or unaffordable. There was only

one of the Festival Days that Maljun held dear, and this was
not it.

With an already sour mood, Maljun encountered yet another
crush of spectators on the Levar's Way as he attempted to walk
to the launderers. To cross the road as a temple's priests were
passing might be interpreted as sacrilege, or at least disrespect.
Maljun woefully looked up the street, knowing any route
around the procession would be many blocks away. His old
joints protested at the thought of such a long detour, and he
sighed.

Maljun's attention was redirected by a heart- and ear-rending
wail at his feet. A brightly dressed, dark-skinned little girl sat
on the ground, her face scrunched up in a mask of despair,
mouth open and gasping in preparation for another volley of
sound. In her hands was a crumple of sticks and string that
was a dismantled shiribi puzzle.

Maljun clicked his tongue and lowered his tall, thin frame
to kneel by the child. "No need for such fuss, little mistress.
It can be rebuilt. It isn't broken. Look." And in a few moments,
Maljun reassembled the puzzle.

The child blinked and closed her mouth. "Howdjoo dooit?"

Maljun obliged, secretly proud to show off the trick that his
master Aritoli had taught him. And Maljun had been rather
pleased that Master Aritoli had been surprised and not just a
bit put out with the speed with which Maljun had learned it.

The girl learned the trick much more quickly. Nearby, other
peals of dismay erupted from young throats, and the child
jumped up and ran to them, shouting, "Don't cry! Lookit! You
can put 'em back together!" Showing off the newly learnt skill,
the child passed the trick along like a contagion until the whole
blockful of youth was infected with the knowledge.

Maljun stood again, his knees creaking with the effort. *With
so many shiribi puzzles about*, he thought, *the White priests
should be going by about now*. Peering over the heads of the
spectators, Maljun saw that this was so. The Church of Truth
had a large representation in the procession and the priests,
male and female, were still striding past. The hems of their
long, white robes stirred up the dust and bits of colored paper
to swirl in clouds around their feet. Maljun found himself
pitying whoever was responsible for their laundry.

The priests closest to the spectators were tossing out little shiribi puzzles, which the Church had adopted as a holy symbol. The puzzles were fragile and fell apart nearly as soon as the children touched them. It was a cruel trick, but in consonance with the beliefs of the Church of Truth. Several of the priests bore signs and placards with the messages: ''All is Illusion,'' ''Disbelieve your senses,'' and ''Everything you know is Wrong.'' For good measure, two wizards among the priests made various buildings along the route seem to disappear and reappear as they passed. The spectators were amused and applauded, which Maljun suspected was not the reaction the priests were hoping for.

There was a gap of about half a block in the procession behind the Church of Truth contingent. Apparently the next temple's votaries had not wanted to be at the White priests' heels. Maljun was not surprised. There came sharp reports from down the street to his right—a *crackety-crack-crack* like fireworks. The spectators all craned their necks in that direction and Maljun saw his chance.

As fast as his aging legs would take him, he dashed across the Levar's Way into a dim, narrow alley. He immediately slowed to a walk, puffing. A figure in a white, hooded robe entered the other end of the alley. As the person approached, Maljun said, ''If you've lost your fellows, they're already passed by. They're likely near the House of Responsible Life by now.''

The individual stopped and pushed back her white hood. Maljun recognized the narrow face and deep-set, vaguely vacant dark eyes. It was Sister Vanta, whom Master Aritoli had thwarted in the affair with the Council mural, and who was inadvertently the cause of his knowing the solution to shiribi puzzles. Maljun paused. Protocol demanded that An Enemy of the Master be treated with great disdain by The Servant, to be ignored or even given a Class Five Snub, if the situation permitted. But she was blocking the route.

''You,'' Sister Vanta said, in a tone of mixed wonder and irritation. Her voice was low and reminded him of the winter wind blowing through the boughs of bare trees. ''I had expected—'' Then she laughed and Maljun felt a chill. ''I have not listened to my own teachings.'' She shook her head with a wan smile.

Maljun stepped forward, uncertain what to say. "I . . . I must—"

Sister Vanta pulled a small votive box out from her sleeve. "Alms?" she said.

Maljun drew himself up to his not-inconsiderable height and administered a Snub Class Two. "I'm sorry, madam, I cannot spare the coin." He tried to brush past her, but she caught his arm.

Her head tilted upon her neck in a way Maljun could swear was unnatural, and she fixed him with a look that was not quite pity and not quite amused surprise. "You misunderstand," she said softly, "you all do. It is I who bring alms for you."

Maljun blinked in what he hoped was a correct demonstration of nonjudgmental disbelief. "Indeed?"

"The alms of truth. The gift of our faith. I wish to give it to your master, as we give to all who veil their eyes with illusion."

Maljun decided it was time for The Polite But Firm Dismissal. "My master is well aware of your beliefs, madam. However, if you would like to make an appointment to present—"

He was interrupted by her laugh, low and throaty. "Appointments are attempts to use one illusion to capture another, as foolish as catching sea breezes in the painting of a fish net. Your master would not see me, yet he will, in the Moment when all things run together. But I will give this tithe to you. You, perhaps, need it even more than he." She handed him a crumpled piece of pure white paper. Then she continued down the alley toward the Levar's Way and faded into the afternoon sunlight.

Maljun folded the paper neatly without reading it and put it in a pocket. He continued his trek to the launderers, reflecting for the who-knew-how-manyeth time about the vagaries of being In Service to an art critic and minor wizard who had chosen to live an Interesting Life. This had tended to make Maljun's life Interesting also, and Maljun still felt himself lost, on occasion, in the jungles of protocol such a life led him into.

Without further impediment, Maljun reached the launderer on Lyme Way. There he ransomed Master Aritoli's favorite black silk shirt, paying the launderer a fee that Maljun denounced as exorbitant, though it was actually only stiff. A

similar scene was enacted at the fruit-seller and the baker before
Maljun finally could head for home.

In the drawing room of Master ola Silba's Oyster Street
townhouse, Maljun meticulously unfolded the paper Sister
Vanta had given him and held it up beside a glass-chimneyed
oil lamp. Nothing, as he had suspected, was written upon it.
But he had lived with his master long enough to have observed
a few things and he held the paper directly before the lamp.
Ghostly watermark writing came into view.

> All that is the world is Illusion.
> All seeming order is Chaos misunderstood.
> All that glorifies the Illusion is Evil,
> and blocks the path to Truth.
> All Life is the dream of a dream,
> All Truth is nothingness,
> All that Is is dust.
>
> In the Final Days,
> The Truth shall be revealed
> And Illusion banished
> Forever.

It was nothing the Church of Truth had not said in one tract
or another that Maljun had seen. Yet he was disturbed. Could
the note be a threat to Master Aritoli? A man who supported
and encouraged arts that glorified "illusion" would clearly be
thought evil by the Church's standards. Torn between the con-
flicting duties of Informing Master Of Possible Threat and Not
Bothering Master With Trivialities, Maljun refolded the note
and put it back in his pocket.

Master Aritoli had gone to celebrate Remembrance Night at
a party where they would drink semipoisonous liqueurs out of
crystal goblets in the shape of skulls. Upon being informed of
this, Maljun had nearly shuddered. But Master Aritoli had
assured him that the best of healers would be on hand "just in
case." It seemed likely Master Aritoli would not wish to be
bothered with so trivial a threat as the note, considering the
level of risk in his normal social life.

Remembrance Night was also not Maljun's favorite time of
Festival Week, but he had rituals to perform and traditions to

follow. After dusting the furniture and tidying Master Aritoli's bedroom in case he should bring home a guest, Maljun prepared for himself a light supper and retired to his quarters.

Maljun's room was spare but elegantly furnished; a long, narrow bed of oak, a wardrobe on whose door was carved a hound's head, a desk, a night table, and a small chest of drawers. From the bottom drawer, Maljun pulled out his Rod of Service and set it on the desk. It was a baton of teak, two handspans long. Maljun had received it when he came of age under the tutelage of the Society of Servitors. All those raised and trained in that house received one upon completion of their First Tier of study, and embellishments were added with each further accomplishment. On Maljun's baton was a copper band signifying his completion of bookkeeping courses, a blue tasseled cord for Protocol Class 7, a red tasseled cord for Advanced Househusbandry Class 4, as well as other symbols and marks.

The Rod of Service also contained Maljun's luck. All those taught by the Society were encouraged to invest their magic when they turned eighteen. The Society held that the master and household one served should be spared the random effects of unbound luck. However, the Society did not encourage the common use of sorcery on the job. "If you must rely on magic to do your work," they taught, "then you are not paying proper attention to detail." Apprentice Servitors were taught only five spells and advised to use them very sparingly. Learning other sorcery was strongly discouraged. The Society specialized in producing servingmen and -women who disdained wizardry for hard work and planning.

This was considered somewhat odd in Liavek. There was, after all, the Goldthorne House, whose servers (commonly known as the Wizards of the Wardrobe) were trained to use their magic extensively. But their fees were exorbitant and their turnover rate was reputed to be lively as their graduates moved on to more prestigious work. And there was the rumor that one sharp-tongued master woke up one morning as a toad. As a result, the nonmagical Society of Servitors found itself with no lack of clients.

Master ola Silba had told Maljun that he had chosen to pick a servingman from the Society for blatantly self-centered purposes. He wanted no servant whose magic would outshine his own.

Maljun lit a honey-colored candle beside the Rod of Service and lightly rested his left hand on the baton. It was a night to remember the dead, but Maljun had few to dwell upon. He did not know his father, and his mother he only recalled as a warm, rough pair of hands that left him at a stranger's door. There were teachers he had been fond of, his first master (a kindly old woman who had loved colorful birds), and a fishmonger's daughter he had known long ago. But that was all. He went over his memories of each, honoring what their lives had given him. He wondered what his Protocol teacher would have said concerning the note from Sister Vanta. His memories gave him no answer.

He realized that memories were not what he needed. With an unavoidable twinge of guilt, Maljun pulled out of a desk drawer a small cloth bag containing rue, sage and other herbs, and a dash of certain powdered fungi. He opened the bag and sprinkled a little of the contents in a pattern on the desktop. He laid the Rod of Service on top of this and murmured the few words for one of the five spells he was allowed—the foresight spell.

There came no vision—there never did. Its effects were small and subtle. The wise servant would find confirmation of what he already knew. The bewildered servant would find only more bewilderment. True, clear foresight was impossible, as the pattern of Events To Come was continually being reshaped by other people's actions. Maljun did not know when the spell would reveal its workings, but it would probably be at the time and in the manner that caused the most nuisance.

Maljun put away the baton and the herb bag, then blew out the candle. He changed into his nightshirt and crawled into bed, still unable to pinpoint why Sister Vanta's message bothered him. *For all I know*, he thought, *it was her infernal references to dust.*

Maljun dreamed he was in an enormous palace, with corridors and doorways that stretched into infinity. He had been here before, in his dreams. Far down some of the corridors, members of the Society of Servitors walked and nodded to him. This particular wing of the palace was his bailiwick; he was

in charge of its maintenance, and he was quite comfortable
with the fact that it was part of a much greater, improbable
structure. As he strode down one vault-ceilinged hallway, he
felt something disturbing and made a turn to the right. Before
him was a corridor he had not seen before, yet he knew it was
still part of his charge. Several doors down there was an enormous gap in the wall and ceiling where they had fallen in. The
floor was littered with broken stone and dust motes danced in
the diffuse light spilling in through the hole.

Just his side of the gap was a woman of indeterminate age,
wearing a long skirt and apron, and a kerchief around her head.
She regarded the damage pensively. Maljun saw to his fasci-
nation and horror that the corridor beyond the hole was dis-
integrating slowly into the cloud of dust motes. It reminded
him of a sidewalk painting whose colors were running in the
rain. "What is it?" he breathed.

"It is Not, yet," said the woman. Maljun thought of at least
three interpretations of her words, but he felt shy of her and
did not ask what she meant. "Take heart," she went on.
"You've seen to prevention of this sort of damage before."

"Ah, yes," said Maljun, "it's all well and good to fill up
a crack here and remortar a brick there. I can't prevent total
collapse."

"You'd be amazed," said the woman, gently, "what a little
mortar in the right place can do."

"What brought this all on, anyway?" said Maljun with an
awkward sweep of his arm.

"It must have been the reference to dust," said the woman,
strolling back down the corridor, passing him without another
glance.

Maljun blinked, and the light of dawn sneaked in under his
eyelids and poked him. He sat up in bed and yawned—then
paused as he saw the dust motes dancing in the rays of the
rising sun.

The third day of Festival Week was Bazaar Day, and it was
not Maljun's favorite holiday either. Master Aritoli threw himself into the thick of the marketplace, voicing his views on the
quality of the crafts for sale. Maljun preferred to stay at home
and balance the household ledgers. The dream remained clear
in his memory, so Maljun concluded that it was the result of
the Foresight spell. As usual, the results were exceedingly

unclear. The dream seemed to mean there was a calamity that was occurring or soon to occur in his sphere of influence. It also implied there was some small thing he could do to prevent it. *But what could it be?* He tossed down his quill pen in disgust and started as he saw blots of ink spreading on the ledger. He mopped futilely at the spots, recalling a maxim of the Society: "Despair is the most loathsome of emotions. It gives one apparent justification to ignore all practical solutions to one's problem, and ruins one for useful work."

There came a knock at the front door. Maljun answered and saw it was a messenger boy in the red, gold, and white livery of the Levar herself. The boy bowed and held out an envelope. "For Master ola Silba," he said.

Maljun took the envelope, but as he reached in his pocket for a coin the boy turned and trotted off. Maljun shrugged and closed the door. He pulled his hand out of his pocket, pulling something out with it. He was clutching the message from Sister Vanta. He looked at the envelope. It was the same kind of paper. He felt his stomach jump and he immediately went to the lamp and held up the envelope to its light. Naturally, nothing could be seen through its double thicknesses. Maljun put the envelope on the desk. *It may be a coincidence*, he thought. *Perhaps they both buy from the same papermakers.* To open one's master's mail without permission was a Class 9 Offense, and justifiable cause for firing. Maljun doubted Master Aritoli would go so far, and Maljun could claim he was Seeing to The Master's Well-Being and Continued Safety. But Maljun had no wish to abuse Master Aritoli's trust and so he left the envelope alone.

Master Aritoli came home that evening, his arms laden with gifts and purchases, including a cream-colored bedsheet, a straw broom, and a bright purple cummerbund for Maljun. Sighing inaudibly, Maljun put away the bedsheet and the broom in a closet, and hid the cummerbund in the bottom of his wardrobe, resolving to wear it when no one but the master was present.

"What is this?" Aritoli called from the drawing room.

"Sir?"

"The envelope on the desk. Was there post delivery today?"

"Oh." Maljun rushed back into the drawing room. "No,

Master. It was delivered by a messenger from the Levar's Palace.''

"Why didn't you mention it sooner, Maljun? Such an over-sight is unlike you." Aritoli took a letter opener off of the desk and slid it inside the envelope.

Maljun held his breath, wondering if the envelope itself was a trap.

But Aritoli opened it with no mishaps and snorted as he read the note inside. "It's yet another invitation."

"From the Levar, sir?"

"Not quite so lofty. It's from the Countess ola Klera. D'you remember her, Maljun?"

"Yes, Master."

"She's a Regent to the Levar now. Says she would be hon-ored if I were to be present at the grand fireworks display tomorrow night. Well, I did have other plans, but I suppose I must attend, mustn't I?"

Maljun sighed with relief. "As you wish, Master."

"Are you all right, Maljun? You look a bit out of sorts."

"No, Master, all is well. Shall I draw your bath now?"

"Yes, Maljun, that will be fine."

These fears are foolish, thought Maljun as he made the bath and prepared a light meal. Master Aritoli partook of them both and then dashed off to another party, dressed to the eyeteeth in color-coordinated tatters.

That night was Beggar's Night, and that, too, was not Mal-jun's favorite Festival Week celebration. It encouraged folk to dress untidily and behave uncouthly. Maljun preferred to re-main home and discourage the children who would show up begging at the door.

He began a cursory tidying-up of the drawing room and noticed the white envelope still sitting on the desktop. With a snort at his own imagined fears, Maljun snatched up the open envelope and held it up to the lamp, just to prove—

There was watermark writing on the paper. The upper flap bore the message: "A Grand Illusion shall cast all other illu-sions away.—Geth Dys." Geth Dys was another of the Levar's Regents, as well as one of the highest priests in the Church of Truth. Maljun put down the envelope, put on his tall hat and gray cloak, and stepped out into the night.

Striding down the laughter-filled streets, Maljun mused that it was certainly a night the Church of Truth would appreciate. Reality overturned and Chaos everywhere, for what was revelry but an unraveling of social order? And on this night that had begun as a token of justice to the very poor, nobles and their children thought it fun to dress in a manner they would never otherwise tolerate and behave like those whose daily existence they'd rather ignore.

Nonrevelers going about their business this night were having some difficulty passing through the streets. Maljun found that coins paved his way when flung far enough aside to send the ragged imps scrabbling with greed into the gutters.

Maljun began to regret his use of the foresight spell. *By a small deed I might prevent a calamity. I do not even know if I am on the trail of the right calamity. It is a very large world and I am but one ant struggling to keep the nest tidy.*

As he plodded onward, Maljun recalled what he knew of Sister Vanta. She had bought the Shatter-Eye School of Fine Arts and had taught the painters to add magic to their wild, disturbing abstracts. She had also arranged for one of her artists to be given the commission of a mural in the chambers of the City Council. What the magic in the mural would have done, Maljun could not recall, but Master Aritoli had managed to interfere before it could do its damage. Revenge might well be on Sister Vanta's disordered mind. Maljun shook his head. Master Aritoli's flamboyant life made him often a target for vengeance. It certainly added variety to Maljun's duties.

Maljun stopped, seeing suddenly he had reached his destination. He was in the great square of the Fountain of the Three Temples. Directly ahead of him was the huge, round fountain, in its center the statues of playful Kil spouting water. Behind that rose the spired bulk of the Levar's Palace, gaily lit for the Festival Days. On the edges of the square, he noted the partially completed wooden risers and scaffolding, seats and reviewing stands for dignitaries and guests for the Grand Fireworks on Restoration Eve. *The Levar's court always sits here,* Maljun thought, *where the view of the Palace is best. Members of the Council will be placed in front of the Red Temple. And the other guests*— Maljun paused. Aritoli would be such a guest, and their reviewing stand was directly in front of the Church of Truth.

Maljun sat on the half-built riser and sighed. *It might be here, at the celebration . . . but what will it be? What will they do?* He saw at his feet another of the little broken shiribi puzzles, perhaps left over from the Procession of Faiths. Maljun picked it up and absentmindedly put it back together.

"What are you doing here?" said a man beside him.

Maljun started and looked up to see a white-robed priest staring down at him.

"You should not be here now," the priest continued, "these constructions are . . . unsafe, until they are completed. Besides, aren't you a little old to go a-begging?"

Maljun stood. "You misunderstand, Brother," he said, and held out his hand with the rebuilt shiribi in it. "It is I who give alms to thee." Maljun dropped the puzzle into the White priest's palm, then turned and hailed a footcab for home.

The chores that remained to Maljun that night were to lay out Aritoli's morning dressing robe, to turn the bed and scatter fresh-cut herbs on the sheets, to prepare equipment for serving breakfast (for two, possibly), and to estimate the cost of purchases by the master during Bazaar Day to note into the ledger book. As he did these, Maljun wondered if he should inform the master of his worries. *I do not know enough about the threat, if there is one. I doubt the Master would turn down an important invitation on my whim.*

The following morning Maljun fixed breakfast for one, a rumpled and morose Master Aritoli who looked all of his forty years old, his long black hair disheveled and his moustache awry.

"Had you a pleasant night, Master?" said Maljun, serving the spiced fish and dawnfruit juice.

Aritoli made a strangulated noise that indicated he surely had not. He offered nothing further, and Maljun did not pry.

"Are you going to the launderer today, Maljun?"

"I had not intended it, Master. But if you require it, I will gladly do so."

"I'm afraid I do. Drop this off there for me, won't you? Least I can do for the lady." Aritoli took from a chair arm a rose-tinted silk wrap-dress that had been artfully cut into tatters, and placed it in Maljun's hands.

Maljun observed the large purple wine stain (a costly dry red, he noted by the scent and color remaining) down one side and the fish-egg salad stain on what might have been the front.

The remnants of various other condiments spotted the hem, and at the neckline was the unmistakable debris of a cinnamon cream pudding. Maljun could not help but wonder what might have been left on the table after . . . whatever had led to this mess.

"I don't understand it. Not even my Mid-year day."

Maljun paused. "Is there something I should be aware of, Master?"

"Hmm? No. You wouldn't believe it, either. I'm going back to bed. Wake me before the fireworks start, eh?"

"Er, Master?"

"Yes, Maljun?" Aritoli sighed.

"Are you certain you must attend the fireworks this evening?"

Aritoli frowned. "If you are asking whether I am ill enough to decline an invitation from the new Regent of the Levar and an old friend, the answer is, of course not. I have a reputation of wild living to uphold, remember? Although, I confess, I am beginning to feel too old for this."

"In that case, Master—"

"What is it, Maljun?"

"May I accompany you?"

Aritoli's dark brows slowly rose, and he appeared to be stifling a laugh. "I did not know you were interested in celebrating Festival Night, Maljun. After all these years, have you at last come to appreciate the jollier things in life?"

Maljun felt himself almost blushing. He truly did not care for the frivolities of Festival Week. He had no interest in overindulgence in food, drink, and improper behavior. "For your well-being, Master, I would like to attend with you."

"Ah. Pity. I was hoping you wanted to unbend a little. Yes, you may come along. Now, if you will excuse me, the mattress calls."

"Thank you, Master. Sleep well."

Maljun quickly cleaned up the breakfast dishes, bundled up the stained ruin of a dress that Master Aritoli had entrusted to him, and stepped out into the street. His daily forays against the subtle, indefatigable forces of decay, seemed to have more grim significance now. Maljun realized he had to do what he once swore to himself that he never again would—ask advice.

It would not do to arrive at his destination by any conveyance except his own feet. He walked the eight blocks to the part of Liavek known as Old Town, to the street known simply as Stone Way, to the large, brooding house that looked like it might be a comfortable home, to those who had never lived there.

The gray brick walls were immaculately clean, the black paint fresh on the iron fence. The window boxes contained just the right number of inoffensive white flowers—"widow bonnets" they were called. Standing on the doorstep, he felt half-remembered fears fluttering in his stomach—memories of holding a warm, rough pair of hands, of hearing beloved footsteps departing, of feeling abandoned and lost. The Society of Servitors liked to tell foundling children that one of their parents was noble and the other was a whore in order to encourage pride tempered with humility.

Maljun rapped on the perfectly varnished door. In just the correct number of moments he heard footsteps approaching and the door smartly opened. It was a Third Tier student, Maljun noted, wearing the black trousers with white hems and black jacket with white cuffs and collar.

"Good afternoon, sir," said the student, "won't you please come in."

"Thank you," said Maljun, always a little embarrassed to receive the courtesies he was used to giving. He stepped into a wood-paneled hallway that led to an achingly familiar vestibule. There was the long, curving stairway down whose banister he and—whatwashisname? Kraquillo! that was it!—little Kraqui and he would slide down in the middle of the night until they were caught. And there, behind the stairs, was a closet with a secret panel that led to the laundry chute and out into the courtyard where he and Lilam, the fishmonger's daughter, shared a first kiss. From somewhere to his right there came the laughter of children and the rapping of a wooden stick on a table. *First Tier, Protocol 1 class, I'll wager*.

"Sir?"

"Tell me, young man, is old Watslatl still teaching Protocol these days?"

The student snorted. "That old Titch mummy—begging your pardon, sir. Yes. They say he'll teach it forever. You've, er, been here before?"

"I'm Twelfth Tier, young man. And you should be careful

in your familiarities to strangers. I might have been a relative of the old Titch mummy.''

The student blushed. ''I am most sorry, Servitor. Er, who was it you came to see?''

''I've no appointment, I'm afraid. But my errand is of some small urgency. I was wondering if Servitor Jussive might be willing to see me.''

The student visibly gulped. ''Who might I tell him is waiting?''

''I am Maljun Nivelo.''

''Yes, Servitor Nivelo. Please make yourself comfortable.'' Unsuccessfully attempting a measured step, the student not-quite scampered up the stairs.

Maljun sat in a solid wooden chair, unable to make himself comfortable, but at least trying to dwell on the pleasant memories. Before long, the student returned, more dignified this time. Doubtless Jussive had words with him. ''You may go up now, Servitor.''

''Thank you.''

The oak door at the top of the stairs was opened by Jussive himself. He was an old man, in his eighties, but scarcely bent with age. He carried his dignity like a well-worn cloak, and his walnut skin sagged only a little around the eyes and the corners of his jaw. ''Maljun,'' he said with a smile of genuine warmth that surprised Maljun, ''won't you please come in?''

Maljun found himself bowing his head as if he were a school-boy again. *There must be something about our vocation that preserves. Few Servitors have died young.*

''It has been a long time since you've visited. It is always a pleasure to see my best pupils. Would you like tea or kaf?''

It would be an insult to refuse, so Maljun said, ''Tea, please, Servitor.'' He remembered the Servitor's office as a place of dread, although he had received praise here as well as punishment. It astonished him to realize that his own room in Master Aritoli's house looked much the same as Jussive's.

Maljun sat in the familiar hard wooden chair—it seemed smaller than it used to—beside Jussive's plain oak desk. Jussive sat gracefully on the opposite side and Maljun knew that he had just pulled a cord to set a bell ringing down in the kitchens and some poor First Tier would be frantically loading the tea tray, making sure everything was perfect. Maljun knew because he often had been that First Tier student answering that bell.

"We are very proud of you, you know, Maljun. Your master yearly sends us letters telling us how pleased he is with your service."

"He does?" Maljun blinked in surprise.

"Yes, accompanied by a sizable contribution of funds, for which we are quite grateful."

A bell chimed and a dumbwaiter slid open in the wall. Jussive pulled out the pewter tea tray with pewter pot and mugs and poured the tea with only a slight tremor in his hands.

"So," said Jussive, "have you chosen to spend your day off with us?"

Maljun shifted uncomfortably in his chair. "Actually, Servitor, I am here on my master's business—in a way. I am here to ask advice."

Jussive clicked his tongue. "A man of your skill—what is the problem?"

Maljun explained.

"Ah," said Jussive. "You see why the use of the foresight spell is discouraged. One should focus on one's work rather than those greater events that the spell may reveal. It is distracting and leads to inattention and sloppiness."

"But, Servitor, this may concern my master's life and health. The dream implied it was my business."

Jussive sighed and tapped his thumbs together. "If we all do our duty as we should, we need fear nothing from the Church of Truth and their like. Our very beings are devoted to the concept of Order. Against that, no empty-headed fool can prevail. Remember from your Protocol 1 course—He who gives a prudent obedience wields a small power of his own. If you must, tell your master about the messages. If you must do other magic, keep to the Blessings and the Restorative. Otherwise, do nothing that would not be your normal duty."

Maljun nodded and allowed the conversation to drift into trivialities. But he was not satisfied. Jussive may have read this in his face, for as they parted, the ancient Servitor clasped Maljun's hand and said, "Remember. A prudent obedience. Do your duty. Naught else."

"I shall," said Maljun. But he felt his duty was more than Servitor Jussive would allow, and obedience far from prudent.

Outside, Maljun hailed a footcab, selecting one with an old though hale runner. With enough coinage, Maljun helped the old one remember what launderer might be willing to work this day.

"Dykhe on Merchant's Way," said the wizened runner. "He was complaining the other night at the Jackal's Den as to how he'd be scrubbing his arms off today."

"Take me there, if you please."

"Surely. It's your nose, young man."

Maljun discovered the meaning of the runner's remark as he stepped off at the doorway of Dykhe the Launderer. Vapors of lye and other caustics assailed his nostrils as he went inside. In the dim light, he saw enormous wooden vats at the far end of the room, several people bent over them, pumping away against the washboards. Maljun coughed and covered his mouth with a handkerchief. One of the workers glanced up.

"Master Dykhe?"

The fellow put down his task and walked up to Maljun, wiping his hands on a towel. His wiry hair was sticking out at all angles and his skin was swarthy except for his forearms, which were bleached ghostly pale. "I'm Dykhe. Whatever you want, you'd better want white. My vats are all being used for this one job, but I might be able to toss yours in with."

Maljun held up the rose-pink silk gown that Master Aritoli had entrusted to him. "I think not, sir."

Dykhe laughed. "No, you'd not want that delicacy in with this lot. You'd be lucky if anything was left of it, and the white robes would doubtless be offended, besides."

"White robes?"

"You know, the Truthies. This stuff is theirs," Dykhe said, jerking a thumb back toward the vats.

Maljun caught his breath. He remembered a saying from his Philosophy courses: "In an ordered universe, all events have their place, cause, and purpose. There is no such thing as coincidence." *Was it the foresight spell that led me here?* "I am surprised," said Maljun, "that they do not employ a wizard for such a purpose."

Dykhe spat toward the corner. "I asked them that myself. They didn't want their clothes 'contaminated with extraneous magic,' they said. Apparently they plan something special tonight. I tell you, I wouldn't want to attend *their* Festival party. Those folk give me the shivers.''

''I understand.''

''I suggest you wash that in a bathing tub with some gentle soap. I'll sell you some, if you like.''

''Thank you.'' Maljun paid the launderer a little extra for the soap. As he left the launderers, he glanced up the alley beside the shop. There, hanging on poles, was a row of drying white robes rustling in the breeze like a parade of ghosts. A fat woman emerged from behind the end of the row, carrying an empty basket nearly as large as she. She stepped into a side door and, to Maljun's relief, did not appear to see him.

Looking both ways, Maljun ducked into the alley and snatched from the closest pole one of the robes. Fortunately, it was only slightly damp. Maljun rolled up the robe and wrapped the pink dress around it. He tiptoed back to Merchant's Way where a bleary-eyed passerby gave him a strange look but said nothing.

He stopped again at the Fountain of the Three Temples on his way home. The risers and review stands were finished, and from the decorations already adorning them, Maljun saw his guess as to who would sit where was correct. The great marble and tile basin of the fountain itself had been drained, and men in bright red jackets were setting up frameworks in the fountain for firework displays. Children flocked around the men like sparrows to bread crumbs, and Maljun moved closer to listen to their conversations.

''Can I help?'' called one little girl.

''No,'' laughed the workman. ''Come to our guild when you are of age. You're too young to join the Lightning and Thunder Show.''

''Aw, it looks easy. I can do it.''

''See this finger?'' said the red-jacket. ''It's been blown off and healed back on four times. I was lucky somebody found it each time—once a dog nearly ran off with it. And I tell you, it hurt a bit more than a stubbed toe. So don't be so eager to come jumping into our job.''

''You had more than this last year,'' said an older boy. ''Is this all?''

''No,'' said a red-jacket. ''The rest of it's up there.'' He twisted to point up at a flat-roofed tower of the Levar's Palace.

On top of the tower was a spherical structure of metal struts. "All the big stuff will be coming off that."

"It looks like a shiribi puzzle," Maljun said.

The red-jacket barked a laugh. "Very astute observation, sir. So it is. At midnight it's going to rise into the air—"

"Hey," said the other red-jacket, "don't give the grand finale away. Let it be a surprise."

"Do you think that will be safe?" asked Maljun.

"Sir," said the red-jacket, standing straight and slapping his chest, "we are professionals!"

"Of course," said Maljun, reassuringly. "And whom might we congratulate for this brilliant idea?"

The red-jacket cocked his head and frowned. "I'm not sure. Regent Geth Dys commissioned it. You know, the White priest. Said it would please Her Eminence. 'Scuse me, I have to get back to work."

"Of course." Maljun inclined his head and stepped away. *I am a fool. What little act can I do to stop the disaster that will happen when this puzzle falls apart? I am in no position to do anything. But perhaps—*

Maljun knocked at the only portal of the Levar's Palace he was likely to be admitted at. The hearty young woman who answered the Servant's Door showed him into an antechamber furnished only with one straight-backed chair. The corners of the chamber were piled with Festival decorations—fern fronds and rare, sweet-scented flowers. Paper streamers and racks of colorful, wide silk ribbons lined one wall. Maljun sat in the hard chair, enjoying the holiday atmosphere in the room. *If this is illusion, why would anyone want it to end?*

Before long, a short, plump woman bustled in. Maljun stood and held out his hands to her. "Vilei," he said warmly.

"Uncle!" The plump woman rushed to press her cheek against his. As she stepped back, holding Maljun's hands, she said, "Uncle, it is so good to see you! But why do you pick the worst of times for a visit?"

Although, given his background, it was possible they were related, Maljun was not actually her uncle. He had helped tutor her when he was Seventh Tier and she was only Third. They had become good friends and Maljun was very proud of her when she was hired to serve in the palace. Maljun smiled sadly.

"Sometimes the worst times seem the best, Vilei."

There came a crash and squabbling voices from a nearby hallway. Vilei looked over her shoulder, then back to Maljun with a little frown. "Couldn't you come back tomorrow? We have so much to do, and two of us have taken sick, and the cleanslippers keep changing what they want for tonight's decorations and—"

Maljun drew from beneath his cloak the Rod of Service. He took Vilei's hand in his and placed the baton in it, folding her fingers over the dark wood. "It is important, Vilei."

"Oh." With a sigh, she said, "I suppose you'd better tell me, then." She released the baton and sat heavily on the chair, spreading out her aprons.

Keeping his voice low, Maljun told her about his fears.

Vilei's frown deepened. "Geth Dys has been very concerned about that construction. I'm quite certain he'd want no one tampering with it."

"I am sure," said Maljun, "that the structure will perform just as the Regent wishes."

"The Regent wouldn't want to harm anyone!"

"Shh. These people do not see the world as we do. Pain and suffering, to them, is just another illusion. Now, do you know when the fireworks are to begin?"

"Shortly before midnight, I think. Yes, it must be—that's when several of us end our shifts and Piri was looking forward to catching the Lightning and Thunder Show."

"Then the large display goes off after midnight?"

"Just at midnight, I should think."

"Excellent," said Maljun. "Perhaps there is a little something we can do."

"Uncle, before I hear this idea of yours . . . tell me—is this something the Society would approve of?"

"Sometimes, Vilei, one must be obedient to the teachings of one's heart, as well as the teachings of one's elders."

"They wouldn't, eh? Very well. Say on."

His next stop was to a S'rian weaver on Loom Lane, to whom he'd often given his master's mending. In addition to being an expert weaver and seamstress, the woman was also adept at weaving low-level magic into her work. It was rumored she had studied under Granny Karith herself.

"You come empty-handed, Maljun. I believe I already finished those trousers of your master's."

"So you did, Okari. I've come to buy something off-the-shelf, if you've any such items remaining."

"I've a few little things. Most customers seem to want amulets to ward off drunkenness, as gifts for their spouses. If that's what your master wants, I'm fresh out."

"No, Okari. The purchases today are my own. I would like a woven pectoral with a protection spell."

"I believe I may have one left. I sold quite a few before Remembrance Night. Ah, here it is. It's just a warding of sorcerous harm from another person, not a general 'all accident' protection, or warding of physical blows or infestation by trolls. It will last until the end of Restoration Day. Will it do?"

"Yes, Okari, it should do admirably. And now a mask. A simple one that makes the wearer's identity invisible to magical seeking. This spell need only last for one day also."

The weaver crossed her arms on her chest and tilted her head coyly. "Maljun, if I did not know you, I would deny your request. Sounds like a pickpocket's gear."

"Nothing like that, I assure you."

"Well, I don't have a mask with such a spell already made."

"Could you make it by sundown?"

"For five levars and a promise that I'm not participating in an illegal endeavor."

"I do not believe it to be illegal. But it is in a good cause, I do assure you. Will seven levars ease your misgivings?"

Okari crossed her arms and breathed a heavy sigh. Under her breath she murmured, "May These Events Not Involve Thy Servant." Shaking her head, she said louder, "Well, I shall have to get to it then."

That evening, in the footcab beside his master, Maljun sat stiffly, trying to ignore his growing fear.

"Maljun?"

Maljun nearly jumped. "Yes, Master?"

"Forgive me if I seem to pry, but why are you bringing along a broom to the festivities?"

"It is a . . . tradition of my family. For Restoration Day. Something I must do at midnight."

"I see." Aritoli paused. "Did I mention that that's quite a fetching mask you are wearing this evening?"

"No, Master. Thank you. I thought it would suit the, uh, festiveness of the occasion."

"Hmm? Did Okari make that?"

"Yes, Master."

"Thought it looked like her work. And what is in that cloth bundle you are carrying?"

"A cloak, sir, in case it should become cooler later."

"A white cloak?"

"White is considered very stylish this season, sir."

"I see."

The clatter of the footcab's wheels on the paving stones was the only sound between them for some moments. Aritoli pulled out of a pocket the invitation he'd received and fingered it thoughtfully. "It would seem that we are in for a most . . . diverting evening."

"Indeed, Master. Indeed."

And so it was that, shortly before midnight, Maljun stood behind the risers on which Aritoli and many other minor nobles sat. He slipped on the white robe he had borrowed from the launderer's and pulled the hood far down over his face. Holding tightly the baton that held his invested luck, he tried to draw upon that magical power, so dearly bought with the hours of his mother's labor at his birth. Looking up at the imposing, bare white facade of the Church of Truth, Maljun wondered if it would be enough.

As the cheering of the crowd and the noise of the fireworks became louder, he walked up the marble steps of the church. Before the silverwood doors with their silver-chased handles, Maljun began to slowly sweep in a pattern as old as Liavek itself. It was a simple spell, dedicated to healing and rebuilding. It assumed and reinforced the concept of Order, and a universe where everything has its proper place.

Maljun felt a quiet joy along with his apprehension. For Restoration Day was his favorite holiday, and this spell his favorite of all magic. All his life had been dedicated to the maintenance of order and harmony in other people's lives, thereby finding order and harmony in his own.

One of the silverwood doors banged open and a white-robed figure came out.

Maljun kept sweeping, watching the straw bristles of his

broom. A white-slippered foot stepped in the broom's path.

"What are you doing?" said Sister Vanta.

"A celebration," Maljun answered, and swept the broom over her foot, continuing the pattern.

She jerked her foot away as if it had been burned. "This is quite unlike your style."

"Is it?" said Maljun, not stopping. "I hardly think you know what my style is."

"Is it not this?" Sister Vanta did something colorful with light in her hands. An image formed, perhaps of a person's face. Maljun paid little attention and continued his sweeping.

Louder cries of admiration came from the crowd now, shouts of "Look up there! Look at that!" Maljun prayed that Vilei had managed to get near the tower with the construction. If so, about now she and several other palace servants should be sweeping in the same patterns as Maljun, doing their Restoration Day spells a few hours early.

"Who are you?" said Sister Vanta.

Maljun did not respond. Finally, he felt his hood yanked back and the mask torn from his face. He saw Sister Vanta gape a little in astonishment.

"Not the one I feared, not the one I laid my traps for," said Sister Vanta, "but his servant."

Maljun could not resist a small smile of triumph and a bow. Bright light exploded over the reviewing stand and Maljun, starkly reminded of his purpose, began to sweep and mutter again.

Sister Vanta grabbed his broom handle. "Stop."

"Anger, madam, is an inappropriate response to an illusion." Letting go of the broom, he began to sing the restoration spell and walk in the pattern he had swept.

Sister Vanta gestured in the air. Maljun felt a warming on his chest and was thankful for Okari's pectoral. Something caught at his ankle and he lost his balance. Scrabbling at the air, he fell, landing hard on his forearms. Sister Vanta had tripped him.

"Why?" whispered Sister Vanta.

"To serve," gasped Maljun, "is to set in order. The simple broom against the dust. It is my duty."

Sister Vanta shook her head. "Do you know to what suffering you would doom the world?"

"And joy," said Maljun, "and contentment, and the satisfaction of achievement in one's labors against ruin and chaos." His arms hurt very badly. He wondered if they were broken.

"So wrong," said Sister Vanta, sadly. "So very wrong. You will not know the value of the gift I will give you. Such pity I have for you. Your love for the illusion has blinded you to truth. I will spare you the tormented dream you would experience in your aging body. I will spare you that to which you condemn others. Rejoice, gentle servant, for you shall receive oblivion."

She pulled on his shoulder, turning him on his back. Her hand slipped into his robe, and she pulled out his Rod of Service.

"No!" Maljun realized he had concerned himself so much with personal harm that he had given no thought to protecting his luck vessel. Sister Vanta, a much more accomplished wizard, had easily been able to locate it. He tried to hold her wrists, but his arms blazed with pain and she slipped from his grasp. As he watched in horror, the symbol of his learning, his trade, his life, turned to powder between her hands. He reached out to it, screaming, feeling as though something was torn from his being. His luck, the power of his soul, was escaping.

As Sister Vanta raised her arms for the final spell that would finish him, Maljun wanted to weep. He feared for his master, he wished he could see one more day in Liavek, he wished he could say good-bye to Vilei, he wished he could see the fishmonger's daughter one last time. He felt a great weakness overtake him—and darkness followed.

Master Aritoli was looking down at him, joy on his face. "Had enough time off, lazybones?"

He was in his own bed. "Master—" Maljun tried to sit up and felt as though he was made of lead.

Aritoli, laughing, grasped his shoulders and gently pushed him back down. "A jest, please! I beg you, Maljun. Lie back. Rest. Rest all you want. By Irhan, man, it's good to see you still among the living."

"How—how long has it been since—"

"Five days, Maljun. Gods, you had me worried. It's a good thing Mistress Govan is so fine a healer."

"Five days," Maljun murmured. "The dusting ought to be done, and the garden—" He tried to sit up again and Master Aritoli again pushed him back.

"Rest, I say! There is no rush for you to return to your duties. There is someone from the Society who volunteered to fill in for you. He's doing just fine and he'll stay until you are fit. In fact, he wanted to speak to you as soon as you were able." Aritoli jumped up and called out the door, "He's awake!"

As Maljun tried to puzzle out who would have volunteered to fill in for him, someone came through the door. It was old Servitor Jussive. Maljun's mouth dropped open.

Jussive nodded to Maljun and turned to Aritoli. "If you please, Master, I would like to speak with him privately."

"As you wish." Before stepping out, Aritoli pointed at Maljun and said, "Rest. That's an order." Then he closed the door firmly behind him.

Jussive sat slowly onto a chair beside the bed and looked at the far wall. "I advised you to remain constant to your duty."

Maljun felt schoolboy fears well up in him. "So I did, Servitor, as I saw it."

With a little snort, Jussive said, "Would you like to know the consequences of your actions?"

Maljun nodded.

Jussive looked down at his hands. "You know we never reissue Rods of Service. If one is lost, the server is never given another. You must be dismissed from the Society."

Maljun closed his eyes.

"There are reasons for this. You came perilously close to betraying all that the Society has striven for."

Maljun opened his eyes again, feeling even sicker.

"Because of what you have sacrificed, I will tell you what it is you nearly destroyed. Our founder, Endophili of Tichen, understood the fragility of our world and the danger from those who welcomed its end. Fleeing some danger that is not recorded, she came to Liavek and began the Society of Servitors. Her experiences had taught her a single important lesson— power lies not in the great, but in the small. A thing so great as a mountain can be worn down by drops of rain, yet grains of stone can become a thing as great as a mountain.

"Order and harmony is maintained not by some mighty power, but by the individual actions of many lesser folk. Endophili had observed how servants seem to keep the world in order, and that was the power she wished to harness and enhance. The spells we teach we claim are simple ones. That is both the truth and a lie. We dare not use great spells lest we catch the attention of the great. Therefore we use little spells, which in combination in the same place for the same purpose become very powerful indeed. As fragile threads can become a strong rope. Though many have wished to destroy or disrupt life in Liavek since we have been here, none have succeeded.

"But you exposed our spells in public, outside their normal pattern of use in a way that caught the attention of the great. Sister Vanta may have learned of our web of influence. Or she may not. But you see the risk."

Maljun nodded solemnly.

Jussive sighed and leaned back, closing his eyes. "Vilei was fired from her position in the palace and returns to us in disgrace."

"I am so very sorry," whispered Maljun. "Servitor . . . the fireworks—did we not at least prevent some damage there? My master yet lives, unharmed I see."

Jussive snorted again. "The fireworks? They did precisely what they were supposed to."

"What—"

"What did you think would happen?" Jussive snapped. "Your spells were only the Restoration spells, intended to let everything act according to its nature, and so they did. That infernal puzzle rose into the air, on cue. It hovered over the center of the square, firing gouts of colorful sparks, which fell to the ground *harmlessly*. And, as intended, the construction burst apart in sprays of white and silver that vanished in the sky. I saw it. It was a very pretty effect."

"No—no fireworks fell on the spectators?"

"What did you expect, man? The Church of Truth may be foolish, but it isn't bloodthirsty. The Regent and Church are dangerous, but not in the way that you believe. Their battlefield is the mind and the casualties are thoughts, not bodies."

"Then," said Maljun, "I have risked my life, the livelihood of others, and the security of all Liavek for a misunderstanding.

Perhaps it would have been fitting had I not survived.''

"The good servant does not have time for self-pity," Jussive muttered. "And I have not had my full say."

"What more?"

"Well. As it happens, Regent Geth Dys was to give a speech as the firework sphere disintegrated. A very beautiful speech, as I understand it, that would have captured the imaginations of the crowd. A speech about the joy of letting go of one's illusions . . . that sort of thing. But he was distracted by a group of servants who were doing a spell counter to the philosophy of his speech. It seemed to bother him considerably."

Maljun imagined a frustrated Geth Dys flapping his white sleeves and he almost laughed.

"By which time, your Master Aritoli had, apparently, become bored, so he began entertaining the audience with sorcerous fireworks of his own. This so impressed everyone that by the time the Regent was ready to speak of the evil of illusions, people were enjoying the illusions too much to listen. After they laughed at his first lines, the Regent gave up in disgust.

"Of course, your master would not have been available to provide such pleasant display, had you not foolishly taken his place in confronting Sister Vanta. Master ola Silba confided to me later that, had you told him of your worries, he might well have been the one on the steps, not you. And surely whatever spells Sister Vanta had prepared were tailored for his mind."

"So," said Maljun, a small hope dawning, "by little actions, a greater danger was averted."

"One could look at it that way."

"Still . . . Vilei . . ."

"Oh, don't concern yourself too much with her. The Regent ola Klera has offered her a position as Head Steward of her household. She should do well enough."

Maljun closed his eyes and sighed. "I am very glad."

"As I have said, the power of the Restoration spell is great, but subtle."

"And what should I do now, I wonder," said Maljun.

"Well," said Jussive, standing, "Master ola Silba has said nothing about being dissatisfied with your service. Once you are well enough, I presume you can resume your duties."

"But not as a Servitor."

"In name, no. We cannot allow it. If anyone asks, I must tell them you were secretly studying with the Goldthorne House, and that your training was none of ours."

"So I can no longer do the spells I know."

Jussive shrugged. "Should you survive the next months until your birthday and succeed in reinvesting your luck in whatever object you choose . . . well, we cannot take from you what you have learned. You will do what you will. Now, you should rest and I must return to your duties. I believe your master said he needed a particular scented oil for some intimate gathering of friends." Jussive rolled his eyes and started toward the door.

"Servitor?"

"Yes, Maljun?"

"Do you—do you think I did wrong?"

Jussive frowned and looked at the ceiling. "Wrong. Well. Let us say that perhaps you exercised a prudent disobedience, and let it go at that. Good day to you."

Procession Day/Remembrance Night: Processional/Recessional

by John M. Ford

Daylight's on the windowsill
Come you who are faithful still
Celebrate the work of will
Do not let us pass you by
Raise the stainless banners high
Take the streets and testify
Separate reasons reason how
Faith and confidence allow
Schisms shall be merry now
Practice, all you souls in clay
Toleration for one day
This anon shall pass away
Now the hour is growing late
God (to each his own) is great
Homeward now, and contemplate
Lamps glow even, candles spark
People keep the light and mark
All the uses of the dark
Now the flags are furled and stacked
Marching costumes neatly packed
Faith reflects on mortal fact
At the end 'tis all the same
Something always snuffs the flame

Everybody knows its name
Many rest so very deep
Those above this vigil keep
Some must watch while others sleep
In the darkened streets below
Laughter's heard, and lanterns throw
Stark light on a shadow-show
Children on the streets alone
Wearing masks of black and bone
In the shapes of things unknown
Overhead the raven sings
Down below walk flapping things
Decked with horns and claws and wings
Now the fleshless grin appears
Now the masquers' chorus cheers
Hail the Lord of Human Fears
Though their elders shield the eye
Trembling as He passes by
Children know they cannot die.

A Necessary End

by Pamela Dean

THE FIRST THING I ever promised Verdialos was to keep a journal, and that was also the last thing I promised him. He says that an honorable child requires promises, but that to an honorable adult they are a hindrance. I can't decide, and nor could Deleon or Jehane when I asked them, if it is harder to be honorable or to be an adult. In Liavek by all common understanding, I would have been an adult four years ago; in Acrivain I would not be one yet. Verdialos does not count years; he keeps rather a calendar of changes, turning points. Nor does he count the ones I would count, the large events, the plain changes, the crossroads with signposts. He adds up events so tiny I am not always certain they happened at all, like the plots of those Morianie plays my father hates so. This is the way he reckons his own life also; and so when the largest thing of all happened to Verdialos, he shrugged his shoulders at it.

I will never understand him. But I promised him that I would keep a journal, and I never promised him to grow up. So here speaks the honorable child Nerissa Benedicti, who owns a remarkable cat.

It is difficult to write unless you know whom you are writing to. My poems I wrote to myself, my stories to Jehane my sister, who always found them no matter how well I hid them. My first journal I wrote to Verdialos. This one is for him, but not, I think, to him. It will no doubt end up in the Green Book with

the other, in that motley section at the end reserved for oddities.
One day someone will have to copy it fair for the printer. I
think my writing is quite clear and regular, but fashions in
handwriting change as everything else does; so one day some
other Nerissa will hunch over this paper, with ink on her second
finger and her hair sticking to her neck, and wonder why it is
that all people who wish to kill themselves have such very bad
handwriting. Then she will wonder if, perhaps, this is in truth
the way the Green priests choose their members, if all the
questions and the prying and the sympathy and the sly suggestion of every other remedy imaginable are a game and a
toy; they are looking for folk who cannot write clear, so that
they will have work for the young ones in ten years, or fifty.

It isn't so. They mean it. You should know this also, you
other Nerissa. Are you hunched there under that weight of
misery that's like the hottest and dampest day even Liavek can
offer, holding you in your chair? If you're copying this, either
the weight has lessened a little, or you are among those who
can plod along under it. Are you young, as I was? If you are,
I can say that this may be like the new teeth growing in and the
spots on the face; it may pass. If you are not, I can say
that if you mean it, the Green priests will let you have your
way in the end. You won't think so. You'll ask, as everybody
does, when was the last time a Green priest died even in an
accident, let alone in the manner he had planned as if it were
a new naval treaty. You'll make jokes about it all, maybe; or
you'll make grave statements about the true purpose of the
House of Responsible Life.

But they mean it. One way or another, they will take that
misery from you. Let me tell you about Festival Week in the
year 3320.

Divination Eve

On the eve of Divination Day, Verdialos and Etriae asked
me to supper, as they had done every month or so for the last
three years, ever since Verdialos found me loitering on the
banks of the Cat River trying to discover the depth of the water.
I have thought since then that I was going about the business
of killing myself very foolishly; Verdialos, approached with

this opinion the first time I ate with them, agreed with me but said that when he was looking for people who needed the House of Responsible Life, he considered their intentions, not their wisdom. He and his wife have a longstanding argument on this topic; Etriae holding that people who truly intend to kill themselves will take the trouble to discover how actually to accomplish it, while Verdialos says people who wish to kill themselves often have not the strength for such discoveries. I learned not to mention the subject with both of them present.

Often, this past year, they had invited me and my best sister Jehane, or me and my brother Deleon; once, even me and my silly sister Livia, although that was not an enlivening evening and was not repeated. But this time they just asked me.

Their house is on the Street of Flowers, not far from the House of Responsible Life. The house is two hundred years old, built in a frenzy of admiration for the Hrothvekan architecture of that time, which is to say, of brick, and very tall and spiky. Hrothvekan brick is red, but all the old houses on the Street of Flowers are of gray bricks. Most of them are painted bright colors, Liavekans being what they are; but Verdialos and Etriae's house is just gray, and very scrubbed-looking. The door is red, and inside everything is white and yellow and brown and gray. It used to make me sleepy, but now seems merely comforting. They have nothing green in it except the clothes they wear to work in. Coming from the House of Responsible Life, which is green everywhere a building can be green, until Jehane says it looks moldy, one can understand their leaving the green in the garden.

It's not a large house. Etriae took me all over it the first time I visited them, while Verdialos cooked the supper. They have a lot of spindly Liavekan furniture that looks odd in so solid a house, and they have even more printed books than my father has; and up on the third floor they have two empty rooms. Etriae told me, in approximately the tone one might use to say this was where she did the sewing, "These were to be for the children." She did not seem to expect an answer.

After that first supper, Etriae always did the cooking. Verdialos had served a dish so spicy it made me sneeze and hurt my throat like the spotted fever. He was more amused than hurt; Etriae got rather sharp with him about it. But this time, on the last sparkling cold evening in the month of Frost, she was the one who let me in the red door. She was almost as tall as I am, but very dark, with a flat nose and wide mouth and huge black eyes that took up most of her narrow face. Calla, who works with Deleon at the Desert Mouse theater, says that if one could give Verdialos half Etriae's distinction, they would both be very handsome to look at. I think they are very well as they are. Calla is too much concerned with appearances.

Etriae always spoke firmly, as if to make up for the fact that Verdialos said everything as if he were thinking of something else. "He *will* do it," she said, following me into their sitting room. "He says you'll be able to eat it."

I said I was sure he was right, and we sat down rather awkwardly near the fireplace. I've always found it hard to visit with people who don't keep cats; but cats make Verdialos wheeze. He and Etriae had a monkey when I first met them, but it was very shy—the only reason, Etriae said dryly, that she could bear it. It died a year later, and they did not get another. I asked my brother Gillo how long monkeys lived; he said that the small sort I described generally managed about ten years. Their not getting another monkey therefore made me uneasy, and not just because of the subsequent difficulty of conversation. Sometimes I brought my own cat, and we would sit in the garden awhile and watch her chase the moths. But she was out wandering today.

It had been dark outside for some time, but the only light in the room came from the fire. This made it easier to sit without speaking, but I was still grateful when Etriae finally did.

"How are you getting on, Nerissa?" she said equably.

"Very well, I think," I said. I wondered what the question meant. Verdialos did not tell her everything, although he certainly told her things I did not want him to mention. If I left the answer at very well, I thought, we would just have to be uncomfortable again. I could hear Verdialos chopping something in the kitchen. I held my right hand near the fire and showed Etriae the ink ingrained in the skin of the first two fingers. "I've got only fifty years to go in copying the Green Book."

"What will you do then?"

"I hadn't thought. It will take several more years, I think; people nowadays are very voluble about everything. The first stories I copied were hardly half a page, but fifty years ago everybody wrote six or eight pages, and I know there are some coming that are more than twenty." I added, when she said nothing, "I shouldn't complain. My own is much longer than that."

"Had you thought of moving out of your parents' house?"

Verdialos had certainly been talking to her. Well, if she liked to do his work for him, it would not harm me to answer. I said, "Yes, but I should need somebody to live with, unless the Green House cares to pay me more than it does at present."

Etriae smiled, as one who has been asked if iron might float and fish fly in the foreseeable future; I said, "I'd thought to ask Jehane to live with me, but she's gone to Granny Carry to learn weaving. And Deleon lives with Aelim. And I couldn't really bear to live with Livia or Isobel." I didn't even think of my two other brothers, not until I was writing this down.

"Haven't you a friend or two you might share rooms with?"

"Well, there's Thyan; but she's quite happy living above the Tiger's Eye. And she'll marry Silvertop eventually."

"What about Calla?"

"I couldn't live with Calla. She'd always be making me uncomfortable for my own good."

Etriae grinned.

"Yes," I said, "Verdialos does that. Well, I don't need two of them; and at least I invited him to begin, if not perhaps to continue as he's done."

"But you feel you could live with Thyan, if her circumstances permitted it?"

"Well—I'm not certain. She makes me feel ungrateful and petty."

"Verdialos's mother was very skilled at that," said Etriae.

"No, Thyan doesn't do it on purpose. It's just—her family sold her to Snake, because they couldn't feed her. She can remember the first time she got enough to eat, when what I remember is once being sent to bed without supper. She says what she remembers most vividly is the *second* time she got enough to eat. But she spent her first eight years being cold and hungry and neglected; there wasn't room or time for her. So why is she briskly working for Snake while I'm skulking in the House of Responsible Life?"

I stopped talking. I knew how Verdialos got me to go on at length, but that Etriae could manage it also I had not known, til now. Her method was altogether different; something to do, perhaps, with how very matter-of-fact she was about all her questions.

Well, now I had asked her one. What I wanted her to say was what I had half worked out for myself; that there are cruelties of the heart as sharp as cruelties of the body; that to be bought by Snake might be better than to be kept by my parents; that I had a sensitive nature and Thyan a sturdy one and this was somehow a virtue in me. I wanted to hear somebody else say all these things. Verdialos would never do it, whether he thought so or not.

Etriae said tranquilly, "We are all fashioned differently. We can but work as we are made."

That was not the sort of thing Etriae said. It sounded to me either too simple to need saying, or else not true; Verdialos would come out with such statements to see if I would argue, but that was not Etriae's way. "Who said that?" I asked her.

She looked pleased. "Lerre ola Advar. You won't have got to her yet if you're still fifty years out. She was one of mine." I hoped, if Verdialos ever said that of me, he did not say it in that tone of voice, cool, reflective, and rueful. Etriae went on, "A most ingenious child, and one of whom you thought, though we are not allowed to, that the sooner she made her ingenious end the better for all. She wanted to take other people with her, and not for love."

"Just a short way to shedding her responsibilities?" I ventured.

"No; that would have been more forgivable."

"For what, then?"

"I'm not sure," said Etriae. "Perhaps some complex variation on the old simplicity that misery loves company. But not that only. She really did want to die, spectacularly if not horribly; and she knew there were others who did not, and it was they whom she wanted to take with her."

"Did she?"

"One of them," said Etriae. "She married him just in order to do that; she was very clever, turning the rules of the House and Verdialos's and my situation against us."

This was the most uncomfortable conversation I had had in months; far worse than all the mind-writhing ones with Verdialos about what was wrong with me, and my family, and all

the world. I did not know what she wanted me to say. Verdialos
had told me soon after we met, when I expressed astonishment
that a sworn suicide should be married, that his death was
bound to Etriae's in ways that he could not speak of. He wanted
to take Etriae with him, when he went. And though she was
presumably not unwilling, I had in fact never heard her speak
of death as Verdialos would sometimes talk of it. So after a
while I became irate, and said, "Forgive me, Etriae; but what
is the difference between the situation she contrived and the
one you and Verdialos have concocted?"

"To the mind, very little," said Etriae. "To the heart, very
great." She said this so peacefully that I knew she had been
hoping to make me ask that question; and whatever malice or
thoughtlessness in me she had tugged on to make me ask it
did not hurt her in the least. I had not in fact wished to hurt
her, yet the realization that I could not hurt me.

"I don't understand," I said, both truly and at random.

"It was the same method," said Etriae, and she gave me a
smug and secretive smile. "If it's your marriage that holds you
back, my own advisor said to me long ago, then best use your
marriage. Sometimes, she told me, it's the flesh that is reluctant, and sometimes it's the spirit. For the reluctant flesh there
are remedies." She looked into the fire, still smiling. She did
not seem to be contemplating death; she looked into the fire as
a cat will look at you when you have fed it six shrimp and may
yet feed it a seventh; she looked at nothing pleasedly, as Livia
would when she came back from walking with her lover in the
twilight.

I felt myself turning extremely red, which in the light of the
fire did not show. And Verdialos came to the door and called
us to supper. He had made the same dish as the first time. It's
a chicken dish with a lavish addition of strips of red pepper,
which look dangerous but are in fact sweet, and an even more
lavish addition of round black seeds that look like poppy, and
harmless, and will in fact take the bumps off your tongue.
There were fewer of them this time, and he had made also a
peculiar dish of melon and tomato that ought to have been vile
but was very nice, and counteracted the black seeds a little.
There was some Ombayan bread, too, to stretch out the hotness
and make each single bite less alarming, though the final effect
was the same. I managed to eat enough to make both Verdialos

and myself happy; I knew my cat would not scold me for failing to bring her any of what she smelled on my breath.

Whatever unsuitable revelations Etriae might make, whatever unspeakable things Verdialos might make me say, when the three of us were together we were always comfortable. We talked lightly of a new translation of the Tichenese poet Seng; of the prospects for snow during Festival; of Etriae's new secretary, who spelled as if he were asleep and insisted on making all his letters separately as if he were a printer; of my cat's latest exploits; of my new niece, and a new playwright who did not cast his dialogue in verse, and five peony trees that Etriae had ordered from Saltigos for next spring that had unaccountably arrived yesterday and were presently occupying both the children's rooms.

Long before we would have talked ourselves out, Etriae looked at Verdialos and said, "It will be midnight soon, Dialo; you'd better take Nerissa home so you can get back before the bells go."

As always, I said, "I can walk," Etriae said I couldn't, I said we could call a footcab, and Verdialos said he would walk me home to settle his dinner and find a footcab to come home in. Etriae kissed Verdialos; gave me the kind of one-armed hug she always bestowed, as if she wanted to make sure the object of her affection didn't feel trapped; and watched us down the pale brick path to the dark street.

It was very still and chilly. The stars were sharp and far away. We saw nobody, not a City Guard, not a stray cat. Verdialos walked quickly for such a short man. We went down narrow winding ways, striking echoes off stone, and emerged in time onto the Levar's Way, which was also empty. Liavekans are cautious about Divination Eve, in case anything they begin then should leak over onto the day; and fanatically conservative about Divination Day itself: do nothing, they say, that you would not gladly do. I always wonder if it's my ill fortune or their blindness that they think to stay home with one's family is safer than to venture among strangers. When I was very young, I could trace each catastrophe in the papers my father read to some slight or unkind word or outright squabble committed by my family on Divination Day. Then I grew scornful of all such beliefs; and now I do not know what I think.

I said so to Verdialos, and looked down in time to see him

smile. In the starlight his face was mostly eyes. He said, "That's a proper philosophy for your age."

"What age is disbelief proper for?"

"A much greater one," said Verdialos. "Disbelief must be earned."

"Has my father earned it?"

"Possibly," said Verdialos.

"And does belief need to be earned?"

"Belief needs to be honored," said Verdialos, rather sharply. He has a great many peculiarities, but perhaps his real fault is to be both definite and pompous about the gods. Since he does not plan to go to any of them after his elegant and beautiful death with Etriae, this attitude of his seems, in fact, not earned. I thought about saying so, but a long bristly shape shot out from behind a tree, made a series of wavery chirps, and wound itself around Verdialos's ankles.

"Hello, Floradazul," I said to my cat.

She acknowledged me with a low noise rather like the bleating of a goat, but went on trying to trip up Verdialos. To my considerable surprise, he sat down in the dust and let her climb into his lap. She commenced an enormous purring, and Verdialos said, "She's very heavy." His voice was already clogging up.

"She's still growing, too," I said. "I think this time around she's got some ship's cat in her, though they're mostly striped."

"So is she," said Verdialos thickly, and rubbed her ears. Floradazul rose up in his lap and bashed the top of her head into his chin so hard I heard his teeth click together. Her purring was phenomenal. Verdialos sneezed, and went on, "Etriae showed me one day. She's black with black stripes. Look at her carefully in a good light."

Floradazul bashed him again; he grunted, and then sneezed twice.

"Dialo, you won't have any peace from now on. I told you not to give in to her."

"I thought the attraction was all in my avoidance," said Verdialos, and sniffed vigorously. I gave him my handkerchief. Floradazul turned around three times and settled in his lap, still rumbling. Verdialos stroked her and blew his nose.

"Think how much avoidance she has to make up for," I said.

"Must I?" said Verdialos, and coughed alarmingly. "You'd better take her, Nerissa; this is exactly as bad as I thought it would be."

I picked up Floradazul, who protested but didn't struggle and absently went on purring. Verdialos sneezed again and stood up, shaking dust off his robe. "Who's awake still?" he said, looking past me at our house.

There were two lights, one on the first floor and one at the very top. "Papa must be reading poetry. And that's my room. Mama leaves a light on sometimes."

"Well," said Verdialos. "Try not to fret yourself too much; I'll see you on Procession Day."

"I still say it's a pity the House of Responsible Life won't march in the parade."

"You wouldn't if you'd seen how we used to do it," said Verdialos.

Something in the relish with which he said it made me think he was probably right. Just the same, I said, "It does get wearing staying indoors with a swarm of misplaced children."

"Ah," said Verdialos. "But thereby we garner strays from all the other faiths and make ourselves pleasant to harried parents by returning their offspring unharmed." His tone was ironic; he was probably quoting some proclamation of the order's Serenities, who worried sometimes about the House's reputation in Liavek. I smiled; he reached up and pushed back from my forehead a strand of hair Floradazul had loosened. "Good night," he said, and sneezed, and walked briskly away down the empty street, taking my handkerchief with him.

His other fault had always been that he was profoundly undemonstrative; Etriae and I had occasionally shaken our heads over it. It seemed unlikely to me that asthma made one affectionate.

I looked after him for a long time, not precisely thinking. Into the unoccupied spaces of my mind there stole Floradazul's view of matters: she liked the way I smelled, although the translation of her olfactory abilities to my senses made me want to cough; she wanted my arm to be fatter so both hind legs would rest securely on it; she had been stalking a lizard that went under a stone and stayed there until she was bored. This ability to see through her eyes and nose has never seemed to me of much use, but when The Magician of Liavek bound my luck to my cat, so that I would not die until she, my only responsibility, died also, he had insisted on including this power.

Floradazul began to struggle and complain, and we went in.

The clock in the hall was just striking twelve; Verdialos was going to be late and Etriae anxious. Well, if tardiness and worry were the worst things that happened in the new year, nobody would have cause to fuss. Floradazul, still muttering, finally kicked me in the stomach, leapt to the floor, and streaked for the kitchen. Cook would have left her something. I sniffed: woodsmoke, tallow, dried roses and orange-blossom, beeswax, cabbage, and something complex that was either chicken with rosemary or else eels doctored with such a lot of herbs that they might as well have been so many parsnips. Floradazul would eat either; that was all right.

I went on standing there. The house creaked around me. Down the long hall in my father's study there was a rough and substantial rustle. He was reading one of his old plays, the huge ones on paper so thick you kept trying to pry each page into two or three. I wondered which it was: *Five Who Found Acrilat*, *Thy Servants and Thine Enemies*, *Maladromo and the Five Muskrats*. Deleon and I had read them all surreptitiously and been smacked or scolded, when discovered, for touching the manuscripts; lately, though, my father had taken it for granted that we had read them, and would talk to me sometimes about them. My mother doesn't care for poetry.

Do nothing that you would not gladly do. I walked down the hall and tapped on the door.

I had not set foot in his study in five years. It was the same as ever, a frail but enormous bamboo desk entirely surrounded by books, some on shelves and some not. There was a path to the desk, with waist-high stacks of books and papers on either side of it. The desk held a lamp and a pewter mug and what my father was reading; it was the tidiest desk I had ever seen, even in the House of Responsible Life, and the untidiest study, too. In a stack near the door lay plans for the invasion of Acrivain. They were at least five years old, but not dusty. We had been forbidden in no uncertain terms by Granny Carry, who in the usual Liavekan way has great but not official power here, to stay in Liavek while yearning for Acrivain. She said it caused a great deal of trouble to Liavek; and I daresay she

ought to know. My parents had taken her ruling badly, and
still argued about it; but in fact long before she issued it my
father had given up on political meetings and taken to beer and
poetry instead. And both of them had made only the sort of
fuss that means nothing when my brothers and sisters began
to leave home.

My father looked up. In Acrivain he was unprepossessing,
but in Liavek, with his stature and his tightly curled white hair
and his bony pale face, I had seen people turn to look at him
in the street. He looked benevolent enough, because of the ale
that had been in the pewter mug. I thought I had better speak
first just the same.

"I'm home," I said. "Happy Divination Day. What are you
reading?"

And that is the best question in the world, certainly in my
house and quite possibly in any. An entire speech practiced on
eight children in turn about their family responsibilities, the
vulgarity of Liavekan superstitions and holidays generally,
one's habit of being sociable only when it was inappropriate,
and any story handy about what trouble some action or possession of one's had caused in one's absence, all died for lack
of breath. He turned the huge manuscript to face me, and I
saw it was not a play at all. It was a cycle of poems by the
Morianie poet Kamissor, that purports to be an herbiary but is
in fact an allegory about love and art. Its herbal information
is correct but not illuminating. I realized, scanning it, that it
was from here Deleon must have gotten the verse form he used
for two of the characters in his first play. I wondered if he
knew, and if my father had noticed.

"Do you still like it?" I said. I could tell by the color
of the ribbon that it was a long time since he had opened this
one.

He had been wanting to grumble, so he grumbled a little
about the work's uneven structure. But in ten minutes he was
reading the old Acrivannish aloud; his pronunciation was not
as good as my grandmother's, but he had a nice grasp of the
rhythms. When I saw him begin to get testy I yawned, and
was promptly sent off to bed as if I were eight and not eighteen.

Jehane was sitting on my bed, her long legs tucked under

her and her yellow hair falling out of its braids, reading a story I was not yet ready to show her. "Put that down!" I said.

Jehane turned pink and did so. "It was right where it always is," she said.

"Well, you don't live here anymore. I was going to bring it along to Granny's in a decent civilized fashion, after Festival."

"You should have thought I'd come home for Festival."

"This isn't your room."

"Gillo and Givanni have filled up my room with bolts of bad silk," snapped Jehane.

My mother had said something of the sort several days ago, but I had paid no attention. "Well, you might have just rolled them down the stairs."

I said this so that I could say later I had thought it would make her laugh; in fact I knew that tonight it would not. Jehane was very even-tempered, but when she chose to become cross, she became very cross indeed. She only scowled at me. I said, "Why are you home at all, in this state of mind?"

"Because it's Grand Festival Week. Granny wants us to try our hands at celebrating a major Liavekan holiday. I finally got her to say I could come back on Bazaar Day; she wants to show me how to bargain for thread and what ready-made fabrics are worth the buying."

I said temperately, "I just spoke to Papa; he seemed quite reasonable."

"Yes, after I spent two hours soothing him down. He was at me at once about why I don't come home more often."

That was very likely true, and the ease I had been silently congratulating myself on won from somebody else's efforts. "You come too often, if anything," I said; another remark that sounded supportive but was not. I was very ruffled that she had read that story. Until last year every sister that I had pried constantly and Jehane's prying was the least of it, because she loved me; now, with all of them out of the house, even Jehane made me furious.

Jehane rose off my bed and stalked for the door. "If you left as you ought," she said, "you wouldn't notice."

Tardiness, worry, and family quarrels. The mere fabric of everyday life.

Divination Day

I have never seen anything like that Divination Day for good intentions gone astray. Everybody came home: Marigand and her husband with the new baby; Gillo and Givanni with Livia and Livia's husband; Isobel from the Theater of Golden Lights; Deleon from the Desert Mouse, with Aelim in tow. Aelim was also a player, and, like Calla, small and beautiful; unlike Calla he was both silent and understanding. If he had not either winked at me at strategic moments or engaged me in obscure linguistic speculation—for how should I be expected to know why the old Acrivannish verb forms had no future tense—at others, matters would have been a great deal worse than they were.

The children who had lived away from home for some time, like Marigand and my two older brothers, knew how to deal with my parents, but found their habits of discourse with the recently departed children no longer adequate. The recently departed children ought not to have come back so soon. Deleon had run away ten years ago. We had found him again by going to see his first play. I knew that he and Aelim had asked our parents to supper; moreover, our parents had gone. But Deleon had not been back to the house he grew up in until now, and he looked like somebody with a bout of stomach fever, unless Aelim made him laugh. He and I shook our heads at one another a time or two, to prevent one or another angry outburst; but we found sensible conversation impossible.

By Divination Night, my mother, my father, Gillo, Marigand, and Marigand's husband had all shouted furiously; Livia, Givanni, and Isobel had all burst into tears; Jehane had said so many sharp things that my mother told her to go to her room, which provoked a hysterical outburst of laughter from almost everybody and made my mother burst into tears in her turn; Deleon had been sick twice into the pan in my room provided for Floradazul, who fortunately was in the habit of disdaining it except in very rainy weather; and even Aelim and the baby were beginning to look fretful. Floradazul had fled outside and gone to sleep at the top of the olive tree. Aelim and Ebullo—Livia's husband—sat quietly, looking dark and

somber and Liavekan, like spectators at some play in an unknown language. I looked at my tall, pale family with all its
yellow hair and its faint lilting Acrivannish accent, and they
seemed very strange to me; my own face in the hall mirror
looked as foreign as somebody's from Ka Zhir.

We all went to bed early; Aelim and Deleon went home,
which they had not intended to do until after dinner next day.
My parents were silent on this alteration in plans after Aelim
and Deleon left, but we all heard about it at breakfast, in a
kind of antiphonal discussion that told us they had talked it
into shape half the night. I don't know why I ever wondered
that our family has produced two players and a playwright.

Birth Day

Aside from this performance, which after all was rude only
to the absent, on Birth Day we were all tremulously polite, as
people who are too frail and injured to make much effort but
know what is right to do. My mother packed up the lot of us
in the late morning and took us to see Granny Carry. Jehane
bore her bag of clothes and a look of grim anticipation; she
was not staying at our house until Bazaar Day and she looked
forward to Granny's discovering precisely why.

It was gray and windy and threatening rain. This did not
prevent large parties of people in bright clothes from running
up and down the streets, laughing and singing and playing on
drums and penny whistles. The taverns and restaurants had all
set out their tables and chairs in the streets again, that they had
taken in at the middle of the month of Wine, which had been
cold this year. A few hardy souls were chortling around some
of these tables; I hoped their drink was warming. Even the
unbelievers don't wish to be sick on Procession Day.

I caught Jehane's eye and smiled at her. "You know they'll
behave themselves at Granny's," I said.

She smiled back, unperturbed. "She'll know by the manner
of their good behavior just how things have been."

Granny let us in serenely, gave us a brazier of coals for our
hands, tea for our throats, and cats for our laps. Gillo and
Givanni and my father had never been here before. Givanni
was comforted by the cat; the other two simply stayed silent,

drinking their tea and looking as if they expected the loom to leap at them or the wall hangings to fall on their heads.

I remembered our ceremonial visits to Granny when I was small. My mother would make imperious pronouncements about Liavek, and Granny would contradict her, and so far as I could tell, they parted each feeling the victor. Today, my mother asked Granny how she did, and how Jehane was getting on with her weaving, and even how the cats were finding the cold weather. Granny dealt with the first two of these questions in an unnaturally gracious manner, but to the third she replied shortly, "Cold," and thereafter settled back in her wicker chair to watch my family try to behave itself. When we left, Jehane did not come with us; and Granny looked as pleased as a cat in a basket of clean laundry.

The rest of the day went rather better. We were trying for the first time the Liavekan custom of celebrating everyone's birthday on this first day of Festival Week (it was the second day of Grand Festival, but Divination Day is not counted, it simply occurs). This meant that everyone's favorite food must be cooked, and everyone's favorite game played at least once, and everyone's desires in the matter of foolish or impractical acquisitions taken into account. Cook, no one having told her otherwise, had made enough of each favorite dish for twelve; when all the serving plates were on the table, there was no room for us to eat. We dispersed all over the house, dropping crumbs and not being scolded for it.

The present-giving was more complex, and elicited a good deal of sarcastic commentary; nobody in this family has ever been able to give another member of it a proper present. The only person who liked what I gave him was Aelim; I had unearthed a mold-spotted glossary to the plays of Petrane, given to me by my father when he got a new one, and Aelim behaved as if it were bound in gold and leather. I myself received a green silk cushion that Floradazul would shred in a tenday; a pen of the wrong size and a bottle of ink of the wrong color; a very beautiful green glass statue of a Kil that Floradazul would enjoy breaking; a white shirt, a red shirt, and a yellow dress that I could not wear to work in but were in fact welcome, if respectively too wide, too short, and too long; and a rocklike loaf of brown rice bread from Livia that made my eyes mist up, although neither Floradazul nor I could possibly eat it.

Givanni was not kind about his own rock of bread, and unfortunately Livia did not take his remark as the other givers had taken everyone else's. The repercussions of this lasted until bedtime. I lay wide awake with a monstrous headache and a purring cat on my stomach, thinking that all the rest of them must have been very pleased indeed to go away rather than upstairs. Later, I thought they might have been relieved to go away but not quite sorry that they came. And I wondered if Granny might have discerned the possibility of just that outcome when she watched us visit her. I went to sleep finally, to dream confusedly of Floradazul's breaking the statue and a great many other things I do not in fact own. I wondered if her dreams were getting into mine. In the morning I found out that I had probably heard in my sleep the thump and rumble and crash of the fireworks by the Cat River.

Procession Day

My parents had decided that celebrating Procession Day was too much to ask of anybody not born in Liavek. I was very much afraid that they planned some ceremony for Acrilat, who (even if Granny had not ordered us to abandon It) had never done any of us the least good. (Verdialos says that what good we think the gods do us is not the point, but I had learned, by the time he said so, not to argue with him on such subjects.) But when I suggested I might stay home with them instead of going to the House of Responsible Life, they were not in the least perturbed; in fact, I had some difficulty in persuading them that I did have to go after all. They did not exactly know that the House was a religion, and the thought of me copying away in there instead of watching the crazy Liavekans parade their mutually incomprehensible and contradictory gods all through the streets soothed them eventually.

I was late for work, if I had been working; but in fact except for the people detailed to deal with lost children, nobody was doing anything but talking and drinking Saltigan wine. Saltigan wine makes me sneeze, rather like Verdialos with Floradazul; Etriae found me some lemon water.

Calla was there, although the Desert Mouse would be performing one play this evening and a different one on Festival

Day itself and yet a third on Festival Night. She was extremely somber, and was wearing a short dress in an unnatural green that made her look sick. With Calla, this meant that either she was sick, she wanted people to think so, or there was some symbolic value in looking sick under the circumstances. She was handing out honeycakes to a swarm of at least twenty children; she smiled when she saw me, gave me one also, and bit into the last one herself.

"The streets don't look that crowded to me," I said.

"Most of these aren't lost," said Calla. "They were lost last year, or the year before, and liked it so well they came back. Some of their parents leave them off at the front door and collect them at dusk."

"I suppose 'House of Responsible Life' does have a soothing ring to it," I said.

"Either that, or they hope the children will take to the philosophy and cease troubling them," said Calla.

"What's the matter?"

She took a very large bite of cake, looking at the floor; when she had finished chewing, she gave me a long opaque look out of her great yellow eyes and said flatly, "I don't look forward to remembering the dead tonight."

I didn't ask whom she had to remember; it might be her father, perhaps, or someone of whom I knew nothing. Now that Deleon was restored to us, I had only my grandmother to think of, and a blue-and-cream cat with green eyes that had once been Floradazul. Cats have nine lives in Liavek—Liavekan superstitions having an irritating tendency to be true—and Floradazul was on her second, through annoying a camel. My black cat was clearly still my cat, my very same cat; and yet from time to time I missed the blue-and-cream, and would think of her on Remembrance Night.

"What play are you doing tonight?" I said.

Calla chortled. "Such a ruckus!" she said. "We always do *Firethorn and Mistletoe*, you know; and Deleon wanted to write a tragedy specially for Remembrance Night, and he went after Thrae and after her, and finally she told him he could write it when he was dead himself and knew something about it; and Aelim laughed, which meant Del couldn't even be properly affronted."

I felt rather affronted for my brother, who was after all going to be a fine playwright; but I had to laugh too. Calla seemed quite over her somber mood; we went and helped Etriae do farcical readings from her Deck of Hours until Verdialos came downstairs with a smudge of ink on his nose and said it was time to go outside and watch the procession.

I had seen one or two others, and this was much the same. I wish now I had paid it more mind, but I had fallen into one of those futile cogitations that seem to follow along with the age of eighteen, concerning why I did not enjoy such spectacles as I used. If I had attended to it, I should likely have enjoyed it just as well. As it was, I stood between Verdialos and Etriae, with Calla in front of me so she could see better, exploring my likes and dislikes in weary and pleasurable detail.

Etriae said in a breathless voice very different from her usual cheerful tones, "Dialo."

And Verdialos said, "Yes—Nerissa, get down." He pushed me, with considerable force for so slight a man, into Calla, and we both fell to our knees in the cool dust, whereupon there was an enormous volley of barking cracks, a bare instant's silence, and a rash of screaming. I could smell gunpowder.

"Sorry, I lost my balance," said Calla breathlessly beside me; and then she said, "*Nerissa.*"

I had hair and dust in my eyes; the first thing I saw, swiping the hair away, was a finger of red paint sliding over the ground between Calla's bare brown knee and my smudged skirt. Then I smelled a smell that made me think of copper, perhaps of the time I had put a half-copper piece in my mouth to tease Deleon, when I was very young. I looked up. It was not paint. It was all over Verdialos and Etriae, dappling their green clothing like the light of sunset through leaves; it had spattered the screaming onlookers. Verdialos and Etriae lay in two ungainly heaps, several feet apart, as if whatever had made the noise had happened between them and flung them asunder. Verdialos, whose face I could see, looked absent; Etriae looked as if she were sleeping as Verdialos would tease her about sleeping, with both arms doubled under her head as if she were afraid they would get away from her. She did not smell like sleep, and none of this sounded like sleep. There was a little drift of smoke mingling with the dust, and a string of spent firecrackers fluttered by on the wind and was gone in the crowd. It was still Festival.

I sat back in the dust, and felt the sticky touch of the finger of blood. I didn't move; there seemed nowhere to move to. Various onlookers were shaking their heads over Verdialos and Etriae, and demanding a healer; eventually one surfaced and shook her head too. Calla was crying, quietly and with great dignity; on the platform of the theater she did it far more loudly.

A number of onlookers had made it their business to run into the House of Responsible Life while the healer was shaking her head. Probably as a result of their efforts, three or four of the Serenities in their green robes now came slowly down the steps, carrying green curtains, or perhaps rugs. They spoke to the healer; she didn't want them to move the bodies but seemed unable to explain why. "The City Guard won't like it," said a young woman, rather loudly. This did not impress the Serenities, although it seemed to make the healer happier. It was true that, while the bodies themselves were not blocking the procession, all the spectators were. It was only the followers of Irhan who were being discommoded, but I supposed they deserved their parade too. The Serenities covered Verdialos and Etriae up and lifted them one by one and carried them into the house.

After a short time, in which the bright winter sun changed the smell of the blood, a City Guard captain arrived, with a lieutenant and another guard whom I recognized. Rusty and Stone; they used to take Deleon and me home when they found us wandering about the city looking for places to kill ourselves. I wondered why Verdialos had not found both of us much earlier; how much easier that would have been for everybody.

I stood up, and helped Calla stand up. Some of her friends from the House handed her handkerchiefs and took her off somewhere. I went on watching the captain; she was easier to pick out of the crowd than either the redheaded Rusty or the gigantic Stone. Partly this was because she was not moving around so much; and partly it was because she had a stern and splendid face, rather like the statue of the northern goddess Valerian who had tried and failed to take the Acrivannish from Acrilat; my mother has a miniature of it in her parlor. She had black hair like Valerian's, and a very definite voice.

I remembered her. When the Serenity Gorodain was killing wizards and leaving them to glow green, a number of Liavek's citizens, not altogether unnaturally, I realize now, though I did not think so at the time, came and threw things at the House

of Responsible Life. Captain Jemuel had come with the City
Guard, sent the rioters smartly away, and spoken pleasantly to
Verdialos. She had been brisk and ironic and had generally the
air of somebody doing what she knows how to do; like Gillo
building a chair for Isobel's doll.

She did not look that way now. She looked like Deleon when
they made him paint in watercolors, like Livia when they tried
to make her knead bread; like me, I expect, when they tried
to teach me to dance. She hated what she was doing so much
that she knew she could not possibly be quiet enough to do it
well. I wondered what it was she was doing, that was not what
she did in her work. Perhaps it was just that she knew Verdialos.
She ran up the steps and into the House of Responsible Life,
and came out again shortly, looking more confounded now
than grim.

"Dialo, you would," she said to the splashes of blood in
the dust of the street. "Pharn take you, right in the middle of
Hell Week." She looked at me. "You'd better sit down," she
said, though I was quite steady. She did not look accustomed
to being argued with. I sat down on the wall. The healer and
the young woman were having the pleasure of explaining to
Rusty why the bodies had been moved. Jemuel watched them
for a moment and then said to me, "Lieutenant Jassil says your
name's Nerissa Benedicti? What happened?"

"I don't exactly know. Verdialos saw something; he turned
and pushed me and said to stay down. Then there was a lot of
noise and a great deal of blood."

"What sort of noise?"

"Like the fireworks."

"You'd better come along with me; we can't talk here. Can
someone come with you?"

She dispatched Stone to find Calla, and Rusty to look for
something; then we all waited about until three more City
Guards appeared and she told them what to do; and the three
of us set off walking. Captain Jemuel looked like Aelim in the
throes of a grammatical dilemma; Calla was an unlovely yellow
color and kept stumbling. Perhaps I should have chosen someone less fond of Verdialos; or perhaps this would prevent her
from thinking before she was ready.

We walked a fair distance, among the celebrations; Calla
stopped crying and began to expostulate. Captain Jemuel didn't

answer her. Finally we came to the clutter of buildings around the Levar's Palace, and went into a room, and sat down. Jemuel gave us some extremely bitter kaf without asking if we wanted it, and went away for some time. The room was very plain and scattered with papers. When she came back, she dropped another pile of papers on the desk and sat down behind it. Then she asked a number of questions about what had happened; and about what might have happened, too, but neither of us was any good to her at all. About halfway through the conversation something Calla said made her face change, and I realized that she had thought one or the other of us might have killed the two of them, and now she did not. At that point she dug a sealed paper out of the new pile on the desk. The seal was an enormous blob of bright green wax with a V and an E in it. It was cracked across the middle.

Jemuel tapped the paper against her palm. "I asked Dialo to tell me how he planned to die," she said, "so we wouldn't have to waste time looking into it, when he finally got around to doing it. He said it was none of my business. But he turned up a few days later with this. He said I could open it after he was dead. And I have, and this is not how he said he planned to do away with himself, or Etriae either."

I gaped at her; I remembered Etriae's pleased and secretive face. Of course, one would not have to write much to show one had not intended to die bloodily at noon in a Festival procession. Jemuel did not look either shocked or puzzled. "It appears they meant to die in bed," she said to me. "Would you know anything about that?"

"It's not the sort of thing you tell your novices," I said tartly. She probably knew more than I did at this point, and in any case I did not propose to discuss the matter with anybody. It would be in the archives, but she could think of that for herself, and battle the Serenities for it, too. Surely she could find out what had happened without knowing anything besides what was in Verdialos's letter.

Jemuel looked both impatient and thoughtful, but did not press the issue. After finding out where we would be if she wanted us, she sent us back to the House of Responsible Life in a footcab. Neither of us said anything. The cab's owner whistled "Eel Island Shoals" off-key all the way there.

The Serenities of the order were just calling a meeting; they asked for me but not for Calla. Calla, shaking her head and muttering something about *Firethorn and Mistletoe*, kindly gave me a hug and went away.

I found the meeting unnerving. Everybody else there had been a member of the House for at least ten years; I couldn't think what they wanted with me. It became evident eventually that, first of all, nobody else would admit to knowing anything about what Verdialos and Etriae had been doing in their work, and, second, that the two of them had left in the House's archives a paper disposing of all their possessions, and with the exception of a few books and keepsakes distributed among the older members, everything was mine.

I had a house. That would set Jemuel off again, I thought, while the Serenities were reading aloud the list of what in the house was mine and what was for each of them. Jemuel was very good at asking questions, and anybody getting a straight account of what went on in my family would not be surprised for a moment at killing two people for a chance to get out of it. I wrote her a note with the news in it, saying she might look for me in the Street of Flowers if I were not at home or at the House of Responsible Life. One of the children could take the message for a copper or two.

The Serenities talked on. I wanted my cat. I wanted to walk by the Cat River and consider the depth of the water. But I found myself beginning to feel angry. Somebody had killed Verdialos and Etriae, probably with a gun, out of a huge crowd, and Jemuel had not sounded very hopeful of finding out who. Leaving aside Verdialos and Etriae, who were no longer concerned in the matter, it seemed to me that for many reasons I was the one injured here.

I sat in the large room used for meetings and for entertaining lost children, the Serenities talking around me, and thought. Once I had run to The Magician with my problems, or to Granny Carry; of late, the problems being more interior than otherwise, I had run to Verdialos. It was Festival Week; one would not find Wizard's Row, and in any case the last time I saw him The Magician had expressed a desire not to see any of my family again, in effect turning our welfare over to Granny. Granny had been dealing with that in her own fashion, but I felt as if my family were on trial and I would do none of us any good by asking her for help. And, again, it was Festival, and she would be occupied.

Possibly, too, I was being unfair to Jemuel. She had caught Gorodain, after all. I got up suddenly and went out of the room. She had caught Gorodain, and after a considerable uproar and a great many violent headlines in all the half-copper papers, they had taken his luck from him and sent him off to Crab Isle. I still remembered a discussion between my father and Isobel concerning what would have been done to him in Acrivain. So. Nothing I had heard about him from Verdialos or anybody else made me doubt that if he chose to leave Crab Isle and come back to Liavek, he would do it. And having no luck any longer, if he wanted to avenge himself on Verdialos, he would have to use a gun.

Would he wish to avenge himself on Verdialos? Everybody at the House of Responsible Life was remarkably muddled about what exactly had happened. Verdialos had flatly refused to discuss the matter; I once overheard Etriae telling him in tones of considerable exasperation that, whatever it was, it couldn't possibly be as damaging as the wild tales that were going around among novices and Serenities alike. Verdialos replied dryly that it was petty to think so, and Etriae threw two folders of letters from the parents of lost children at him, and was obliged to ask me to pick them up and sort them while she went for a walk to cool her temper.

Gorodain had killed six wizards and made them glow green; everybody agreed about that. It was less generally agreed that it had taken the combined talents of Jemuel, Verdialos, and The Magician to realize what Gorodain had done and to catch him. It was reported variously that Gorodain had been caught trying to kill a healer, or the little girl she was treating, or a toymaker who lived in the neighborhood of the healer, or The Magician himself—having practiced, as it were, on six lesser wizards first. It was reported also that whichever of these had in fact been his victim was in fact killed and then brought back to life by The Magician, or else by the children's healer if the victim was reported as The Magician. This last prompted a long and convoluted debate over whether wizards could bring back the dead. Verdialos, appealed to on this point, said in the same flat tone with which he had been refusing to discuss the matter for three months, that bringing back the dead was the prerogative of the gods alone, and not all of them. But of course he would say that, whether it had any bearing on what had happened or not.

It seemed clear at least that Gorodain, adhering to the tenets of the old Green Faith whose members visited death on others, not themselves, had killed six wizards, and that Verdialos had either helped to catch him or at least not defended him or helped him. I thought of going back to the Guard station; then of sending another message. But as I considered the form it would take, I began to see that there were holes in the fabric of my thought. I was still certain I had discovered the truth, but felt Jemuel would laugh at me. I stopped pacing the halls and went into the nearest room.

It was Verdialos's, of course, habit having taken over when thought was elsewhere. I sat down at my own table. I felt extremely tired suddenly; again, I wanted my cat. And then I considered my cat. My cat that was a magical artifact. My cat that had my luck bound into her by The Magician, so that I might die when she did but neither before nor after. My cat that, because The Magician had refused to make a magical artifact that did nothing, would let me see what she saw but understand it as if I were seeing it with my own eyes. Could she show me what Jemuel was doing or what frame of mind she was in?

I had not practiced this when there was any distance involved. I did not know where Floradazul was; she might have found it noisy enough outside that she would retire to our garden and sleep under the stone bench, occasionally waking up and smacking a spider for its presumption. I shut my eyes and wandered among the red and green and yellow sparks and the lost lines of what I had seen just before, but that did nothing. I looked at my hands; I looked at Verdialos's books, at the green-and-white rag rug, at the scarred wooden leg of his desk. Finally I leaned back and looked at the ceiling and let the focus of my eyes drift, as cats do when you think they are staring you out of countenance but in fact they don't see you at all. And that showed me, in a slow and jumbled fashion, the world through Floradazul's eyes. She was down by the docks, sniffing the fish and eating the fish scraps and being scratched behind the ears by passing children and idle sailors.

This was all very well as far as it went, but it was a far cry from nudging her in some direction useful to me. She didn't know I was there, and Acrilat only knew what she would think of it if she did. I tried to remember where the Guard offices were, but I had not paid attention when Calla and I were walking with Jemuel. Near the Levar's Palace, I thought. I sat staring aslant at the rough plaster ceiling, patterned with thin sunlight through the branches of the tree that grew outside the window, thinking of the smells we had encountered on our way.

Floradazul suddenly shook herself from the embrace of a small fishy boy and bolted down a narrow alley so fast it made me dizzy. She could climb walls with dispatch, too. Luckily Jemuel's office was not far from where we had been; I should have hated for us to end up somewhere that just happened to smell like its neighborhood. The Guard offices were in fact in the Levar's Palace itself, which was only reasonable, and had their own entrance, which was fortunate. Floradazul sat on the steps for a few moments and then slid in when somebody left. He smelled of wool and dog; I don't know what he looked like. Once inside, Floradazul recognized more smells and tried to trip Lieutenant Rusty up as he leaned against the wall playing with the innards of a shiribi puzzle. Floradazul liked the idea of the string, but Rusty was not interested in playing. He said, "Get that thing out of here!"

From somewhere else in the room, Stone's voice said, "Aw, Rusty. It's that ghost kid's cat. And there's nothing to do."

"There will be. All right, but whatever she pisses on and whatever she claws up, you can explain to the captain."

Rusty had always asked kindly after Floradazul, and even once spoken of getting a cat after he retired. He was either a consummate hypocrite or in a foul mood. Probably the latter, if he had to work during Festival. That might account, too, for the change in Jemuel.

Jemuel came in, looking enormous from a cat's-eye view. "Is Lani still around?" She sounded harried, and smelled extremely interesting.

"Not a chance," said Rusty, aggrievedly.

"Well, send somebody after him. And you might as well read this. Stone, if that cat—"

"It won't," said Stone, also aggrievedly.

"Nothing new here," said Rusty, reading.

"The pig's blood is new," said Jemuel. "You couldn't tell that just by looking, could you, Lieutenant?"

"We knew it wasn't theirs, anyway," said Stone; he had understood that she was displeased without precisely knowing what she was displeased about. "Not a mark on them."

I tried very hard to be just a cat sniffing an old but interesting spot on the floor; there was no need for thought in that.

Rusty, still reading, said nothing; Jemuel said, "Lani says it was pig's blood. He says further that neither of them should be dead at all as far as he can see; and he's gone out to celebrate, the son of a camel, because, he says, obviously, given what they were, they did it on purpose."

"That's the first thing you thought, too," said Stone helpfully.

Jemuel breathed out violently through her nose and said, "That's not the point. If they killed themselves, we still need to know how, or we won't know for certain that they did." She rubbed her hand across her forehead and added, "At least they weren't glowing green."

Rusty stood up and tossed the sheaf of papers onto the table. "Come on, Stone," he said. "I know where Lani will go first."

"Take that cat when you go," said Jemuel.

Stone knew how to hold a cat; and the leather vest he wore over his uniform made a comfortable station for claws. Floradazul rode happily with him through the bright crowded streets of Liavek; and I went with them, feeling slightly seasick. They came to a narrow stucco building front crammed in between a brick one and one of smooth pink plaster. Its ornate sign said simply, "Ale," and that appeared to be all they served you inside. If, that is, one can get ale tinged purple, or greeny-yellow, or reddish-gold. Lani turned out to be a thin dark boy with very short hair, sitting alone in a corner with a glass of the greeny-yellow stuff. He was younger than I am, probably, but whatever life he led had made him both more tired and more assured than I ever fear or hope to be.

He received Rusty's admonishments and Stone's insults with perfect good humor, scratched Floradazul behind the ears, and reiterated that the blood in question was pig's blood, concealed in several bags under clothing. Verdialos's clothes always looked too big for him, but I remembered Etriae looking rather bulkier than usual. I thought she had just put on more clothes against the cold. No, said Lani, patiently, nothing was in the least wrong with either of them except that they were dead. No, not poison; no, not disease; no, not magic either. He finally snapped at them to go and vex Mistress Govan, who had taught him all he knew, with his deficiencies, supposing he really had any, which he begged leave to doubt. He then drained his glass, rubbed Floradazul's head again, and walked out. Stone and Rusty, arguing, sat down and had some of the purple ale. They didn't seem to like it. Stone spilled a puddle of it on the table and offered it to Floradazul. She didn't like it either, and sneezed so violently that I jerked suddenly back to my stiff neck and one foot asleep, in a green room full of shadows. I had found out rather more than I bargained for; and if nobody had shot them at all, then Gorodain had not shot them.

It was Remembrance Night, and so I remembered the dead. I was very angry with them. They had left me; they had made a mystery of it; and for what? To get me out of my parents' house? It could not be that simple. It had, grotesque amidst all the marks of genuine loss and tragedy, the flavor of a practical joke, a play for two before an unwitting audience. I thought of Calla. "I don't look forward to remembering the dead to-night." Yes, indeed, I had discovered something. Doing anything about it would have to wait 'til morning.

I did not go home, to my parents' house or to the brick house on the Street of Flowers. I sat in my wooden chair in Verdialos's room, trying to think of my grandmother, who had taught me Old Acrivannish and the proper making of wedding cake with lard and honey and rye flour. Songs and talk and laughter and shrieks ebbed and swelled in the streets outside; the sharp glancing light of lanterns bounced across the room. After a long time I heard an irritated mewing in the street, and went down to let my cat in.

Bazaar Day

The Desert Mouse had a new coat of white paint over its much-peeled stucco; it looked like the cakes Jehane used to make, on which she thought a liberal application of frosting sufficed to correct all structural defects. The wooden carving of the theater's entry porch, formerly painted lumpily in bright yellow, had been scraped and picked out carefully in six colors. They had been alternating between Andri Terriot's rejects from the Levar's Company and Deleon's so-called Acrivannish plays, and it must have been working beautifully. Liavekans have very odd taste.

I went in quietly. They were rehearsing something; it sounded more like Deleon than like Andri Terriot. There was more talk than action and the verse was sparer than Terriot's. Deleon appeared to be simultaneously playing the part of an old woman and instructing his fellow players Calla and Lynno how to say their lines. Thrae, who owned the theater, stood off to one side looking sardonic; but when she said, "Let's stop and consider, please," all three of them ceased yelling and went over to her.

Calla saw me and nudged Deleon. He looked at Thrae, who nodded, and swung himself off the platform. "Nissy? I thought I was supposed to meet you on Restoration Day? Did Aelim misremember?"

"Aelim never misremembers," I said. "I wanted to ask you something. Do you use a lot of pig's blood?"

Deleon hardly blinked. "We used to," he said. "But Naril's gotten so clever we haven't much use for it these days. Why?"

"Where did you get it, when you needed it?"

"From a butcher, dear sister," said Deleon, kindly enough; he was somewhat of a flowery frame of mind, from repeating his own poetry all day. "We used Roani Sirro on Canal Street, usually. It wasn't all pig's blood," he added, looking at me rather anxiously. "He would give us chicken's or goat's or whatever he'd had a call for that day. Does that matter?"

"How much would it take to look as if two people had bled to death?"

"Nerissa, what are you plotting?"

"Nothing. How much?"

"Holy preservation, Nissy, I don't know. Thrae? Where's Malion?"

"Cleaning out his desk," called Thrae. "He's feeling about as friendly as a sick tiger; I'd leave it until tomorrow."

"It's all right," I said to Deleon. "Just let me talk to Calla." She was, I thought, listening to us instead of to Lynno; but that might have been mere curiosity.

Deleon looked at me. "Something's happened."

"It certainly has. And when I've done with Calla she can tell you all about it."

"Calla's worse than Mistress Oleander, when the fit's on her," said Deleon. He pulled my hair, said, "Give my best to your cat," and called to Calla that she should talk to me in the players' room while he and Lynno discussed Lynno's lines.

I followed Calla into the back of the theater. She was wearing red and still looked sick. She looked straight at me and said, "I couldn't tell you, Nerissa," in the way one would say, I can't reach this shelf, I can't throw that ball so far, iron sinks in water. I looked at her hard, and believed it. Verdialos and Etriae were not wizards, but they could be a most potent combination.

"Why did they tell you at all?"

"For the pig's blood."

"Did they say they would kill themselves?"

"No," said Calla. "They didn't say what they wanted it for. But what else could it be? I knew."

She knew, I thought, but she might have been wrong all the same. I remembered a few pranks in the past, with pigs' bladders—there it was, pigs again—filled with water and dropped down the stairs; or the day somebody had baked slips of paper with rude messages written on them into all the honeycakes. Nobody had ever been held to account for these antics, but I remembered also how Etriae would turn the Deck of Hours upside-down and run riot through it, and what Verdialos thought was funny. They might not have planned to be dead, but they were. I still thought of Gorodain, who had known them for years and was very astute, however mad he might be.

I said to Calla, "I told Deleon you'd tell him what happened. If you'd rather not—"

"No, I ought to; Malion will go out in disgust soon and buy the *Cat Street Crier*." She signed. "Deleon will be solicitous; he can't help it."

"I know; that's why I'm leaving before you tell him. Say I'll see him day after tomorrow, just as we planned." Calla smiled; I added, "Ought I to tell you to break your leg now?"

"No," said Calla, with a remarkable combination of rue and cool irony. "I think a broken heart is sufficient to ensure a good performance." She gave me a good long time in which not to answer, and then said, "Will you come to see us?"

"I'll try."

"Bring your sisters," said Calla. "They laugh so charmingly."

I patted her on the shoulder and went away.

It was impossible to walk anywhere and not buy something. If you refused to buy, eventually they would grin and give it to you. I was given a leather harness suitable for holding six or seven knives, a small copper pot, and a tangle of marbles and wire that I suspected was a failed shiribi puzzle, but was asserted by its giver to be an ingenious device for getting the sand out of spinach in one washing. I gave in finally and bought a linen bag of catmint for Floradazul and a linen hat, without catmint, to keep the sun off my head. It was hot for year's end. I almost bought Etriae a fan of peacock feathers; the merchant in question, thinking I disliked it after trying it out, pressed upon me instead a clip for the hair, also of peacock feathers attached to a band of copper. Perhaps Calla would like it.

I needed somewhere quiet to think. The House of Responsible Life, between the lost children, the allegedly lost children who wouldn't go home, its two lost Serenities, and the necessity of celebrating their death with a party even larger than had been planned for Festival, was in an uproar. My parents' house would be quiet if they had gone to Marigand's as they intended, but not if they had stayed home to scold me. I would not go to the Street of Flowers until I found out in precisely what manner I had come to own it. To have, I thought, suddenly furious, the responsibility of it. A fine example they had set, if they had meant this. A fine example whenever they died; I was supposed to have a cat and nothing else, not an entire brick house full of nooks and crannies and linens and oddments and drains that needed attending to and windowseats for kittens. And five peony trees, I thought gloomily, that were no doubt languishing in the attic this moment.

I went back to the House of Responsible Life, locked the door of Verdialos's room, and began rummaging in his desk. It was not in very good order and, besides containing several unpaid bills and several more that had been paid twice, was graced with a number of peach pits and a mummified mouse. Floradazul had no doubt put it there to begin with, but that it should have been so long undiscovered must still be laid at Verdialos's door.

I found his notes concerning Calla, and nobly forebore to read them. I could not find the ones about me; and he had not taken on anybody else for so long that those writings would all be gathering dust in the archives. I shuffled through the account books again, and found finally a tall black one ruled for figuring that contained six pages of ancient household records, and Verdialos's own journal.

I closed it over my finger and sat frowning at the polished floor. Sometime after that a young man with his hair in three braids knocked on the door and delivered an indignant Floradazul with the remark that she had eaten all the cream off the largest fruit sculpture and then been artistically sick in a whole series of ingenious locations. That was all right, finding them all was giving the children something to do, but did I know where Etriae had kept the stomach potion, because several of the children had gotten sick too in sympathy; and the willow-bark; and the collection of odd mugs and glasses, because there were a great many people here; and where she had hidden the cask of beer she had taken away from him and two of his friends last week? I told him where Etriae kept the medicines and the glassware, and disavowed knowledge of the beer. Then I looked at Floradazul, but she had curled up and gone peacefully to sleep in a corner.

I took my finger out of the journal, sighing. Etriae had meant to give them that beer on Festival Night; but if they wanted it on Beggar's Night instead to help celebrate her death, who was I to thwart them? I went out and downstairs, found the braided boy, told him where the beer was, and returned to Verdialos's room. I supposed it was mine now.

If I did not read the journal, how would I discover what I wanted to know? It was not reasonable to go a hundred miles to Crab Isle to see if Gorodain was still there. It occurred to me that Captain Jemuel would be likely to know such things as whether exiled criminals had escaped and whether anyone had seen them. She might know also how reasonable it would be to think Gorodain might want to kill Verdialos and Etriae. I did not much want to talk to her; probably, in any case, it being Bazaar Day, she would not be working. But I could not read that journal without at least making some other attempt to find out what I wanted to know.

I left Floradazul sleeping and found a footcab. There were if anything more of them about than usual; I supposed the job gave one a good chance to observe the festivities without losing a day's earnings. The owner of this one, a perfectly cheerful young woman, tried to sing that most melancholy of songs, "The Dry Well of Dondar," but kept forgetting verses and starting over. She didn't mind, but I paid her feeling that even if throwing the dice yet again *would* lead me alive out of hell, I didn't want to hear about it.

I went up the steps Floradazul had climbed, and opened the door she had slipped through. The room where she had found Stone and Rusty was empty. I had to wander a little before I found Jemuel's room. I saw nobody else, but she was there behind her desk, making patterns on its paper-strewn surface with an appalling number of empty mugs. It looked as if she had collected them with an eye to washing them and then forgotten about it; but surely Guard captains didn't have to wash their own crockery.

I clapped my hands gently, and she looked up. Her hair needed combing and her eyes sleep. She did not look in the least surprised to see me.

I was surprised, if gratified, to see her. "Are a great many terrible things happening?" I said foolishly.

"I wouldn't say a great many," said Jemuel. "Cheeky's blew up on Divination Day; I can hardly wait to see how many crazies that sets off in the next four years. And your two Green priests went on Procession Day. Aside from that, less than the usual mayhem and more than the usual weirdness." When I said nothing to that, she added, "Are you enjoying your house?"

"I'd rather have Verdialos and Etriae," I said. Jemuel merely looked at me; I added, "I wondered about Gorodain."

"I wondered about him, too," said Jemuel. "He's on Crab Isle."

"Couldn't he have come off it?"

"Not easily," said Jemuel. "But I sent Lieutenant Jassil down there yesterday. They were giving away rides on the train to Saltigos." Her mouth twitched; I wondered what Rusty had had to say about the train. Jemuel said with finality, "Gorodain's on Crab Isle.'' She leaned back in her chair and stretched.

''Couldn't he have left and gone back?''

''Even assuming he would want to,'' said Jemuel, ''no. Lieutenant Jassil spoke to him. He ought to be dead.''

That was what my father and Isobel had thought also, but as an answer to the question I had asked it did not seem satisfactory. ''Do you think I killed them?'' I said.

She sat forward again and moved a few of the mugs back and forth on the desk. ''I wish I'd never asked Dialo for that paper,'' she said. ''Without that, we'd assume this was the way they'd chosen, and roll our eyes, and forget it.''

''But someone would have killed them before they were ready.''

''Do you know how many—'' said Jemuel, and let her breath out, and shook her head at her desktop.

I said, ''And with the paper, what will you assume?''

''Is that the kind of joke he'd play?''

I thought of saying yes, but Verdialos would not have liked it. ''Not exactly,'' I said. ''Too subtle. Now the pig's blood, *that* is the kind of joke he'd play.''

That was the wrong thing to say, and though in fact her expression altered very little, I knew it. Explaining Floradazul to that weary and experienced face was more than I could manage. ''Calla told me,'' I said.

''That's more than she did for me,'' said Jemuel.

I could not tell what she thought; her air toward me shifted according to what I said. She did not look at me at any time as I would look at someone who had killed two people for offering nothing but kindness. But she had probably seen a great deal worse than that. ''If I killed them,'' I said, ''how did I do it?''

''Well, that's the question, isn't it,'' she said.

I went back to the House of Responsible Life and read Verdialos's journal. He had very bad handwriting. Once I had found the dates I wanted, I had no desire to read the rest of it. The problem of Gorodain had occupied his mind almost to the exclusion of anything else; but in the passages I scanned finding the right ones there were a number of things I did not want to know, or wanted very much to know only if Verdialos or Etriae had seen fit to tell me. I had never thought for a moment that Verdialos doubted what he was doing, but here were the tracks of that doubt. It appeared that after a number of years of loving Etriae devotedly and regarding everyone else with the tolerant indifference of a well-fed cat, he had suddenly found himself growing fond of people again. I was one of them. He had loved me; truly he had. I was almost immediately ashamed to be so pleased about this: it had held him back and caused him much distress. But I was pleased just the same.

This account ended in the middle of a sentence; I finally found its other half written upside-down in a book otherwise occupied by gardening notes. Five years ago the tomato-worms had been very bad; the lost children had rebelled at being made to pick them off the tomatoes.

Floradazul woke up halfway through my reading and required to be taken down to the party and made much of. They were lifting their glasses to Verdialos and Etriae as I came in. Somebody handed me a cup, and somebody else gave Floradazul a dainty confection of fish and cucumber. She bolted the fish, ejected the cucumber neatly, and pushed her head into her benefactor's ankle. I drank the entire glass. It was Saltigan wine. I sneezed three times and felt obscurely comforted.

My reading had seemed very promising when I left it, but when I returned it petered out into a series of murky philosophical speculations and rapidly jotted notes that were agitated and evocative, but not informative. If he had been writing a poem for Remembrance Night, it might have made more sense. All I could gather was that although Gorodain had indeed killed all those people, something else had happened also. Gorodain was a magician; the deaths of the six wizards were the culmination of some project stretching back thirty years at least, a project fueled by his adherence to the old Green Church. He had not crept about Liavek at night with a ball of green lightning in his fist or a bottle of green poison in his pocket, as some of the stories said. He had sat in his high room in this very house and done subtle things with sorcery; and just like Verdialos and Etriae, the wizards he killed were dead without a mark on them—and without any pig's blood, either. But if he had killed from a distance by magic, and his luck had been taken from him, then he could not have done what was done to Verdialos and Etriae.

I turned to the most recent pages. "I have sent Calla for the pig's blood," I read. "It will do her good to be in something she cannot meddle with." Although that was just what I would have said of Calla myself, it made me angry to read it. At the bottom of the page was written clearly: "Quard—toyshop near Wizard's Row."

I read it all again, several times; eventually I fell asleep on the floor in a position very uncomfortable to wake up in. I woke up not because I was uncomfortable but because somebody was banging on the door. It was the braided boy, very red about the eyes, with Floradazul; and the Serenity Ressali with a series of apologetic questions. Etriae had kept the records of children recently lost, and they had several downstairs who might need to be identified, asked questions, and probably returned to their parents.

Festival Day

The Serenity Ressali, a thin old woman with skin the color of a much-handled half-copper and short white hair like the burst pod of a milkweed plant, appeared to have had a great deal less sleep than I. This didn't impair her concentration, but it made her testy. I could only be grateful that Etriae's methods of working were considerably tidier than Verdialos's. I found Ressali what she wanted, explained the system so that she would not have to ask me again, and went down to the kitchen for some breakfast. The kitchen looked as if the entire Green Order had drunk itself halfway into the next world right there; the only person present, cooking barley porridge with bacon in it amidst a crowd of dirty pans, was the cook. He was red-eyed, too, but entirely pleasant. I discovered that he expected to sleep until evening, and most of the House with him. I thought this sounded an excellent plan, if I had had a bed to sleep in.

I ate the porridge, secured a jug of very strong black tea, and went back up to Verdialos's room with designs upon the curtains that were never fulfilled. In clearing up the stacks of notebooks I had piled on the floor, I began leafing through them again, in the daze a certain degree of tiredness can cause. And I found that Verdialos kept two journals. The one I had found first was, shall we say, the heart's gloss upon the mind's text; this one just told what had happened.

It was still rather difficult to make out. Why Gorodain had chosen to assassinate those particular six wizards was not clear; Verdialos was more concerned with how he had done it. Perhaps it was just the challenge of the method; that's a philosophy not alien to the new Green Order. Gorodain had killed those wizards, yes; but not with his hands, and not merely through some spell. Through the spell, he had induced somebody else to do it. A toymaker named Quard. And he had meant those six to be the first of many; maybe, though Verdialos seemed to fear more than to know this, the first of all.

On a page by itself Verdialos had written, much more clearly than he usually did, "Quard to Gorodain, 'Death serves no man's wish, nor does it wear one face. Death is particular to all it touches.'" On the next page, he had scribbled, again by itself, "Quard to Jemuel, 'Justice is another thing entirely.'" I hunted about for the first journal and found again a passage that had especially puzzled me. "If it serves no man's wish," Verdialos had scrawled, "then it will serve mine no more than Gorodain's. But if it is indeed particular to all it touches, then might it not serve my particular wish while disdaining any scheme for the world's dissolution? Have all of us in the Green Order indeed been condemned by that we seek, or might our modest plans still meet approval? I suppose time will tell. We strive to choose our deaths; that death might choose or spurn us we have not thought of."

I went back to the mind's journal, and read, "I have quarreled with Etriae for the first time in thirteen years. She will not come with me to talk to Quard. I am afraid to go, not for the obvious reason but because he has so very sharp a tongue. I do not know the latitudes of his choice or the climate of his heart—supposing after all this time it is other than icy. I remind myself that he seemed fond of children. What he would not do for me, or even against Gorodain, he may possibly do for Nerissa. Etriae is not afraid, and therefore she will not come. Matters have been so easy these last years; this is no doubt a salutary lesson in the true difficulties from which we study to extricate ourselves gracefully. I am going tomorrow. I trust he will be—"

And that was the last page of the book. Nothing had been torn out. He must have found some blank pages in some other and continued on. I rummaged for a long time, but found

nothing. I supposed it might be at the house in the Street of
Flowers. I drank the last of the tea and scratched my sleeping
cat between the ears. If Gorodain had made Quard kill six
wizards, could he have made him—no, not without his luck;
I kept forgetting. Besides, Verdialos had thought of going to
see Quard, and had apparently not seen him since they met
over Gorodain's arrest. Nobody had sent Quard anywhere. But
the lack of apparent cause was the same in Verdialos's and
Etriae's deaths as in the wizards'. I opened the heart's journal
again and looked at the end. Quard. A toyshop near Wizard's
Row. As an address, it was about as useless as could be imagined.

Restoration Eve

I went out anyway. It was early evening, a golden one piling
up with blue clouds in the east, and a very sharp wind. I went
back inside and borrowed Etriae's sheepskin jacket, and Floradazul spotted me as I opened the front door and insisted on
coming too. When I bent and tried to push her back inside she
jumped on my shoulder and settled, purring. She was a great
deal heavier in her second life than she had been in her first,
and had fish on her breath. I took her along anyway. Her basket
was at my parents' house, but I remembered we were getting
on for Festival Night, and Liavekans might do anything. A
large and protective cat might be just the thing.

The streets were crammed, the alleys filled to their walls;
even the small pathways and side turnings that Deleon and I
had discovered long ago held clots of people drinking, or dancing, or dicing, or playing music, or having races with black-
beetles, or all at once. Some of them had built bonfires. From
every pillar and balcony blue streamers snapped in the wind
and blue lanterns shot shaky bars of light like moonshine over
the moving faces and the walls of houses. Nobody paid me
any mind. I got to the Street of Scales with no mishap, and
walked along it to Healer's Street. Wizard's Row was not there,
of course; but I trudged up and down all the streets around
where it would be, and found not a single toyshop. I wondered
if Wizard's Row had gotten absentminded and taken some
neighboring buildings with it. I watched the long deep light of

evening turn Bregas Street into something cozy and minute, and thought.

I did not know how Wizard's Row disappeared; I did not know if it took more effort to keep it elsewhere or to make it vanish every time someone undesirable appeared, and then put it back again. If the latter, perhaps I could send Floradazul to find it. I went along to the Lane of Olives and slipped in the side door of the Desert Mouse, bumping my head on its low lintel and wondering if Deleon had ever done so. The players' room was empty. I was missing the play. I sat down at Deleon's table, which had laid ready on it a red hat, a tambourine, and a wreath of firethorn. Then I looked at my cat, who was sniffing Calla's clove water and wrinkling up her whiskers at it. I unfocused my eyes at the wall with its fans and gongs and old cloaks, and thought of the way we had come, and of Wizard's Row where it ought to be, remembering the smell of damp brick and dry grass and pot-boil and beer and camel. Floradazul, much as she had done before, shook herself and dashed out the door. I closed it, and leaned back in my brother's chair, and went with her.

Wizard's Row was there, though I deduced this mostly by a strong and peculiar smell I had never encountered before, but that Floradazul associated with snails and strange cats. She had followed Jehane there once, and been fed snails. I had to let her wander at this point, not knowing what the street with the toyshop might smell of. I considered glue, and sawdust, and paint and cloth. Floradazul trotted around a corner and stopped suddenly, looking upward. Over a shut door in a narrow storefront there hung a dancing puppet. It kicked twice in the wind, which was what had caught her eye; and then stilled absolutely, although the wind still ruffled Floradazul's fur and whirled the dry leaves in the little street. She went on looking at the sign, in case it might jerk again; she twitched her nose, and again there was that most potent and peculiar smell. I wondered if cats could smell magic. I got up in a hurry and followed her.

She greeted me with a happy chirrup, but refused to come any nearer than she was to the shop in question. I raised my hand to knock, and then shrugged and pushed the door open. Nobody was there, so I went in. It was almost dark outside, but there were lamps lit in here.

The store was much larger than it had seemed from the outside, and though a little dusty it did not look neglected. It was full of dolls and wooden blocks and houses and cloth animals and shiribi puzzles and painted miniature things and puppets. Behind the counter sat a life-size puppet, its long arms leaning among a scattering of paint pots, a brush appealingly held in one clever hand. It was finished except for the eyebrows and the hair; with those, indeed, it would be alarmingly lifelike. I thought it would be heavy to maneuver; and what a large theater one would need for a whole group of them. I moved a step farther to see if its pale skin was porcelain or painted wood, and it raised its head and looked at me with eyes as green as olives.

My lungs wanted to gasp and my throat to shriek, but for a mercy all I did was stand there like a threatened rabbit, quivering just a little. It was not a puppet at all, but a person; and yet what was petrifying was that even looking at me and breathing, he still seemed like something living inside a made body, not like a person who cannot get out whether he will or no.

"Master Quard?" I said, not very loudly.

"I'm sorry, the shop is closed," he said. He had a nice voice, but it was all in the way his throat was made, not in the force of who used it or how he felt. "Ersin ais Tairit, down by the docks, sells a very nice line of wooden boats and animal puppets."

"I don't want to buy any toys."

"That's fortunate," he said. After that first appalling moment, he had not looked at me; he was painting the face of a small wooden doll dressed in green, very delicately. "There are far more comfortable places not to buy toys. A good Festival to you."

"Sir, my name is Nerissa Benedicti, and I want—"

He looked up. Other than that, his face did not alter, but his voice did. It was less pleasant but more human. He said, "Verdialos said you were a child."

"He thinks of me as one, I expect."

"Say rather he knows my weaknesses."

"He knows everybody's, sir. But truly, he doesn't count things as ordinary people do."

Quard smiled, neither pleasantly nor cruelly. "No. No, he does not, not now."

"Do you know how they died?"

"You might say so." He had bent his gaze on the toy again.

"Did it hurt them very much?" I said, without in the least wanting to.

"I didn't ask them," said Quard. "Very likely it did. It's in the nature of things."

"What happened to them?"

"They called death," said Quard, "and death came."

"It isn't supposed to be that easy."

"It isn't," said Quard. "Never think so."

"It isn't supposed to be that easy for *them*," I said, very angrily.

"Young lady," Quard said, not as most people use the words, but as if they meant "beloved sister"—and why I of all people should make that of all comparisons I truly don't know. Quard said, in his gentle, unkind voice, "You want to know what it is like. You need simile as others need—what they need. But it is not like anything. There is nothing about it to make grasping it one hair easier." He ran a finger over the bare skin where he should have had eyebrows. He had the intent stare of the nearsighted, but I did not believe there was anything wrong with his vision. The dense green of his eyes made it hard to think.

I swallowed, and said, "Well, how did they die?"

"Somebody else called death too late, and death did not come," said Quard, with no expression at all. "Death, having not a conscience, maybe, but a way of counting, came for these two who called a little too soon."

"How do you know?"

He reached under the counter and took out a folded paper. On it was a large blob of green wax imprinted with a seal, a V and E together. It was whole. Scrawled under the seal in Verdialos's wildest writing were Jemuel's name and title. "This is from Verdialos," Quard said. "I think you had better tell Jemuel where you got it."

I opened my mouth to ask how he knew I was in trouble with Jemuel, and stopped. "He ought to be dead," she had said of Gorodain; not as a judgment for what he had done, but as an explanation of why he could not have left Crab Isle. Gorodain had induced Quard to kill the wizards. Gorodain, some of the stories said, had killed someone who had not remained dead. Wizards, had said Verdialos flatly, cannot bring back the dead; that is for the gods alone, and not all of them. Gorodain had tried to contrive the death of the world, and Quard had said to him, Death is particular to all it touches. I did not know precisely what Gorodain had done, but I knew whom I was talking to. I wondered what ways of counting he had, how the laws of his addition worked. He had taken two for one; for a very great one. Would he take three? I put my hand out for the paper, and did not ask him.

"Thank you," I said.

"We'll meet again," he said. He looked at me and smiled. It was a frightening smile precisely because it was entirely human while his eyes were not. This was the face that death had worn for Etriae and Verdialos. "Not soon," he said, "as time passes. I am young myself, you know, in time. And my heart is not icy."

"Good-bye," I said.

Restoration Day

I had been longer in the shop than seemed reasonable; it was very dark, the sky was sown with stars, and the last hurrah of the fireworks was drowning them momentarily in green and red and yellow and white, when we stepped onto Bregas Street.

I thought of taking the paper to Jemuel, in case she was still brooding in her office; but she would be furious at having had her time wasted. I looked vaguely around for a messenger, but even if I had found a willing one, they were probably all drunk. Jemuel would have to wait until the new year.

They were still celebrating at the House of Responsible Life. Calla was there, only mildly reproachful, with everybody except Deleon and Aelim. She found me some sweet Tichenese wine that did not cause sneezing but in time made for great drowsiness, and Floradazul and I went upstairs and slept under Verdialos's table, with Etriae's jacket for softness.

Floradazul bit my nose rather hard at eight in the morning, and I was very stiff, so I got up. There was a vast silence over the entire House, and a disorder that looked like the aftermath of a hurricane. I righted two chairs and carried an armful of pewter goblets out to the kitchen, noticing that although everything had been brought out from the cupboards and nothing whatsoever put away, very little was actually broken. I picked up a broom in the kitchen, brought it out to the entry room, where people had been spilling sugar, and stopped. I leaned the broom against the wall, and creaked outside, and heard only a lark high up in the cold sky. Floradazul was complaining in a mild way about breakfast.

She complained a great deal more before we got to the Street of Flowers. We met nobody, not a City Guard, not a stray cat. Etriae and Verdialos's house stood like a column of stone in a field of blooming trees. I rather liked the effect. I pushed open the green bronze gate in the brick wall and stood looking at the front garden. Etriae had planted whitegrass, which keeps its shape all winter and looks like a ghost grass; and firethorn, which holds its leaves and berries through the cold; and juniper, which is exactly the same dusty green all the time. The grass was still green, and the patch of mint was making one last attempt to bloom. Another frost would stop all that. I went up the walk, trailed by a very loud cat.

One of the six square panes of glass in the window to the right of the door was broken; the bits must be on the floor inside. Somebody had left a stack of coppers on the brick sill. It is entirely possible that Liavekans are the only people in the world who behave better on their holidays than at other times. Or perhaps Verdialos and Etriae just had good neighbors.

I opened the door and went in. Etriae used lemon oil for cleaning; I could smell that, and drying herbs, and, when I put my head into the kitchen, a lingering aroma of kaf. I went back to the front room, looking for what had broken the window. Floradazul darted under a hammock chair and sent a red wooden ball rolling across the floor. I left her rattling it madly about the room and climbed the stairs, past the snowflake window in improbable purple on the first landing, and the room Verdialos and Etriae had slept in, on up to the little rooms under the roof with their slanting ceilings. The rest of the house had been cold, but up here the sun was coming in the back windows.

There were two peony trees in terracotta pots in one room, and three in the other. It looked as if somebody had stuck a number of interestingly shaped sticks into the dirt, like children playing at gardening. But rosebushes are just the same. When

you water them they burst out in leaves. I pushed a finger into
the soil of the nearest pot. Yes, Etriae had been watering them,
and trusting that she would be able to put them outside before
they outgrew their pots. I hoped Wind would be a mild month
this year.

I sat on the floor. If I watered those peony trees, I would
be lost. I was still very angry with Verdialos and Etriae. They
had in fact killed themselves; they had left me quite deliberately, in such a way that I must run about Liavek seeking how.
They had made a joke meant to be seen through. And still I
could think of no other reason than that they thought I would
be better out of my parents' house. That was rank folly. They
had been happy, I thought; they had work they liked and friends:
they could have waited. They ought to have waited until I
solved my problems myself; I'd have gotten around to it. I
needed them to provide, not a roof over my head, but a shelter
for my spirit.

And that, I thought, had been a responsibility. What business
had they abandoning it? They had shunted off on me their
house, their work, their abominable peony trees. I stood up.
And, of course, myself. Oh, they were so clever; it was as
good as a poem. But I was still angry. If I were leaning on
them too heavily, surely there was some less final way of
disentangling themselves?

I leaned on the wainscoting and watched the new sun shine
on Liavek, striking a remote glint on the Levar's Palace and
gilding Old Town like one of the little houses in Quard's shop.
The tiled roofs of the neighborhood curved along like some
strange red sea. They wanted to die, I thought. Despite any of
this, truly they did. So when the moment seemed right to them
in any case, they changed their plan and they did it. With a
great deal of care, planning, and perfect good cheer. Still, why
change the plan and cause a scandal for the House of Responsible Life? I thought of Calla, who had been made not to
meddle; of the Serenities, who worried perhaps too much about
what Liavek thought of them; of myself, who, confronted with
Verdialos and Etriae dead as they had first planned, in some
abandon of pleasure, might have thought them no different
from Lerre ola Advar. I thought that there were probably others
in the House who might have needed some shock or some
adjustment. I thought very briefly of Death, whose heart was

not icy. But I was still, faintly, angry with them. And I thought, suddenly, if I were to kill myself, who would be angry with me? Deleon, Calla, Jehane, perhaps Aelim, certainly Livia. Not so many in the usual manner of counting, but a multitude in another.

And my parents. It would be a poor return, even for Mama and Papa. They would never understand, as long ago Deleon and I had dreamed of making them, all their own weakness and folly and blindness that had made us think dying a fitting revenge. They would think it my own weakness, my own folly, my own blindness. And it would be. I did not want to make anybody feel as Etriae and Verdialos, killing themselves, had made me; not even my parents.

The House of Responsible Life has always dissuaded more suicide than it has encouraged. Usually the process takes less time, and proceeds nimbly in a round of classes explaining in lovely detail the horrors of this or that death. Anybody who stays that course is welcome to devise his own. But Verdialos, sparing me that round, nevertheless made his own death, if less ugly than a natural one might be, still far uglier than anything I had managed to imagine. He used other signposts, and took me the longest way round that is, they say in Acrivain, the shortest way home.

When I went downstairs to get the water for the peonies, I took the red ball away from Floradazul and set it on the low wall by the gate, in case it might belong to one of my neighbors who would want it back.

Bazaar Day: Ballad

by John M. Ford

A fat brocaded merchant sang the praises of his
  merchandise
His audience a soldier and a beggar bent and gray
The beggar no more drew his eyes than common rats or
  summer flies
His mind was on the man in steel, and on his monthly pay

"I'll sell you guns and powder and I'll sell you pikes and
  shining swords
And drink to blunt your senses to the daily thrust and cut
I'll dress you up in bronze and cords, and finally in six pine
  boards
And then sell you the hammers for to nail your coffins
  shut."

The soldier smiled and reached into his purse, and then the
  beggar said
"Do you recall this hammer that you sometime sold to
  me?"
The soldier frowned and turned his head, and signed against
  the Eye, and fled
The merchant's eyes turned evil then, quite terrible to see

"Why should I know your hammer? Is there reason that I
  ought to do?

Or do you mean to tell me?'' and his voice turned very
    hard:
''That you're a thief I know is true, perhaps you've other
    talents too
So if your story's good enough, I might not call the
    guard.''

The beggar said, ''I soldiered once, a green recruit from up
    the hills,
My company supplied from you when first we mustered in
It's not the shine on swords that kills, it's steel that pays
    the butchers' bills,
I learned that proof the hard way, from your worthless
    piece of tin.

''It might have been on mountainsides, it might have been
    in meadows gay
It might have been in forests or upon a hill of slag
It might have been by night or day, it doesn't matter
    anyway
The murky morning after no one rallied to the flag.

''Alone against one final foe, my situation mighty tough
I had to strike, and hot, or I should nevermore be free
Your other goods were shoddy stuff; your hammer it was
    good enough
To kill the man who tried so hard to do the same to me.''

The merchant said, ''My sorry friend, now even if your
    story's true
You cannot have a reason to be angry, sir, with me
Let credit fall where credit's due; you're here because I
    dealt with you:
I think you got your money's worth: how can you
    disagree?''

The crooked little beggar turned the shining hammer in his
    hand
Said, ''Let me end my story, then you tell me what it's
    worth:

I think you still don't understand: I said I killed the bloody
    man,
I never said I fought him anywhere upon the earth.''

And now the twisted beggarman looked bigger than these
    words can tell
With thunder in his bootheels and the lightning in his eye
"You never gave a spit in hell for anything you couldn't
    sell,
But I've come up from underground with something you
    can't buy!''

He struck the hammer on the stone; it made the cobbles
    quake and ring
The merchant started pleading and the wind began to wail
The air began to crack and sing as tents and poles and
    everything
Came down like so much paper in the fury of a gale

There's darkness on the Merchant's Row and stillness in the
    great bazaars
An emptiness in doorways and a silence in the stalls
The merchant and the man of wars are gone into the
    summer stars
They're gone into the thunder when the final hammer falls

The True Tale of Count Dashif's Demise

by Jane Yolen

THERE ARE MANY stories told about the death of Count Dashif but none, my lords and ladies, is worth a copper coin. They are fabrications, obfuscations, taradiddles, and lies; all tales spun out by wretched tellers for pitiful profits and nebulous rewards.

There is but one true history, built fact upon fact, which has been told down through the years in my family, father to son, father to son over and over. It has been polished by our tongues until it shines like a ripened olive, like a water-smoothed stone, like the jewel in the Levar's best crown. We have kept that truth alive by this process of mouth-to-ear resuscitation and with but a little bit of encouragement, my Excellencies, I shall pass it on to you this Beggar's Night.

Encouragement comes in many forms, and not all of them are hard, round, and golden. But I will not begrudge you the payment of even such a small coin.

The Count Dashif was neither the blood-soaked murderer nor the magic-forsaken princeling you have heard of in other tales. He was a man—not a mad god. He had his magic, more hidden than even he knew. And he had his long list of hates. What he did not have were his right hand, his left leg, and his right ear. But it was his nose, my Elegancies, that finally did him in. That nose—and another part of his anatomy that modesty—and an empty pocket—forbids me to mention.

But a coin can loosen even the tightest of tongues, as long as we are on the subject of anatomy.

Tori was the count's name, though no one alive dared use it. It was the small form of Toriff, but believe me, there was nothing, my Magnificencies, small about him. Of this I have ample testimony from shop girls and street girls, and the published diaries of Countess Neelya, plus the whispered confidences of a small, dark-haired thief.

Still, the tale I would tell is not a bawdy barracks round; nor is it of the count's greatness of manhood. It is about the shortness of his years, for he died at the moment he most wished to live. And it was all on account of his nose, my Graces. And that *other* piece of his anatomy.

Dashif had a daughter, a girl of no great beauty except in her bedazzled father's eyes. And another daughter and a son who were uncommonly pretty but of no importance to this tale.

The girl of whom we speak had been raised in a tosspot inn and had eyes the color of certain blue flowers that grow only by the side of roads and wastes. Her mind had sharp angles. Her tongue was like a knife. In other words, my Graciousnesses, she was a child of her father, and the more beloved thereby. She was, in fact, the only person in the world he cherished, and he was determined to polish his gem to a high gloss; though like a miser with his treasure, he kept her hidden from the light.

So, rather than presenting the girl at court and acknowledging her as his daughter, Dashif let the world think she was just another of his flirtations. And she was rude enough to enjoy the speculations.

The girl was named Kaloo, which, as you know, my Graciousnesses, is the name of the honey bear, the one that chortles as it digs into a hive. She was like honey to the count. He could not keep away.

He came to the inn to collect her on a Beggar's Night like this to find—of course—that her stepfather who owned the inn was playing at dishboy and the dishboy (as was the wont along the waterfronts) was innkeeper for the evening. The boy was a handsome lad, though a bit thin in both hair and what lay beneath. Taking his night's role too seriously, he was attempting to enjoy Kaloo's favors. She, while not adverse to a kiss or two in a dark corner, was resisting his bolder thrusts.

The boy was just leaning his nose into Kaloo's cleavage, newly revealed by one of the elegant dresses her father had purchased for her, when Count Dashif strode into the inn. He roared once, which was all the warning he ever gave his enemies, and pulled out two pistols from his waistband. Though the Count could not fire yet for fear of hitting his daughter, the roar itself was sufficient to undo the dishboy. Losing his courage and his bowels at more or less the same moment, the boy raised his face and tried to flee.

It was a mistake. Once absent from Kaloo's side, he presented a remarkable target. The Count fired at the two places he felt had so recently attempted to violate his precious child. One of them was the boy's nose.

The Count almost always hit what he aimed at. However, since the two targets this time were at opposite ends of the boy's anatomy—that word coming up rather often in this narrative, as such worthies as yourselves will have already noted—he hit only the boy's nose, smashing it beyond the skill of any leeches in Liavek. The other bullet sailed between the boy's legs and buried itself in the hearth.

Then Dashif took his daughter by the arm, dragging her away to the House of Seven Pleasures where the latest play by May Gan B'russtt was to be performed. Dashif and his daughter, being of similar natures, enjoyed the play enormously, forgetting the bit of bloodletting that had preceded it.

Now the boy, my Exultancies, had not forgot. Indeed, he was not able. Though the leeches had cleaned him up and sewn him up, they had only been able to fashion for him a nose out of a silver spoon boiled down and crudely reshaped. It looked like the topmost peak of the Silverspine Mountains, with a sprinkling of little points like dead trees.

He was ruined forever. The silver nose picked up the heat of the kitchen and held it, so he could no longer work there. And, as for his manhood, though it had not been physically injured, the shock to his desires precluded any pleasure whatsoever. He was unable or, as they say in Ka Zhir: *Though he lost not the pen, the verses were gone.* A remarkably graphic people, the Zhir.

What was he to do? He had lost his means of livelihood, for being a dishboy was all he knew. His silver nose marked him.

And all desires but one had fled. He would have done himself
in had he the passion for it. But his one passion was this: to
kill the Count.

He knew he could not himself call Dashif out. His training
was in pots, not pistols. He thought and thought all that day
and decided that the only thing to do was to hire a wizard,
though he had no coins with which to pay.

He walked slowly to Wizard's Row and knocked on the very
first door he saw. It was the *only* door he saw, for all the
wizards, save a Tichenese spellmaker named Frost, were off
enjoying Festival Day. And of course, when wizards are not
at home, their homes are not . . . er, at home.

"Come in," the door intoned.

Unnerved, the boy leaped back. Then, taking his courage in
hand, he knocked again.

"Enough with the knocking already," the door said, its
accents shifting drastically. "Would you like me to knock on
you over and over?"

"No, not really," the boy said, "since I am not a door."

"Well, I am not a door either," said the door as it creaked
open. "I am ajar!" It began to laugh uproariously. "Get it?
A *door—ajar?*" Its laugh tapered off to a giggle.

Adjusting his nose, which had fallen to one side, and refusing
to be drawn further into a conversation that consisted of old
jokes, the boy walked in.

The Tichenese wizard's house consisted of one long hall.
There were many doors off it and they were all opening and
shutting with a fluttering movement that the boy realized was
faint laughter. He could see no rooms beyond them, just brick
walls. It was, though he did not know it, the cheapest kind of
housing on Wizard's Row. Frost could afford no better. He
was not a mighty wizard, nor was he likely to become one,
but then my Supremacies, what Tichenese can?

"May . . . I . . . help . . . you?" came a sepulchral voice.

"Get it?" the front door cried out again and the fluttering
laughter from the other doors flamed up for a moment before
lapsing into silence.

"May I help you?" This time the voice was normal.

The boy turned toward the sound and there was Frost. Typical
of his race, he was dark as oak bark with hair just as rough.
The boy had seen many such in the inn.

"Are you the magician?" he asked, his voice squeaking on the final syllable like a Tichenese woman in labor.

"We prefer the term *wizard*."

"Are you the wizard?"

"I am."

"*A-jarrrrrrrr*," tried the door one last time.

The wizard waved his hand dismissingly and the door slammed shut. "And what do you want of me?"

"I wish to kill a certain count."

Now if the wizard had not been Tichenese and new to the Row, he would have known at once that there was but one count worth killing. And that one count to be avoided at all costs. But he was, my Preeminencies, very new. And very Tichenese, which is to say he reveled more in what he did not know than in what he did.

"That should not be so difficult. How will you pay me?"

The boy had been pondering that very question all the way to Wizard's Row, scratching up under the silver nose where scabs and stitches itched in equal measure. It was as he walked, between one itch and the next, that he had realized the extent of his wealth and determined that should his plan succeed, he would work hard never to be poor again.

"I will give you this silver nose," he said. "And I will also give you my good right arm for a year."

"What earthly use have I for a severed arm?" puzzled the wizard out loud. The Tichenese are quite literal. He must have been a sore burden to his door.

"I mean, sir, that I will work for you for a year."

"I have a door already," said Frost. "But . . ." He reached out toward the boy's face. "The silver nose intrigues me. Were you born that way?"

The hall doors fluttered briefly.

"When is a nose not a nose?" asked the front door. When no one answered, it shouted, "When it comes to the bill!"

The wizard made a sour face and waved his hand. The door turned into a curtain and blew about in a desultory wind.

"Not born with it," replied the boy. "That was the Count's doing."

So they struck a bargain and the boy went back noseless to the inn where, at the wizard's instructions, he carefully dug the bullet out of the hearth. Frost *did* know about correspon-

dences and attractions, for those, as you know, my Ascenden-
cies, are the very first lessons any real wizard learns.

The boy also talked his way back into the innkeeper's good
graces by the simple expedient of groveling. And having his
wages cut in half. And though the hole in his face was grotesque
(he tried fashioning a nose out of a different substance daily),
it was no more grotesque than some of the inn's regular customers. One-eyed Jok, for example, or Half-an-ear Emma, or
the redoubtable Wil of the Quarter Leg.

So there they all were, three days after Restoration Eve, the
inn fairly empty and the innkeeper asleep in a chair by the
hearth. The dishboy, his nose this day fashioned out of the stub
of a cheroot that had the added attraction of smoking gently as
he worked, cleaned the pots and pans. Kaloo, back in her
ordinary inn clothes, polished the silver, one spoon short.

The door was summarily flung open and in stomped Dashif.
"Kaloo," he chortled in his joy, "I have good news."

He was immaculate in a white ruffled shirt that smelled of
sweet closet herbs. His trews were of wine-colored velvet. His
doublet matched the trews, though threaded through with gold.
As ever, his brace of pistols were snugged into the waistband
of his trousers and there was—though none but Kaloo knew
of it—a finely honed knife down in his right boot. It made
walking the more difficult thereby, but he was never without
that particular blade.

It was, my Extremities, the moment of truth.

Realizing who had come in, the dishboy picked up a certain
bottle that contained the bullet he had dug from the hearth, and
walked out of the kitchen. He held the bottle before him like
a gun.

Dashif, who had recently given up the weed, smelled the
smoldering cheroot and turned to take a deep draught of it with
his own quivering nose.

It was his first and his final mistake.

The charmed bullet burst out of the bottle and sped toward
the place where it had last been lodged—Dashif's left pistol.
Said pistol was snugged, as I have said, in the waistband of
his pants.

Ah, my Benevolencies, your imaginations leap before my
simple tale. I am sure you have guessed the start of it. But
not, I warrant, its ending.

The bullet tore through that part of the Count's anatomy of which I have been too modest but to allude before settling itself in the barrel of his gun.

In agony, Dashif pulled out both pistols and fired off a round each.

He hit the dishboy's cheroot with one shot, with the other spread the boy's legs. Kaloo caught first her father, then her erstwhile lover, and lay them each before the hearth. Then she ran for the local leech.

The dishboy did not die, though the Count did. Not of the wound, which was famous but not fatal. Many jokes were told of it, and not a few by the wizard's door. No, Dashif died of mortification after the Zhir wrote of him in their broadsides, one of which found its way into his hands:

> The Count counts not on gun or pen,
> Who once counted great among mortal men.

Kaloo inherited both the inn and a large portion of the Count's estates, which was the good news Dashif had been bringing her. She immediately married the dishboy, for though she had only found him handsome before, without his nose she found him exciting. She made him remove his prosthesis when they made love, hanging it from a special nail above their bed.

As for the Tichenese wizard, my Tremendousies, he wore the silver nose at the costume party he gave every Beggar's Night from then on. But he never—no never—learned to laugh at the jokes of his door.

Festival Day: Catechism

by John M. Ford

Ninepins that thunder when bowling them down,
Eight horses driving the nobles to town,
Seven-starred oaths and a feeble excuse,
Six-spotted dice always rolling a deuce,
Five-finger exercise hitching your pants,
Four-footed clumsiness trying to dance,
Three shots of rum and a headful of foam,
Two City Guards come to usher you home,
One resolution no more to get tight—
Count off the hours of Festival Night.

Six Days Outside the Year

by Will Shetterly

Divination Day

IN THE MIDDLE of a cool and sunny morning, on a palace balcony high above the noise and bustle of the harbor of Ka Zhir, Prince Jeng spooned iced cream with hazelnuts from a yellow porcelain bowl. "How is my father?"

"He woke with a toothache a few minutes after midnight." The old slave's wrists were enclosed in gold manacles to display his position and his worth. A hand's length of iron chain dangled freely from each manacle to show that Advisor L'Vos could be bound again. "The dentist removed the tooth."

Jeng clicked his tongue against the roof of his mouth before taking another bite of the sweet cream. "Though his pain ends, his bite is weakened. A good sign on Divination Day, or a bad?"

L'Vos shrugged. "He says he is an enlightened despot. To believe that the events of one day may shape the course of the next four years is foolish."

"My father and I are remarkably alike." Jeng's voice changed subtly. "Does he suspect?"

"The King always suspects. His recent illness only reduces his ability to act on his suspicions."

"And he still favors my cousin."

"Your cousin ended the island revolts—"

Jeng grunted and waved his hand for silence. The grunt must have sufficed; the Prince remembered too late that while Advisor L'Vos's vision encompassed the future of nations, his eyes had been replaced with black marbles after an attempt to escape.

Jeng turned away from the sightless gaze. Far below, sailors and slaves and officers and overseers worked within view of the palace of King Thelm of Ka Zhir, every Zhir's overlord. A steam-driven cart rolled along one pier, bringing bags of coffee and sugar to a freeladen ship that flew Liavek's blue pennant from its highest mast. "Twenty-three years of peace," Jeng said, not caring whether L'Vos understood what that meant to him. Twenty-three years since Liavek's navy had destroyed Ka Zhir's at the Battle of Gold Harbor. "My cousin would reinforce our friendship with Liavek. More fool he."

Jeng licked his spoon clean, tasting sweet cream and cold silver, and turned back to L'Vos. "What does the King think I'm doing?"

"What you wished. The wood is for a summer house. A careless messenger allowed a letter with architectural plans to be seen by a spy; I've been assured that the house would be beautiful, should you decide to build it. The cloth is for tents to be erected there, for a festival when you surprise the King with the gift of the house. Your Thunder Fist Marines have been brought inland for training on unfamiliar ground, and will display their new skills to His Majesty in the spring, undoubtedly when you give him the palace."

"And the water-gas manufactory?"

"I think he thinks your magicians seek to build a new sort of bomb, and your hired Tichenese have come to work with them."

Jeng laughed, and placed another spoonful of iced cream on his tongue. The dessert was very good; he would try it with mango this evening. The dockworkers scurried below. Could they suspect that Ka Zhir's harbor would, within a few years, no longer be the only mouth of a hungry nation, that the eldest surviving son of King Thelm had begun to wrest the nation's dependence from the untrustworthy clutch of the sea?

Jeng turned from the palace window. "The King thinks these are all parts of a gift from a loyal son."

"Yes, Prince Jeng."

"But he believes that the loyal son is preparing a revolution."

"Suspects. None of your plans occur near the sea. You cannot hold the capital without the navy, and the navy is loyal. He sees the beginnings of a pattern and waits to know its final shape." The old man paused, then added calmly, "His assassins wait, too."

"If I feared the Black Cord, I would not be worthy of my father. How do the tests go?"

"Very well. If the winds permit—"

"The winds will permit. Haven't my magicians ensured that the winds will permit?"

"Of course."

"Good." Prince Jeng's thoughts were no longer on his plans, for there was nothing more for him to do. His part had ended when he ordered it begun. His people would succeed, and he would be his father's favorite by the end of Grand Festival Week. Perhaps three bites of the cream and nuts remained. He could taste each, thick and cool and sweet in his mouth. "Hold out your hands."

The iron chains rattled as L'Vos obeyed. Jeng set the porcelain bowl into the slave's palms. "Eat." The Prince's voice held no hint of his smile as L'Vos fumbled for the spoon, then brought a dollop of cream and hazelnuts into his mouth.

"It's good," L'Vos said, with no more feeling than the Prince.

Jeng laughed. "My dessert," he announced, rewarding L'Vos with the knowledge that he had not been poisoned. "You may finish it."

"Thank you."

Jeng looked up at the King's balcony. "What will my father think," he asked, "when I give him Liavek?"

Across the Sea of Luck in the Canal District of the city of Liavek, beside the steps to a gray windowless brick building, a single blue flower of Worrynot grew in a small terracotta pot. The presence of the contraceptive plant was the only suggestion of the nature of the business practiced behind the bland face of the house named Discretion.

A young man with plain brass bracelets on each wrist drew

the bell chain. After a moment, the door opened, admitting him from a cool and sunny street that smelled of fish and salt and hickory smoke and a distant baker's fresh bread, into a warm and dark greeting room that smelled of frankincense smoke and jasmine perfume. A slender woman in black silk trousers and blouse touched one finger to her forehead in a mockingly affectionate greeting. "I would not have expected you today, Master Magician."

He did not know if she knew his name; he had not cared to learn hers. She always addressed him with the same amusement, as though they knew each other's weaknesses. Perhaps they did: she served Discretion, and he visited it.

"Oh?" he said. "No one spends Divination Day here, hoping twenty-four hours will guarantee four years of pleasure?"

The woman laughed, the sounds of her amusement surprisingly husky from her narrow chest. "Not one. The superstitious fear a day within these walls will ensure that the next four years' pleasures all bear an exorbitant price." She indicated a door carved with scenes of the Kil making love and war beneath the sea, which led to a spacious sitting room with thick carpets and low couches. "Are you superstitious, Master Magician?"

"I do not need to be."

She raised an eyebrow. He had not meant to brag, and he did not care to think about what he had truly meant. "Aychiar," he requested.

"No one is expected to be available today." The woman, opening a low rosewood cabinet to reveal cloudy bottles filled with liquids and powders, reached for an amber Hrothvekan wine that he had drunk on his last visit to the house.

He shook his head. "Aychiar is here?"

"I could see." She stepped toward the hall.

"I would appreciate it." When the woman glanced over her shoulder, he set a stack of gold ten-levar pieces on a delicate mahogany tea table.

He could not tell if she counted the coins in that glance, but her smile became, if anything, more cruel or, perhaps, more pitying. "I suspect he is in," she said. "Will you wait in the sea room?"

"Of course." He knew the way and went, wondering only if she had left him alone as an act of trust or of kindness, or if the House was so very shorthanded on the first day of Grand Festival Week.

The sea room was painted in pale blues and aquamarines. The beams of the ceiling were bare cypress, and the floor had been sprinkled with white sand. Two oil lamps burned in niches carved into either wall. The oil smelled of cinnamon. The bed was a thick mattress covered with sheets the color of hyacinths or bruises.

He waited for several minutes, standing motionless in the center of the room, telling himself to leave the House and making no effort to do so. When the door opened, a bare-chested youth in loose blue trousers entered. The boy's expression might have been boredom, or he might have just woken. His hair was a mat of black braids; his skin was as pale as a Farlander's or a dead man's. A pack of tattooed cats raced up his left arm and around his thin shoulders. "You," he said. It might have been the boy's usual greeting, and not a sign of recognition.

The man opened his robe, letting it fall. He kicked it aside with a sandaled foot. Then he kicked off the sandals and waited, wearing nothing but a black silk loincloth.

"What this time?" the boy said.

The man could not make himself answer. Far away, in another room or in another world, someone plucked lazily at a cittern, spilling notes at the farthest edge of the man's hearing.

The boy demanded, "What?"

The man lifted his chin, a tiny beckoning gesture.

The boy, smiling, reached into a fold of his baggy trousers and withdrew a black pearl-handled flick-knife banded in burnished steel. When his wrist twitched, the knife opened as quietly as a book, its blade the length of a human hand. The boy crouched, the flick-knife low before him, his body twisted away in a fighter's stance, and smiled again and stood erect.

The man nodded.

The tip of the knife cut an inch into the man's left shoulder and separated skin and muscle in a diagonal line from his collarbone to a point near his navel. In spite of his resolve, the man grunted. He and the boy looked at the wound, watching flesh part like butchered meat. Naked bone glistened for the instant before blood filled the cut.

The distant cittern played the first seven notes of "Rag Woman's Luck," then repeated them.

"I wouldn't do this on Divination Day," the boy said.

"The advice is a little late."

The boy shrugged.

"We earn our luck," the man answered, thinking the words sounded true and not sure what he meant by them.

The boy nodded and lifted the knife. "How much?"

"Until I fall and cannot stand."

The knife leaped out, a kiss that traveled from the man's right cheek to his chin, slicing the corner of his lips in its passing. "And then?"

The man tasted his blood. Speaking heightened the pain, so he enunciated extravagantly. He tapped the skin above his heart. "Kill me."

The cittern notes raced each other, a mountain folk reel played for unseen, insane dancers.

Birth Day

Rangzha Fon did not enjoy intrigue. He enjoyed comfort, and he enjoyed wealth (for that was the best way to ensure continued comfort as a citizen of Ka Zhir). He enjoyed living in lands far from King Thelm's court (for that was the best way to ensure continued wealth as a citizen of Ka Zhir). If Rangzha Fon's idea of comfort had not included the amenities of a prosperous city, he would have sought a post as an ambassador to a trading town like Gold Harbor, where Zhir diplomacy was a matter of blatant threats and more blatant bribes, or to the inland matriarchy of Ombaya, where Zhir diplomacy was politely ignored. But Rangzha Fon's idea of comfort included fine restaurants, fine theaters, fine magicians, and fine courtesans, so he had come as the Zhir ambassador to Liavek in the hope that its uneasy peace with Ka Zhir would endure.

The presence of the slender woman standing before his desk assured him that it would not.

"You recognize this." On her thumb was a ring with an ebony stone inlaid with a white bird of prey.

He nodded; that was all she expected, so he would give her as much. This philosophy had served Rangzha Fon for the forty-seven years of his life. Through his office window came a beautiful Liavekan song about fate and the aroma of a street vendor's roasting almonds, beckoning Rangzha Fon to loiter outside on the curb where he could hum off-key while sharing nuts with the embassy guards and the passersby.

Rangzha Fon rested a hand on his belly, sighed inaudibly, and gestured toward several thin cotton cushions. "Please. Be seated."

"My name is Djanhiz ola Vikili. You do not know me?" The woman crossed her legs and sat gracefully. She was very dark and very tall; though he had three cushions and she, two, she remained taller than he. Her hair was a cap of tight gray coils cut close to her skull, and her face bore a light tracing of weather or age. If she was a magician, she was not vain in the ways he understood.

"No," Rangzha Fon replied. In Liavek, Djanhiz was conspicuous for her height and for her skin's hue; since she could hide neither, she used them in her disguise. Travelers from many nations came to trade and study and live in the City of Luck. During his twenty years here, Rangzha Fon had been visited by his short, swarthy, and rather sullen Zhir countrymen in their bleached cotton tunics and trousers, by very dark and excessively courteous Tichenese in long brocaded robes of sea-green or saffron or indigo silk, and even by ghost-white, round-eyed Farlanders in high-collared wool jackets and heavy boots. He had never been visited by any of the tall, ebony-skinned women of Ombaya, but he had seen them striding through Liavek's streets in their hooded linen tunics and tight trousers. In her green-and-gold tunic and her tan trousers, Djanhiz would pass as a comparatively short and pale Ombayan, a people who had never been Liavek's enemy, and never be recognized as a tall and dark Tichenese, a people who had never been Liavek's friends.

When she smiled at him, he added, "You wear the Ombayan clothing like a native, but not the accent." He kept his tone courteous. Djanhiz frowned, and her glance carried a new weight of respect or suspicion. "Speak with more sibilance," he suggested. "Perhaps a lisp—"

"Thank you."

Her voice said he had gone too far, so he nodded and waited, wondering why a Tichenese woman in Ombayan clothes came to Liavek with the ring of Prince Jeng of Ka Zhir.

Djanhiz looked around the pleasant clutter of his office, the shelves of books that filled one wall and the collection of masks from many cultures that covered another. "I need your help."

He could not deny her, whatever she asked, but he was grateful that she had not ordered him. "I am your slave," he answered in Zhir.

She lifted an eyebrow and said in Tichenese, "We are the hands, another is the mind."

"What does my prince require?"

"We must capture The Magician of Liavek before Festival Night."

Rangzha Fon kept his smile while he nodded. The muscles of his stomach tightened to check his fear in case the woman was making a joke. The muscles of his face tightened to check his amusement in case she was not. "The Magician's house is on Wizard's Row," Rangzha Fon said gently. "And Wizard's Row is never to be found during holidays. If we did find it, the house is guarded—"

The dark woman shook her head once. "I have encountered The Magician before. That is why your prince accepted my aid in this matter."

"Ah." And why you offered it, Rangzha Fon thought. Her expression disconcerted him, and he glanced at the wall of masks. The painted leather Casoe god of sandstorms and murder watched the world with the same mad serenity.

Djanhiz reached across his desk to center his letter opener, a knife of chipped jade, on top of an unfinished report to King Thelm. "Fortunately, we do not need to find The Magician. We only need to find one of his friends."

"What use is magic?" a woman asked, and The Magician stopped to listen. The speaker, small and boyishly slim in multicolored cotton trousers and a maroon silk shirt, stood with legs wide and arms akimbo on a boulder in the Levar's Park. Her head, shaven as clean as a ship's captain's, reflected the afternoon sun. A small crowd of people eddied at her feet, waiting to see what entertainment she offered.

"What will magic profit you?" she called, and The Magician smiled, knowing she knew her audience.

"Who would hire a magician?" The bald woman grinned

and shook her head. "Only the very wealthy. Only those who need a service that will last no more than a few hours or a few days. Certainly not those who need a service that will last a year or more."

He knew too well the limits of his trade. The intricate rhythms of many drummers came from a crowded open-air restaurant, accompanied by the laughter of dancers and the smells of cinnamon Festival cakes and spiced apple wine. The Magician began to walk on.

"Who would become a wizard?" the bald woman asked. Again she paused, and so did he, telling himself that he stopped to watch a fleet of toy sailboats racing across the Children's Lake.

"Spend years studying magic when you might be studying life? Knowing you're as likely to die as to live when you finally try to invest your birth luck in some object to become a magician?"

On the little lake, a schooner as large as a swan took the lead. On the far shore, a small girl jumped and cheered. On the near shore, a red-bearded man waded knee-deep in the water, awaiting the schooner's arrival. Most of the toy ships had sails or pennants of rich Liavekan blue, but a sloop bearing the yellow of Tichen closely followed the schooner, and a Zhir warship raced aft and starboard of the Tichenese sloop, so close together that they threatened to collide.

"You must love power much and life little, to risk everything to become a magician."

The Magician glanced back at the speaker. He wanted to ask her what she knew of life and power, but he did not care to call attention to himself today. He touched his left hand to the bracelet on his right wrist, and felt his birth luck throbbing there, ready for any use he might find for it.

If he could find a use for it, he would not be wandering the Levar's Park in search of entertainment.

The red-bearded man who cheered the schooner seemed familiar. The Magician imagined him with a shaven chin and wearing a blue sash over his gray tunic, and recognized Lieutenant Lian Jassil of the Levar's Guard. Did that mean the girl—He glanced back at her. Sessi Jassil had grown a head taller since she and her brother came to 17 Wizard's Row, and her dark hair had been cut short. People changed so quickly when they remained in the world.

"But you do not need magic!" the bald woman cried. "You do not need magicians! With every year, we learn to harness the natural forces of the world—" The race had attracted several of her listeners, so she pointed it out to the rest. "Like those boats, powered by the wind. Like the trains of the Levar's railway, powered by steam. Like the airships that will soon ply Liavek's skies, lifted by great bags of water-gas and powered by small engines—"

"It's Featherlake's Folly again!" someone yelled from the audience.

"The engines are new, and lighter—" the bald woman replied. The Magician saw where her speech was going, and saw also that she had lost the crowd's interest. The Margrave of Featherlake had built an airship twenty years earlier. It had risen from a field outside the city walls like a newborn calf struggling to its feet, then sagged and burst into flame. Some said the fault had been the engines, some said the design, some blamed poor construction, others claimed the magicians had acted to keep their monopoly on the air.

"Adding a big balloon to the Festival fireworks?" someone else yelled.

"Wait!" the bald woman said. "Soon you'll see the Luck of Liavek fly over this park!"

"Fly to pieces!" another heckler called.

The bald woman shook her head. "The Tichenese have designed an airship that will carry one hundred people or more. Will Liavek be kept to the seas while Tichen rules the sky?"

A new boat, modeled after the Farlanders' razored galleons, threatened to steal the lead from Sessi Jassil's schooner. The girl put one hand to her necklace and made a tiny gesture that only a wizard might recognize. The sails of her schooner filled with a sudden wind. The Magician smiled, thinking that was appropriate; the purpose of magic was to cheat: to cheat nature, to cheat death. Then he laughed, for the schooner listed in the wind, toppling toward the razored galleon, and the Tichenese sloop and the Zhir warship both rammed its stern. The razored galleon escaped the tangle, only to veer off course. A simple fishing boat, probably carved by a parent or a grandparent from Minnow Island, took the lead. It reached a small, delighted boy, and a group of congratulators surrounded him.

Atop her boulder, the bald woman still talked about the chance to buy shares in the Luck of Liavek Airship Company, but most of her audience had wandered to newer diversions. The red-bearded man was wading out to fetch the capsized schooner; his sister was walking around the small lake with her head bowed, as though her muddy toes fascinated her. Someone had stretched ropes across Lake Levar, and two acrobats began a comic act on them. A young wizard created illusions of fanciful, improbable, yet exquisite flying creatures. A troupe of people in brightly colored gauze danced in complex patterns for the patrons of the open-air restaurant. There was nothing entertaining in the Levar's Park. The Magician turned to leave.

Sessi Jassil looked up, catching his eye. She threw her arms wide and began to run toward him. "Master Trav! Master Trav! It's me, Sessi!"

He could hurry into the crowd as though he had not heard. He could disappear in smoke or rise into the air, and let her wonder if he had heard her. Instead, he smiled. "Hello, Sessi. I remembered that you raced boats every Birth Day."

"Oh?" She stopped before him and let her arms come to her side. "I cheated."

"I saw. You're coming along. I hadn't invested my luck until I was twice your age. Don't worry; most first-year magicians trying that trick would've blown every boat up into the trees."

"Well." She glanced down again. "Cheating and winning would've felt wrong, anyway."

"Ah."

"But cheating and losing feels really stupid."

The red-bearded man approached with the toy schooner in both hands. "Master Marik," he said.

The Magician nodded, acknowledging another of his names. "'Lo, Rusty. How's Hell Week so far?"

"Someone burned down Cheeky's yesterday. A temple or a tax collector's, anyone could understand, but a good tavern should be sacred."

"You'd think—" Trav Marik let the sentence die. On the boulder, the bald woman pointed in triumph. From over the trees and rooftops came a cylindrical bag as long as one of the Levar's triremes. Beneath it hung a wooden platform shared by a bulky engine and a single pilot.

"The Luck of Liavek!" the bald woman called. "We'll dock here for the rest of the Festival Week. Interested investors may ride . . ."

The Magician felt the air for unusual magics, but there were none. The Luck of Liavek came on, ponderous and ugly, no faster than a landsailer, as remorseless as the future, driven by a grinning girl who sat in a cage of levers and cords. The crowd cheered, seeing nothing more than another Festival Week novelty. Trav Marik felt his throat grow thick with a feeling he did not recognize. Unnoticed by Rusty or Sessi, he turned to go, certain that the bald woman was right. The age of magic had ended.

Procession Day and Remembrance Night

The Pardoners had always been Sessi's favorite of the many religions who marched in the Procession of Faiths. They danced and sang in the streets in comradely chaos, with no apparent intent to display their devotion to any other gods than those of celebration. Several Pardoners parodied priests of other faiths: A man draped a wine-stained white sheet about his shoulders and announced, "All is illusion!" "Oh?" said a woman in a red blanket. "Then I'm not doing this." She slapped the man, and he spun about, whirling his arms and saying, "Uh, n-n-no, I guess not." "Or this," said the woman, giving him a loud kiss while yanking his moneybag from his sash and tucking it into her own. "Well, n-n-no," said the man in white, rolling his eyes, and all the spectators cheered. "Or this," the woman said, kicking the man in the rear, who jumped high, grabbing his buttocks. Sessi held her arms around her stomach and laughed as though she could not stop.

"Ah, the subtleties of Liavekan humor," said a woman behind her.

"Well, if you knew a little about the Reds, the Faith of the Twin Forces, and the Whites, who're the Church of Truth—" The man's voice reminded Sessi of the Zhir sailors who frequented the docks and the Canal District.

"Is there any reason why I should?"

"Probably not," the man said.

Perhaps forty people in golden robes came next in the procession, singing gentle, ecstatic, wordless notes. They were interrupted by something like firecrackers exploding at the far end of the street. Before Sessi could look, someone behind her touched her bare neck. She gasped; the touch stung like a wasp. She could not hear her own voice in the concatenation of explosions or the babble of the crowd. She started to turn, to confront the foreign couple to tell them that she didn't think this was funny at all, but the street had begun to whirl as if the world was a tornado and she stood at its eye. Then she was not standing. Someone caught her shoulders. Someone said, "Poor dear's had too much excitement. She'll feel better when she's safe at home." Someone lifted her and added, "We all will."

"Night leaps upon the unresisting body of the day," said a moustached man in black clothes, "much as I shall leap upon you, my dear."

His companion, a handsome woman whose scarlet jacket and tight trousers were a subtle mockery of the man's, laughed delightedly. "With twenty seconds of enthusiasm followed by an hour of drunken apologies?" Her amusement emphasized her exotic features, the small nose and high cheekbones characteristic of mixed Liavekan and Tichenese ancestry. Her face had been powdered as white as a corpse's.

The couple strolled arm in arm through Liavek's oldest graveyard, a place of urns and mausoleums and high marble beds littered with leaves and human bones, as though they passed through a crowded ballroom. Directly before them lay a glass case containing a perfectly preserved old woman, plump and coiffed and dressed in an elegant, archaic fashion. Glowing letters at the woman's feet proclaimed, "Kaelin Marik, 2906–3013. 'All things considered, I hope I'm dead.'"

The woman in red, sipping a black liquid from a green glass skull, pointed, sputtering, "Ari, look!" A drop of her drink dripped from the corner of her mouth, leaving a dark path on her powdered face. She winced, dabbed at the drop with her sleeve, then drank from a ruby vial that the man gave her.

He rested both hands on a silver-topped cane and studied the old woman's body. "She is surely an artistic piece now, the creation of her own life and her embalmer's skill. But it's the whole of the presentation, the audacity of the setting, that truly makes . . ." His words trailed off as he looked up at the neighboring mausoleum, a miniature fortress with walls of gray lava.

The woman followed his gaze. A young man in a green robe, apparently immune to the evening breeze, sat cross-legged on the slate roof.

"Forgive us for intruding," the woman said. "We were—" She shrugged. Her embarrassed smile hinted that a blush lay beneath her white powder.

"Remembering the dead," said the young man. "What could be more natural on Ghoul Night?" He swept his hand wide to indicate the dark graveyard or, perhaps, Liavek beyond. The air smelled of dried leaves and mold. A nighthawk pirouetted in the sky, streaking the twilight with the white bars under its wings.

The man in black reached for the woman's arm as if to lead her away, but let his hand fall and addressed the seated man. "Haven't we met? At a party—"

The young man touched both hands to his forehead. "Indeed we have, Aritoli ola Silba. I am The Magician of Liavek."

"I think he's drunk," said the woman. "Whoever he is."

"I am The Magician!" the man cried. "The woman you admire was my first wife."

"I meant no disrespect," Aritoli said softly.

"Of course not." Trav smiled at the woman. "He admires so many wives. How is your husband, Countess ola Klera?"

"We should go," the woman whispered.

"Please, no." Trav, still cross-legged, floated down from the mausoleum and bobbed in the air before them. His robe was stained and torn. "It is a Remembrance Night party. Surely you'll share drink and conversation with an . . . old friend? No, old acquaintance, but new friend." Extending his legs to the ground, he added, "Never drink and fly."

"I shall try to remember that," said Aritoli. "There was a notice for you in this evening's *Cat Street Crier*. Have you seen it?"

"I'm not in need of clients." Trav laughed. "You have not asked me about Gogo. You remember Mistress Gogoaniskithli?"

Aritoli nodded. "A charming creature."

"Indeed," said Trav. "When she intends to be, and when she does not. Did you know that we lived together for almost two hundred years?"

"No," said Aritoli. "I considered living with someone once. For an entire week, I considered it. Ah, the mad passions of youth."

The nighthawk cried, and they all glanced at the sky.

Trav shrugged. "My apologies, ola Silba. I had not meant to bore you. What're you drinking?"

"Green God's Nectar," said Countess ola Klera, lifting the heavy glass skull in her right hand. "Ari and I began with a drop a day to build up a tolerance. We still need the antidote after every drink." She indicated the ruby vial in her other hand. "A taste of death, a taste of life—"

"Ah, something new. Delightful." Trav held out both palms. "May I?"

The Countess glanced at Aritoli, who shrugged. She gave Trav the skull. "If you want a sip . . ."

Trav raised the skull to salute each of them, and then held it toward the dead woman in the clear coffin. Putting the skull to his lips, he drained half of the contents.

Aritoli said, "You are a damned fool, Magician."

"Thank you." He gave the skull to the Countess. "I began my study late in life, but I am a clever pupil." His last words rasped from his throat.

"Drink this!" The Countess held out the ruby vial.

Trav shook his head. Sweat burst out upon his brow.

"Even if your magic keeps you alive," Aritoli said, "you must feel a terrible burning."

Trav nodded. He reeled about, grunted something that might have been pain or farewell, and staggered away. High above, the nighthawk cried again, a brave and lonely sound in the darkness.

Bazaar Day and Beggar's Night

Lieutenant Lian Jassil raised his fist to pound upon the naked wood of the front door to 39 Beach Drive. A gleaming brass gargoyle's head rose from the oak beneath his hand like a swimmer surfacing in a pool. Its teeth glistened like fresh-forged daggers as it said, "Dawn is vastly overrated. Consider carefully before you decide to share it with us."

"My sister is missing, Didi."

The head retreated, and the door swung wide, revealing a dark hallway. Gas lights lit themselves when the lieutenant stepped within. Small orange flowers grew in a pot on a wall shelf, scenting the air with a smell like tangerines.

Two kittens, one tiger-striped and one beige, ran in to circle his boots. The first backed away to watch from under a corner cloak rack. The tan one stood with its hind legs on the toes of Rusty's boot as though it intended to climb him, so he stopped to stroke it.

A small woman with hair like a cloud of copper coils came barefoot down a stairway, tying the sash of her short white robe as she walked. An incoherent voice called querulously from behind her. She answered over her shoulder, "A friend! Go back to sleep, Vay!"

Rusty stood and touched the fingertips of both hands to his forehead in respect. "Mistress Gogoaniskithli."

The woman shook her head, and her hair bounced as though in water. "I said a friend, Rusty. What's happened?"

He held out a creased scrap of rice paper. Gogo scanned it once. He knew the words perfectly: *If you value Sessi Jassil's life, have The Magician come alone one hour after sunset on Beggar's Night to the gate where a Liavekan captain surrendered his pistol to three sorcerers.*

"That's the Tichenese embassy," Gogo said. "But it would not be like them to kidnap a girl. Or to leave a note directing the kidnappers there."

Rusty nodded. "It's a meeting place, nothing more. But without The Magician . . ." The kitten bashed its head against his ankle, so he picked it up and stroked it, trying not to think of how much it would delight Sessi.

Gogo lifted the note. "Who brought this?"

"A girl from a dockside inn. She said a tall woman paid her to deliver it. No reason to doubt her. The description wasn't very helpful. Middle-aged woman. Dark skin, gray hair. An accent that the girl described as 'funny.' No one else in the inn remembered the woman. During Festival Week, that's not surprising.''

Gogo handed back the note. "I could disguise myself as Trav. Illusion's a simple spell.''

Rusty took the note in his left hand because the kitten had gone to sleep in his right. "It's a simple spell to detect, I hear. We'd use a Guard magician, if we thought that'd work. I don't like involving Master Marik, but I'm afraid for Sessi.''

Gogo set her hand on his upper arm. "I'm sorry. If there's anything I can do—''

"The Magician. That's all.''

"No one knows where he is. His house has not been on Wizard's Row for months. He's The Magician. He could be anywhere.''

"Wizards can't find him, either? I thought he had duties as The Magician of Liavek—''

Gogo released his arm. "His spells are intact. The entire community of magicians will know well in advance if Liavek's attacked by magic, or if armies come by land or sea. But this is . . . a private matter.''

Rusty rubbed his brow with his free hand. Something like a headache wanted to settle on him, but he could not let it. He had slept several hours in the last few days; that had to be enough. "My parents put notices in all of the half-copper sheets, asking him to find us, asking people to tell us where he might be. There's no response, so far. I hoped he might tell a friend where he was.''

"I consider him a friend, but he doesn't consider me one.'' Rusty glanced at her, and she added, "I tried to help. I tried until I realized that I was the only one trying, and he was content for things to remain as they were.'' She moved her chin, indicating the upstairs. "So I moved in with Vay, and Didi joined us. We're happy now. Is that wrong?''

He made a sound that she could interpret as she wished. "There's no one else he might see?''

"There's Tenarel. The Ka'Riatha. But I doubt he'd go to her. She'd tell him what she thinks of the way he's been behaving.''

Rusty nodded and handed the kitten to Gogo. He would return to his parents' home and wait with them, before he had to go back on duty. A Guard should be very good at waiting.

"He's given up, Rusty. I would've seen it a century ago, if I hadn't loved him so much. I don't know why. Maybe he's retreated too far from the world. Didi and I were falling with him. That's why we left the Row, finally."

"You don't have to explain—"

"I'm not making excuses! I'm trying to warn you!"

He blinked, realizing that he had not been listening for the meaning behind her words. "We won't find him?" He shook his head. "I can't stop looking."

Gogo's hand rose for a gesture of emphasis that she did not complete. She let it return to stroking the sleeping kitten. "It's all you can do. So do it. I'll try to find him, too. But you should worry less about finding him and more about whether he'll care to help you, if you do find him."

"I see." Rusty scratched the kitten's head, then turned to go. "Thank you."

"Wait!" Gogo held a red playing card in her hand. "Take this. Vay and I're going away for a few days. We might be back by Festival Night. If you need me before then, tear this card, and I'll come."

Rusty woke to a pounding that could only be Stone's fists on his door. His first thought was that Captain Bastian would lecture him for being late. As he opened his eyes and saw the plaster ceiling of his mother's living room, he forgot Bastian and Stone. He sat up from the wicker couch, saying, "Has anyone heard—"

His father shook his head and opened the front door. Stone stood in the hallway, clutching his blue beret in one huge hand. "Master Jassil," he said. "I'm sorry. Really, I am." Tears fell from his eyes. "We looked everywhere. We talked to everyone."

For some reason, his parents and Stone turned to stare at Rusty. He sat on the couch and began to pull on his boots, saying, "We keep looking." He smelled hot kaf and buttered toast in the kitchen, but he wanted to act, not to eat.

His mother's face was very grim, so he added, "The Magician likes her. He'll help." What point was there in repeating Gogo's warning?

"The Magician likes money," his father said. "Little else."

Not even that, anymore, Rusty thought. He repeated more

firmly, ''He likes Sessi. He'll help us find her.''

''I've got a hundred and twenty-one levars saved,'' Stone said. ''He can have that.''

''Oh, gods,'' said Master Jassil, slumping into his chair and covering his face with his hands. Mistress Jassil put an arm around his shoulders and said very calmly, ''She's not dead.''

''We'll find The Magician,'' Rusty repeated, and Stone followed him out the door.

The streets were a maze of carts and spread blankets at midmorning on Bazaar Day. What was not offered freely was sold for its cost, or so every seller swore. Within a few feet of the Jassils' door, a tailor invited passersby to feel embroidered silk robes to appreciate their quality, a baker gave out bits of warm brown bread and honey cake, a woman and a man in garlands of Worrynot kissed anyone who sought an embrace. A girl offered rides on her camel, and three identical boys sang a song that stated that every purchase was an exchange of gifts.

Through this bustle, an unshaven young man in a green robe strode toward Rusty and Stone without a glance to either side.

''Magician!'' Rusty called in disbelief.

''I can understand advertising in *The Liavekan Herald*,'' Trav replied. ''But did you really think I read *The Old Town Inquisitor*?''

Several Tichenese guards in quilted yellow robes stood with shouldered muskets at the gate to their embassy. Golden Festival lanterns hung from the walls and on poles beyond them, as though a sea of moons swayed restlessly in the night.

Trav stepped beneath one. He wore a blue cotton robe, low boots, and black trousers; his hair and his skin still smelled of peppermint soap. He smiled, knowing this would be a good place to attack him, and he had done all he could to be a fine corpse.

A small boy ran up to him with a folded bit of rice paper in both hands. ''Are you Master Spider?''

Trav coughed something like a laugh. ''I think I'm Master Fly tonight.'' He touched one hand to his forehead and bowed.

The boy squinted. ''The letter's for Master Spider.''

''That's a courtesy or a mockery. But I'll be Master Spider.'' He gave the boy a silver coin and ignored his thanks. The note

said: *Shall we meet in the rear gardens of the Zhir ambassador?
Walk briskly, and you will arrive on time. Do not travel by
any other means or route, and do not dawdle. There are a
thousand ways in which you can fail in your mission, and only
one in which you can succeed.* It ended, *You're still a magician.
Destroy this.*

The message seemed to confirm what the earlier note's reference to a Liavekan captain's pistol had suggested. Djanhiz
ola Vikili had returned to Liavek. Knowing the identity of one
of his opponents told him surprisingly little. Djanhiz ola Vikili
had twice failed to capture or kill him; her second failure had
resulted in the permanent loss of her magic. Whether she came
now as a Tichenese agent or for her own revenge made no
difference, though he wondered if the Zhir played a major part
in this, or if Djanhiz simply preferred embassy grounds, where
Liavekan officials could not interfere.

At his nod, the note ignited in his hand.

He hurried through crowds of laughing beggars, many of
whose sores were paint and whose tatters were velvet and otter
or artfully shredded silk. He wondered if Djanhiz ola Vikili
had expected the Festival to impede his progress through the
city. He could not tell if he was followed, and did not care.
He would play the game fairly, and by doing so, he would
win. Sessi meant nothing to Djanhiz, so she would be freed.
And he meant everything to Djanhiz, so he would finally die.

The Zhir embassy was a large whitewashed building, note-
worthy only for decorative iron bars on every window and a
high stone wall that enclosed it. The embassy's inhabitants had
gone to sleep or had left for the more exciting quarters of
Liavek; every barred window was dark. Two Zhir musketeers
stood at the front gate. "I believe I'm expected," Trav announced.

"I believe you're invisible," one guard answered, stepping
aside so Trav could pass.

He followed a brick path around the building to the only
source of light, a three-legged iron brazier that had been placed
in the center of a tiled patio. When Trav came near, Djanhiz
ola Vikili stepped from under a tree and began snapping her
fingers, setting a moderate, steady tempo. She recited, "You
will not speak or so disrupt in any way this little song. Four
verses tell what you must know. The girl dies if you interrupt."

He nodded, pleased that Djanhiz expected him to trick her and wondering what he might have done if he had intended to try.

"A man and she wait somewhere near. He watches while you hear me speak. If my lips pause at any point, he'll cut her throat from ear to ear."

Trav glanced at the quiet windows of the embassy and saw no signs of anyone's presence.

"You need not wonder if I lie. I know the vessel of your luck. Discard it now and back away, or leave and let your small friend die."

Centuries of habit made him reluctant to expose and abandon the container of his power; this amused him when he considered his resolve. His smile grew, and he wondered how Djanhiz interpreted his humor.

"The final verse must now be said." Her voice might have quavered as she began the line, but her expression preserved infinite confidence.

Trav rested his left hand on the bracelet around his right wrist and felt his birth luck pulsing there. He could do anything now, except kill himself. Anything he did would result in Sessi's death. Yet the power tempted him. A last magical feat that Liavek would remember forever. . . .

"The watcher's knife is at her throat. In sixteen syllables—"

He tugged at his wrist, suddenly sure that he had waited too long, that the knife in the hand of Djanhiz's hidden companion would part Sessi's throat before Trav could comply.

"—we'll learn if you prefer—"

He felt his vessel sliding free in his left hand.

"—her live—"

He dropped the vessel onto the patio and hurried backward.

"—or dead." Djanhiz smiled. "I congratulate you on your choice."

His right hand lay on the flagstones. As he took his fourth or fifth step away from it, he felt his magic dwindle and disappear, lost to his senses and his control.

Djanhiz picked up the hand by the tip of its little finger. It dangled like a small, dead animal. Djanhiz glanced at Trav, as if about to speak, then smiled and threw the hand onto the coals of the brazier.

He started forward without thinking, moving close enough that a shadow of his birth luck caressed him.

Djanhiz said, "Remember the girl!"

Trav nodded and backed again. The brazier had darkened when his hand fell into it. As the hand began to smoke, Trav gasped and dropped to his knees. His birth luck whirled about him, wild and strange, a storm that he perceived as silver light and tamarind scent and something like burning honey. Then his birth luck fled, freed from the prison that had been his severed right hand. Every spell that he had ever made dissolved in that instant.

His sight left him, and so did his balance. He fell forward, bruising his left hand and his right stump on the tiled patio, then vomited.

Djanhiz sighed. "I suppose it was too much to hope that your own magic kept you young. You still trust Gogo with your life, though she left you? Or another? It is a weakness, Magician."

His vision returned, though there was nothing he wished to see. He wiped his chin and rose unsteadily, sneering as he said, "It'll keep me alive until I invest my luck again." He and Gogo had always used their magic to keep each other alive during their birthdays, when their magics failed as their birth luck returned to their bodies. Gogo had left Trav at the end of the month of Fruit and found or hired someone else to help her through her next birthday. Without telling him, she had renewed the spell that would keep Trav alive through his. He had cried then, though not since.

Djanhiz said, "Take off your clothes."

He glanced at her and began to undo his sash.

She laughed. "Because I remember when you walked freely into Chiano Mefini's trap, and I would know what preparations you might have with you now."

He stood naked in the night while Djanhiz ran her hands over his clothing and prodded his coin purse. Frowning, she stepped closer to him. Her eyes narrowed, and she reached out, touching a thin pink slash across his chest. He almost grabbed her hand, then remembered the knife at Sessi's throat. She said, "It would've been easy to heal that entirely. It must itch—" Her fingers moved to a shorter reddish line just beneath his sternum, a puckered line as wide as two fingers.

She held his gaze. After a moment, he nodded and glanced away. She prodded the wound with her fingers, and he cried out, bringing his left hand and the stump of his right wrist up to cover his chest.

"You disgusting—" Her full lips curled, but found no words. He waited, wondering if she could understand, or if her loathing would help him understand himself.

"I'd planned to kill you quickly," she said softly, "if another's magic kept you young. I couldn't decide between water and fire, whether to sink you in the sea or let the fish clean the living flesh from your bones, or to close you in an oven until even your bones were ash. I doubt anyone's spell would keep you alive then. But now I suspect that keeping you alive would be the crueler thing to do." She smiled again. "We've nine months before your birthday and the return of your luck. That's sufficient time to decide."

"No!" Trav drove his left fist toward her face, forgetting everything for a moment. Her smile disappeared, but her left arm came up in the smooth movement of the experienced martial artist. Her right hand knifed into his solar plexus. He fell again and lay on the ground, hugging himself. When air returned to his lungs, he began to cry.

Djanhiz touched her ring to his bare arm. He felt the bite of a needle, then nothing. As the world retreated, Trav wondered if that had been an act of convenience, or of kindness.

Festival Day

His mother met Rusty at the door to her apartment. "Here," he said, thrusting a folded scrap of rice paper at her. "Where's Dad?" He glanced past his mother and saw that the apartment had been hung with small blue lanterns and sashes. A blue glass chipmunk sat behind a bowl of candied cashews, Sessi's favorite Festival treat.

"Sleeping." The hollows of his mother's eyes were dark, and he hoped he had not woken her. She took the note. Sessi's abductor had written, *The Magician has arrived. Expect Sessi Jassil on Restoration Day. She will be healthy and unharmed.* "Bastards," she whispered.

"She's all right."

"You believe that?"

He glanced at the blue glass chipmunk. "Why would they send the note, if she wasn't?"

"To gain time to escape, my son, the Guard lieutenant." When he winced, she said, "Why not send her home now?"

"My best guess? Because she knows something that would hurt them. Something that won't matter tomorrow. Who they are, maybe how they'll leave the city. The Guard is still watching for her, in case she's not in the Zhir embassy."

"Can't a magician verify that Sessi's there, at least? Just knowing whether she's alive—"

Rusty shook his head. "The Zhir aren't the most sophisticated wizards, but every Guard magician says they outdid themselves in laying blankets of secrecy spells on their embassy. Four of our wizards are trying to find a path through. I asked if Gogo could help. They say it's not a matter of power, but of patience. Let Gogo enjoy Festival Week. Someone should."

His mother sighed and touched his cheek. "You should be resting."

"I can help Sessi as much on duty as off. 'Sides, the Guard needs everyone during Hell Week. Sessi's kidnapping isn't our only case."

"Sessi will never forgive herself if The Magician dies for her."

"We're looking for him, too. Bastian's agreed to tell the Zhir that we followed Marik to their embassy, but she's not hopeful. Any search that the Zhir allow us will be a joke. They'll move their captives from room to room ahead of us like a damned shell game. If we really press them, they'll kill Sessi and Marik and bury them in the cellar. So we wait."

His mother nodded. "Don't sneak in by yourself."

"Mom! You don't think—"

She smiled and shook her head. "You're in the Levar's pay. It'd be an act of war. It was enough to stand by while The Magician sacrificed himself. Don't expect me to let my son throw away himself and his city."

Rusty bit his upper lip, then said, "What do you expect of me?"

"What you expect of me." She hugged him. "We wait."

● ● ●

Ceramic dolphins swam from chandeliers and wall lamps in every room of the Zhir embassy, excluding the basement and the south guest room. Rangzha Fon stood in the doorway of the south room and wondered why he had always thought it so beautiful; he would repaint it when his visitor left. He said carefully, "It's dangerous to keep The Magician alive."

"Would you kill him? You're welcome to try." Djanhiz adjusted the front of her bright yellow Festival gown. "You could chop him into tiny bits. Would each bit continue to live, do you think, no matter how small you cut it? You could fill a tub with lye and lower him into it. Would that amuse you?"

Rangzha Fon shuddered.

"We are safe," said Djanhiz. "If your tour did not convince the Guard that only Zhir are in these walls, it did convince them that they could not find the girl or The Magician without occupying the building. We've nothing to fear from The Magician so long as he's drugged. Liavek's remaining wizards are celebrating Festival Night in their various ways. By the time anyone learns of your prince's plans, it will be too late. Now we only wait to see if his plans display genius or madness."

"Why do you drug The Magician? The Guard won't return until Festival Week's over and Jeng has . . . acted."

Djanhiz turned to him and grinned. He flinched when she extended a long-fingered hand toward him. Smoothing the front of his Liavekan evening jacket, she said, "You're off to hear speeches, see fireworks, light a Festival lantern or two, and celebrate like any of the Levar's most honored guests. Do you really enjoy worrying?"

Rangzha Fon nodded again.

Djanhiz laughed. "Then let me tell you a bit of esoteric magical lore. If a master magician—and The Magician is certainly that—does not invest his luck or has his luck freed—and we have done that for Master Marik—he still has access to his power during the nine minutes or so of each day that correspond to the moments of his birth."

"May Thung feign mercy!"

Djanhiz shrugged. "So we keep Trav Marik unconscious. Tomorrow we can convince him to reveal the exact time that he was born, and then ensure that he never has a chance to use his birth-moment magic." Djanhiz glanced out the window at the dying light of the day. "He should be coming to, soon. Can you feed him his dinner without me?"

Sessi sneezed into her hand, wiped it against the wall, and wrapped her wool blanket more tightly around her. The Magician remained unconscious on the other cot, where the fat Zhir and the old Titch had thrown him the night before.

She knew her windowless cell very well after two days. Two walls were cool, damp stone, telling her that this room was probably in a basement. Two walls were thick wooden planks. Iron rings hung from the ceiling beams; Sessi did not want to know their purpose. The only light came through the narrow bars set into the door. When she stood on tiptoe and peeked through the bars, she could see an iron lamp standing close to their door, and a shadowy hallway lined with more sturdy doors like theirs. She hoped those rooms were normally used for storage. A guard always waited at the end of the hall, but the only people who ever entered the cell were the fat Zhir and the tall Titch.

Something blocked the light, and the door rattled open. The fat Zhir, wearing evening clothes, entered with a tray holding two bowls of soup and two mugs of water. Placing the tray by The Magician's cot, the Zhir locked the door with a key that hung around his neck and said, "He hasn't stirred since lunch?" The Magician, semiconscious, had been spoon-fed by the Zhir and the Titch, and then had gone back to sleep.

Sessi shook her head. Wanting to test a suspicion, she reached for the bowl and cup that were closest to The Magician.

The Zhir slapped her hand. "No! The Magician's has a special medicine. It's only for magicians. It'll help him rest."

The Zhir lifted The Magician's head, and he groaned. "Wha—Where?"

"Shush," the Zhir said kindly. "Drink." He held the cup to The Magician's lips. "You'll feel better."

Sessi tried not to watch the Zhir feed The Magician. She made herself finish her own bland dinner, thinking that food was strength and she would need hers, if a chance came to escape. The Zhir helped The Magician with the nightpan, then set it and their dishes into the hall. Sliding a clean pan back in the cell, he said, "Rest well," and fled.

Sessi counted to twenty-five to be sure that the Zhir had

gone. She reached across The Magician's bed to grab his far shoulder, then turned him onto his side. His eyes flicked open once, and he said, "Uh?"

As his eyes closed, Sessi whispered, "Please don't bite," and stuck her fingers down The Magician's throat.

Trav woke on his back in a dark room to the sensation of something damp and scratchy moving across his face. He reached for it, and a child said, "Oh, thank the Twin Forces! I thought you'd never wake up!"

He rolled over, tangling himself in a rough blanket. Someone had taken his clothes. Feeling for the edge of the bed, he remembered that someone had taken his hand, too.

"I saved some of my drinking water," the child said. "Go on. They didn't need to drug me." He could not see her face clearly, but she was small and short-haired, wearing a flowered tunic and a braided necklace. She had been holding a blanket, which she dropped.

"Sessi?" He sipped from her wooden cup. There was only a taste of warm water, enough to tell him how very thirsty he was. His head ached and his chest felt hollow. "Drugged?" The room smelled of vomit, and the taste in his mouth told him whose.

"Yes. I don't know what, but it's something to keep you unconscious. I made you throw up. It was really disgusting."

"Sorry."

"And it still took hours for you to wake up. We've got to get out of here!"

"They destroyed my luck piece." Trav knew that he should care, but he could not.

Sessi whispered, "They didn't destroy mine." She touched the pendant of her necklace, a blue stone chipmunk. "Didn't think a little kid could've invested her luck yet, I guess. But the only magic I know is wind and orange smoke and an illusion that looks like a kitten if you turn your head sideways and squint."

"Not terribly helpful."

"No," Sessi agreed.

Trav let himself fall back onto the cot and draped his arm over his forehead. He might have a fever; he could not tell. "Then we stay here."

"We have to try something! The Zhir are attacking Liavek tonight!"

He squinted at her. "That's ridiculous."

"It's true! That's why they want you out of the way. When I woke up after they captured me, they were talking about airships and the Levar and Festival Night and marines and holding the palace and like that." She nodded to herself. "We have to do something, Master Trav."

"Yes." Trav closed his eyes. "Let me rest." All of Liavek would be celebrating Festival Night. Gogo would be celebrating too, in her new home, with her new friends. Would she miss him? He might have been celebrating, too. He tried to remember what had become of his friends and his life. He knew a city's worth of dead people.

She shook him. "You're The Magician! The Levar depends on you."

He laughed. "Hardly. There's the Guard for worldly troubles, and half the inhabitants of Wizard's Row to deal with magical ones." But the inhabitants of Wizard's Row vacationed like other Liavekans. How many of Liavek's greatest magicians were in the city? How many of those looked for danger during Festival Week? They all knew—

They all knew that the Levar's Regents had paid The Magician very well for a web of spells that would detect any magical threat that came to Liavek, or any mortal threat that came by land or sea.

He thought of the smoking ruin of his right hand. Every spell that he had formed had dissipated when it burned in Djanhiz's brazier.

His loss did not matter to Liavek. The city's officials were not fools. Other magicians had been hired to set magical defenses around Liavek, too; the city's fate could not depend on one person's well-being. More magicians had added their own spells out of love of Liavek and the Levar. Sessi's fears were ludicrous.

"Master Trav?" Sessi said hesitantly.

He twitched his head for silence. Something besides his headache and his weakness nagged at him. "If any worldly threat came by land or sea," he said, remembering the *Luck of Liavek,* bulky and slow and carrying no more than a passenger or two as it floated quietly over the Levar's Park. A thousand of those would fill the sky. What wizard would think to set spells to watch the air for dangers that did not come by magic? How many experienced soldiers would be needed to seize the palace and the Levar, if they could arrive without warning in the middle of the chaos that was Festival Night?

"The Zhir and the Titch didn't say anything about land or sea," Sessi whispered. "They said airships."

"The entire idea's ridiculous," Trav answered. Then, wrapping the blanket tightly around himself, he stood and began to study their prison.

Fek Zhang dreamed of being a boy in his mountain village near the city of Ka Zhir. When he woke, his first thought was relief that he would not have to explain to his mother how the goat's milk had spilled. His apprehension returned when he realized that he had fallen asleep at his post in the basement of the embassy in Liavek, and smoke and screams came from the prisoners' room.

Something must have knocked over the hall lamp (for surely no wind could have blown in this closed place). Fek Zhang grabbed a fire bucket and ran to scatter sand over the flames. He looked all around the narrow hall, wondering how a cat or a dog could have crept past him while he slept.

"In here!" the girl prisoner called. "It's burning in here!"

Fek Zhang could not see within the cell; smoke and darkness hid the room from him. Drawing his pistol from his sash and bringing its hammer to full-cock, he unlocked the door. "Come out! There're buckets—" Orange fumes billowed from the open door, as if driven by wind. Fek Zhang coughed and blinked, and something leaped for his face. Through his watery, half-blinded vision, it seemed a demonic caricature of a kitten.

Fek Zhang screamed and fired his pistol. The kitten disappeared with the sound of his shot. Fek Zhang gasped deeply and watched for the thing's return.

The Magician of Liavek, naked and filthy, stepped from within the smoky cell. Fek Zhang lifted the pistol, and The Magician smiled. "Hello. Don't you wish you had time to reload?"

Fek Zhang tried to club the man with his flintlock's barrel, but The Magician blocked the blow with his right forearm and drove his left fist into Fek Zhang's stomach. Within a minute, the fight had ended. For the rest of his life, Fek Zhang maintained that he would have beaten the one-handed man, if only the misshapen kitten had not returned in the form of a girl-demon that climbed on his back and clawed at his eyes.

Though Rusty's shift had ended and he should be somewhere asleep, he waited in the alley across from the Zhir embassy. A dark woman had left early in the evening, and the ambassador had departed soon after. He did not know how many servants remained, and wondered whether he should ignore his mother's warning and enter. Near midnight, he saw a slim man in ill-fitting Zhir trousers and tunic leave by a side door. Rusty nodded to Stone, and they both moved forward. When Sessi stepped into the street behind the man, Rusty and Stone began to run.

Rusty caught Sessi in a hug and, laughing, whirled her around. Only then did he notice that her one-handed companion was The Magician, and The Magician was walking quickly away.

"Master Marik!" Rusty called. "Thank you! What happened—"

"Alert the guard," The Magician answered. "The Zhir may invade this evening. Protect the Levar."

"You're sure?"

"Not at all. Do it anyway. Look for Djanhiz ola Vikili. Sessi can describe her. A Tichenese woman who was once a wizard. You'll want the Zhir ambassador, too, I think." One of the new pedicabs wheeled by and The Magician called, "Taxi!"

"Wait!" Rusty yelled after him. "Where're you going?"

"For a ride on an airship. Beautiful night for one, don't you think?"

"Faster!" he called from the padded bench of the pedicab, though they took a corner on two of the cab's three wheels and he had to grab the side of the seat to keep from falling. He wished he knew the time. He wished he had calculated the exact minute when his birth-moment magic would return. He feared his luck would come too soon to be of any use to Liavek, if there was any substance in Sessi's mad suggestion.

"That's a joke, right?" the wiry driver answered without

looking back. "You want to pump the oak 'til it's broke? Or you want to let me?"

His strength was half of hers, after his stay in the Zhir embassy. "Sorry. It's important."

The driver laughed. "I'm getting you to her as fast as I can."

Festival lanterns hung at every pole and window, transforming the City of Luck into a city of light. Each major intersection was blocked with revelers who danced to bands playing music from every culture of the known world. Liavek's avenues were impassable, so they raced through alleys and back streets until the cab rolled into the Levar's Park.

Trav found a coin purse in the Zhir guard's trousers and tossed it to the pedicab driver. "Thanks, Master!" she yelled as he leaped from the bench and ran toward the *Luck of Liavek*.

The airship shifted at its mooring in the middle of the meadow like a lazy tethered elephant. Trav saw no one near it. The fireworks had begun across Lake Levar, attracting most of the people who passed Festival Night in the Levar's Park. A rope ladder hung from the netting around the pilot's platform, so Trav scrambled up, snatching at its wooden rungs with his one hand. Midway up, he heard the bald woman call, "Who comes? I'm armed!"

"A passenger! I'm not!"

"It's the middle of the night!"

"Do tell?" He gained the platform, wondering if she would kick him off.

"Oh, luck of a chipmunk. We need the money." She took his elbow with a firm grip and helped him over the low wall of netting. She wore wool trousers and a leather jacket; a blanket had been spread near the pilot's chair, which was built into the front of the wood and wicker platform. "When and where do you want to go?"

"Up. Now." A wave of dizziness rolled over him, surely the effect of his haste.

"Right." Her gaze inventoried his cheap, ill-fitting clothes, and perhaps his desperation, too. "Come back tomorrow, when you're not drunk or stoned. If you're just stupid, don't come back at all."

"Now. I'll pay—" He patted empty pockets and wondered how much money he had given the taxi driver. Fireworks exploded above the lake. He told himself that the glow before his eyes was only their reflected light.

The woman shook her bald head. "No crew to launch us, no crew to bring us in. The field isn't lit for landing. Come back tomorrow."

"I'm The Magician. Going's vital for Liavek's safety."

"I'm the captain. Staying's vital for my safety."

"Oh, gods." He doubled over, feeling the world grow bright as though the sun shone for him alone. His nose filled with the scent of cinnamon.

The captain set her hand on his shoulder. "Puke over the rail if—"

Trav straightened up, as strong and as clear-headed as if he had never been captured by Djanhiz and the Zhir. "Take the controls."

"Don't speak—"

A fireball appeared at each of his fingertips. "I'm The Ma—"

She hit his hand, destroying his concentration. "Damn it, man! Water-gas is inflammable."

"Sorry." The flames imploded silently. "Take us up."

"No."

Trav imagined the mooring cords untying themselves like restless snakes. "Take the controls."

The captain dropped a hand to the long knife at her hip. "Never."

"I'd rethink that." He pointed. The brilliant lights of Festival Night sank slowly beyond the platform rail. The *Luck of Liavek* drifted toward Lake Levar and the fireworks beyond.

"How'd—" She ran to the engine at the rear of the platform and began to crank it. "Grab my bedding!" she called. On the fourth turn, the engine's explosive protests became a rough roar. "Stuff the blankets in that locker!" As she took her seat, she pointed at a chest built onto the platform. "And haul up the ladder!" The ship's wooden propeller turned faster and faster behind them. "You damned fool!" she shouted. "You endanger my ship!"

"Sorry!" Trav shouted back. "I'm The Magician."

"I know you're a magician! Didn't I say you're a fool?" The *Luck of Liavek* turned lazily toward the south. "I've spent my life building this ship and you toy with it as if it was a bauble conjured out of dreamstuff—"

"I'm sorry."

"As though the rest of us had no—" She glanced back at him. "What?"

"I'm sorry. And I'm a fool. Please, don't land."

"Land?" The captain laughed without humor. "Not 'til dawn. Not even then, if we can't find a sober landing crew."

"You'll be paid well, whatever happens. This is the Levar's business. Please. Take us higher. Over the sea."

She studied him, and he thought he had failed. Then she nodded. "All right."

At least two minutes of his magic were lost. "Can we go faster?"

"Engine and fuel and the two of us make a lot of weight. You could jump."

"Ah, no, thanks." He pictured the platform and its load, then thought of feathers. The city of Liavek dwindled more quickly beneath them.

She opened her mouth, closed it, and said, "You did something?"

He nodded. "What else would speed us?"

Surprise and delight came to her face. "An engine of the finest steel, twice as large as this one. A propeller to match. A larger gas bag, long and sleek like a rigid eel. And twice the fuel!"

He nodded again, then grabbed the low wall of netting to keep from falling as the transformed airship surged forward. Its nose lifted until the captain did something with the dangling cords around her seat; the platform became level again. The engine seemed smoother and louder, a beat for tireless dancers, and the wind whipped at Trav's borrowed clothes. He realized he was cold, and glanced at the captain. She'd turned up her leather hood. He made himself a jacket to match hers.

She grinned at him. "I've dreamed of a ship like this. But why do you want an airship when you could magic up something that didn't care how the natural world wanted things to behave?"

"Because my power will be gone in four or five minutes. And I need to concentrate on something besides staying in the air."

"Ah. Let my ship's true weight return slowly, then, not all

at once. Even then, I'll be playing tricky games with the controls to keep us aloft when the *Luck* reverts.''

He nodded, noting that and ignoring it. He probed the skies around him, casting intangible nets for humans in the air. He found gulls and owls and nighthawks, and then, a mile away, two people high above Liavek. He smiled grimly, thinking he had found Sessi's Zhir invaders a few moments before they would act. His smile changed when he realized that two magicians were celebrating Festival Night in their own way, then changed again when he realized who they were.

"Be happy, Gogo," he whispered.

"What?" the captain called.

"Nothing. Be quiet." Catching her scowl, he added, "Please. There's no—" And then his nets found the Zhir, perhaps thirty miles away. Not a fleet of small airships, but three leviathans of the air, each carrying ninety soldiers. He thought of fireworks, and knew how easy it would be to imagine skyrockets within the explosive water-gas bags of the Zhir's huge ships.

Would the explosions be visible from Liavek? Three balls of fire would hang in the sky like exploded stars. Would the flames consume the Zhir soldiers? A passing sailing ship might find flotsam that hinted at alien vessels and unknowable calamities. Would the Zhir soldiers die screaming as they fell onto the hard, green waves of the Sea of Luck? Would the fall to the sea kill the burning airmen, or save them? The passing sailing ship might find charred swimmers who dared not speak of their mission or their fate.

Trav touched one Zhir's mind, and discovered impatience after twelve hours in the air and a fear of leaping from the airship at night to circle down on a fragile glider onto a strange city; the hope of landing safely in the bright, confused streets, of being one of those who made it to the palace to seize the Levar and close the palace gates before any semblance of resistance came against them; the hope that his parents would be proud of him. . . .

A minute or two of Trav's birth luck remained, at most. He remembered the captain's warning and commanded the *Luck of Liavek* to begin its return to its original weight and form.

He thought he could see three dark dots on the southern horizon, though they may have been imagination.

He pictured a tiny, turbulent fist of air over the Sea of Luck that beat itself into a spiral of wind. Something resisted his will; weather had its own desire and its own momentum that he must master or coerce, if he could. He imagined the spiral whipping faster, driving itself against the night breezes, becoming a storm between Liavek and the three Zhir airships. He wrestled with the raw stuff of the sky, shaping a hurricane to protect the city he loved.

His birth-moment magic ended without warning. He sagged against the netting, weary and cold, then made himself stand.

If he'd succeeded, the effects of the storm would continue, and the winds would drive the airships southward, away from Liavek. One or all might crash, but he could think of nothing better that he could have done for the Zhir or for his conscience. If he'd failed, a battle would be fought in Liavek's streets. Whether Liavek endured or fell, he would share in each death on either side.

"Didn't expect that," the captain said, throwing a bag of sand over the netting and pointing. A small dark turbulence built in the distance like a wall between them and the southern stars. "Thought it was going to be a nice night."

Trav glanced at her, then laughed to himself. "It's going to be a great one."

She shrugged. "If you say so. Mind if we head back? I don't want to be caught if that comes our way."

"No, not at all." His teeth chattered, but he did not care.

"Take one of my blankets." She moved around her seat to open the locker. "Sounds like you could use it."

"Thank you." He looked away. The black clouds hid the southern stars. Though the storm grew larger, it did not seem to be approaching them. Moonlight rolled over the waves of the Sea of Luck below them. To the north beyond the harbor islands, Liavek beckoned, a city etched in light.

"Fortunately," the captain said, passing him the blanket and reaching again into the locker, "I keep a few refreshments on board for special occasions. Happy Festival Night." She lifted out a bottle and two glasses, then smiled, and Trav laughed for no other reason than joy.

Restoration Day

Rangzha Fon returned to his embassy with his evening clothes stained and rumpled. He wore a mask of a blue chipmunk around his neck and sang a Liavekan love song that he had learned from a desert tribesman who did not understand the words. Between them, the lyrics had become "Dippa didi wokka wie," which seemed to express all that Rangzha Fon wished to say. He carried a large teak box in both hands.

"You are drunk," Djanhiz ola Vikili told him as he entered his office.

"Excellent." Rangzha Fon placed the teak box in the center of his desk, hung the new mask among the others on the wall, then fell into his chair. "Would've been a shame to waste all that wine."

"A Gold Harbor ship came into Liavek this morning with many shipwrecked Zhir marines aboard."

"Poor shipwrecked Zhir. Missed Festival Night."

"The ship that was wrecked was an airship."

"Oh," said Rangzha Fon, and when Djanhiz ola Vikili seemed insufficiently pleased, he repeated it. "Oh."

"The Prince's ships were caught in a storm."

"Well." Rangzha Fon waved his hand, still smiling, but realized from the demands of his stomach that the wine's quality had been less than it had seemed. "Storms happen."

"There should not have been a storm last night. If The Magician had not escaped, there probably would not have been a storm, don't you think?"

Rangzha Fon burped.

"How elegant," said Djanhiz ola Vikili. "Several of your shipwrecked countrymen have asked for asylum in Liavek. Their story has perplexed the Liavekans. Messages have traveled between Liavek and Ka Zhir."

Rangzha Fon nodded. "You're a very smart person, Mistress ola Vikili."

She slammed the palm of her hand against his desk. "I am a captive in this embassy, Rangzha Fon. And so are you! The Liavekans will arrest us if we step outside. Jeng will not help us, because we have failed him. What will we do?"

"A very smart person," Rangzha Fon repeated. "But you worry too much. Don't worry about the Liavekans outside."

She raised an eyebrow.

"I invited them in." Rangzha Fon clapped his hands.

Two Liavekan Guards in gray and blue stepped into his office, led by a red-bearded lieutenant with weary eyes. When Djanhiz ola Vikili reached toward the jade letter opener on Rangzha Fon's desk, the lieutenant drew his pistol and aimed it at her heart. He said, "My part in this business has been to watch and to suffer and to do nothing at all. I would be most grateful if you attacked me."

Djanhiz's hand remained over the jade knife, then drew back. She stared at Rangzha Fon, making him feel almost sober, and he reminded himself that her magic had been destroyed years ago. "Why?" she said softly.

"I'm the ambassador," Rangzha Fon answered. "King Thelm had his magicians send a gift to the ambassador to present to the Levar." As Djanhiz glanced at the teak box, he fumbled in his robes. "A scroll, too. But I think I'll give his gift to the Levar's Regents, and let them give it to the Levar, if they want." He met her glance. "Go ahead. Look."

Djanhiz ola Vikili reached out with both hands and lifted the hinged cover, revealing the head of Prince Jeng of Ka Zhir.

"Scroll says, 'Accept this proof of Ka Zhir's friendship with Liavek. Though Thelm's bite is weakened, his pain ends.'"

Every year, Sessi dreaded the arrival of Restoration Day. It meant the end of Festival Week, the end of celebrating life and the return to living it. Yet every Restoration Day, she decided this was really her favorite day of the year.

The Street of Old Coins bustled with people, mostly its inhabitants but also visiting friends and family, ostensibly cleaning up after the excesses of Festival Night but actually sharing gossip and leftover holiday food. The youngest kids picked up trash and the older ones swept and scrubbed, and no one minded that their work was interrupted by impromptu games, like now: Sessi and six friends chased each other with straw brooms, swatting and laughing. Her mother usually did chores that she had wanted to do for months; today she was in the front yard, painting their shutters a joyful blue. Her father usually napped in a chair on their balcony, claiming the day's best use lay in restoring himself, however that was done. Neither of her parents seemed to be devoting themselves fully to their pastimes. Now and then, they would glance at her or at each other and smile.

As she chased the cute boy from the next block, determined to swat him twice as many times as he had swatted her, a hand fell on her shoulder. She gasped and spun, flailing with the broom.

The Magician stood still, letting her hit his shoulder, and said, "I'm sorry, Sessi. I didn't mean to startle—"

"Master Trav!" She hurtled into his arms. He caught her awkwardly, then she felt his grip grow tighter for a long moment.

When he released her, he said, "I wanted to say thank you, and I wanted to say goodbye."

"You're going away?"

"For a little while, anyway." He laughed, and she laughed too, because she had not seen him really happy for the longest time. "I'm going to build and design airships. Remember the captain of the *Luck of Liavek*? We'll be partners. Each day when I've got my birth-moment luck, I'll create and test our new designs. Next year, we'll build a proper manufactory and start producing ships that won't disappear when my magic does. Want a ride on the first?"

She nodded. "Who'll be The Magician, then?"

"Gogo. She'll keep giving you magic lessons, if you want them."

Sessi nodded again.

"Listen," he said, squatting so they were alone in the crowded street. "It's all right if you're scared sometimes. Do you have nightmares?"

She gave the tiniest nod.

"Me, too."

"You're The Magician." She looked at his face and said, "Were."

"When you're The Magician, you'll have nightmares, too. Different ones. Don't let them rule you, and you'll be better for it."

"Me? The Magician?"

He laughed and nodded. "If you work hard. If you don't

let the bad things scare you too much. If you remember that luck is something to share. If you never give up, no matter how pointless it seems." He stood up. "That's probably a good exit line. I should go."

She touched his sleeve, the empty one where a hand had been. "There's Festival cake. With almonds and cherries and chocolate sauce."

He looked away, destroying their moment of privacy in the street. Sessi's friends still chased each other. A little kid had fallen and begun to cry, but his older brother was already picking him up. An old woman in a wheelchair played a game of shan with the university student who lived across the street. A group of singers made a merry hash of "Pot-boil Blues." The smell of fresh bread came from the bakery around the corner. Someone hawked the latest edition of the *Cat Street Crier* with surprising enthusiasm for Restoration Day: "Storm destroys Zhir airships! Abducted girl returns safely! Beautiful weather for Restoration Day! All the news of Liavek for only half of a copper!"

"Well," said the man who had been The Magician. "There's more to life than a good exit line. A slice of Festival cake would suit me very well indeed."

The Levar's Night Out

by Patricia C. Wrede

TAZLI IFINO IV LARWIN, Levar of Liavek, pressed her nose against the heavy glass window pane and scowled down at the dome of the palace. From where she sat in the highest chamber of the northeast tower she could see antlike figures in the streets below, laughing and hanging colored lanterns and garlands of evergreens from the Silverspine Mountains in preparation for the celebration of the evening's Festival parties. Some were already hurrying off to change into their Festival clothes. Everyone in Liavek, from the poorest beggar child to the richest merchant, would be celebrating the turning of the year in the company of their friends. Everyone except Tazli Ifino iv Larwin, Liavek's Levar.

" 'Go to a public celebration? Out of the question! She's the Levar,' " Tazli muttered, her tones a fair imitation of the Countess ola Klera's. She dropped her voice half a note, to the calmer and more reasoned tones of Merchant Councillor Pora Dannilo, and continued, " 'I'd disagree, except that it's her true birthday. When one's birth luck is so unpredictable, it's best to stay indoors.' Bah!"

So she, ruler of Liavek, was confined to the palace from— she cocked her head; yes, the conch-shell horns had sounded from the Black Temple several minutes ago—from now until midmorning tomorrow, during the full period of her mother's labor, with a little extra time on each end just to be sure. She wasn't even going to get to go to the party downstairs in her

240

own ballroom or watch the fireworks from the specially built benches in Fountain Court just in front of the palace; Geth Dys, priest of the Church of Truth and the third of her trio of Regents, professed himself worried about the impact of her uncertain luck on the foreign dignitaries who would attend.

Tazli wrinkled her nose and stuck her tongue out at the white marble of the temple of the Church of Truth on the other side of Fountain Court. She supposed she ought to consider herself lucky not to be incarcerated for all of the last two days of Festival Week. It had taken her three co-Regents half an hour of wrangling to agree that she would be allowed out of the palace at noon the following day, when her luck period was safely over, to participate in the traditional street-sweeping on Restoration Day. "The Levar of Liavek doesn't get to go to any parties; she just gets to clean up after them," Tazli muttered. "Some birth luck!"

Something small and blue flashed across the dome of the palace below and vanished from Tazli's sight. Tazli blinked, wondering whether she had imagined it, then shrugged and looked out across the city. She had been coming up to the tower rooms ever since she had realized that Resh, Scarlet Eminence of the Faith of Twin Forces and until a few months ago her Regent, was afraid of heights. She had insisted on observing the custom of leaving out bowls of nuts for Rikiki, the chipmunk god, for a similar reason; it was a safe way of annoying Resh. Both habits were with her still, though none of her current Regents found heights or chipmunks bothersome.

"I'll cut off all their heads when I'm Levar; that'll bother them," Tazli said, but she knew she wouldn't.

The light of late afternoon was fading fast; soon the first groups of celebrants would come down the street, lighting the paper lanterns as they passed. It was considered lucky to light one of the Festival lanterns, so long as the sun was down. "Luck!" Tazli said in tones of disgust, and pushed herself away from the window.

"Nuts?" said a high voice from the ledge she had just vacated.

Tazli jumped, staring at the window and thinking instantly of assassins. But assassins would hardly be asking about nuts. Cautiously, she leaned forward and peered out once more. A chipmunk was sitting on the ledge outside the windowpane.

His fur was bright blue. *"Rikiki?"* Tazli said incredulously.

"Yes," said the chipmunk. "Where nuts?"

"I think there are some in a bowl around the corner," Tazli said, feeling stunned.

"Good!" said Rikiki. "Like nuts!" His tail twitched once, and he walked through the windowpane as if it weren't there. Tazli stared as he jumped down to the floor and ran out of the room; a moment later, she heard crunching noises in the hallway. Still bemused by the sudden appearance of a god, even an extremely minor one, in the northeast tower room of the Levar's Palace, Tazli walked out into the hall. Rikiki was just finishing the last three nuts from the shallow bowl on the floor outside the door.

"Nice nuts!" said Rikiki. "Thanks, nice nut lady!"

"I'm not a nut lady," Tazli said, offended. "I'm Tazli Ifino iv Larwin, Levar of Liavek!"

"Oh!" said Rikiki. He tilted his head to one side and stared up at her with his beady black eyes. "Nice Levar lady?" he said in a doubtful tone.

"I am referred to as Her Magnificence," Tazli said with dignity, though she was not sure that gods were among those required to use this form of address. She was not used to being uncertain about protocol, and it made her more irritable than ever.

"Too long!" Rikiki said decidedly.

"Well, you may call me Tazli," Tazli said graciously. She wondered how many rulers were on a first-name basis with a god; the thought cheered her up a little.

"Good," said Rikiki. "More nuts, Tazli?"

Tazli blinked at him, then called for one of the palace servants to bring her another bowlful. She was annoyed at the time it took, but most of the staff had already begun their own celebration, or joined the official party in the ballroom. Rikiki disappeared under a cupboard when the servant arrived at last, and Tazli did not mention him. She had been known as the Mad Child of Liavek for too long to say anything that might rekindle unpleasant rumors.

The servant returned quickly with an enormous green glazed bowl of walnuts. Tazli was startled at the quantity, until she saw the sympathetic expression on the man's face. He knew as well as the rest of the staff just how much of the Festival celebration Tazli wouldn't see.

Tazli's scowl returned. "You may go," she said brusquely.

"Yes, Your Magnificence," the servant said, bowing.

"And see that I'm not disturbed until tomorrow morning!" Tazli shouted after him as he closed the door behind him. She was still scowling as she set the bowl on the floor.

Rikiki ran out from under the cupboard. "Nuts!" he said joyfully, and dove into the bowl. He disappeared almost completely; the tip of his blue tail was all that Tazli could see protruding from among the nutshells. She sat cross-legged on the floor and leaned her chin into her hands, listening to the crunching noises and happy squeaks from the green bowl. "Everybody has fun at Festival but me," she muttered.

"What?" said Rikiki, poking his head out of the rapidly diminishing heap of walnuts.

"I said, everyone but me has fun on Festival day!" Tazli repeated angrily.

Rikiki's eyes went wide. "No fun? That bad!" He munched several more walnuts, shells and all, then ducked back under the pile. An instant later the contents of the bowl vanished except for Rikiki, who sat on the smooth porcelain and looked cheerfully up at Tazli. "Nuts for later," he explained. "Now have fun!"

"Some fun," Tazli said. "Me and a blue chipmunk, having a Festival party in the northeast tower."

"Not here," Rikiki said impatiently. "Fun place."

"But they won't let me leave the palace," Tazli said, then wondered if perhaps they might. Rikiki was a god, after all. Her scowl returned; it would be just like her Regents to listen to a blue chipmunk after they'd ignored *her* wishes completely.

"Don't care," Rikiki declared. "Nice Tazli want fun; Rikiki fix." He jumped out of the bowl and scurried over to the window and up the wall to the window ledge. "Hold tail," he commanded.

Tazli stood up and reached for the chipmunk's tail. She felt nervous and excited and a little doubtful. "Careful!" Rikiki warned, and walked out of the window, pulling Tazli behind him.

The next few minutes seemed like a dream. Afterward she had a clear memory of crawling down the outside wall of the

tower like a three-legged fly, headfirst with one hand clutching
Rikiki's tail. Partway down it occurred to her that this was not
a very dignified position for the Levar to be in. She lifted her
head, intending to point this out to Rikiki, and saw the flagstones of the courtyard far below. Her hand tightened on Rikiki's tail, and she decided not to mention the matter just then.

When they reached the base of the wall, Rikiki pulled his
tail out of Tazli's hand and scampered off. Tazli, who had not
quite made the transition from the vertical wall to the horizontal
courtyard, was sent sprawling across the gray flagstones in a
thoroughly undignified manner. Muttering curses that she had
overheard from the palace guards who had drawn Festival Day
duty, she climbed to her feet and looked quickly around to see
whether anyone had noticed.

No one had. There were, in fact, only two other people
besides Tazli in that section of the courtyard, and they were
just disappearing around the northeast corner of the palace.
Oblivious to the unusual arrival of their Levar, they were heading for the main entrance, where a loud voice was announcing
the early arrival of the Chancellor of Colethea. Tazli felt a bit
miffed.

"Tazli!" Rikiki called insistently from somewhere near the
bottom of the outer wall.

"Shh!" Tazli hissed as she ran across the vast emptiness of
the courtyard. She scooped the chipmunk up in one hand and
swerved toward the small door midway along the outer wall.
It had been installed during the reign of Andrazi the Lucky,
and since then had served as an inconspicuous way into and
out of the palace for spies and secret messengers of the Levar,
second assistant cooks late for work in the palace kitchen, and
ambassadors from Tichen who wanted to visit the palace un-
remarked. Tazli had once heard a guard refer to the door as
"the Ambassador's Gate," presumably because the Tichenese
ambassadors used it nearly all the time, except when they came
to the palace for official functions such as the Festival Party.

Because of the ambassadors and spies, the door was never
locked; and because it was Festival, the guard who should have
been standing beside it was somewhere else. Tazli yanked it
open and slid through just as four guards in full dress uniform,
their breast plates polished to a mirror hue and their blue capes
flung jauntily over their left shoulders, marched around the

corner from the rear of the palace. She pulled the door shut behind her and leaned against it, panting, wondering whether Rikiki or her birth luck deserved the greater credit for her escape.

The street on the north side of the Levar's Palace was wide but relatively empty. A laughing couple in Festival finery were coming slowly up the far side, admiring the evergreen garlands, and several people in ordinary clothes were hurrying in the opposite direction, presumably heading home to change. A black-haired girl about two years older than Tazli was hanging blue streamers from the bottoms of the Festival lanterns. She stepped back to eye her work, and saw Tazli.

Tazli stiffened, but the girl only smiled and said cheerfully, "Well, what do you think? Are they too short?"

"Too short?" Tazli took a more critical look at the streamers. "You're right; they'd look better if they were longer."

"That's what I told Darik," the girl said with great satisfaction. "But he thought the Levar's guests would find longer ones inconvenient, and he said no one would notice if the proportions were wrong."

"I've noticed," Tazli said. "You'll have to change them."

The girl laughed. "I don't think your opinion will weigh much with Darik; you're not the Levar, you know."

Tazli opened her mouth, and shut it again just in time.

"What have you got there?" the girl went on.

"Nothing that concerns you," Tazli said, putting her chin up. She didn't know what would happen if the girl recognized Rikiki, but she suspected that it would cause nearly as much fuss as if she herself had been identified.

"Oh, something for your Festival costume," the girl said. "Don't worry; I won't tell anyone. What is it?"

"Fun?" said Rikiki, sitting up in Tazli's palm. "Have fun now!"

The girl's eyes widened. Before she could shout for help, or for everyone to come see, Tazli was running again. "Hey, wait!" the girl called, but Tazli did not stop. As fast as her legs could carry her, she ran toward the rear of the palace and plunged down the hill toward the Cat River.

"Wheee!" said Rikiki. "Faster, nice Tazli!"

Tazli obliged as best she could, dodging carts and footcabs and people carrying baskets of last-minute supplies up to the palace. "Hey, watch where you're going!" one of the pedestrians said as she whipped past him, nearly upsetting the basket of peaches he was carrying. "Must be some fine Festival party, if you're in such a hurry to get to it!" a woman called from a passing footcab. Tazli did not bother with a reply to either.

Halfway down the hill, she ran out of breath and slowed to a walk. A nervous look over her shoulder told her that no one was following her, though several of the carters gave her amused looks. She glared at them, but it only made them chuckle harder. Disgusted, she turned away and continued toward the bottom of the hill, trying not to pant.

In the palm of her right hand, Rikiki stirred. Tazli relaxed her fingers, which had closed around him when she started to run, and he immediately began combing his ruffled fur with quick strokes of his paws. He looked like a cat washing itself at triple speed, and Tazli had difficulty in suppressing a laugh.

Rikiki looked up. "Fun ride!" he said. "More?"

"Not now, Rikiki," Tazli said between breaths. "Maybe later."

"All right," Rikiki said in a regretful tone. Then he brightened. "Go fun place now?"

"Which way?"

Rikiki sat up and pointed back the way they had come.

"No!" Tazli said automatically. "If we go back past the palace, somebody's sure to see us and we'll get caught. We'll have to go around."

The streets on this side of Temple Hill had originally been laid out as part of the palace defenses, and they twisted and turned and doubled back on themselves in a thoroughly confusing fashion. The golden sunset had dissolved into purple darkness by the time Tazli finally reached the east bank of the Cat River. Tazli turned south, toward the harbor, intending to follow the river a little way and then turn east again toward Rikiki's "fun place."

She soon discovered that she had made a mistake. The Canal District began near the foot of Temple Hill, and Tazli was quickly lost in the mazelike web of waterways. Streets turned into narrow corridors between high wooden buildings outlined in Festival lanterns, linked by the stone bridges that arched across the canals. Lanterns hung from the bridges, too, though as Tazli went farther the strings of delicate paper and imported bamboo lamps gave way to simpler, less expensive lights. Even the boats and barges were decked in lights that glimmered against the water like reflected stars.

The streets were full, but hardly anyone seemed to be in a hurry. After a while, Tazli gave up trying to find her way and let the crowd take her where it would. Rikiki did not seem to mind; he sat quietly in her hand and blinked complacently at the passersby while he washed his whiskers. Tazli herself was amazed by the diversity of the crowd. She was accustomed to the silk-robed nobles, ambassadors, and merchant princes who found their way to court; her only real experiences with the common folk of Liavek were her brief dealings with the guards, spies, and servants at the palace and her view of colorful, cheering crowds on those occasions when she had been allowed by her Regent to participate in a procession or ceremony. She had come to think of them, on the few occasions when she did, as a sort of large, faceless mass of interchangeable parts, all of which, in one sense or another, belonged to her.

But it was not possible to think of the people who now laughed and called and cheerfully jostled one another on all sides of her as either faceless or interchangeable. An enormous man with a shaved head and a gold ring in his ear nodded to a woman dressed in leather who was as dark-skinned as a Tichenese. A boy in a colorful tunic sprang onto the stone rail of one of the bridges and did a handstand to the whistles and shouted encouragement of his companions. A woman with dark, liquid eyes leaned laughing out of an upper window and pelted three admiring youths below with dates while they pretended to recite a long (and very bad) poem that seemed to be about her elbows. A red-haired man in the gray vest of a City Guard went by amid calls of commiseration from the crowd at his having to work on Festival Night. A woman with graying hair and a seamed, weatherbeaten face sat in a doorway throwing dice with a fat man in the brown robes of a Pardoner and a younger, short-haired woman with an ivory-handled dagger in her belt. To Tazli, they were more exotic than Ombayan tiger-flowers, and she watched them all with wide eyes.

As time went on, more and more people joined the throng, though Tazli would have sworn there was no room for them. Some carried lanterns or torches; about a quarter wore outlandish costumes of one sort or another. Tazli began to feel trapped by the sheer number of merrymakers that surrounded her. She was also cold, and all too conscious of the fact that she had not eaten since midafternoon. Then she saw an unoccupied niche near one end of a bridge. Thankfully, she darted into it, shivering in the sharp wind that was blowing off the harbor.

A hand fell on her arm. "What's this?" said a deep voice, and suddenly she was surrounded by a masked group of torch-bearers. One woman wore a leopard-skin and carried a long spear in one hand and a feather in the other; beside her was a man in mud-colored garments and a hideous, wrinkle-faced mask; another man wore a robe of Liavekan blue, painted with gold symbols, and a fist-sized, diamond-shaped piece of glass bound to his forehead. The man who held Tazli wore an old-fashioned long robe, also painted with wizard's symbols. Tazli saw with a start of horror that his right arm ended in a stump; then he waved it and she realized that it was only a coating of wax and clay, covering his real hand.

Tazli tried to hide Rikiki behind her back, but the one-handed man's grip prevented her. The movement made him glance down; a moment later he straightened with a laugh.

"Kosker and Pharn, it's Ryvenna and Rikiki! That's luck for you!" He let go of Tazli's arm and bowed with a flourish. "Allow me to introduce my companions, madam. This"—he waved his false stump at the leopard-clad woman—"is Ibinrun, whom Ombayans name as the first woman. This"—he turned to the blue-clad man—"is Calornen, the wizard Levar. That is a troll." The man in mud-colored garments pushed his mask forward almost into Tazli's astonished face, and the man with the false stump thrust him back with a good-humored curse.

"Here we have Anjahaz Girandili, the famous Tichenese caravan master," the man went on, indicating a woman in a flowing abjahin with a dagger stuck through her belt. He bowed with a flourish. "And I, of course, am the great wizard Marik One-Hand."

"You're all people out of stories!" Tazli said, forgetting her windborne discomfort.

"Clever girl! I knew you'd see it. You must join us, you really must," the one-handed man said. "We'll take the prize for sure."

"Wait a minute, Jinji," the leopard-clad woman said. "We have opinions, too; it's not as if you're in charge of this group."

"Yeah," said the troll. "Why should we add another person to split the prize with?"

"*If* we win," murmured the wizard Levar, but Tazli was the only one who seemed to hear him.

"Niv's right," the leopard-clad woman said, nodding toward the troll.

"We don't have anyone from the old S'Rian stories, Elit," the one-handed man said. "And this girl is perfect!"

"Perfect?" Elit said in a skeptical tone. "Ryvenna was the most beautiful woman in seven cities."

"Don't be so literal-minded. Besides, we need something from S'Rian. Ryvenna and Rikiki would be just the thing." He lifted his left hand from Tazli's arm and gestured dramatically.

The moment her arm was freed, Tazli lifted Rikiki onto her shoulder. He was watching the costumed group with great interest, and she hoped he would have sense enough to stay quiet and perhaps hide under her hair.

"Jinji's got a point," the woman in the abjahin said in a thoughtful tone. "I heard that Danesh Fels is one of the judges, and you know how he feels about his S'Rian ancestry."

"Where'd you hear that, Voshan?" the troll said.

"Does it matter? The point is that with Danesh judging we'll make a better impression if we have someone in the group who represents S'Rian."

"Then we'll say that Niv is that storm god of theirs, instead of calling him a troll," Elit said.

"Don't be ridiculous," Jinji said, waving his false stump for emphasis. "Niv's costume is entirely wrong for the S'Rian storm god. Besides, we can't go improvising at this stage of the game."

"Then why are you so set on letting this girl in on it?" Elit snapped. "And what's wrong with Niv's costume, anyway?"

"For one thing, Shissora is a snake," the wizard Levar said dryly. "But you aren't really considering taking this child to Ishvari's place, are you, Jinji?"

Jinji stared at him with a blank expression. "Whyever not?"

Tazli had been listening to the argument with growing irritation; it was all but identical to the "discussions" her three Regents held about her plans and duties. Tazli was tired of having her decisions made by other people. "Because I don't want to come," she said. She lifted her chin and glared at the wizard Levar. "And I'm not a child. I'm fourteen today." The wind made her shiver again, partly spoiling her gesture.

"Today?" Niv said, backing away. "Jinji, I really don't think—"

Jinji's eyes narrowed, and he studied Tazli speculatively. "It could be just what we need. A little extra luck . . ."

"Birth luck's too unpredictable," Elit said. "And she's not interested, and we're late. Come *on*, Jinji, quit wasting time."

The group of revelers began moving off, all but the wizard Levar, who was still watching Tazli. "Hurry up, Daviros!" Voshan called. "We'll lose you!"

"I'll catch up with you later," the man called, waving them on. "I want to see this young lady on her way first." Tazli stiffened, and Daviros bowed and added, "If she'll permit me, that is."

"There isn't time," the woman in the abjahin said. "We'll be late as it is."

"Yes, do you want us to lose our chance completely?" Elit said. "I thought you needed that prize money just as badly as the rest of us."

"And even if we lose, there'll still be free food," Niv said.

The mention of food reminded Tazli that she had not eaten since midafternoon, and that she had done a great deal of running and walking since then. Rikiki seemed to have fallen asleep on her shoulder, and he had been quiet enough so far. "All right, I'll come with you," she said suddenly.

Daviros looked at her in surprise. Jinji smiled broadly, and Voshan laughed. "I thought you looked hungry," she said.

"But, Jinji," Niv said with an uneasy look in Tazli's direction, "what if her birth luck—"

"It's her luck, not yours," Jinji said.

"But—"

"Come on, come on," Elit said, prodding Niv with the butt end of her spear. "Worry on the way, if you must."

As they started off again, Tazli shoved her way to a position beside Daviros. "Tell me about this prize you're after," she commanded.

Daviros looked down at her with surprise, but answered readily enough. "Ishvari has decided that her place is going to be the next Cheeky's, and to get things in motion she's offered a prize to the group that comes to her Festival party in the best costumes. The prize will be twenty-five levars.''

"*Twenty-five levars?*" Tazli said, amazed at the fuss these people were making over what seemed to her a paltry sum.

"She got her suppliers to join in," Daviros said, mistaking the reason for her astonishment. "And the losers will all get free food."

Tazli blinked. "Don't people always have food at Festival parties?"

"Not when the party is in a tavern," Daviros said. "I doubt that Ishvari will lose by it, though; she's still charging for the drinks."

Frowning, Tazli considered the matter. It sounded a little like the shipping arrangement that the Tichenese had tried to make last year, where all Liavekan merchants would send their goods with Tichenese caravan masters in return for special treatment at the border. What was it her former Regent had said when he turned the offer down? "It is not your perquisites that interest Liavekans, but your prices. I believe the merchants are able to judge those without official interference." Tazli looked at Daviros. "Does Ishvari charge more on Festival Night, then?" she asked.

"Naturally." Daviros studied her briefly, then said, "Look, I know you're an adult if you've turned fourteen, but Ishvari's place can be pretty rough at times. Try to stick close to us."

Tazli did not have an opportunity to reply, for they had reached their destination. Ishvari's was a wide wooden building that looked as if it might once have been a warehouse. The lower floor had been painted, but in the darkness it was impossible to make out what the colors were. On either side of the door hung an iron ship's lantern, spitting and struggling to get a few dim rays of light out through the unwashed surface of its glass.

Elit pushed open the door, and a wave of noise and warm smoke spilled out into the street. Tazli heard calls of greeting and saw several mugs raised high above the heads of the crowd; then she was inside. The warmth was more than welcome, but Tazli nearly choked on the smell of mingled smoke and ale and fish and roistering humanity.

"Stay here; I'll go find Ishvari." Jinji had to shout to make himself heard. Tazli felt Rikiki stir against her neck as Jinji shoved his way into the crowd and disappeared.

"Fun place?" Rikiki's voice said in her ear.

"I don't know," Tazli answered, glad that no one was likely to hear the chipmunk over the sound of the crowd. "Be very quiet and don't say anything where anyone else can hear you, all right?"

"All right, nice Tazli," Rikiki said.

Jinji reappeared and beckoned. With some difficulty, the group followed him to the far end of the room. A benchlike wooden table had been pushed against the wall between two small doors, one marked "OUT," the other "KEEP OUT." A tall, angular woman with stringy hair and a stained apron stood beside the table, watching them with narrowed eyes.

"They just finished showing the costumes, but I got Ishvari to agree to let us have a chance," Jinji said, jerking his head in the direction of the angular woman. "Up on the stage, everybody."

With some difficulty, the group clambered up onto the table. Jinji positioned everyone to his satisfaction, then handed Tazli a small paper bag. "Hold this," he said, and nodded to Ishvari.

Ishvari put two fingers in her mouth and gave an ear-piercing whistle. The crowd quieted at once. "Last entry for the costume prize," the woman called.

"Sirs and madams," Jinji cried loudly, bowing with a flourish. "Allow me to present to you legends from Far and Near! This is Ibinrun, named by the Ombayans as the first woman, who chose the feather of luck from the gifts offered by the Mother's servants. This is Calornen, the sole Levar to invest his luck and become a wizard. Here we have a troll, one of those invisible and malevolent creatures who torment their chosen victims both in this world and the next, or so they say. Here is Anjahaz Girandili, the Tichenese caravaneer, whose exploits in the Great Waste made her a legend in three cultures. I myself am Marik One-Hand, who destroyed the luck of seven wizards during the Saltigan wars, and this"—Jinji gestured triumphantly at Tazli—"this is Ryvenna, the wizard's daughter, with Rikiki and her magic bag of chestnuts!"

Tazli felt a sudden sinking feeling, but her brain would not work fast enough to tell her why. On her shoulder, Rikiki sat up. In a piercing voice that carried to the farthest corner of the room, he said, "Nuts? Nuts for Rikiki?" and dove headfirst into the paper bag that Jinji had given Tazli to hold during the presentation.

There was a moment of frozen silence, and then the room exploded in cheers and applause. Tazli stared; then she realized that everyone thought it was some kind of trick. A little of the tension went out of her shoulders. Ishvari was conferring with a small, dark man and two women in gaudy clothes whom Tazli assumed were the judges.

Rikiki's head poked itself out of the top of the bag. "No nuts in here!" he said indignantly.

"Shh!" Tazli said. "I know; it's not my fault, Rikiki. Jinji didn't have any nuts."

"Jinji not have nuts?" Rikiki said. "Poor Jinji!"

Ishvari whistled for silence once again. "The prize for the best costumes goes to Legends Far and Near, by popular acclamation." She poured a handful of gold coins from a small bag and showed them to the crowd, then replaced them and handed the bag to Jinji. "Next year, get here on time."

Rikiki turned his head and stared at the bag in Jinji's hand. His whiskers twitched, and Tazli's sinking feeling returned. She backed away and squatted down to slide off the table as Jinji opened the bag and prepared to count out the proper share for each member of the group. Five large pecans fell out of the bag into Jinji's palm. Jinji's face turned purple.

"There!" Rikiki said happily. "Now Jinji have nuts. Rikiki fix!"

Jinji heard him. With a roar of utter rage, he dropped the bag and pecans together and lunged at Tazli. Tazli fell off the table, banging her elbow and losing hold of the paper bag with Rikiki in it. Something wet splashed onto her arm, and a fat woman above her said angrily, "Here, now! Watch what you're doing!" An instant later, Jinji's hand closed on Tazli's shoulder and shook her violently.

"My money! What have you done with my money, you little thief?"

"Let me go! How dare you?" Tazli was at least as furious as she was frightened. She hit out at Jinji and missed. She struck again and found her hands full of the cloth of Jinji's robe. A blow fell on the side of her head, and she let go of the robe. "Stop it!"

Another blow fell. She heard other angry voices around her,

and the sounds of breaking crockery. "You break it, you pay for it!" Ishvari's voice called, clear and harsh above the tumult. Tazli raised her arm, hoping to deflect Jinji's next blow. She was just in time. Her hand slid on wax; then she felt the bare skin of Jinji's wrist. She grabbed it and clung in a futile attempt to stop him.

Suddenly the arm she clung to shivered in her grasp and then collapsed into a hard, round ball. The grip on her shoulder also vanished, and Tazli fell forward onto her knees, half under the table. Dimly, she saw the crumpled folds of Jinji's wizard robe piled on the floor in front of her. The shattered remnants of his false stump lay scattered to one side; there was no other sign of Jinji himself. She heard someone gasp, "The girl's a wizard!" but she was too stunned to take it in.

The folds of the robe twitched, and a small blue head appeared. "Tazli all right?" Rikiki said in a concerned tone.

"Rikiki, what have you done?" Tazli wailed.

"Never mind that now." Daviros's voice was almost in Tazli's ear, and she jerked in surprise, banging her head against the edge of the table. "You need to get out of here, quickly. Come on."

Tazli scooped Rikiki up in one hand and Daviros dragged her to her feet. Most of the crowd seemed to be fighting and throwing bottles and mugs; only a small half circle of people near the stage table had stopped to stare at Tazli with hard, startled eyes and murmur uneasily among themselves.

"This way," Daviros said, pulling Tazli toward the door marked "OUT."

Tazli started to object, but thought better of it. As they reached the door, the small, dark man who had been among the judges of the costume competition shoved his way to the front of the crowd. "If I might talk with you a moment—" he began.

"Not now!" Daviros snapped, pulling the door open. He whisked Tazli into a dark hallway and hurried her down it, around a corner, and through another door. Tazli found herself standing next to a large, smelly bin of discarded fish heads and other refuse.

"Ugh!" Tazli said, wrinkling her nose in disgust. "This place is awful!"

"Girl, that's the least of your worries," Daviros said grimly.

"Being a wizard isn't going to be any help to you at all if one of those characters gets a knife in you." He nodded back the way they had come. "And none of them would think twice about it, for twenty-five levars."

"I'm not a wizard," Tazli said. "But I am hungry. And—"

"Hush!" Daviros raised a hand and leaned toward the door they had just passed through.

Tazli opened her mouth to object that Daviros had no right to order her around, but she closed it again without speaking. She had heard enough talk from advisors and merchants and nobles and emissaries to know when someone meant what he was saying, and Daviros had meant it about the knife. A gust of wind came down the alley, briefly replacing the smell of decaying refuse with the scent of smoke and salt water. Tazli shivered. Her Festival Night was not turning out at all the way she had hoped.

"Someone's coming," Daviros whispered. "Run."

Slipping and sliding on the damp, unpleasant surface of the alley, Tazli ran. Behind her, she heard a shout and the sounds of fighting; then she dodged around a corner and into the crowded street. She wormed her way between the people until she found herself between a chestnut-haired woman in flowing desert robes and a heavyset man in a leather vest, both of whom were considerably taller than she. Somewhat protected from sight, she concentrated on putting as much distance as possible between herself and Ishvari's tavern.

Five streets and two bridges later, Tazli relaxed a little. She paused in a doorway to put Rikiki on her shoulder, and discovered that she was still holding the hard, round object she had found herself clutching when Jinji disappeared. She opened her hand to look at it and saw a medium-sized hazelnut. It seemed to glow faintly silver in the darkness.

"Put away," Rikiki's voice said in her ear.

Tazli turned her head. The little chipmunk was trembling, his tail a rigid bar behind him, his eyes fixed on the hazelnut in her hand. "Put it away," he repeated, and there was an unprecedented intensity in his tone of voice.

"All right," Tazli said, and slid the hazelnut into her pocket. Rikiki stopped trembling. "What's the matter, Rikiki?"

"Rikiki has no sense," Rikiki said unhappily. His tail drooped, tickling her back. "Sorry, Tazli."

"I don't know what you're talking about," Tazli said. "You did all right getting us out of the palace." A thought struck her. "Do you know how to get away from all these canals?"

Rikiki's tail lifted. "That way," he said, and pointed. Tazli hesitated, then stepped out into the crowd once more. At least the wind seemed to be dying down.

The crowd remained dense, cheerful, and slow-moving. Even with Rikiki's directions, it took Tazli nearly half an hour to work her way out of the Canal District. At last she found herself on a straight street with no bridges in sight. It was lined with two- and three-story houses that, to Tazli, looked small and cramped. "Where are we?" she said.

"The Street of Dreamers," said a matter-of-fact voice behind her. "Are you lost?"

Tazli turned and saw a slim, dark-skinned woman with wiry hair. Beside the girl stood a small, white-skinned, pale-haired man who was studying Tazli with interest. "She looks lost," he said. "And if she is, she could—"

"No," said the woman. "You are not going to talk a perfect stranger into helping with one of your experiments. You are not going to do any spells at all on Festival Night. We are going to go up on Snake's roof and watch the fireworks and make sure nobody sneaks anything out of the shop, and that is all we are going to do."

"I need someone who is lost to hold the fur," the pale-haired man said to Tazli as if he hadn't heard a word his companion had said. "Thyan can knot the belts together, but it won't work if I don't have someone who is lost to hold the fur."

The woman, who was presumably Thyan, rolled her eyes. "I told you, no, Silvertop. He gets this way sometimes," she explained to Tazli. "Well, most times. Nearly always, in fact."

"Oh," said Tazli. "Um, how do I get to the Levar's Park from here?"

"Don't tell her," Silvertop said quickly. "If you do, she won't be lost anymore, and—"

"Straight down this street to Park Boulevard, then turn right," Thyan said. "We're headed that way ourselves; you can join us, if you don't mind Silver here."

"Thank you," Tazli said. "I don't mind." At least she would have some idea where she was going.

"Why did you do that?" Silvertop asked Thyan in an aggrieved tone as they started moving again. "Festival Night is the only time this has a chance of working, and Snake's roof was the perfect place. All I needed was someone who was lost."

"And about six layers of plate armor for when Snake found out," Thyan said. "You're lucky she'll let you up on the roof at all, after you spilled blue paint all over it last year."

"I got it off again, didn't I?" Silvertop said. "Well, most of it." He looked thoughtful for a moment. "Maybe that would work."

"What?" said Thyan in tones of deep misgiving.

"If I used paint instead of the feathers, and some gunpowder instead of the six needles, it might work even if I didn't have someone lost to hold the fur."

"*No*," said Thyan. "Absolutely, positively not. You'll blow up the shop, or yourself."

"Don't be silly, Thyan," Silvertop said. "There are much easier ways of doing explosions; that's not what I'm trying for at all."

"I don't mean the spell, bubblehead. I'm talking about the gunpowder."

"Oh," said Silvertop. "Well, I suppose I could use fish oil if I had to. But I need the paint."

"You don't need anything," Thyan said firmly. "You aren't going to do any spells tonight. You are going to watch the fireworks. And if you are very good, I'll let you have some of the brandy."

They reached a wide, well-paved boulevard and Thyan stopped. "The Levar's Park is straight up that way," she said to Tazli, pointing. "Have fun!"

"That was the original idea," Tazli muttered. She smiled and thanked Thyan, then turned the corner and left. Silvertop was still babbling incomprehensibly about silver buttons and Zhir fish-knives, but he remembered her presence long enough to nod farewell.

Slowly, Tazli made her way toward the Levar's Park. From there it would be easy to get back to the palace. She was cold and hungry and very tired, and she had never been any of those before, much less all three at once. At the palace she could have a fire—a large fire—and she could order date bread and yellow cheese and chocolate for herself and nuts for Rikiki. Nuts for Rikiki . . . Tazli fingered the hazelnut at the bottom of her pocket. Where had it come from? She turned her head. "Rikiki," she started.

The dull boom of the first fireworks cut off the rest of her sentence. Was it midnight, already? Tazli turned back in time to see the blue sparks falling down the sky. Park Boulevard was wide enough to provide a surprisingly good view, and traffic halted almost completely. The crowd murmured as the dim trail of the second and third rockets shot upward from the Levar's Park, and a chorus of "oohs" and "aahs" greeted the dazzling display that followed. Tazli forgot about Rikiki and stared in delight with the rest.

Since Festival Night was the climax of Festival Week, the fireworks were more spectacular and went on longer than on any of the previous evenings. Rockets flew up from the Levar's Park and burst into circular patterns of sparks; others rose from the market and left a trail of small, bright explosions; still others shot from the towers of the Levar's Palace itself in streamers of blue and white fire. The grand finale lit up the street with all the colors of the rainbow, until it was nearly as bright as day.

Once the fireworks were over, the streets slowly began to clear as people headed home or to private parties. Tazli was able to make better progress, though she still found herself jostled and pushed. It was still cold, and she shoved her hands into her pockets. Her fingers brushed the hazelnut.

"Rikiki, where did this come from?" Tazli asked, pulling the nut out of her pocket to show to him.

"Put it away!" Rikiki said.

"All right, but what is it? Why does it bother you so much?" Tazli said as she put the nut back into her pocket.

"Jinji," Rikiki said.

Tazli frowned, trying to remember. "I thought you turned his levars into pecans, not hazelnuts."

"I did," Rikiki said. "The hazelnut is Jinji."

Tazli turned and stared. "Rikiki! How—I mean—"

"I may be stupid, but I'm still a god," Rikiki said bitterly. "That's how."

"I don't mean that," Tazli said. "I meant the way you talk. You don't sound as—as—"

"As stupid," Rikiki said. "I'm not, now. Not quite, anyway."

"Oh," said Tazli. Two half-drunk men looked at her curiously, and she quickened her step. Two blocks later, she reached the Levar's Way and turned right. A quick look showed no sign of the men, and Tazli turned her attention back to Rikiki. "Is that why you were so bothered about Jinji?"

"Yes," Rikiki said in a dull tone. "I shouldn't have done it. Ten more minutes, and I wouldn't have done it."

The despair in Rikiki's voice hurt to hear. "If you don't want Jinji to be a hazelnut, we'll just find someone to turn him back," Tazli said firmly. "Liavek has plenty of good wizards, and none of them will turn down a request from the Levar."

"There aren't many who can undo a spell cast by a god," Rikiki said glumly. He hunched together into a miserable little ball on Tazli's shoulder. "I should never have gone near the palace."

"It's not your fault," Tazli said. "It's my birth luck, and anyway I'm not sorry it's happened." She found, to her surprise, that she meant what she was saying. She was cold and tired and hungry, but she felt better and more alive than she had since the day the garbage-picker had come to the palace and taught her how to begin to be happy.

"This is *your* birthday?" Rikiki said.

"I thought you knew," Tazli said. "Don't you remember my telling Jinji and Niv?"

"I . . . didn't make the connection," Rikiki said. "It comes of being stupid."

"What connection?" Tazli said. "What are you talking about?"

"Birth luck," Rikiki said. "I think—I think we had better go and see the Ka'Riatha."

"Who?" Tazli said.

"The Ka'Riatha. She's the only one likely to untangle the mess I've made."

They had reached the bridge over the Cat River and she could see the towers of her palace, ringed with lanterns and silhouetted against the stars. The warmth and food available there held a strong appeal, but she saw no reason why she couldn't have both comfort and the Ka'Riatha. "All right. We'll go back to the palace and I'll tell someone to bring her."

Rikiki gave a snorting chuckle that tickled Tazli's ear. "She wouldn't come."

"Everyone comes to the Levar's summons," Tazli said, frowning.

"Not the Ka'Riatha," Rikiki said positively. "We have to go to her."

Tazli glanced at Rikiki. He was serious, she could tell. She looked at the palace towers again. She had never felt so hollow in her life, her feet hurt, and she would cheerfully have traded the coronation tiara for a wool blanket. She looked at Rikiki again. His tail was quivering with tension; this obviously meant a lot to him. With a sigh, Tazli turned away from the palace. "How do we get to this Ka'Riatha person?" She said.

"Thank you, Tazli," Rikiki said in a low voice. "She lives on Mystery Hill; just stay on the Levar's Way until we're past Temple Hill, and then we'll go through Old Town."

Following Rikiki's directions, Tazli skirted the base of Temple Hill to the Two-Copper Bazaar. To her surprise, even this late on Festival Night there were people haggling over tables of feather masks and Zhir shoes, hand-painted pottery and wax candles carved like faces, wooden bowls and tiny marble statues.

Several times Tazli found herself exhorted to purchase such useful items as a knotted leather necklace guaranteed to repel trolls, or a set of hooks from which to hang strings of onions in the kitchen. She paused only once, to look more closely at a table filled with dolls and headdresses and bracelets, all woven out of straw. The old man behind the table watched her intently, and as she turned away he caught her hand and pressed a small straw butterfly into her palm. "A Festival gift," he said when she tried to explain that she had no money with her, and he refused to take it back.

At the far end of the Bazaar rose Mystery Hill. Light still streamed from the windows of many of the houses, but the Festival lanterns along the streets were beginning to burn out. The people who still remained outside were mostly in groups, some sitting around bonfires, some dancing, some moving slowly but purposefully from one party to another. Tazli climbed the hill slowly, thankful that the streets were relatively straight. When she reached the top, she stopped to rest underneath a huge cypress. "How much farther is it?" she asked Rikiki.

"Not far," Rikiki said. "The middle of this street."

"Good," Tazli said, and pushed herself away from the tree trunk.

The house to which Rikiki directed her was near the center of the hilltop, a small, neat building with a low fence enclosing the garden at the front. A gleam of light showed from one of the windows at the front. As Tazli put out her hand to open the gate, a dark shape with pale, glowing eyes rose hissing from the top of the fence. She gave an involuntary squeak and jumped backward, and the shape settled back, watching her with those strange, unwinking eyes.

Rikiki made a chirruping noise, then said, "It's all right now; she won't scratch."

"She won't *what*?"

"Scratch. It's one of the Ka'Riatha's cats."

Feeling a little foolish, Tazli went back to the gate and opened it. The cat on the fence watched her every move, but this time it remained silent. Tazli stepped into the garden.

The strong smell of herbs and evergreens rose all around her. She started toward the door, but Rikiki put a paw on her ear. "Go around to the back," he said. "She's probably still out there."

Tazli gave a half shrug; she'd followed Rikiki's directions this far, and there was no reason to stop now. Peering into the shadows, she made her way to the rear of the little house. As she rounded the corner, she stopped short.

The back garden was even more strongly scented than the front. Beyond it on a low rise was a jumble of huge stones; they reminded Tazli of the abandoned rubble of the Gold Temple that still lay behind the Red Temple, just off Fountain Court. In an open space beside the house was an iron brazier, half full of dying coals, and beside it stood an old woman, leaning on a cane. Her hair gleamed silver in the starlight, but her face was in shadow.

"Come out where I can see you or go away," the woman said. "I haven't time to waste playing hunt-the-feather."

Slowly, Tazli moved forward. She stopped beside the brazier and found herself being studied by a pair of bright, penetrating eyes. "Are you the Ka'Riatha?" she asked.

"I am." The eyes fixed on a point just above Tazli's left shoulder, and the old woman's eyebrows lifted. "Rikiki," she said in a resigned tone. "I might have guessed. And on the busiest night of the year, too. Who've you brought with you?"

"Tazli Ifino iv Larwin," Rikiki said in a small voice. "The Levar."

The Ka'Riatha snorted. "Hummph. You've really made a mess of things this time, haven't you?"

"It's worse than you think," Rikiki said. "It's her birthday."

There was a moment's silence. "You'd better come inside," the old woman said.

"I would like to know what this is about first," Tazli said, staring hard at the Ka'Riatha.

"Would you, indeed." The Ka'Riatha sounded mildly interested, at most, and entirely unimpressed.

Tazli tried again. "I am not accustomed to people holding conversations about things I don't understand."

"No wonder you haven't learned much," the old woman commented. She turned her back on Tazli and opened the back door of the house.

"How dare you talk to me like that!" Tazli cried. "I'm the Levar!"

"Then why did you come here?" the Ka'Riatha said.

Tazli's anger and frustration suddenly drained out of her. "Because it was important to Rikiki," she said. "And I expect it still is." Sulkily, she moved toward the open door.

"Hmmph," said the Ka'Riatha as Tazli entered the house. "Perhaps there's something to you after all." She gave Tazli another penetrating look, then gestured at a wooden bench draped in a thick wool throw. "Sit down and warm up a little. Don't mind the cats."

Thankfully, Tazli let herself down onto the bench. A large orange cat rose from the opposite end, glared at her, and stalked off. Rikiki jumped off of her shoulder, and Tazli found herself curiously aware of the absence of his few ounces of weight. She picked up the throw and wrapped it around herself. It made her feel warmer, but not happier.

The Ka'Riatha was doing interesting things with a collection of jars and unfamiliar pottery from a shelf beside a large fireplace. "The tea will be ready in a few minutes," she said.

"Ka'Riatha—" Tazli started.

"Call me Granny," the old woman said firmly. "Most people do. And while we're waiting, you can explain how the Levar of Liavek comes to be wandering around the city on Festival Night with no one but Rikiki for company."

"Is there time for that?" Rikiki said from the end of the bench.

"There had better be," Granny said. "Tazli?"

"It just happened," Tazli said. She had decided that there was no point in arguing with this strange old woman, any more than there had ever been any point in arguing with her Regents. The Ka'Riatha had an even greater air of confidence than they had, and she was clearly unimpressed by Tazli's position. "Rikiki came up to the tower room and asked for nuts, and I gave him some, and then he said he would take me somewhere for Festival, so we crawled down the outside of the palace. Only I got lost in the canals. Then we ran into a group of people who thought we were pretending to be Ryvenna and Rikiki for Festival, and they took us to a tavern to be in a costume competition. We won, but Rikiki turned the prize money into pecans, and Jinji got mad and tried to hit me, so Rikiki turned him into a hazelnut."

Granny's expression, which had been faintly amused, tightened abruptly. "Have you got the hazelnut?" she demanded.

"It's right here," Tazli said, taking it out of her pocket. She glanced at Rikiki, who looked back at her over his shoulder, then jumped off the bench and vanished from Tazli's sight. With a mental shrug, Tazli held the hazelnut out for Granny's inspection. Granny immediately plucked the nut from Tazli's hand, and Tazli felt a sharp tingle run up her arm as the old woman's fingers brushed her palm. "Ow!" Tazli said, rubbing her hand.

Granny was studying the hazelnut, and she ignored Tazli's exclamation. After a moment, the old woman nodded. "A year and a day—nothing unusual. I'll keep this; it will be safer."

"Safer than what?" Tazli demanded.

"Than leaving it somewhere where Rikiki can get at it," Granny replied. "Or would you prefer to let Rikiki eat it?"

"Can't you just break the spell?" Tazli said. "That's what we came for, so you could break the spell and turn Jinji back into himself."

"It doesn't work that way," Granny said. "He'll just have to wait out the year and a day. If he's lucky, he'll learn something from it."

"Is that all you can do?" Tazli felt dizzy and light-headed, and she was too warm. She dropped the wool throw and stood up, swaying slightly.

"Rikiki!" Granny said sharply.

Tazli saw a fuzzy blue blur come toward her from the corner of the room. As it neared her feet, it suddenly sharpened into focus. She blinked and shook her head. "What happened?"

"Sorry," said Rikiki.

"And well you should be," Granny said. "Be more careful in the future." She looked at Tazli. "Sit down, and I'll get you some tea."

"What *happened*?" Tazli repeated.

"Rikiki got too far away from you for comfort, that's all," Granny said, handing her a plate containing a slice of buttered nut bread, a wedge of paper-white cheese, and two small, puffy pastries that smelled as if they were stuffed with crab.

Cats materialized from all the corners of the room and converged on Tazli. "Watch out, Rikiki!" Tazli said, momentarily distracted.

"They won't bother him," Granny said. "They know better. Cream and sugar?"

"Yes," Tazli said. "What did you mean, Rikiki got too far away from me?"

"Festival Night is his luck period," Granny replied. She gave the chipmunk a dark look. "Thanks to his carelessness, his birth luck has gotten tangled up with yours."

"Gods have birth luck?" Tazli said.

"Rikiki does," Granny said. "Why do you think he's been getting smarter all night? Or hadn't you noticed?"

"Well, all right, but then what did you mean about our luck getting tangled?"

"What I said," Granny replied. "It's a little like what happens when a wizard invests his birth magic in a luck piece."

"That's impossible," Tazli said. "You can't just invest your luck without training!"

"You can't," Granny said. "And you didn't. Your luck isn't invested in anything at all, right at the moment; it's simply caught in Rikiki's luck. Since Rikiki is a god, his luck is stronger than yours, and when he moves away from you he takes your luck with him. That's why you felt dizzy a minute ago.''

Tazli took a large swallow of tea and lifted her plate out of reach of the cats. ''How long will this last?''

''Until the end of your luck period,'' Granny said. ''If we haven't done something about it by then, your luck will dissipate the same way a wizard's luck does if he's unsuccessful at investing it.''

''But . . . but if a wizard tries to invest his luck and fails, he dies!'' Tazli said. ''That's why the Levar is never allowed to do magic.''

''It's one reason, and a pretty poor one, if you ask me,'' Granny said. ''But you're going to do some tonight. Unless, of course, you'd prefer to die young and let that fifth cousin of yours in Saltigos take over the city.''

''No!'' Tazli said, angered as much by the thought of Esveri Aranda iv Larwin, Chancellor of Saltigos, running *her* city as by the thought of dying. ''What do I have to do?''

''Follow directions,'' Granny said. ''First of all, when is the exact moment of your birth?''

Tazli hesitated, but the old woman already knew that this was her birth period; knowing the exact moment couldn't make much difference. ''Seven fifty-six in the morning,'' Tazli said.

Rikiki gave a surprised squeak. Granny looked startled, then thoughtful. ''We've four or five hours to mend matters, then. Just as well; this is going to be trickier than I'd thought.''

''Why?'' Tazli demanded. ''What's so special about seven fifty-six in the morning?'' The old woman did not answer, but Tazli persisted. ''It's my life. I ought to know.''

''The peak of my luck time is then,'' Rikiki said. ''That's why the Ka'Riatha said untangling your birth luck from mine would be tricky.''

Granny stood up and crossed to a shelf on the opposite side of the room, where she picked up something Tazli could not see. ''What are you doing?'' Tazli demanded.

''I'm going to lock the gate so we won't be disturbed by visitors,'' Granny said. ''Fortunately, Jehane is a sound sleeper and has learned to limit her snooping.''

''Who's Jehane?'' Rikiki said worriedly.

''My apprentice in weaving. Don't fret; she has no interest

whatever in magic.'' She went out through the front door and returned a moment later to replace the gate key on the shelf.

"What kind of magic is this going to be?'' Tazli asked uneasily.

Granny looked at her. "I'm going to guide you through the process of investing your luck.''

"Will that get it untangled from Rikiki?''

"Probably, but it doesn't matter,'' Granny said. "If your luck's successfully invested, being without it won't kill you, and it won't matter if a little of it stays stuck to Rikiki.''

"This is impossible,'' Tazli said. "One person can't help another invest her luck, or there wouldn't be so many deaths when people try.''

"Normally, you'd be right. This time you're not.'' Granny sighed and picked up a lamp and a small fleece of unspun wool. "This is going to be a joint investiture. It's my birthday, too. Now, come along; we haven't much time. You'd better carry Rikiki. It'll be safer for both of you.''

Feeling rather stunned, Tazli picked up Rikiki and followed Granny out the back door and down a flight of stairs into the cellar. They paused only long enough for Granny to wave her cane over an area of the floor, which melted into a second set of steps, leading downward. Below was a large cave, empty except for a set of heavily laden shelves carved into the stone and a wine rack near the foot of the stairs. "Wait here,'' Granny said.

The old woman crossed to the shelves and began selecting things: a wooden drop-spindle, six small brass lamps, a box of colored chalks, a smooth-surfaced, irregularly shaped lump of black stone, two new candles. With the chalk, she drew an intricate diagram on the floor of the cave, positioning the brass lamps at carefully spaced intervals. The black stone, the wooden spindle, and the unspun fleece she had brought down to the cave from upstairs went in the center of the diagram.

"It's ready,'' she said at last. "Tazli, come here and listen carefully. You are going to have to follow my instructions exactly, or we'll probably both die.''

Tazli swallowed hard and nodded. Granny handed her a candle and began explaining what she was to do. It did not seem very hard—Tazli would have to walk behind her through the maze of the diagram, lighting every other lamp from the candle she held and thinking about birth luck. When they reached the center, she was to put Rikiki down and concentrate as best she could on the drop-spindle, which Granny would make use of until the end of the ritual. She was to ignore everything else that went on; Granny was particularly firm about the necessity of making no sudden moves or unexpected noises.

"What about the rock?" Tazli asked, looking at the black stone in the center of the diagram.

"That's for me," Granny said. "Ignore it. Are you ready?"

"Yes," Tazli said. She felt completely incapable of saying anything more. If this did not work, she would be dead within four hours and Liavek would have a new Levar. She thought about the straw butterfly in her pocket and wondered whether the new Levar would understand about Liavekans like Ishvari and Jinji and Silvertop and Daviros and the old man at the Two-Copper Bazaar. She did not think she understood them herself.

"Good. Another minute or so, and—" The old woman stopped and swayed as if something had struck her, and the black rock in the center of the diagram began to shimmer.

"What was that?" Tazli said. "Are you all right?"

"That was my luck returning to me," Granny said. She sounded tireder than she had a moment before.

Tazli looked at the glowing rock. "I thought a wizard's spells collapsed when his luck time came."

"They do," Granny said. "That's not my doing, nor is it a wizard's spell. It's a gift to keep me going until my luck's reinvested."

"Keep you going?"

"I'm older than I look," Granny said shortly.

"Ka'Riatha," Rikiki said, "are you sure you want to—"

"Of course I'm sure," the old woman snapped in a more normal tone. "Light your candle and let's go. Remember, once we've started, don't stop for anything. And don't smear the diagram."

Granny lowered the wick of her candle to the flame of the lamp she had brought with her, and Tazli did likewise. The fire dimmed, then rose high and smoky as the two candles caught. Without another word, Granny started into the chalk maze. Tazli took a deep breath, thought of her birth luck, and followed.

At first, nothing seemed to happen. Tazli walked slowly and steadily along the narrow, twisting path marked out on the floor in blue chalk, and tried to think of birth luck. It was more difficult than she had expected; thoughts of Rikiki, of Granny, and of Liavek itself kept intruding. She found it strange that a god would have a luck period. Were gods born the way people were, or did they come into being in some other fashion that determined their luck time?

Granny paused to light the first of the brass lamps, and Tazli blinked. As the wick caught, a flicker of red light ran across the surface of the diagram. Birth luck, Tazli thought, forcing her mind back toward the subject she had been told to think of. Is all birth luck red? Granny passed the second lamp, and Tazli stopped to light it herself. This time the light was orange, and a little stronger than before. Ignore it and think of birth luck, Tazli told herself firmly.

The lighting of the third lamp made a clear yellow light shine from the diagram when Granny lit it; the fourth, which was Tazli's, brought a bright green glow. Tazli began to feel light-headed. The fifth lamp produced a medium-blue flare of light and the mental sensation of having lost something and then having forgotten what it was that was lost. The sixth and last of the lamps lit the cave with a dark bluish-violet light. The sense of loss intensified. Tazli staggered, and her foot nearly scraped one of the chalk lines.

Granny reached the center of the diagram. Turning to face Tazli, she set her candle on the floor beside the rock and picked up the spindle and fleece. Tazli set down her own candle and let Rikiki jump off her hand to crouch beside it; then she turned to watch the spindle as she had been instructed.

Granny had tucked the spindle under one arm and was teasing one end of the fleece into a peak. There were beads of sweat on her upper lip, but her expression was merely intent, not grim. She twisted the wool and pulled, twisted and pulled, and a six-inch strand of yarn hung from the end of the fleece.

With a practiced motion, Granny flipped her arm so that the fleece wrapped itself around her wrist and out of the way. Her other hand brought the spindle forward, and she quickly knotted the end of the yarn to a short nub at the base of the spindle. She twisted and pulled at the fleece again, and brought the additional length up and around to wrap twice around the top of the spindle. Then, with a quick, strong snap of her fingers, she set the spindle turning and let it hang free from the end of the fleece.

Tazli felt something pulling at her, tugging her in all directions at once. The revolving spindle seemed to turn with considered slowness in the air before her eyes, and the cave seemed to turn with it. The spindle slowed further, or the cave spun faster, until it seemed that the spindle was a still center around which Tazli, the cave, Liavek, and all the world beyond swung in steady, solemn circles.

The pull intensified, and Tazli feared she would be torn apart. Then the pull shifted and came together, until it seemed to come from the spindle itself, drawing part of Tazli's self out of her to wrap around the wooden shaft, twisting and winding and binding a piece of her soul in with the lengthening yarn.

With a soft click, the spindle hit the floor of the cave. Everything stopped; then there was a last sharp tug and Tazli fell backward, gasping. Her hand slid against a dry chalk line, and she looked at Granny in horror, afraid that she had ruined everything.

Granny's face was shiny with sweat, but she was smiling. From her left hand a slim wool thread, faintly glowing, stretched down to the spindle.

The spindle stopped turning and the glow vanished from the thread. "Well done!" someone said beside Tazli.

Tazli looked up. An unfamiliar young man dressed in blue silk was standing next to the puddle of wax that had been her candle. His hair was light brown, and his eyes were the same bright blue as Rikiki's fur. He smiled and put out his hand to help her to her feet. "Who are you?" Tazli demanded.

"Rikiki," said the young man. He sounded apologetic and rather sad. "If you've got any questions, you'd better ask them quickly. I've only got about five minutes before my luck period ends and I turn back into the stupidest god in Liavek." He looked at Granny. "At least you've managed to negate the results of my latest muddleheadedness. My thanks, Ka'Riatha."

"It's my job," Granny said. "But the thanks are welcome nonetheless." She detached the yarn from the drop-spindle and wrapped it around her wrist.

"Is that what my luck is invested in?" Tazli asked.

"It is, and if you were going to ask for it the answer is no," Granny said. "You don't know the first thing about using it, and letting an untrained magician loose in the Levar's Palace is a recipe for an even bigger disaster than letting Rikiki loose there." She paused to give Rikiki a grim smile. "Although this time I may have salvaged more from the mess than you think."

"What do you mean, Ka'Riatha?" Rikiki said warily.

"I'd been wondering whether it wasn't time for me to find someone to train to succeed me," Granny said. "Now I won't have to. As for the rest—we'll see."

"You're going to make the *Levar* an apprentice Ka'Riatha?" Rikiki said.

"Why not?" Granny said. She began picking up the various items that had been used in the ritual of investiture. "She's got S'Rian blood; all the Levars have, from the very beginning. Her luck period is a better match for your birth hours than any Ka'Riatha's since Vesharan, and she's got a certain amount of natural talent. And it's about time this city was run by someone who knows the difference between herring and mackerel."

"The Ka'Riatha has always stayed clear of politics."

"Things change."

"I—" Rikiki stopped and gave Tazli an uncertain look.

"Do you have an objection?" Granny said. "If you dislike her, of course, it's out of the question."

"No," Rikiki said. "I don't dislike her."

"Then it's settled." Granny looked at Tazli. "Don't stand there like a beached whale; pick up the lamps on your side. If you're going to be my apprentice, you'll have to learn where things go."

"Don't I get any say in this?" Tazli said. The idea sounded interesting, but she knew that the way something sounded was not a reliable guide to how enjoyable it would actually be. "What does this apprentice Ka'Riatha business *mean*, anyway?"

Granny looked at her approvingly. "It means that in addition to your duties as Levar you will have a great many lessons from me, mostly in regard to the use of magic, at least at first. You need training so that next year you can invest your luck for yourself. There will be occasional ceremonies I shall expect you to participate in, and later you will learn a good deal about the gods that their priests won't admit to, and a considerable amount of history that you won't find in the palace library. If you succeed, you will become extremely powerful; in return, you will have the responsibility of safeguarding the people of S'Rian, who have become the people of Liavek, and of untangling some of the unfortunate results of having too many gods interested in the same city. You will also be charged with keeping an eye on Rikiki in various ways. Is that a sufficient explanation?''

"It's all I'm going to get, isn't it?'' Tazli said, and Granny smiled slightly. "What happens if I don't want to be your apprentice?''

"You go back to the palace and give your Regents whatever explanation you think appropriate for your whereabouts all night. Next year on Festival Night your birth luck returns to you; if you are reasonably intelligent, you will not attempt to invest it, since you will have had no training. It's unlikely that you'll see me again. Rikiki—'' Granny shrugged. "Rikiki is another matter.''

"You'll see me again,'' Rikiki said. "Though I can't promise—'' His body shimmered like smoke and shrank in on itself; an instant later a blue chipmunk sat where the brown-haired man had been standing. "—that when you do I'll be able to hold an intelligent conversation,'' the chipmunk finished. He blinked, and his head snapped in Granny's direction. "Ka'Riatha! What did you do?''

"I didn't do anything,'' Granny said. She sounded extremely smug.

"Then why doesn't he sound as . . . as silly as he did when he was a chipmunk before?'' Tazli demanded.

"Because there's still a tiny bit of your luck mixed up with his,'' Granny said. "It's no problem for you, but I wasn't sure what the effect on Rikiki would be. I must say that this is most satisfactory.''

"Will it last?'' the chipmunk said anxiously.

"As long as luck does,'' Granny reassured him. She glanced at Tazli. "Well? Made up your mind yet?''

Tazli looked from Granny to Rikiki and back. She thought about returning to the palace and her Regents, and what she would tell them. She thought about the amount of time it took just to be the Levar, and of how much more it would take to be both the Levar and the Ka'Riatha's apprentice. She thought about the way the whole world had seemed to whirl around the spindle. She thought about the people she had seen and met during the course of the night, greedy and generous, kind and self-absorbed, quarrelsome and cheerful and, above all, varied. She thought about Liavek.

Then she bent and picked up the nearest of the brass lamps. She blew it out and walked to the next one. "Where do these belong?" she asked, and Granny, with an amused and understanding expression, told her.

Restoration Day: Plainsong

by John M. Ford

On the day after, when there is finally time to consider
  things,
The citizens think on this piece of their invisible history:
On Festival Night someone makes a choice in the City,
Not a reasoned but a random one,
Which the chooser does not and never will know is special.
For if it goes one way, all remains as it is and was,
And if the other (but you've guessed this,
Haven't you), the entire City that calls itself Luck
Will vanish, towers, palaces, hovels, brothels,
Sewers, street lamps, viaducts, dustbins,
Stone and wood and brick and iron and tile,
To the last bolt and peg, all gone
As if the earth had but dreamed them,
The people gone too, their absent relatives
Suddenly cloudminded as to their even existence.
What would be left? Perhaps old S'Rian,
Bustling again, its trees full of chipmunks,
Or perhaps a bare beach, one bent tree, perhaps some Other
  City,
With a name and a culture and a population all its own,
New for an instant, then old in the mind
As all cities become.
And all this comes from randomness:
Whether or not someone feeds a stray cat,

Wears red or blue to the revels,
Has that one glass of wine too many,
Tosses a coin to a beggar, or which way that coin lands.
It hardly seems fair
(To those who persist in demanding the thing
Of the persistently unfair world)
That this great city, these spires and parks,
These three hundred thousand only moderately damned
  souls,
Should hinge on a coin toss:
Yet the coin falls the same for kings and beggars,
For priests and mathematicians alike a die has six faces.
To influence the fall is to cheat, to cheat is unfair,
Thus is it proven.
And now here diverge the two ways of the Mystery,
On the one hand:
Count up the years of the City,
Assume the coin is cast for each of them, comes down in
  each of them,
And in all those centuries of spinning it has always landed
  right.
Half a chance in a year, half half in two,
And by the long division of probability
The chance of the City's continued being
Is cut thinner than hair by the philosopher's razor.
It is impossible.
And that is what gives it its chance:
For life is impossible, after all,
The million articulations of bone and skin, blood and flesh,
The soft wet puzzle with the loose parts,
Its every step a stumble caught in time,
The city that walks
About a city it and those like it have built
From trees and stones and sand molten clear:
What are a few flipped coins against all of that?
This is the argument of perspective.
Now the other way to approach the paradox
Is to say that perhaps the coin does not always land right.
Suppose that the city *is* damned, some years.
If you were there, you would never admit it.
If you were not, how would you tell?

Ships go down and the sea closes over them.
A thing of which the only evidence extant
Is only the evident existence of things
Admits no negative.
This is the argument of perception.
Some still refuse to believe in the choice at all,
Uncomfortable with the uncertainty,
Yet uncertainty is a divine comfort:
If there are two ways the world can go,
And even the gods cannot tell which,
Then there is an absolute route of escape.
The gods do not play all the pieces,
The coin is ours to toss, fumble, drop.
The ineloquence of the hands speaks volumes:
Coins slipping through the fingers,
The wobbling point of the drawn sword,
Torn stitching at the clasps of clothes.
God may be in the details,
But free will is in the accidents;
Predestination dies in a pratfall,
Whoops, hallelujah.
On the morning after Festival
People think on these things and deny that they do,
They reglaze windows, mend walls, right weathervanes,
Silently thankful that there is still a wind to stop out and
    measure,
Near to weeping that the sun is in their eyes, ache in their
    joints,
Looseness in their bowels, real, real, real;
All over the redeemed City they are working joy-blind,
Shaping pots, baking bread, sewing fabrics and wounds,
Making with their hands the ultimate prayer
Of those who endure in the hope of the truth of the world:
Please, you gods and fellow mortals,
Let us do it right,
Let us do it right, this time.

278